BLAZE

DONNA GRANT

St. Martin's Paperbacks

This is a work of fiction. All of the characters, organizations, and events portrayed in this novel are either products of the author's imagination or are used fictitiously.

BLAZE

Copyright © 2017 by Donna Grant.
Excerpt from *Heat* copyright © 2018 by Donna Grant.

All rights reserved.

For information address St. Martin's Press, 175 Fifth Avenue, New York, NY 10010.

ISBN: 978-1-250-10955-2

Printed in the United States of America

Our books may be purchased in bulk for promotional, educational, or business use. Please contact your local bookseller or the Macmillan Corporate and Premium Sales Department at 1-800-221-7945, ext. 5442, or by e-mail at MacmillanSpecialMarkets@macmillan.com.

St. Martin's Paperbacks edition / June 2017

St. Martin's Paperbacks are published by St. Martin's Press, 175 Fifth Avenue, New York, NY 10010.

10 9 8 7 6 5 4 3 2 1

To my kids—
I love you more than you'll ever know.
Thank you for bringing such light into my world.

ACKNOWLEDGMENTS

A special shout out to everyone at SMP for getting this book ready, including the amazing art department for such a gorgeous cover. Much thanks and admiration goes to my fabulous editor, Monique Patterson, who I can't ever praise high enough.

To my incredible agent, Natanya Wheeler—here's to dragons!

Hats off to my street team, Donna's Dolls, along with the fabulous readers on DG Book Talk. Words can't say how much I adore y'all.

A special thanks to Gillian and Connor and my family for the never-ending support.

CHAPTER ONE

London, England
January

The press of people, the noise, the mayhem was going to drive Anson mad. He'd never minded it before.

Then again, his entire way of life hadn't been hanging in the balance.

A man slammed his shoulder into Anson as he walked past. Anson fisted his hands and kept his growing ire under control. To think that he'd walked the streets of London just seven months before, loving that he could get lost amidst the millions of mortals.

Now, he craved the solitude of his mountain. To have the sixty thousand acres that was Dreagan to roam uncharted and unchecked. To take to the skies in his true form, flying from cloud to cloud.

Unfortunately, Dreagan would have to wait. Anson had been tasked with a critical mission. His gaze landed on the two females in his charge. Kinsey, the taller of the two had her dark brown hair up with her face hidden by a baseball cap as she sipped her coffee. She was carefully concealed behind people while taking pictures of everyone who entered the office building.

The second woman, Esther, was a trained MI5 agent

who used those skills now to fade into the throng of people. Esther was perfectly average from her brown hair and eyes to her height, but her training had given her the ability to change her appearance as needed.

Her hair was pulled back in a bun, and she wore glasses. The dowdy clothes, as well as the way she hunched her shoulders and looked down, made her appear as if she were afraid of her own shadow. It also caused others to forget her as soon as they saw her.

This was their third day watching Kyvor and learning the comings and goings of those who worked at the tech company. With Kinsey's computer abilities, and Esther's spy skills, the girls were quickly learning all there was to know about the top executives.

And they'd already found their target.

Sitting on his hands babysitting wasn't something Anson did well—or willingly. He was a fighter, a warrior, a Dragon King who was used to taking care of a situation himself, not watching. Or waiting.

Then again, he couldn't—and wouldn't—say no to watching the future mate of a Dragon King. That's what Kinsey was. She and Ryder had fallen in love despite everything that had worked to keep them apart. It was up to Anson now to make sure she remained safe and unhurt until they could return to Dreagan.

Not that Esther was any less important. She might not be a future mate, but she was the sister of one of their closest and most trusted allies—Henry North.

Having two such women to keep an eye on made Anson nervous. Both were reckless and rash. It should be him investigating Kyvor. Alone.

But that was difficult to do since the tech company had files on each of the Dragon Kings.

He blew out a weary breath. All those eons of hiding,

believing no mortals knew of the dragons who lived in Scotland and made the finest whisky in the world.

Perhaps it had been foolish to believe their ruse would never be discovered. Yet it had worked for thousands of years. The humans had never known of their existence, and the Dragon Kings were able to live with a sliver of the freedom they'd once enjoyed.

Anson pulled his baseball cap low and moved off the sidewalk when a security guard at Kyvor's doors looked his way. How easy it would be to end all of this.

All he had to do was shift. In one instant, everyone would see him in dragon form. With a swipe of his tail, he could clear the roads. With one breath of dragon fire, he could obliterate the buildings.

He didn't wish to harm humans. But he was tired of pretending to be something he wasn't. He was a dragon.

A Dragon King.

And he missed his Browns with an ache that went so deep it pierced his soul.

Now, as he looked at the mortals, he felt . . . revulsion. Because they had dug into his world and that of his brethren, everything had changed.

Hiding was becoming more difficult. Not only did Kyvor have information on all of them, but the video that showed the Kings fighting—and shifting—was also very much still in the news, even all these months later.

Never mind the fact that the Kings had been battling the Dark Fae at the time, and the Dark had used magic. The humans saw what they wanted, though, and that was dragons with other mortals.

How wrong they were. If only the humans knew what was living among them. But that wasn't his concern.

No longer would the Kings be allowed to go about their days in relative obscurity. Kyvor may not have released the information they'd obtained, but it was only a matter of time. More importantly, the Kings needed to know who at Kyvor had gained such information.

That's why Kinsey and Esther had decided to infiltrate the company and destroy everything. It was a long shot, yet one that had to be taken.

For every Dragon King.

For every mate.

For peace.

Anson ran a hand over his chin. Peace. That word should mean so much but rarely did. At one time, there had been harmony between dragons and mortals.

It had seemed to only last a heartbeat, though. Then all Hell had broken loose. The next thing he knew, dragons were crossing the dragon bridge with the Kings remaining behind.

The plan was to bring the dragons back one day. Anson snorted. That wasn't likely to happen. He'd realized that ages ago, even if he did still hold out hope of seeing his clan.

"She's here," Esther's voice said in his ear.

Her British accent was soft and smooth, but she had the ability to do different dialects with ease whenever she wanted.

He rubbed his ear with the earpiece. Esther had made him wear it so they could all keep in contact. He could've easily heard them with his enhanced senses, but the same couldn't be said for the girls.

"I see her," Kinsey's Scottish brogue came through the earpiece.

Anson's gaze locked on the leggy brunette they were speaking about. She arrived at Kyvor like clockwork every morning at 7:33.

There was a smile in Esther's voice when she said, "Devon Abrams is the key."

The woman wore impeccable clothing tailored to fit her body and her curves. She carried a handbag that Kinsey cooed over in his ear, while Esther admired how fashionable her hair always was.

Today, Devon had her shoulder-length hair in soft waves that seemed in contrast to her more severe navy pencil skirt and white top. The sky blue jacket that fell a few inches short of her skirt tied the entire ensemble together.

Or so Esther said through the earpiece. Frankly, he couldn't care less what Devon wore. She was a means to an end, and the sooner they got to that end, the better.

Though he could—and did—admire Devon's beauty. She had the walk of a woman who was used to being in charge, someone who was no stranger to accomplishing her goals.

"She'll never turn," he whispered into the mic.

Kinsey sighed loudly. "She's not going to be an easy flip, that's for sure. Devon is loyal to Kyvor and working her way up that corporate ladder fast. I wish she would flip to make things easier."

"Liar," Esther said with a chuckle. "You want to hack the system again."

"You're right," Kinsey said, anger tinting her voice. "After what they did to both of us, I want to make them pay."

Anson looked at the two girls. It wasn't the first time he'd wondered if he should have backup. Though it was kept tightly controlled, there was a fury that burned in both women that demanded to be unleashed.

And it was directed at Kyvor.

The tech company hadn't just dug into Dreagan and the Dragon Kings. They'd used both Esther and Kinsey in the worst way. With magic.

The power that had taken had alerted the Kings that

there was a Druid out there they needed to find—and quickly. Playing with someone's mind took considerable strength and ability. Whoever this Druid was could pose a huge problem.

While the girls looked to erase all the files on themselves and Dreagan, Anson would search for any clue as to who the Druid was while keeping the females safe.

"I want to go in tonight," Kinsey said.

He knew it was too soon. "Nay."

"We can do it," Esther argued.

"No' yet," he stated. "Soon, though."

That seemed to pacify them. Not that he could blame them for their urgency. He wanted his own kind of justice against those at Kyvor, but even he knew not everyone was to blame.

He needed to know who led the investigation, who'd ordered it, and how they'd gotten their information on all of them. The fact that Kyvor knew all of the Dragon Kings and specific information about them was troubling.

Because there was only one person who knew those kinds of details—Ulrik.

Ulrik had been banished from Dreagan long ago, and because of that, he had his own agenda against them. The Kings were fighting enemies on all sides, and Anson wanted a win sometime soon.

He needed it after everything that had been lost—and that which could still be taken away.

His gaze swept the area, looking at each face. It wouldn't surprise him if Ulrik were there. Everywhere the Kings went, Ulrik managed to show up.

So far, Anson had been out of luck seeing his old friend. It wasn't as if he wanted to talk to Ulrik. Some of the other Kings had and didn't have anything good to say about the experience. It was probably better if Anson didn't talk to him.

Because he didn't want to talk. He wanted to punch Ulrik in the nose.

All of this, everything that had happened beginning three years ago, was all Ulrik's fault. The spell Con had put into place to prevent the Kings from feeling anything deeply for the humans would still be working had Ulrik not had his magic unbound by Darcy.

Because when Ulrik's magic returned, it had shattered the spell, and the Kings had begun to fall in love. That created a distraction for everyone because now they had mates to protect and shelter, as well.

Anson's gaze located Kinsey among the humans. He'd seen her with Ryder, had witnessed the deep love between them. It was the kind of love his sister used to dream of. The kind she'd longed to find.

He used to tune his sister out as she spoke of romance. Now, he wished he could go back in time and soak up every word, look, and gesture.

She hadn't found her true love. She'd found death at the hands of a human instead. It was for that reason that he'd joined Ulrik in the war with the mortals.

But slaying humans hadn't given him the satisfaction he'd hoped for. It just made the emptiness within him grow. Over time, he'd let go of his hatred. It hadn't been easy, but it's what his sister would've wanted.

She'd only seen the world at its best. Not once had she seen the ugly, cruel side, even when it had been right in front of her. She'd refused to accept it. That had brought her death, but even as he'd held her in his arms while the life drained away, there was no anger inside her.

The mortals hadn't seen the dragons as anything other than beasts. They didn't know the dragons had families and friends. He wasn't sure if it would've mattered had the humans known.

A look at the state of things now showed how little the

mortals thought of life. The depravity they leveled against each other—including children and animals—turned his stomach.

The humans were like unruly children with no discipline and no one to guide them, doing whatever they wanted, however they wanted.

Thousands of years of the same wars, same crimes, same cruelty. Nothing changed.

And nothing ever would.

He looked at the Kyvor building. Maybe it was time someone took a stand and did something. Perhaps it was time the Dragon Kings returned to the sky where they belonged.

CHAPTER TWO

Can't Get it Right

It was great to have a job that she was good at and loved. The lift doors opened to the twentieth floor with a *ding*. Devon walked out with a smile in place. She enjoyed hearing the hum of the office as everyone went about his or her tasks.

From the moment she'd first walked into the Kyvor offices six years earlier, she'd known the company was where she would make a name for herself.

There was something about the building and the people. Kyvor wasn't just one of the top technological companies in the UK. They were amongst leaders in the *world*.

And she was proud to be a part of it.

It was because of the leadership that she had excelled, had been allowed to continue climbing the corporate ladder as if she were the only one on it. Nothing was going to prevent her from being CEO one day. It was simply a matter of time.

"Morning, Devon," Stacy said.

She smiled at her secretary. "Good morning. Did everything come in for the meeting tomorrow?"

"It sure did," Stacey replied as she followed Devon into the office. "I put it on your desk."

Devon hung up her purse on the coat rack, followed by her jacket. Then she made her way to the desk. As soon as she saw the black folder with gold lettering, she smiled. She pulled out her chair and sank into it as she lifted the file.

"You're going to kick ass tomorrow," Stacy stated.

She certainly hoped so. The next promotion would move her to the twenty-fifth floor—that much closer to the top. She'd been working and preparing for the past three months for the meeting.

Running her fingers over the embossed lettering on the front flap, she felt calm and more than ready to face the roomful of top executives, including the current CEO, Stanley Upton. But that was tomorrow. Today, she had to continue with her current position.

She set the folder to the side and lifted her face to Stacy. "What's first on the agenda today?"

"I moved your schedule around to accommodate a meeting with Madeline Sharp from accounting after lunch. She wanted to go over some figures for your department."

"That's fine. Before my 9:30 meeting with my senior officers, get me the reports so I can compare the six teams."

Stacy turned and walked to her desk, saying over her shoulder, "I printed them out yesterday before I left. Let me get them."

Moments later, the reports were in front of her. Devon hadn't continued to rise through the company by allowing her teams to fail. She was tough, but she considered herself fair.

When a person or team struggled, she was more than ready to help them find the cause and work through it.

Most times, it was all that was needed to get people back on track. However, there were times it didn't work, and someone had to be let go.

That was the part she hated about her job. Delivering that kind of news ruined everyone's day. But the fact of the matter was, not everyone had the same kind of drive that she did. Not everyone loved their careers like she did.

For ninety percent of the population, their jobs were simply a means to earn money. Only ten percent actually enjoyed what they did.

She wished everyone could love their occupations. It made life so much sweeter. She had good friends and an amazing profession.

There was just one thing missing—romance.

Devon grabbed the top report and scanned the numbers, but she couldn't concentrate. Her mind was on the miserable date she'd had the night before.

Needing something to help her deal with the part of her life she couldn't seem to get right, she signed on to her computer and pulled up her favorite blog—*The (Mis) Adventures of a Dating Failure*.

The blog had begun about a year before and became an internet sensation. No one knew who created it, and no amount of searches had led anyone to the source of the candid and sometimes hilarious stories of a single woman in today's dating culture.

The blog was such a hit that it had been featured in news stories worldwide. What made it so wonderful was that the writer laid it all out there—the so-so, the bad, the ugly . . . and the truly awful.

So many of the writer's dates had gone as bad as Devon's. It helped her feel like less of a disaster in that department. How could she be so successful in her career and so terrible at dating?

Devon stopped her thoughts right there because she

knew it wasn't just her. It was the men. Something had changed in the world. Men were no longer *men*. She wanted a true man. One who wasn't threatened by her success.

One who knew how to treat a woman with respect. One who was faithful and honest. One who wasn't afraid to give his heart.

Devon sat back and began to read the newest blog post titled *Can't Get it Right*.

I thought taking a little break from dating might work. Boy, was I wrong. I even asked all of my "must" questions through our interaction online. He passed those, which led to me giving him my number.

We spoke on the phone and via text for a week before our first date. I actually thought I'd found someone I could have a second date with. (I've learned the hard way not to look for more than that. Sad, I know.)

I've had friends tell me I have rather high expectations. So? Why shouldn't I? Why shouldn't we all? We know what we'd like in a significant other. We know what we're looking for.

That then = high expectations.

Why should I keep that hidden? Why should I pretend I want something other than what I really want? Men certainly don't.

I began this blog as a way to help me *sort through what was becoming a hopeless process. I don't claim to be an expert in anything, but I can—and have—spoken about my horrid dates.*

Last night was no exception. The gentleman I thought I'd accepted a date from turned out to be a frog of the worst kind. I won't post details—for obvious reasons— since this blog has become so popular.

*But let me tell you this . . . internet searches, people.
Do them.*

*I'm going to leave it right there because I'm betting
you can guess why I ended the date early.*

Yeah. Another flop.

And why I always arrive separately for my dates.

Devon clicked off the blog. Dating shouldn't be so hard,
but it was. And since she didn't like to fail at anything, she
kept putting herself out there.

The blog always made her feel a little better about her
current love life—or lack thereof. Because she wasn't the
only one lacking in that department. She really wished
she knew the owner of the blog because she'd love to sit
down and talk with her.

Devon focused back on the reports until it was time
for her meeting. Then she was back in her office, finishing her comparison of the teams to see who needed im-
provement and who was on the right track.

The next time she looked up, it was lunch. She grabbed
her coat and purse and headed to the elevators. Many
times she ate at her desk and worked through lunch, but
today she was deviating from her routine.

She walked out into the cold and looked around, deciding where she wanted to eat. Bypassing the fish and
chips stand, she made her way to a café. The smell of
freshly made soups had her stomach rumbling in eager
anticipation of tasting the delicacies.

As she got in the queue, she read the menu, deciding
on a bowl of smoked haddock chowder and half a toasted
cheese sandwich. She ordered and paid. It wasn't until
she turned to find a table that she bumped into someone.

"I'm sorry," she said and looked up to find an older
man who was frowning at her.

"Watch where you're going," he grumbled.

Devon shook her head. Then her gaze landed outside the café through the windows on a gorgeous male specimen in a thin, blue sweater who had everyone looking his way.

The man was tall and broad-shouldered. Muscular without being overly large. He walked as if he didn't notice or care about the world around him. His cap was pulled low, preventing her from getting a good view of his profile. She wished she could see the face that matched his long, black hair and mouthwatering body.

When he turned the corner and disappeared from sight, she realized she still stood in the middle of the restaurant. Chuckling to herself, she found a table and waited for her food. As she ate, she watched the passersby through the café window, hoping she might get another look at the man.

There was something about him that had drawn her attention and made her forget herself. It could be the way he'd held himself—confidently. Strong and assertive.

She'd always enjoyed men who possessed such traits. Not that she wanted to be bossed around. No, what she wanted was a man. Not these metrosexual guys who cared about getting their nails manicured, waxing their eyebrows, or finding the right pair of shoes.

Where were the men who didn't care about breaking into a sweat? The ones who didn't mind working with their hands and getting dirty?

"Stop it," she berated herself.

It wasn't doing her any good to continue dreaming of the kind of man that obviously didn't exist in London. That kind of guy would be far from the city. Which made it worse for her since her life was here.

But it didn't matter what she told herself. It wasn't that she minded being alone. In fact, she rather liked it. It was the loneliness that got her, and it wasn't going away anytime soon.

All that did was make her focus more on work. It was all she had.

When lunch was finished, she remained a little longer. Everywhere she looked, she saw happy couples holding hands, smiling, gazing into each other's eyes, and kissing.

It made her present situation all the more painful. Finally, she'd had enough and left the restaurant to make her way back to Kyvor. When she looked down the street before crossing the road, she could've sworn she saw a glimpse of the hunk from earlier.

She blinked, and he was gone. Obviously, she was seeing things. For all she knew, the man could be ugly, married, or both.

Making her way into the building, her spirits were dimmed. Normally, it was the office that reminded her of all she had. After the meeting tomorrow, she might take a few vacation days and get out of the city.

Maybe that's exactly what she needed. She'd been working nonstop for months with no downtime. She even took work home on the weekends.

She pushed the button for the lift. Seconds later, it dinged. A man in a steel gray suit moved around her to hold the door open. She looked into gold eyes set in a gorgeous face. His black hair was long and pulled back in a queue. He had a little gray at his temples, but that didn't distract from his handsomeness.

"After you," he replied in a cultured British accent.

She smiled and walked onto the lift. He followed a moment later and raised a brow with his hand held over the various buttons.

"Twenty, please," she said.

He punched the button, then hit thirty for himself.

She'd never seen him before, but obviously, he knew the top executives. She eyed the tailored suit and how it fit his well-honed body. When she looked into his face, his gaze was locked on her.

"Do you work here?" he asked.

She quite liked the way he let his appreciation of her show in his expression. The attention bolstered her confidence. She always did love to flirt. "I do. You?"

"No. I have some interests in the company, however."

The bell dinged a moment before the doors opened to her floor. "Good day," she said and started to walk out.

But he stopped the doors before they could close and said, "It will be now."

She stopped and turned to him. It wasn't until the doors tried to close again that she realized they'd been staring at each other. She looked at the floor before smiling up at him.

"Perhaps I'll see you again," he said.

"I'd like that."

He dropped his hand, and the doors closed. It was only then that she realized she hadn't gotten his name or given him hers. That was too bad because he seemed nice. And he was incredibly gorgeous.

Could she have finally met someone worth a second date?

Devon's smile was back in place as she made her way to her office and her meeting with Madeline Sharp.

CHAPTER THREE

In order to win in this epic battle, they had to choose the right allies. Right now, Anson wasn't so sure the woman Kinsey and Esther had chosen was the right one. In fact, the more he watched Devon, the more he was sure they'd gotten it wrong.

Kinsey picked Devon because she was high up enough in the company to get the information they needed. Esther wanted Devon because she was certain Devon would want the truth once she saw enough to get her looking.

But all he saw when he looked at Devon was a woman who was happy. Did they have a right to shatter that? There was a smile on her face each time she walked into the Kyvor building. That meant she enjoyed her job. Because of that, she wouldn't willingly turn against the company that had given her so much.

Nothing he said could dissuade either of the girls enough to pick another person, however. So he'd trailed Devon during her lunch, while Kinsey and Esther dug into her life.

He'd been surprised to see Devon eating alone. Not that it seemed to bother her. She watched others with curiosity, though he noted that she took particular interest in groups of two. As if she were trying to decipher how each relationship worked.

Several times, she would study couples for long periods of time, her brow furrowed. He wondered what it was that the men who looked her way lacked since she showed no interest in them.

The fact that she was comfortable eating alone told him a lot about her. She was content with herself like few people were. She didn't need someone with her to put her at ease.

It was his job to keep an eye on her, and he had to admit, it was a duty he enjoyed. Babysitting he might not like, but looking at a beautiful woman would never get old. It was during his observation that he saw flashes of loneliness in her blue eyes. And he found himself wondering what could bring about such an emotion.

Now that Devon was back in the building, all he could do was wait for her to show herself again. At least the girls were safely ensconced in the flat that was fortified with dragon magic.

No Fae—Light or Dark—would be able to get past his spells. Because as powerful as a Fae or even a Druid was, nothing was more potent than dragon magic.

He hated sitting around waiting for something to do. Especially when there was a building full of people trying to hurt him and his family. He wanted action.

It was too bad that Asher had been sent to Paris for the World Whisky Consortium. That actually sounded like something fun. Anson would've liked that assignment. Instead, he was waiting for Kinsey's and Esther's plans to proceed while he spied on a gorgeous woman, who was about to have her world upended.

It seemed wrong to bring Devon into their war. He'd

wanted to find a way into Kyvor himself, but no one liked that idea.

There was a nudge in his mind before he heard Constantine say his name. Anson opened the mental link shared by all dragons. *"Aye?"*

"How are things progressing?" Con asked.

He ground his teeth together. *"Slowly."*

"There's been a development. I've sent Dmitri to Fair Isle where an archeologist has found what she believes is a dragon skeleton."

"What?"

"That was my same reaction."

As King of the Dragon Kings, it was up to Con to make such decisions, and Anson was glad he wasn't in Con's place. *"How does Dmitri feel about returning to his home?"*

"About as happy as you were about being sent to London."

"That good, huh?" At least Anson wasn't the only one on an assignment he wished he wasn't.

But every Dragon King made sacrifices.

"I just spoke with Ryder," Con said. *"He reports that Kinsey and Esther found their mark."*

"Aye."

"You doona sound as if you agree."

Anson blew out a breath. *"I still think I could do this with Ryder hacking into their computers while I enter the building. I'm no' sure this Devon Abrams is the one."*

"The lasses are adamant that it's Devon they need."

"I'll do what needs to be done. The girls will be protected, and we'll get the information one way or another."

"Without anything coming back on Dreagan," Con stated in a hard tone.

"That goes without saying."

Con sighed loudly. "*I know we're taking a chance with this.*"

"*A big one, but I agree it needs to be done. I just wish the girls were no' here.*"

"*We're taking a huge risk with you being there. If Kyvor really does know all of the Dragon Kings, then I can no' send anyone else to help you.*"

Anson glared at the building that held the root of their problem. "*It willna be needed.*"

"*This is why I sent you and none of the others. I know you hate inactivity, but you can control your anger until the time comes to unleash it.*"

Con did know him well. "*I'll unleash hell on them.*"

"*I wish I could be there when you do. I'd like to extract my own brand of justice.*"

He heard the longing and fury in Con's words. Now he began to understand the pressure that rested on the King of King's shoulders because part of that was now on him.

"*I'm going to have Ryder send you information on Miss Abrams,*" Con said.

"*Good. I know the girls are doing their own digging, but Ryder knows how to find things others can no'.*"

"*Kinsey has already asked him for help. Knowing Ryder, it shouldna take long.*"

Anson crossed the road and hid behind a building. "*I'll let you know as soon as we have anything.*"

"*Be safe,*" Con said before severing the link.

Anson squeezed the bridge of his nose between his thumb and forefinger. Control. That's what Con thought Anson had. Perhaps it was control, but he wasn't sure anymore.

Most likely, it was the fact that he hadn't been able to act on any of the many—and various—impulses over the last ten thousand years.

Because if he ever let go, if he ever gave up that *control*, he'd likely destroy anything and everything around him.

Did Con comprehend that he'd potentially put a ticking time bomb in the middle of London? The pressure to remain detached from all of it weighed heavily upon Anson.

Why couldn't things be as easy as before the humans? How he longed to once more return to the time when dragons ruled the earth. When all he had to worry about was keeping the peace between his dragons and finding a mate.

Life had been simple then. He hadn't realized it at the time, but looking back, he'd taken it all for granted. Every second of it. Now, there wasn't much he wouldn't do to return to that fabled time.

His thoughts came to a screeching halt when he saw Ulrik walk from the Kyvor building.

"I knew it," he murmured to himself.

Then he frowned. There was something different about Ulrik. Two men flanked him on either side as if bodyguards or something. Since when did Ulrik need guards?

There was also the matter of the gray at his temples. Had Ulrik taken to altering his appearance? If so, why not go further to make it more difficult to recognize him? Just what was the banished Dragon King up to now?

Whatever it was, it couldn't be good. It wasn't coincidence that Ulrik was at the very building the Kings were investigating.

It confirmed what Anson already knew—Kyvor had gotten their intel from none other than Ulrik. The tiny thread of hope that his old friend could be redeemed was now as distant as a memory.

If Ulrik could give up the Kings and Dreagan as

effortlessly as he had to those at Kyvor, then he was beyond saving. Con would have to kill him when it came time for the two to battle.

Because that time was drawing ever closer. Anson could sense that the end was nigh. The only one ever capable of taking down Con was Ulrik, but the once best friends had never fought.

Mainly because Ulrik hadn't wanted to be King of Kings. All he'd ever wanted was to rule his Silvers. That had been shattered when the human female Ulrik had wanted to take as his mate betrayed him.

It was Con who discovered her treachery and gathered all the Kings but Ulrik. In an effort to keep the worst from their friend, the Dragon Kings had cornered the mortal and killed her.

Ulrik, however, wasn't relieved, even when he'd learned the truth of what she was about. Instead, he'd lashed out at the humans, attacking them and starting a war.

After thousands of dragons had been slaughtered, Con bade all the Kings call their dragons and send them to another realm over the dragon bridge. Once they were safe, the Kings turned their attention to Ulrik.

It had taken a lot to stop him. They'd only done it by combining their magic to bind his. Con then banished Ulrik from Dreagan and made him walk the earth for eternity as the very thing he hated—a mortal.

Now, Ulrik was after revenge. He'd set his sights on Con, and wouldn't stop until one of them was dead. If Con won, everything would return to how it was with the Kings hiding in plain sight.

If Ulrik won . . . the mortals would be wiped from the world. The Kings' dragons would be allowed to return, and they could live as intended.

Anson wasn't sure which scenario he wanted. After

so many centuries living among the humans, how different would it be to return to a time before them?

He watched as Ulrik got into the back of a car before it drove away. He wanted to follow it and find out where else Ulrik was going, but Anson remained hidden. Ulrik wasn't his mission. At least, not now.

He opened his mental link and said Ryder's name. As soon as Ryder responded, Anson said, "*I just saw Ulrik.*"

"*He's in London?*"

"*Aye. He got into a black Jaguar.*"

There was a pause before Ryder said, "*Facial recognition just confirmed he was there. The new software I coded last night is in place to follow him.*"

"*We've been looking for him a long time.*"

"*Aye. That's what concerns me.*"

Anson heard the worry in Ryder's voice. "*Meaning?*"

"*Ulrik goes to great lengths no' to be seen. Why would he change that now?*"

"*He wasna alone. There were two men with him.*"

"*Like guards?*" Ryder asked in confusion.

"*Just like that.*"

"*Ulrik doesna need guards.*"

Anson moved to better see the front doors of Kyvor. "*I know. This could be a trick of some kind. It was Ulrik, but no' him.*"

"*I'm enhancing the picture now. Oh, you mean the gray in his hair?*"

"*We're immortal, Ryder. We doona age.*"

"*Whether this is Ulrik or no', I'm tagging him. My software will track his movements so we can see what he's up to. While I have you, I've pulled everything on Devon Abrams.*"

"*Tell me,*" Anson urged.

"*She lives alone with no family to speak of. I've sent*"

Kinsey her address. Seems that Ms. Abrams is squeaky clean. She pays her taxes on time, has a good credit score, and likes to shop for the finer things. However, she doesna overdo it."

"There has to be something she does wrong. No one is that perfect."

"Blackmailing Devon isna going to work. The girls will have to somehow persuade her to find the information we need and then turn it over to us."

"I can no' see that going over well."

"You could always step in and seduce her."

Anson wrinkled his nose. *"Doona even jest about it. Let me know if you find out more."*

"Will do," Ryder said and ended the conversation.

Anson was ready to do a lot of things for his brethren, but seducing a woman—even one as pretty as Devon—wasn't part of his plans.

He'd rather force her than woo her. At least with coercion, he wouldn't be lying to her. At least those were his thoughts at the moment. If he ever learned that she was part of those who had dug into the Kings and had had the Druid use magic to mess with Kinsey's and Esther's minds, then he'd reevaluate things.

Because whoever did that, was going to feel the wrath of the Dragon Kings.

CHAPTER FOUR

Devon read the last of the files, making notes along the way. For the most part, her team was doing well. But she wanted them to do great.

As she put a dot next to the people she would have to motivate to be more productive, her computer screen flickered. She stared at the computer for a moment to see if it happened again.

With a shrug, she took a drink of coffee. It was late, and most everyone else had already gone home for the day. She had another fifteen minutes before she would call it quits.

Her screen flickered again.

Though she wasn't a hacker or a computer guru, she knew enough about the workings to know this wasn't normal. As a technical company, Kyvor prided themselves on having several firewalls in place to stop hackers in their tracks.

So what was going on? She rose and walked to Stacy's desk to check the computer. Unfortunately, there was nothing abnormal about it.

Devon returned to her desk to find her screen black.

As she watched, someone typed *DO YOU REALLY KNOW WHO YOU WORK FOR?* across the screen.

Making enemies on purpose wasn't something she did. Many times, she went out of her way to keep the peace between anyone who felt threatened by her. It wasn't because she feared conflict. She did it to prove that she could be a peacekeeper.

However, there were times she had to demonstrate that she wasn't a pushover. She hated those instances. Being direct and frank wasn't in her nature. Yet in the business world, sometimes there was no way around it.

So as she stared at her screen, her first thought went to her meeting tomorrow and the promotion that could come out of it. Who might be jealous of her ascension through the ranks?

Two people came to mind.

Neither of which could hack into her system. That either meant they had help, or it was someone else entirely.

Her first instinct was to ignore the message. If she played along, it could come back to bite her with regards to her future at Kyvor. She hadn't spent years to get where she was only to give it up over some stupid prank.

She turned off her computer, choosing to ignore the message. Then she neatly stacked the reports she'd been reading and gathered her notes, as well as the folder for tomorrow's meeting and put them in her purse.

Within minutes, she had her coat on and was on the lift down to the lobby. As she walked from the building, her gaze scanned faces, looking for anyone who seemed suspicious.

As soon as she saw a taxi, she waved it over and got in. On the drive to her flat, she kept seeing the white words on the black screen.

What did they mean? Her boss? The company?

Both?

She didn't know Harriet Smythe well. Harriet had hired her and was always willing to give praise when it was deserved. Not once had Harriet helped her as Devon navigated the tricky slopes of office politics or the ranks.

Yet her boss had always been there to congratulate successes.

But what did Devon know of Harriet, really? Not much. In fact, she knew very little about anyone at Kyvor other than her secretary. Stacy had been with her for three years, and in that time, the two had worked closely together.

Devon wouldn't exactly consider them friends, but they were friendly. It was her hatred of business politics and gossip that kept Devon in her office and focused on her work rather than becoming friends with others.

However, she realized that might've been a mistake. If something were going on with Harriet, Devon would never know. She'd shut down anyone who came to her with gossip so many times, that she knew absolutely nothing that was going on within the company.

The taxi stopped outside her flat. She paid the driver and exited before walking up the steps to her front door. As she pressed the keypad with her six-digit entry, she glanced around.

When she didn't see anyone watching, she slipped inside the flat and locked the door behind her. Then she let out a loud sigh.

She dropped her purse on the bench and hung up her coat on the hook before she made her way up the stairs to her bedroom and undressed. Once she was in a pair of leggings and an oversized sweatshirt, she returned downstairs and poured herself some wine.

After a couple of sips, she got out the scallops she'd

bought fresh the day before. She then cleaned and cut the carrots before seasoning them and sticking them in the oven.

Only then did she grab her laptop and look up Harriet Smythe. A picture of Harriet popped up, along with her title at Kyvor. There was a site that listed all the charities her boss was involved with, as well as the humanitarian work.

But there was nothing on Harriet's private life. No mention of a significant other, kids, or even where she liked to vacation.

Devon skimmed several sites, but there was nothing more to learn. Still, Devon wondered if Harriet was hiding anything. With a shrug, she turned to the stove and grabbed a pan to heat.

It wasn't long before the scallops were cooked and she was dishing them onto her plate with the carrots. She took her food and wine to the couch where she flicked on the tele while she ate.

It was an hour later after she'd cleaned the kitchen that she turned to her laptop to see those same six words flashed across her screen in all caps.

"Do you know who you work for?" she read aloud.

This had gone from a prank to something that made her heart pound in her chest. For several tense minutes, she simply stared at the screen.

Then she put her hands on the keys and typed as she spoke, "What do you want?"

The screen went black before the word *TRUTH* appeared.

She frowned. "Truth? What the hell does that mean?"

Devon tapped the keys with her right forefinger and typed, "What truth?"

WHO IS KYVOR?

"I can't help you," she typed.

YOU'RE THE ONLY ONE WHO CAN.

"Why me?"

BECAUSE YOU'LL FIND THE TRUTH.

"What the hell is that supposed to mean?" she asked aloud. Her mind was going wild with the conversation she was having.

She swallowed and typed, "Who are you?"

CONCERNED CITIZENS.

"Bullshit," she replied.

KYVOR ISN'T WHO THEY SAY THEY ARE. LOOK INTO KINSEY BURNS.

Before she could ask who Kinsey was, pictures flashed on her screen one after another until there were dozens, all showing a beautiful woman with long, dark hair and violet eyes.

In some, the woman was alone. Others, she was photographed with an attractive man. Some were of her on the street. Some were of her through a window, looking into what appeared to be Kinsey's home.

KYVOR HAD KINSEY FOLLOWED AND HER LIFE DOCUMENTED.

"Why?" Devon typed before she thought better of it.

THE MAN KINSEY WAS WITH. KYVOR MANIP-ULATED AND USED HER TO GET TO HIM.

It all sounded too fantastical to be true. And yet, she didn't close the computer and walk away.

"Who is the man?"

KYVOR BELIEVES HE'S AN ENEMY.

That didn't really answer the question. "What kind of enemy?"

THINK ABOUT WHAT WE'VE TOLD YOU.

"What do you want from me?"

But there was no answer. The screen went blank, and then the search results about Harriet returned. Devon took the laptop to the couch.

She stared at it, unblinking, thinking of the conversation she'd had with the unknown person or people. They wanted something from her. That was obvious. She wasn't sure why they hadn't just come out and asked for it.

Probably because they knew she'd refuse. Instead, they'd put questions in her mind. Even though she knew it was undoubtedly the wrong thing to do, she had to look into it.

Her gaze went to where she had a piece of paper taped over the camera. No one could see her, but a good hacker would be able to hear and see what she was doing on her computer.

Whoever had contacted her wasn't just a good hacker—they were elite. Most likely, they were watching what she would do. If she played along, they would return with more statements and eventually ask her for something.

If she proceeded down this path, it could jeopardize the career she'd worked so very hard for. She wasn't naïve enough to believe that Kyvor didn't have its secrets. Every company did—large or small.

But the idea that Kyvor had paid someone to follow Kinsey Burns and take such personal photos caused Devon concern. It also whipped her curiosity into a frenzy.

She moved the mouse to the search engine box and typed KINSEY BURNS before hitting ENTER.

Immediately, the page was filled with information and pictures. When she saw one with the Kyvor logo behind Kinsey's smiling face, her stomach filled with dread.

It made it all feel real. Doubtless, because it was.

One by one, she went through the photos. They were all taken at Kyvor events where Kinsey had received awards for her work in the technical department creating software that protected companies from being hacked.

Next, Devon moved to the websites that had Kinsey's name listed. There was all kinds of personal information about Kinsey, including her address in London.

Three hours later, Devon closed the laptop and sat in the silence of her flat. Kinsey worked for Kyvor. The company had had her followed. The question was, why?

No matter how hard Devon looked, she couldn't find any other photos of Kinsey and the man she'd been with. The few males Kinsey had been photographed with were different. Could it really all point back to this one man?

While Devon should be going over her presentation for the meeting tomorrow, her mind was on Kinsey and the unnamed man. And Kyvor.

This was a side of the company she hadn't seen before. One that made her distinctly uncomfortable. If they could do that with one employee, who was to say they didn't do that with everyone?

Devon's head swung around to her windows. She rose and closed all the blinds. Never again would she be able to leave the panes bare for fear that someone was watching.

She glanced back at her computer. Her clearance gave her remote access to the Kyvor computers. She could easily look up Kinsey and see if she still worked for the company.

Just as she sat and put her fingers on the keyboard, she hesitated. Kyvor's computers made a note anytime anyone logged in, whether it was remotely or not. They would see what she was doing.

Quite frankly, she didn't want anyone to know she was looking into Kinsey Burns. That did beg the question: how was she going to find out if Kinsey still worked for Kyvor?

Whether this was all an elaborate prank or real, Devon was now on a mission. Although it would have to wait until she returned to the office the next morning. Then she would be able to see what she could find.

All the while, her stomach knotted as she began wondering what it was the people who'd contacted her wanted. It couldn't be good, no matter what it was. If the hacker could get into Kyvor's computers, then they could find whatever they wanted.

And that's when it hit her. The hacker couldn't get into where they needed. They were going to have her do it.

CHAPTER FIVE

"I think it worked," Kinsey said with a smile as she sat back from leaning over the laptop.

Anson wasn't so sure. He'd observed the entire scene with Devon play out on the computer. Yes, she had answered Kinsey. Devon had even done a search on Kinsey after the conversation.

But that meant nothing.

"It's a start," Esther said as she walked to them with her sweatpants pushed up to her knees.

Kinsey's smile vanished. "We need more, faster."

"Someone should talk to her."

It was then he realized that both women were looking at him. "No' going to happen."

"Why not?" Kinsey asked with a frown.

Ester leaned on the back of the sofa and crossed her arms. "I've seen how women look at you. You could easily catch Devon's attention."

"I'll no' seduce her just to get information. I'm here to make sure Kyvor doesna attack either of you."

Kinsey's violet eyes met his. "I don't want to lie to

Devon either, but it may come to that. She's fully invested in Kyvor. She won't give in easily."

"If it comes down to it, I'll do what must be done," he told them.

Esther ran a hand through her long hair and wiggled her toes encased in Wonder Woman socks, complete with a red cape behind each knee. "We're all anxious to return to Dreagan. I don't know who the Druid is who messed with my head, and I don't like remaining here and chancing running into her again until I'm prepared."

"Me either," Kinsey said and looked down at the computer.

Anson couldn't imagine what it felt like to have someone use magic to alter his thinking. It was a violation. If he ever encountered that Druid, he would be hard-pressed not to kill her immediately.

"Kyvor and the Druid could've muddled with others' minds, as well," Esther said into the quiet.

Kinsey nodded slowly. "I've thought of that."

"You've told me how good the tech analysts are at Kyvor. They won't be able to trace you, will they?" Esther asked.

Kinsey shot her a droll look. "I was head of that division. I taught most of them everything they know."

"And Ryder installed something on Kinsey's computer," Anson added.

"That's right," Kinsey said. "If anyone tries to trace me, they'll be rerouted all over the world a hundred times over."

Esther let out a whistle. "Impressive."

Anson turned away from the girls. He felt like the walls were closing in on him. It had been steadily getting worse ever since Con had refused to permit any of them to shift.

It had only been a few months since that order, and

already he was about to rip off his skin. How had Ulrik endured it for centuries?

Some said Ulrik had gone insane. Anson could believe it. He felt as if he teetered on that precipice daily. If only he could shift. He didn't even have to take to the skies. Being in dragon form would ease him.

That wasn't to be. There was nowhere in London he could chance such a thing. Already the news agencies, military organizations, and MI5 had an eye on Dreagan after the video was leaked.

Any other infractions would only make things worse for everyone at Dreagan. Vaughn, the resident attorney, was working to remove MI5 from the premises.

If Anson gave in and shifted, he would ruin everything the others had been doing to erase the damage the video had wrought.

Though it hadn't hurt the sales of their Scotch. In fact, their whisky was more popular than ever. Unfortunately, so was talk of dragons.

"I knew it!" Kinsey shouted.

He spun around and found her furiously typing on the laptop while lines of code scrolled. "What is it?"

"Kyvor put the same code they installed on my mobile on Devon's computer. It was probably done when she logged in remotely months ago."

"What does that mean?" Esther asked.

Kinsey looked from Esther to him. "It means they've been watching her."

"So they know about our conversation?" Anson asked, his muscles tensing.

Kinsey shook her head. "They'd have to know what to look for. I entered through a back door and masked our conversation."

"But they will see her search of you," Esther pointed out.

Anson pointed to both of them. "Stay here."

"Where are you going?" Kinsey asked as she jumped up from the table.

He strode to the door. "I'm going to keep watch on Devon. I want to see if Kyvor sends anyone."

Anson didn't wait for the girls to reply. He shut the door behind him and hurried down the steps. The flat they occupied was only a few blocks from Devon's.

There were few people out at the late hour. The dark made it easy for him to keep to the shadows, avoiding the streetlamps and headlights from the cars. He moved fast, circumventing anyone he saw on the sidewalk.

By the time he reached Devon's street, he slowed and eyed the areas near her flat. He saw one man staring at Devon's window on the second floor, which was most likely her bedroom.

The light was on, but there was no movement within. The lights on the first floor were also lit, but Devon had closed the blinds.

Anson silently applauded her for taking such precautions. He'd hoped that seeing the pictures Kyvor had taken of Kinsey would put her on edge enough to take such measures.

As he approached, Anson saw a second man. There was no way Kyvor had just sent these two. Most likely, they had been following her for some time. But why Devon? According to Kinsey, she was one of their best employees, who had her eye on the top position and was working her way there.

Then again, Kinsey had been one of their best employees, as well. Was that the pattern? Kyvor took those who appeared to be devoted to the company?

That didn't make sense. Wouldn't it serve Kyvor better to target those who didn't have such loyalties? He knew he would in their position. Kinsey and Devon had been star employees, who spoke highly of the company without being forced to do it.

There was a connection the Kings were missing, something that tied everything together.

Anson came up behind the first man and wrapped his arms around the man's neck, squeezing. The man grasped wildly, trying to break the hold as he struggled to breathe. Anson didn't relent until the man had passed out.

After dragging him out of sight, Anson searched his pockets and found a memory card. He tucked it in his pocket and stayed there for a moment, looking around to see if there was more than just one other human watching Devon.

It didn't take him long to realize the second man was trying to take pictures. Anson wanted to knock him out as he had the first, but if he did, it would alert Kyvor that they were on to them.

Instead, he took the first man's wallet and watch to make it look like a robbery. As he made his way to Devon's flat, he looked at the name to give to Ryder later before he tossed the items into a trash bin.

Anson went to the back of the structure. That's when he saw her standing at the kitchen sink, looking out the window up at the moon.

For a second, he was struck senseless. He'd seen Devon from afar. He'd noted her beauty. But he'd never paid such close attention to her face before. As he took in her quiet, simple allure, he found it difficult to breathe.

Her brunette locks were disheveled as if she'd run her hands through her hair. Her large, pale blue eyes held a hint of sadness, melancholy that struck him right in the chest.

He wanted to know what she was thinking. What would make her brow pucker so? There should be a smile upon her plump lips. And laughter in her gaze.

His eyes traveled down the slender column of her throat to a bared shoulder. An oversized, cut-up sweatshirt never looked sexier.

He didn't want to worry about Devon. He didn't want to care. She was a means to an end, a way for them to fix what Ulrik had done. The fact that he was standing there, staring at her lips meant that she'd become something more than just a means to an end.

"Shite," he murmured.

This was a complication he didn't need or want. But discovering Kyvor already had surveillance on her infuriated him.

He hadn't wanted her to be a part of this war, but Kyvor had made that decision for him. Now, it was time for him to make sure she wasn't harmed as Kinsey and Esther had been.

Devon finished off the last of her wine and washed the glass. As she set it aside to dry, she took one more look at the moon before she snapped the blinds closed.

It was his enhanced hearing that picked up the sound of a camera clicking. While he'd been ogling Devon, the second man had come around the back of the building and began taking pictures.

Anson stopped himself from going after the mortal and destroying the camera. For now, Kyvor needed to believe that everything was as it should be.

He hoped that Kinsey and Esther hadn't frightened Devon too much to change how she dealt with others at the company. If she did, it would alert Kyvor that Devon knew something. And that could only spell dreadful things for all involved.

Anson sent a text to the girls, telling them that Kyvor had two men watching Devon with one taking pictures. He then told them he'd remain at Devon's until the morn and then meet up with them at the office building.

He found a dark, quiet spot to watch the back of the flat since the front was bathed in light. The photographer finished and left shortly after that. It wasn't until the wee hours of the morning that another man appeared and punched in a code to Devon's back entrance. The door swung open.

As the mortal walked into the house without concern, Anson rose and quietly followed him inside. The intruder was looking through Devon's mail before turning on her laptop.

Since the lights were out, it was easy for Anson to remain hidden. He was able to see as well in darkness as he did during the day. The human, however, had to use a small flashlight to make his way around.

The more the mortal poked around in Devon's life, the angrier Anson became. Who did these people think they were to believe they could invade someone's home and privacy without repercussions?

After a bit, the man closed the laptop and made his way up the stairs. Anson waited until the man was at the top before pursuing.

Not once did the mortal look behind him. It made Anson wonder how many nights someone had broken into Devon's flat to look around. If the man hadn't been in all black and sneaking around at three in the morning, Anson might have thought he was a friend of Devon's.

He reached the landing in time to see the mortal standing in a doorway. To the left of Anson was an empty room. There was a door a few feet ahead on the right that could be a bathroom.

Which made the doorway the intruder stood at Devon's bedroom.

Anson quickly closed the distance between them when the human entered the room. When he spotted the man leaning over Devon's sleeping form, he'd had enough.

He gathered his dragon magic and used his power to take possession of the man's body with his mind. There weren't many times he used his power or enjoyed it, but that night was an exception.

With force, he made the man retrace his steps out of the house and walk down the street, right into the side of a police car. Anson watched from the shadows as the mortal tried to explain why he'd run into the moving vehicle.

Anson quickly forgot about the human and turned back to the flat. He checked the back door to make sure it had locked behind him. Then he returned to his hiding place.

But the more he thought about the man inside Devon's home, the more he realized that Kyvor might have something special planned for her. The sooner Devon discovered the truth for them—and herself—the sooner she could get clear of Kyvor.

He refused to think about where she might go, but no matter how hard he tried, he kept seeing her at Dreagan.

CHAPTER SIX

There were times a dream seemed so real that she didn't want to wake from it. And last night's was a doozy. The hunk Devon had seen the previous day was in her flat.

Except he hadn't been wearing a cap. She still hadn't seen his face clearly, but she saw his profile, and it only made her ache to see more of him. In the dream, he'd stood in her doorway, staring at her.

The soft glow of light from the moon and streetlights had allowed her to see his wide shoulders and the mouth-watering way they tapered to his trim hips. He'd stood silently. And she'd wanted him to come to her, to bend down and kiss her.

She stretched, thinking of the dream and wishing it had been real. She sat up and rose to get ready for the day. Even as she replayed the fantasy over and over, her mind kept coming back to the questions posed to her last night. A feeling of disquiet grew.

It wasn't until she was dressed and downstairs that she came to a halt. Something was wrong. She knew it. It was the notion that someone had been inside her home—and not her hunk. Someone else.

She tried to shake it off as she cooked scrambled eggs and toast, but the sensation grew. Her mind drifted back to her search of Kinsey Burns.

Her stomach soured as she realized if a company could do that to Kinsey, it could do it to her, as well. Devon wasn't the paranoid type, but with the new questions, it made her wonder.

So she looked at the facts. Someone had taken pictures of Kinsey, which meant they could do the same to her. For all she knew, her flat was bugged. But she wasn't quite ready to open electrical boxes to search.

Not yet, anyway.

She tossed aside the half-eaten toast and scraped the remaining eggs into the garbage. Without finishing her coffee, she put on her coat and grabbed her purse before walking outside.

With her mind crammed full of awful scenarios, she didn't feel the cold temperatures. She hailed a taxi and gave the address for Kyvor as she got in. Every mile that brought her closer to the office building, the more her stomach twisted in knots.

It was as if someone had yanked off a pair of rose-colored glasses she hadn't known she wore and exposed the dark side of the company. No longer did Kyvor feel like a second home. Perhaps that's what the people who'd contacted her planned.

She wanted to deny all of it. To believe that whoever had reached out to her was jesting and making it all up. But wanting something didn't make it so.

After paying the driver with shaky hands, Devon had no choice but to get out and make her way toward the building's doors. She stopped before she reached them. Then, tilting her head back, she looked up at the tall, elegant structure.

She lowered her head, wondering if her imagination

could be making things worse. She didn't know the people who'd contacted her. The only thing she had was a name and photos. What did that mean, exactly?

What if Kinsey had done something illegal, and Kyvor was merely protecting themselves? It was definitely a possible scenario.

It was the very private nature of some of the photos that tripped her up. If Kyvor wanted to follow Kinsey, they could've done it without taking pictures of her in the shower or getting dressed. Those were the ones that imploded Devon's theory.

Devon glanced to her right, her eyes meeting those of a man. The hunky man she'd seen from the café window the day before. The one who'd haunted her dreams. Their gazes tangled, and her stomach fluttered with exhilaration.

Suddenly, she was bumped into from behind, causing her to look away. When she returned her gaze to where it had been, he was gone. She remained a moment longer, searching the crowds.

What a pity. Had she imagined him? Made him up to help her cope with everything? Shaking her head, Devon tried to get herself under some semblance of control. It was difficult when every instinct urged her to return home.

"What are you doing out here?" Stacy asked as she walked up.

Devon glanced at her assistant and blinked.

Stacy laughed and nudged her toward the door. "Today's the big day. Don't tell me you're nervous."

Nervous? What was she talking about? Then it all came back. The big meeting that could propel her career. Devon hadn't thought about it all night.

"I don't think I've ever seen you at a loss for words before." A small frown marred Stacy's brow. "Let's get to your office, and I'll bring you some tea. That'll surely help."

With no other recourse, Devon found herself allowing Stacy to lead her through the doors and onto the lift. Before she knew it, Devon had reached the twentieth floor and was making her way toward her office.

After she'd hung up her coat and purse, she sat at her desk and stared at her computer. She realized how far-reaching Kyvor's hand was in the tech world. She knew all too well what the company could do.

That kind of power could grant all kinds of access when investigating someone. It didn't matter if they were the queen of England or some random person on a boat somewhere near Bora Bora.

The thought made her physically ill. None of this had bothered her before, but that was because she'd assumed the programs were used in the right way.

How fucking naïve. It was one thing she'd insisted she wasn't. Now, it was as if there were letters hanging over her in fifty-foot-tall flashing neon that spelled *naïve*.

"Here's your tea," Stacy said.

Devon nodded because it was expected.

Her assistant bent and looked at her before putting the back of her hand against Devon's brow. "You look flushed. Are you coming down with something?"

Yes. That *something* was reality.

And it sucked.

She almost asked Stacy if she knew Kinsey Burns, but Devon thought better of it at the last minute. After all, she wasn't sure who to trust.

"You need to cancel the meeting." Stacy straightened, her brow puckered.

"Why would she do that?" Harriet asked as she strolled into the office with her blond hair in a French twist.

Devon actually groaned at the sight of her boss. Her stomach rolled viciously, and she broke out in a sweat. Not because she was sick, but because she was coming to realize with crystal clarity just how screwed—and scared—she was.

"I think she's sick," Stacy said.

Harriet walked closer, her blue gaze narrowed. "Devon, you look like shit. I can't have you stand up in front of a roomful of executives and lose your cookies."

Devon opened her mouth to agree, but Harriet thought she was arguing.

"No. I insist," her boss stated as she took a step back. "We'll reschedule. Go home and rest. I don't want whatever it is you have."

As soon as Harriet had left, Devon rolled back her chair and stood. Stacy was there with her coat and purse. She let her assistant help her with her jacket before walking to the lift.

Devon felt as if every eye in Kyvor were locked on her. It made her want to scream. Mostly because the very thing that had brought her so much happiness, now frightened her. How could a job do that?

The lift doors opened, and she stepped inside, pushing the lobby button. She paid no attention to the others in the lift with her. All she wanted was to go home.

Once more, the pictures of Kinsey taken at her flat flashed in Devon's mind. She couldn't go home since she felt as if someone had been there. For all she knew, Kyvor was watching her.

Her legs felt wooden as she reached the first floor and slowly made her way outside. The frigid air cooled her heated face, but nothing could ease the knot of anxiety within her.

She turned and started walking down the sidewalk. Perhaps a stroll was all that was required to clear her head. She had no destination in mind, only the need to be alone.

Devon had no idea how long she walked. When she finally looked around, she discovered that she was in a section of the city she'd never been in before. As soon as she saw the park, she made a beeline for it.

She sat on a bench and watched others, her mind going over everything again and again. The more she thought about it, the more she began to think of different things that could mean someone was watching her.

Just as she was about to tell herself that she was being silly, a woman stopped near the bench and knelt to tie her running shoe.

"You're being followed."

Devon's gaze lowered, wondering who she was talking to. Then the woman looked up. Devon sucked in a breath because she recognized the face.

Kinsey Burns.

"Get home," Kinsey whispered urgently.

The Scottish accent hardly registered before the woman was gone. Devon barely kept herself from watching Kinsey run off.

She was being followed. Devon's blood turned to ice. There was no faking it when she put her hand to her stomach and gagged.

When she was sure she wasn't going to be sick, she stood and jogged to the street to hail a taxi. The entire ride to her flat, she wondered if there was a car following her, or if someone was already at her home, waiting.

She'd begun to shake from the fear when she exited the cab and walked up the steps. A quick punch of the code and the door unlocked.

But she didn't feel any safer inside.

She walked upstairs and changed into a pair of jeans and a beige sweater before she curled up in her bed. At least she knew Kinsey wasn't dead, but that didn't mean Kinsey's life was exactly her own.

Devon jerked when she heard the buzz of a cell. Since hers was downstairs in her purse, she was more than paranoid when she sat up and pushed aside the accent pillows on her bed to find a mobile phone buried beneath.

Hesitantly, she picked it up and saw the text message that read: HI. IT'S KINSEY.

She quickly responded with: YOU WERE IN MY HOUSE.

YES. WE HAD TO HAVE A WAY TO SPEAK WITH YOU. WE BROKE IN AFTER YOU LEFT FOR WORK.

WE? WHO ELSE IS WITH YOU?

ITS BETTER IF WE MEET.

Devon snorted, shaking her head. I DON'T KNOW YOU. I CERTAINLY DON'T TRUST YOU.

HEAR US OUT. PLEASE.

Devon stared at the plea for several minutes, weighing her options. Her life had been much simpler before Kinsey had come into it, stating things about Kyvor and showing the pictures.

Yet how could Devon forget what she now knew? She couldn't. And Kinsey knew it. Besides, Kyvor was following her. Whether that had just started or they'd been at it a while didn't matter.

The fact was, they were trailing her, and that pissed her off royally. She might work for Kyvor. She may have even given more of herself to the company than she had to anyone or anything else in her life, but that didn't give them the right to invade her privacy.

Devon held her thumbs over the small keyboard on the mobile phone. After releasing a deep breath, she wrote: WHEN?

TODAY. TURN OFF ALL YOUR COMPUTERS AND YOUR PERSONAL MOBILE.

Those cryptic words sent a chill down her spine. She

knew exactly how Kyvor could watch someone through their electronics. She sold the equipment and software to companies. She should've known to turn off everything, but her mind hadn't wrapped around all of it.

To be honest, she still hadn't come to terms with everything. But facts were facts, and right now, she had to act if she wanted to find out more about what was going on.

She made her way downstairs to the sofa. After sitting, she grabbed her laptop and opened it, pretending to try and work for those spying on her. After a few minutes—with some fake gagging—she shut off the computer. Then she powered down her mobile.

Devon returned to the sofa and curled up on it with the mobile from Kinsey clutched between her hands. All the sneaking around made her feel as if her life were in danger, which meant it doubtless was.

Her clearance at Kyvor gave her access to certain classified documents and operations. None of which had given her pause in the past. Now, with what she knew, she itched to go in and take a second look at everything.

She closed her eyes, hoping it would all go away. Meditation only calmed her a little. It wasn't long after that she drifted off to sleep. The dreams were vivid. All of them centered around her being chased by Kyvor.

It was a never-ending cycle of chases, each more horrible than the last until finally, she jerked awake. She put her hand to her forehead and looked at the ceiling. That's when she felt the eyes on her.

Devon sat up and looked to the side. Her gaze landed on the hunk that had been in her dreams. He stood with his arms crossed over his thick chest, his feet shoulder-width apart. He dropped his arms and slightly bowed his head, his gaze never leaving her face.

Finally, she got to see his features. Looking at him

head-on, she was at a loss for words. Gorgeous didn't begin to describe such a specimen. His black eyes were intense, penetrating as he watched her. Those onyx orbs were framed by thick lashes.

His cheekbones were so sharp, they looked as if they could cut. That, along with the scar on his jaw, gave him a sinister look. Yet it was his wide mouth that turned him sensual.

Carnal.

With her eyes locked with his, she had the insane and wanton urge to sink her hands into his thick, black hair and hold his head in place as she kissed him.

She'd never had such a physical reaction to a man before. Lust drummed in her ears, making it difficult to breathe. Her lips parted as she thought about the kiss. Would it be slow and erotic? Or fast and fiery?

Or even better . . . a mix of both.

"Good. You're awake," Kinsey said as she came from the kitchen. "Anson has been standing guard over you for the past hour."

Devon jumped at Kinsey's voice, only just comprehending that her chest was heaving and her toes were curled in the rug at just the thought of kissing . . . Anson.

So the hunk was real. And he'd stood guard over her? Her gaze lowered to his wide chest and continued down to his long legs. Her gaze snagged on his hands that hung at his sides, the fingers of his right hand curling slightly as she watched.

Despite her fears and the unknown of what awaited her, she had one thought running through her head: *yum*!

CHAPTER SEVEN

The way Devon's light blue eyes perused him made Anson *burn*. He couldn't look away—nor did he want to. Desire scorched his veins as his balls tightened and a hunger throbbed within him.

While she slept, he'd looked her over from head to foot and back again. It had been hard to ignore her long legs and supple curves while he'd watched from afar. But now, he had an up-close-and-personal view.

And he more than liked what he saw.

He'd crossed his arms to keep his hands away from the shiny brunette locks that fell to her shoulders. Her flawless visage, however, was what held him transfixed.

There wasn't anything that stood out in particular in her oval face, but as a whole, he thought her magnificently perfect. Her round eyes, her pert nose, her wide forehead, and her plump lips.

It was a good thing Kinsey and Esther were in the flat because he wasn't sure he could keep his distance from Devon.

Then, finally, she woke. As soon as those stunning eyes of hers landed on him, he forgot how to breathe.

Her irises were as clear a blue as the Scottish sky in summer—and just as brilliant.

She ran her hand through her hair as Kinsey walked up, talking, not that Anson paid any attention to what Kinsey was saying. He was too focused on Devon.

Kinsey elbowed him in the ribs. He cut her a look before realizing that she was looking at him curiously. He swallowed and looked away, only to find Esther smiling as if she knew exactly what he'd been thinking.

He nodded to Devon and backed away so the girls could properly introduce themselves. Though he didn't go far. He wasn't sure what was wrong with him. He'd watched Devon for a few days and had never felt such a physical response before.

Did it have something to do with the previous night and the man who'd entered her house? That must be it. Because nothing else made any sense.

"How did you get inside my home?" Devon demanded. "I have a specialized code that no one knows."

Esther finished off the last of her bottled water and walked from the kitchen to the living area. She took the empty chair and crossed one leg over the other. "Kyvor has known it for a while. One of their men entered your house at three this morning."

"What?" Devon asked, her eyes wide with anger and fear.

Kinsey held up a hand. "Anson was here and stopped the intruder before he could do anything."

"Like what? What was the man going to do?" Devon asked, her gaze trained on him.

Anson took a deep breath and slowly released it. "I didna stop to ask him."

"You're Scottish, too."

She said it as if it surprised her. "I am."

"What do you have to do with Kyvor?"

He hesitated, unsure how to begin. It wasn't as if he could blurt out that he was an immortal Dragon King there to end everything to do with the company.

Fortunately, Kinsey didn't have his worries. She said, "We're all involved with wanting to shut Kyvor down."

"Why?" Devon questioned, a deep frown puckering her forehead.

Esther shrugged a shoulder. "Because they're evil and they need to be stopped."

Devon blinked. "Listen, I—"

"Before you continue, look at this," Kinsey said, handing her a laptop.

Anson watched as Devon scrolled through the pictures from the memory card he'd managed to swipe from one of the men following Devon earlier that morning. The more pictures she looked at, the paler she became. Then she set aside the computer and closed her eyes.

His fury ran thick and deep on her behalf. He could only imagine what she was feeling. When she lifted her lids, she looked right at him. He saw her resolve and the beginnings of anger.

"Why are they following me? Surveilling me?" Devon asked.

Kinsey sat beside her on the couch and shook her head. "I haven't figured that out yet. With me, it was because of who I was dating."

"That's absurd." Devon's face scrunched up. "Why would they care who you dated?"

"Because of who he is," Anson replied.

Kinsey pressed her lips together before continuing. "We came to London to find out how much Kyvor knows. We need someone on the inside. I didn't know when I chose you that they might already have you under surveillance."

Devon's eyes grew round. "Chose me? Why would you pick me?"

"There was something about you," Esther said. "I'd classify it as honesty."

The play of emotions on Devon's face as she slowly sank back against the cushions captivated Anson. Her entire world was unraveling, and she wasn't even aware of just how thoroughly everything was about to come apart.

He felt sorry for her. The only thing that made it better was knowing that they would help her distance herself from Kyvor. The sooner she was away from them, the better.

"I've dedicated years of my life to Kyvor," Devon said. "I did a comprehensive investigation into the company before I applied."

"You only saw what they wanted you to find," Kinsey said.

Esther merely replied, "They are the leading tech company in the UK, remember."

As if that said it all. Though he had to admit, it did. Anson remained quiet while Devon absorbed it all. For several tense minutes, she sat silently.

Then she looked at Kinsey and asked, "How do you know I won't go back to Kyvor and tell them everything you've told me?"

"Because once you know it all, you'll comprehend how dangerous they are." Esther then tossed something on the coffee table. "And because I found and disconnected the cameras in your flat."

Devon lifted one of the small cameras the size of a button and looked at it. "Won't they know it's gone?"

"I've looped a recording of all the rooms. It'll give us a little time," Kinsey said.

Devon set down the camera and folded her hands in her lap. "Tell me everything."

"Are you sure you want to know?" Anson asked. "Once you know everything, there's no going back."

Her clear gaze met his. "I don't do anything in half measures. My interest was piqued last night. I did a search on Kinsey on my laptop."

"Kyvor saw that," Esther stated.

"I'm aware of that now." Devon drew in a deep breath. "If you want my help, I have to know everything you know."

Kinsey glanced at Anson before she said, "Some . . . things . . . might be pretty difficult to believe."

"Tell me anyway."

Anson gave Kinsey a nod. There was only so much she would tell Devon. It would then be up to him whether Devon learned the secrets the Dragon Kings fought so hard to keep.

Kinsey smiled. "All right, then. As I'm sure you learned when you searched me, I'm rather good at what I do."

"Hacking," Devon said.

Kinsey's smile widened. "Yes. Computers and software coding come easily to me. Most people never understood me. That is until I met Ryder. If you think I'm good, he's brilliant. He molds anything electrical into whatever he wants. If he can think it, he can create it."

"Does he work for Kyvor?" Devon asked.

Kinsey shook her head. "Ryder and I dated for a while before he returned to his home."

At the mention of that, Devon's gaze shifted to Anson. He saw the question in her eyes, but she didn't ask it. Instead, she turned her attention back to Kinsey.

"For three years, I had no contact with Ryder," Kinsey continued. "Part of my job description with Kyvor was that I would get work orders, sending me to large companies or corporations to overhaul their IT departments or work out bugs. One of my specialties is security systems. A few weeks ago, I got a work order that took me to Scotland."

"Why aren't you telling me the company name?" Devon questioned.

Both Kinsey and Esther looked to Anson. He waited until Devon's gaze slid to him, as well. Then he said, "It's Dreagan Industries."

There was a small flash of surprise in Devon's blue eyes. "Ryder works for Dreagan?"

"Yes," Kinsey answered. "I wasn't aware of that, however. I thought he'd submitted the work order to get me there, but he didn't."

"Then who did?" Devon asked.

Anson leaned forward to rest his forearms on his thighs. "No' anyone at Dreagan."

Devon's forehead crinkled with her confusion. "I don't understand."

"It was someone at Kyvor," Esther explained.

"But . . . why?" Devon shook her head as if she couldn't make sense of it all.

Kinsey gave her a half-smile. "They wanted me at Dreagan. Fortunately for me, Ryder was able to convince the others to give me a chance to discover what had happened. With his help, we hacked Kyvor's computers and found that someone had shut off all the building cameras for a short period. Though we couldn't see the face, we did learn that the fake work order originated at Kyvor."

"From there, Ryder was able to work his magic and found all the pictures of Kinsey, as well as those of them together," Anson added.

Devon swallowed. "Did you contact Kyvor?"

Kinsey's lips twisted in a grimace. "I did. I called my supervisor, Cecil. He was adamant that I remain at

Dreagan and sell them as much as I could. It was talking with him that clued me in that he wasn't running the show."

Anson saw the way the pulse in Devon's throat beat wildly, yet she kept her composure. Her fear was palpable, however. Not that he blamed her. What Kyvor was doing was beyond reprehensible.

"Who *is* running things?" Devon asked.

Kinsey exchanged a look with Esther. "That, we don't really know. There was software on my phone that tracked me. We were able to get rid of it, but the more Ryder and I dug, the more it was obvious that Kyvor wanted something."

"Dreagan." Devon's gaze swung to Anson. "Or someone there."

Anson nodded, impressed with her quick assessment of the situation.

She looked between Kinsey and Esther. "Then what happened?"

"Me," Esther said and lowered her eyes to the floor for a moment. "I was recruited by MI5 because of how well my brother did as a spy. Henry had no idea that I was there or that they'd put me out into the field so quickly. I had several missions that went well. Then I came up with a plan to infiltrate the very people who were spying on Dreagan. We had no names or even an idea of where to begin, but we knew it was Kyvor. I went undercover with a new name and story that was more solid than anything MI5 had ever done.

"I found a flat and began looking for jobs. I was interviewed by Kyvor, but the position went to someone else. MI5 then stepped in and made an offer to that person they couldn't refuse. Kyvor then called me. I went in to start work and walked into a room with a woman—who I now can't recall—and then my memory goes blank until I woke up at Dreagan."

"Why Dreagan?" Devon asked.

But her gaze was on Anson. He had never shared his secret with anyone, and he wasn't sure that Devon needed to know it. The more people who knew the truth, the more chance of exposure for the Dragon Kings.

"Dragons," Kinsey said.

Devon rolled her eyes. "You're talking about that video that surfaced a bit ago about men shifting into dragons. It's a hoax. Why would anyone believe it?"

"MI5 did," Esther replied.

Kinsey shifted to face Devon once more. "Ryder was able to locate pictures from CCTV of Esther in Ireland, at Dreagan, and at a shop in Perth called The Silver Dragon."

"What's special about that?" Devon asked.

This, Anson was prepared to answer. "It's the business of a man named Ulrik. He's an enemy, who has gone out of his way to ruin Dreagan. He uses many aliases in an attempt to keep his identity from hu . . . others."

At his near slip, Devon frowned, but she didn't question it. She looked at Esther. "You don't remember going to any of those places?"

"No," Esther stated.

"I don't understand."

Kinsey sighed softly. "None of us did."

"I was questioned by those at Dreagan," Esther said. "I was so sure that everyone there was some type of villain. Despite my training, I gave up the name of the person I was working for—Sam MacDonald."

Devon raised a brow. "You all look at me as if you hope I'll know that name. I don't."

Anson was both relieved and troubled. If she didn't know anything about Ulrik, then why was Kyvor following her? There had to be something else.

Just as before, he felt as if he were circling the answer, that it was right before him. If only he could see it.

CHAPTER EIGHT

Devon found herself repeatedly looking at the brooding Scot. How odd that she used to think the brogue harsh and ugly. Yet Anson's deep, smooth voice relaxed her. And she wanted to hear more of it.

Devon was relieved that she didn't know Sam MacDonald or this Ulrik. The mere mention of the name set everyone in the room on edge—Anson more so than the others.

"You see," Anson continued, "we believed it was only Esther we had to worry about. That wasna true. I was guarding Ryder's room as Kinsey slept. One night, I heard her scream. When I rushed inside, I found her curled on the floor of the bathroom with her hands covering her ears. Ryder and another friend, Dmitri, arrived then. We could see how much pain she was in, and Ryder reacted quickly. He went to pick Kinsey up, only she stopped screaming when he did."

Devon glanced at Kinsey to see that her eyes were lowered to her lap where she picked at her nails as if the retelling were painful to hear.

Anson rubbed his hand over his chin. "Kinsey lost

consciousness. A moment later, her eyes snapped open, and she stood. But it wasna Kinsey. She was someone else. She didna recognize any of us. We each tried to stop her, but she fought us. She got the better of all of us, but we were able to catch up and follow her to where Esther was being held."

The story was becoming more intense, and Devon was anxious to hear the ending—especially since all three were sitting in her living room, seemingly on good terms.

"Kinsey and Esther began to fight," Anson said. "It wasna long before Esther let out a scream and clutched her head the same way Kinsey had. The next thing we knew, Esther was no longer herself. It was as if someone had flipped a switch and controlled both of them."

Devon got to her feet and walked into the kitchen. It didn't matter that it was just a little after noon, she needed something to settle her nerves, something strong. She poured a large glass of wine and took a drink.

Then she faced the group. "What you're saying isn't possible."

"It is," Kinsey said.

Esther nodded. "Trust us. We know."

"Then that means someone got into your head. Like hypnosis." Devon gave herself a virtual pat on the back for coming up with the answer.

"No' exactly," Anson said.

She took another drink before letting out a laugh. "It's not as if magic were used."

The silence that followed her statement was deafening.

"There's no such thing as magic," Devon stated.

Esther uncrossed her legs. "Actually, there is."

"I wish there were an easier way to break this to you," Kinsey said as she turned on the sofa to face Devon. "But Esther is right. There is magic."

"You're serious." Devon was beginning to wonder if she was going crazy. Why else would she believe complete strangers over the company she'd worked with for years? It was bonkers.

She must be barmy.

Yes. That was the explanation.

Her gaze came to rest on Anson. He looked at her as if he knew exactly what she was thinking. There was no censor in his black gaze. Only acceptance.

It was because of him that she *wanted* to believe the story. But no matter how she turned it, she couldn't. There was no such thing as magic. She'd known that since she was a little girl.

"If you don't believe, then the rest of the story doesn't need to be told," Esther said as she got to her feet.

Kinsey stood, as well and held out a hand to stop Esther. "Wait." She then looked to Devon. "Please, hear us out. You wanted the truth, and that's what we're here to give you."

Devon had told them to tell her everything. It wasn't as if she'd ordered them to only tell her facts that she could confirm. This was their story, and whether or not she believed it, they did.

"Go on," she consented.

Esther didn't bother to return to her seat. She moved to the window and peeked out of the blinds. Anson's gaze was now focused on the floor.

That left only Kinsey, who gave her a half-smile and slowly lowered herself onto the sofa. "There is magic, Devon. One of the types of beings who are able to use it is Druids. Believe it or not, but there are some very powerful Druids walking among us. So powerful, that when those at Dreagan were able to break the spell on Esther, she remembered nothing of her time in Ireland or with Ulrik or at Dreagan."

Devon finished off her wine, hoping it would help numb the feeling of unease that kept growing. Unfortunately, it would likely take more than one glass.

Once more, her gaze moved to Anson. He sat still as stone. His long locks had a slight wave. They seemed to call out for her to run her hands through their inky length. His hair looked as soft as his body appeared hard.

And though she was ogling the fine male form in her living room, her mind had focused on the part about those at Dreagan breaking what they claimed was a Druid enchantment.

She kept that to herself for the moment.

"It took me a bit to come out of the spell," Kinsey said. "I know all of this sounds very unbelievable, but it's the truth."

"And you think all of this involves Kyvor," Devon said.

Anson's gaze slowly lifted to her. "We do. The woman Esther met at Kyvor is the key."

"The Druid, you mean."

He remained silent for a beat. "Aye. The Druid."

"And you want me to find this woman?"

Kinsey jumped to her feet and took a few steps toward her. "No," she quickly said. Then she drew in a breath and said more calmly, "We don't want you in any danger."

"Apparently, I'm already in danger." Damn but why couldn't she stop looking at Anson? It wasn't like he was going to be the one to save her.

She'd learned long ago that the only one who could save her was herself. Knights on white horses existed only in fairy tales. And fiction was far removed from reality.

"We're hoping you can find out who is making the decisions about Dreagan," Kinsey said. "We just need a name."

A name. That sounded simple enough. But an operation such as Kyvor going after Dreagan meant a team of people. "It'll be more than one, though."

"Most likely," Anson agreed.

"And it will probably get worse for you," Esther said without turning from the window.

Worse. Just what she needed.

Kinsey's face scrunched up. "I know we're asking a lot."

"You're asking for me to ruin my life. If I start digging into anything at the company, I will lose everything I've worked so hard to gain," she told them.

Anson's head tilted to the side. "Do you really want to be part of a company that invades an employee's private life? Or worse, tries to control them?"

"No."

With that, Anson stood and walked toward the back of the flat. Dimly, she heard the door close behind him as he left.

"I know you don't believe us," Kinsey said. "It's all very unbelievable, but it's the truth. Please take some time and consider everything we've told you."

Esther faced her then. "And think on the fact that Kyvor has been following you, bugging your home, taking pictures of you, and who knows what else. They did it to Kinsey, and they're doing it to you. Why? More importantly, who else are they doing it to?"

"You can't trust anyone at the company," Kinsey added.

Esther moved to stand beside Kinsey. "Our lives were in their hands, and I hate that. If it weren't for my brother and those at Dreagan, both Kinsey and I would be dead. I owe the people at Dreagan my life. Part of that debt is discovering what Kyvor wants with them and erasing all evidence. We could use your help, but we'll get what we need one way or another."

After a look to Kinsey, Esther walked out.

For long moments, Kinsey simply looked at Devon. Then she released a long breath. "Whether you believe us about the magic or not, think about everything else we've told you. Kyvor is lying to everyone. This is your chance to help us and break free of them. Stand with us to take down this company so no more lives are ruined."

Devon set aside her wine glass. She didn't know how to respond, so she didn't say anything at all.

"Whether you help or not, we'll do our best to keep an eye on you." Kinsey then walked to a bag that leaned against the side of the sofa. She took something out and walked back to the kitchen with a smile as she held out the computer. "This is a clean laptop. Keep it with you at all times. Change the code on your locks every other day. Keep the mobile we gave you. If you want to help, you know how to reach us."

Devon took the laptop and brought it against her chest as Kinsey gathered her items and walked out. As soon as she heard the door close, Devon set aside the computer and hurried to change the code on both doors.

She then stood in her living room, looking around at the home that had been her sanctuary. It had been invaded by men spying on her. And for what? Being an exemplary employee?

It infuriated her that she was being spied upon. In her own home. Of course, there was the chance that Esther had lied about the cameras in her flat, but Devon didn't think so.

She'd seen the pictures of Kinsey with her own eyes. Though she hadn't seen anyone following her, the pictures she saw of herself were proof of that.

And, apparently, someone had been in her house last night. That was mind-blowing. She hadn't been aware of it, even if she had suspected it this morning. It made her wonder if her dream about Anson had been a dream, after all.

How many nights had someone entered her home and walked around, watched her sleep, and gone through her things? It made her ill.

How would she ever sleep again? Every noise would keep her awake. Even taking showers would be difficult. Perhaps she should invest in a weapon of some kind.

Not that it would help if magic were used.

She snorted at that thought. Magic. She'd believed everything up until that point. If only Kinsey and Esther hadn't added in that bit of untruth. They should've known she wouldn't buy it. So why did they mention it?

The only conclusion she could come to was that they truly believed that magic had been used on them. Obviously, it was some kind of hypnosis, which had been shown to be very effective.

When her stomach grumbled, she was reminded that she hadn't eaten. She pulled out leftovers from her Chinese takeout and warmed them up before carrying the cartons to the coffee table. She opened the new laptop and began to eat.

After several bites, she set down the chopsticks and did a search for anything related to Kyvor. It was of particular interest that it took significant digging before she found anything negative related to the company.

The search engine had buried those websites and blogs deep in the millions of pages of data. The only way for that to happen was with big bucks and the knowledge of metadata.

For the next four hours, she dug through pages and pages of information, jotting down names of past employees and anyone who had a grudge against the company.

By the time she came to the last page, her eyes burned,

and her head ached, but she had a list. Over sixty names of those who had spoken out against Kyvor. And every single one of them was an individual, not a company.

Devon rose and stretched her back. She cleared away the food and got a bottle of water before getting comfortable on the sofa again with the computer in her lap and the list of names beside her.

One by one, she did a search on the names. By the twelfth name, she saw a recurring theme: they were deceased. None of them were labeled homicides, though. Each was classified as an accident or suicide.

Just to be sure, she looked up every name on the list. And every one of them was dead.

Devon then put in her name. She hadn't done such a search on herself in over eight years because she was always afraid what she might find.

Surprisingly, there was no mention of the past she wanted kept hidden. Just like Kyvor, that information was buried too deep for anyone doing a cursory search.

Not even the past could keep Devon from doing what she knew she had to do. She sent a quick text to Kinsey, agreeing to help. As soon as it went through, she dropped her head back on the sofa and sighed loudly.

"I hope I'm doing the right thing," she said aloud.

CHAPTER NINE

Somewhere in Western Canada...

Usaeil stared at her reflection in the mirror of her trailer. The filming had wrapped for the day, and everything about the current movie was going swimmingly.

But she felt nothing but fury.

It spoke of her acting skills that she hid it while among the mortals. It was only in the privacy of her trailer, away from everyone, that she let her true feelings show.

Weeks had passed since she'd last spoken with Con. She'd expected him to search her out and apologize. After all, he was the one who'd acted like an ass the last time they were together. He just had to mention Rhi.

Didn't he realize that Rhi was dead to her? It was Rhi who'd left the Queen's Guard—*her* guard. Being Queen of the Light was grueling work.

Everyone wanted something from her, and no one ever considered what *she* might want. It's why she'd begun her acting career.

Her fans adored her. Everywhere she went, females from the age of one to one hundred dressed like her. If that wasn't devotion, Usaeil didn't know what was.

The Light were only concerned with their own desires.

Humans saw what they didn't have and tried to copy it. And they wanted to be her.

She tilted her head as her wealth of black hair fell to the side. Silver eyes stared back at her. Eyes that her recent co-star, the handsome Jason Statham, had called "mesmerizing."

There wasn't a man she couldn't have if she wanted him. Why then was Con being so difficult? Why couldn't he admit his love?

She smiled at herself. Not that it was going to matter. She had taken care of their little *secret*. No longer would that be a bone of contention between them. It was time their love was out in the open for the world to see—and accept.

The Dragon Kings would be thrilled to have her as their queen. The Light would come to accept Con, as well—because the Light loved her so much. They would bend to her will as they always had.

As for Rhi . . . Usaeil fisted her hands. Leaving the Queen's Guard had been the final straw. As soon as the movie wrapped, she would return to her castle in Ireland and announce that Rhi was banished from the Light.

It was the only course available. Usaeil couldn't kill Rhi.

Or could she?

She drummed her fingers on the table. There was one she knew she could turn to to get such . . . dirty . . . work done. Taraeth. The King of the Dark never hesitated to take care of such things.

He'd been happy to kill Balladyn.

She sat back in her chair and shoved her black hair over her shoulder. Hundreds of copies of the photo of her and Con had been hung inside her castle and distributed among the Light.

Soon, everything she'd worked centuries for would

come to fruition. Con had all but ignored her for eons, but she'd known it was only a matter of time before he realized that they were meant to be together.

When he had come to her, it had been the best day of her life. She'd wanted to shout the news to everyone, but she had respected his need to keep their affair quiet.

That had been a mistake. Now that was taken care of. And it wasn't as if she were to blame. She hadn't actually spoken to anyone about him. No matter what argument Con used, he wouldn't be able to be angry over that detail.

It wasn't her fault that the photographer was there, or that he'd snapped a picture of them. She laughed loudly. Con need never know that she'd set up the entire thing.

He would be too focused on blending the Dragon Kings and the Light together to think of anything but their upcoming wedding. Because there would be a wedding.

It was going to be a grand, lavish affair that would echo across the realms. Everyone would be there to fawn over and adore her, including Con.

The Dragon Kings would take members of the Light as their mates and finally be able to have the children the mortals weren't able to give them.

With Rhi out of the way, there wouldn't be anyone there who would dare to disrupt her perfect day with her Dragon King.

She wanted it all.

And she would have it all.

There were only a few more days before they took a small break in filming. That's when she would set things in motion with Taraeth in regards to Rhi.

At one time, she'd considered Rhi a sister. But that hadn't lasted long. Usaeil had recognized the power within Rhi that the Light Fae hadn't even suspected was there.

It would be better for everyone if Rhi never fully realized the potential she had. What a colossal mistake Usaeil had made trying to cultivate Rhi's power to help her grow. It was a good thing she'd seen Rhi for who she really was before the Fae did something impulsive and rash as she normally did—like try to take Usaeil's throne.

It was for that reason that she would have Taraeth kill Rhi.

Well, there might be another reason, as well, but that wasn't even worth mentioning. Rhi hadn't been with her Dragon King in thousands of years. It was over between them.

Wasn't it?

Usaeil swiped everything off her vanity in a fit of rage. That question should never have entered her mind. She had her Dragon King—the *King* of Dragon Kings. She was the one coming out the victor.

It wouldn't be long before everyone forgot Rhi. As a matter of fact, Usaeil had already forgotten the ungrateful Fae.

She took a deep breath to calm herself. Then she snapped her fingers to fix the mess she'd made. With a nod of approval, she stood. Merely a thought had the costume for the movie removed and a slinky white dress and heels in place.

She smiled at her reflection, pleased with her look. After all, there would be a group of adoring fans waiting for her autograph or even a picture. She had to look her best for them.

She exited her trailer and waved at one of her assistants as she headed to the waiting car. Halfway there, she came to a halt when Inen appeared in front of her.

Usaeil glared at the captain of her Guard. "What is the meaning of this?"

"I've been searching for you everywhere," he said and did a quick glance to see if they were alone. "It took me browsing the humans' entertainment news to discover where you were."

She raised a brow. "No one was supposed to be able to find me."

"It's important, my queen." Inen bowed his head and clasped his hands behind his back.

He'd been a faithful Queen's Guard for many millennia. She supposed she could take a moment to listen to whatever he wanted. "Go on. What is it?"

His gaze jerked to her, a frown in place.

When he didn't speak, she rolled her eyes. "I thought you said it was important."

"It's just . . . you're different."

She waved away his words. "Inen, get on with it before I leave."

"There has been an accident at the castle. The Everwoods have been killed."

"The entire family?"

"Aye," Inen said and took a step closer. "Your people need you. They're terrified it was the Reapers who killed them."

At the mention of the legendary Reapers, Usaeil laughed. "They aren't real. How many times do I need to say that?"

"Regardless, your people need to see you, need you to comfort them."

"I'm busy. It's going to have to wait," she said as she walked around him.

"On your movie to finish?"

It was the note of anger and resentment in his voice that brought her to a halt once again. She jerked her head to him and raised a brow. "You dare talk to me like that?"

"I dare to ask a question."

"Yes, Inen, I have to finish my movie. The Light can wait to be coddled until I'm done. If you feel they need more, step in for me."

He held out a copy of the picture of her and Con. "And what of this?"

She looked down at it before meeting his silver gaze. "What of it?"

"Is this Constantine? Have you taken a Dragon King to your bed?"

"I have. Deal with it. Our union will be happening very soon."

He took a step back, his face full of revulsion as his arm dropped to his side. "You can't be serious."

"I've never been more serious. Now, return to the castle and tell everyone that I said not to worry about the rumors of the Reapers. They aren't real."

She continued walking, a smile in place when she saw a group of her fans near her car.

"What do I tell them about Con?"

She rolled her eyes as she stopped. This time when she turned around, she let her anger show. "I don't give a flying fuck what you tell them. It's happening, and nothing anyone says or does is going to stop it."

"You never wanted Rhi and her King together. You actively worked to break them apart."

"And your point?"

"You told Rhi that the Fae would never accept a Dragon King among them."

She shrugged. "That was for Rhi. That doesn't apply to me. You know that."

"Usaeil, please rethink this."

"If you question me again, I'll banish you. Have I made myself clear?"

A muscle worked in his jaw. "Perfectly."

"Good. Now go away. Don't ever interrupt me again when I'm working in the mortal world."

She gave a shake of her head, wondering what he'd been thinking to intrude upon her like that. And if someone brought up the Reapers one more time, she might scream.

They were merely a story, a myth told to frighten young Light so they wouldn't turn to the Dark. Everyone knew that. Why then did every Light suddenly believe the Reapers were real? It was maddening.

She glanced over her shoulder to find Inen still standing where she'd left him. He didn't look pleased. That was something she would have to take care of when she returned to the castle.

"I'm Queen of the Light," she told herself. "I've ruled for over a thousand millennia. I've proven myself to the Light time and again. I've given them everything. There's no reason I can't take some time for myself."

How many centuries had she remained at the castle, listening to all the petty troubles of *her people*? How many centuries had she put aside her wants and dreams to sort out arguments, marriages, and other squabbles?

How many times had she gone above and beyond to help out some ungrateful Fae, who didn't even bother to thank her afterward? How many times had she thought of everyone but herself?

She hadn't married, hadn't allowed herself to think of having a family during that time. It wasn't until she stepped into the mortal world that she realized it was time to take back some of her time, to remember that she could have the things she'd always dreamed of.

One of those was Con.

And she wasn't going to stop until he was hers.

With a bright smile in place, she greeted her fans, basking in their love—as was expected of a queen.

CHAPTER TEN

Devon didn't know what she'd expected after sending that text to Kinsey, but she fully anticipated . . . *something*. Well, other than the thumbs up emoticon.

What the bloody hell did that mean, anyway?

She closed the laptop, unable to look at it any longer. Her mind needed something else to occupy it, so she decided to pick up the kitchen after the mess from that morning and reheating lunch.

Instead of cooking dinner, she opted to eat the rest of the cappuccino gelato. The flat was entirely too quiet, so she put on some music.

The first track from her playlist was *Dragonfly* by Shaman's Harvest. She danced around the living room, eating her gelato and pretending that the world wasn't crashing down around her as she attempted to navigate the unseen road without being crushed.

Using the spoon as a microphone, she sang at the top of her lungs. The song finished, and she turned around, only to freeze as her gaze landed on none other than Anson.

She couldn't think of another time in her life when

she'd been more embarrassed. As she stood there, staring at the god before her, all she could think of was how damn good his lips looked.

A man with a mouth like that had to be an expert kisser. And she really wanted to find out if that were true.

Men like him got women without even trying, which meant he knew how to kiss. At least, that was her reasoning. After all, he'd probably kissed a thousand women. Even after fifty women, the worst kisser had to be a pro.

She bit back the laughter that bubbled up. She had no idea what was wrong with her, and she didn't even try to figure it out.

"Want some gelato?" she asked, holding out the nearly empty carton.

Without a word, he walked to her. He stopped a foot from her and looked pointedly at the spoon. Her mouth went dry as she grasped that he wanted her to feed him.

Holy shit. Could anything be more erotic?

Well, it could, but this was certainly doing it for her.

Devon filled the spoon with the delicious treat and brought it to his lips. Her gaze was fastened on his mouth as those lips of his wrapped around the spoon. Reluctantly, she withdrew the silverware.

"It's good," he said after he'd swallowed.

She nodded, then frowned. "I locked my doors. I even changed the code. How did you get in?"

"You wouldna believe me."

"Tell me."

He shrugged. "Magic."

Not that again. "Seriously. How?"

He lifted a black brow, those dark eyes of his penetrating as they stared at her. "I told you."

"The system I bought is top of the line."

"Anything can be broken into."

Well, that made her feel better. "Wonderful."

"I checked around your block. There is no one watching your flat."

She gave him the carton with the final bit of gelato. "For some reason, I felt as if they were always around."

"They probably were."

"Then where are they now?"

"You've turned off your laptop and mobile. The cameras on their loop will only last so long before Kinsey has to reset them so Kyvor doesna become suspicious."

"Which means they're probably already suspicious."

"It's why I'm here."

She looked around, biting her lip. "Are you hungry? I can fix something?"

"I'm fine. I'll stay out of your way. Go about your night as if I'm no' here."

The snort left her before she could stop it. "Sorry. That's just not possible."

"Would you rather I waited outside?"

Their gazes locked, and though him being near reminded her all too well that she was a woman and he a very viral man, she didn't want to be alone. "No."

There was a tense moment when silence filled the air between them. It was Anson who pulled out a chair from the table and sat.

It was her cue to go about her business. Though her singing into the spoon was officially done for the night. She needed something to do other than ogling him. Devon took the empty container and threw it in the bin before putting the spoon in the sink.

"I didna think you'd agree to help us."

She turned to face him. "Because I don't believe in magic?"

"Aye."

"I try not to think of that part. The rest of the story and what I've learned about Kyvor speaks for itself."

His brow furrowed. "What did you learn?"

"When I did a search of the company, nothing negative came up. That's not natural. Look up any business, any person, and there is a mix of good and bad. Not so with Kyvor. I had to search through hundreds of pages to find the bad."

"But you found it."

"I did. Kyvor must've used their technology to hack all the search engines and change metadata to display what they want the public to see."

Anson stretched out his legs before him and crossed them at the ankles. "That's the theory Ryder and Kinsey came up with earlier."

"That's not all I found. Digging through those hundreds of pages of links to websites, blogs, and news articles, I discovered people who had actively spoken out about Kyvor's practices and policies, as well as some who questioned the ethics of the software and technology used."

"I doona think even Ryder has gone that deep in his investigating yet."

She went to the coffee table and lifted the paper with the names. "Give him this and save him some time. That list is what I've been doing all afternoon. Every name on it—all sixty—was vocal in criticizing Kyvor or someone who works for them. And all of them are now dead."

"All?" he asked, his frown deepening.

"Sadly, yes. And each of their deaths were either classified as an accident of some kind or a suicide."

"That doesna sound right."

She sank onto the arm of the sofa and let the paper fall back to the coffee table. "I'd be lying if I said I wasn't terrified. The smart thing to do would be to forget I ever met any of you, but I can't."

"I'll no' let anything happen to you."

"Thank you," she said with a smile. "But you can't promise that."

His look said he believed otherwise, but he didn't argue with her.

The silence that followed unnerved her. She rubbed her hands on her thighs, trying to find something to say. Everything sounded awful in her head, which meant it was better to stay silent. But the silence was killing her.

"My being here isna suppose to make you uncomfortable."

She looked into his black eyes. "It's me. I do this. I feel like I have to fill the quiet with talk, and then I can't think of anything to say. It's why I don't date. It's just too painful."

"You doona have a lover?"

Her heart skipped a beat at his question. Really, it was the way he'd said "lover" in his brogue. Her nipples tingled in response. An ache deep inside her began that she knew wouldn't go away as long as he was near.

It took her two attempts to answer. Finally, she managed to swallow and say, "No."

"Do you no' notice how men look at you?"

"I don't pay attention." Then she sat up straighter. "They look at me?"

He crossed his arms over his chest. "Aye."

How had she never noticed? Most likely because none of the men around were what she was looking for—present company excluded.

Now he was someone she'd go out with in a heartbeat. The fact that she was constantly breathless around him, her body achy and hungry to feel him, was frightening and exciting.

Needless to say, his statement did a lot for her confidence. She realized she was grinning stupidly and quickly wiped it from her face.

"That pleases you?" he asked curiously.

At this, she laughed. "Of course. To know that someone finds me attractive makes me feel good."

"Then you should feel verra good."

If he didn't stop talking, she was going to really feel good in a minute. Damn, but his voice was as smooth as chocolate and deliciously wicked as sin.

She wanted to hear more of it.

"Earlier, Kinsey mentioned that it was those at Dreagan who broke through the spell of the Druid. What did she mean?"

His lips lifted in a half-smile that made her stomach flutter. "I didna think you believed in magic."

"I don't." She comprehended her mistake and scrunched up her nose. "It's just that it's part of the story that was left out."

"On purpose."

"Why? Am I not trustworthy?"

He didn't look away or try to come up with a quick response. Instead, he said, "Lives are at stake. That information isna given unless it's needed."

"And you don't think I need it?"

"You doona. Besides, it wouldna matter since you doona believe."

Point to Anson. She liked that he didn't attempt to lie. He spoke the truth, no matter how hurtful it might be. It allowed her to trust him.

"You don't like London, do you?" She wasn't sure how she knew that. Maybe it was the way he sat as if on high alert.

He gave a shake of his head. "It's true, I doona. I prefer the mountains of Dreagan."

"I've never been to Scotland. How odd is that?" she asked with a laugh. "I've lived in England my entire life and never ventured north."

"I wouldna call that odd. I'd say it was sad. You're missing what I consider Heaven on Earth."

She wished she could see Dreagan through his eyes, to take in the beauty he was even now imagining. "Will you take me?"

"Aye, lass."

Though she was forthright in business, Devon had never been so in her personal life. The fact that she'd asked him such a thing embarrassed her, but that was quickly overshadowed by the fact that he'd agreed.

When his lips curved into a smile, she found herself returning it.

"What is it about you that puts me at ease?" she asked.

He dropped his arms, his eyes burning with some unnamable emotion that made her breasts swell. "Shall we find out?"

The invitation was out there, waiting for her to accept. Inside, she was screaming "*yes*!" But her brain cautioned her about getting involved with Anson with everything else going on regarding Kyvor.

As much as she was going to regret it, she had to decline. She stood slowly. All she had to do was walk to him. Hell, she didn't even have to do that. She just had to give him a reply. Even a nod would do.

Then he would do the rest.

He would come to her, pull her against his hard chest, and wrap those arms around her. He would lower his head and kiss her. Then . . .

She halted her thoughts right there. It wasn't safe to let her imagination go down that road because once there, she wouldn't be able to refuse him.

"It's been a long day. I'm going upstairs. Make yourself at home." She hurried away before she changed her mind.

But she was sure she heard him sigh as she left.

CHAPTER ELEVEN

Every moment Anson heard Devon in the tub was an excruciating, wicked type of torment. He closed his eyes, letting his enhanced hearing drown out the music she played to focus on her as she lifted her hand from the water.

He clenched his jaw as he imagined the drops of liquid rolling down her arm and onto her chest. Her skin would be dewy from the heat and steam. Had she wet her hair or pinned it up? Most likely, there were dark locks clinging to the damp skin of her neck and face.

A groan tore through him when more water sloshed as if she had moved her legs. When she began to sing along with the song, it caused him to smile since she was off-key and didn't seem to care.

Devon was a particularly troublesome woman because she made him ache and grin all at the same time. No female had ever done that before. The fact that he craved her to such a degree bothered him.

In his very long life, he'd taken various kinds of women to his bed. Seductresses, innocents, dominatrices, liars, thieves, and even submissives.

Each had something that drew his interest, but none had that special combination that would keep his attention for more than a few weeks.

The more he told himself to keep away from Devon, the more he ached for her. Half of him had prayed she would refuse to help them, but when she'd agreed, the other half of him inwardly shouted with joy.

She was an intriguing complication he wouldn't be able to stay away from. There was too much going on at Dreagan, not to mention that they were in a middle of a war that was only going to get worse as the months passed. And yet, he couldn't stop thinking about her, wanting her.

Hungering for her.

The big problem was that she didn't believe in magic. If she couldn't even consider that it existed, how would she ever accept him in his true form as a dragon?

His mood soured at the thought. There hadn't been a single instance over the eons where he'd ever worried about what a female might think of him as a dragon because he never intended to tell them his secret.

Ever.

He'd promised to wed one of the dragons from his clan long before they were sent away. Since he didn't make such pledges lightly, it was important to him that he remain true to his word.

Con had once warned him that there might come a time when that vow would be tested. Anson hadn't believed it to come sauntering into his life with amazing legs, a beautiful visage, and pale blue eyes.

He ran a hand down his face and got to his feet to pace the living area. The last place he should be is inside Devon's flat. He could easily watch the structure from outside as he'd done the night before.

An image of her eyes silently begging him to stay flashed in his mind.

"Fuck me," he murmured in frustration.

He couldn't leave. Devon was scared, and she had every right to be now that she'd begun to see what Kyvor was capable of. How could he, in good conscience, leave?

Kinsey would skin him alive, and he was pretty sure that Esther had ways of doing harm that he hadn't even thought of yet.

It was then that he heard it. The sound was so quick, so soft, that if he hadn't been on alert, he might have missed it. He took the stairs three at a time. When he reached the landing, he stopped and listened.

There it was again. Someone was trying to open one of the windows. He heard Devon get out of the tub. His head swung in the opposite direction when the sound came again.

He took a step toward the spare room in an attempt to take care of the would-be intruder before Devon came out of the bathroom. But his plans went to shite as she opened the door.

With one look, he took in the towel wrapped around her and the hair coming loose from being pinned atop her head. She had her head down and her gaze on the floor, so she didn't see him.

Anson grabbed her before she could run into him. He put a hand over her mouth to stop any sound and turned her so that she was braced against the wall.

Her eyes went wide as she looked up at him. He removed his hand and put a finger to his lips to keep her quiet. She nodded quickly. A second later, the sound came again.

It was then that he felt her grip his arms, her nails digging into him through the sleeves of his shirt. He didn't feel it because he was all too aware of the towel that was slowly coming loose. If he stepped away, it would fall and reveal her body.

His mouth went dry at the thought.

Then he noticed how fast she was breathing, and it had nothing to do with him and everything to do with the person trying to open her window.

Large, blue eyes stared up at him. Her lips were parted, and apprehension filled her face. Without thinking, he placed his hand on the side of her face to let her know it was going to be all right. Instantly, she loosened her fingers.

Minutes ticked by as they waited, but no more of the clicking sound could be heard. That could mean whoever it was had moved on to another part of the flat, or left altogether.

Anson took a step back and turned toward the spare room. He let one hand drift down her arm until their fingers touched. Looking back at her, he gave a nod of assurance. She smiled in answer as she held the towel up with her other arm.

He dropped her hand and walked into the bedroom. No lights were on. It might hinder a mortal, but not him. Moving aside the blinds, he was able to see that no one was at the window. A closer inspection showed where someone had tried to unlock it to get inside. He put his hand on the glass and used his dragon magic to ensure that no one could get in to do Devon harm.

He returned to the hallway but held up a hand to stop her when she started toward him. "No' yet," he whispered.

One by one, he went to each window upstairs and then on the first floor and spelled them. He then did the same to the front and rear doors. Not once did he see anyone attempting to gain entrance into the flat.

It should've relieved him, but it didn't.

When he finally returned to Devon, she stood where he'd left her. She was occupied, attempting to tuck a corner of the towel in to hold it in place, so she didn't see him.

Her head swung to him with her brows raised in silent question.

"They're gone," he said.

She blew out a breath and leaned back against the wall. "So someone was trying to break in?"

"Aye."

"On a second-story window?"

"It appears so."

She shook her head in amazement. "What next?"

"I've learned it's never a good idea to ask that."

Her gaze locked with his as the light from the bathroom filled the hallway. He knew he should return to the living room. It was the best place for him—for both of them. Yet he couldn't leave.

He closed the distance between them slowly, giving her ample time to move away. When he stood before her, he ran a finger down the same cheek he'd cupped earlier. Then he reached up and released her hair.

The brunette locks tumbled down about her face to skim the tops of her shoulders. He slid his fingers into the silky thickness and held her head in place. Just as he was lowering his head to kiss her, she looked to the side, turning her face away.

He released her instantly and took a step back. His willpower might have shattered, but not Devon's. She knew it was folly for them to travel down such a road.

It was lucky that she had the wherewithal to remember what was at stake. For him to complicate matters by taking her to his bed was pure folly.

Putting a finger beneath her chin, he turned her face to him and shot her a quick smile. It was important that she knew he wasn't angry. The relief he saw in her eyes affirmed that it was better they not give in to the desire—no matter how badly the inferno blazed within him.

Anson turned on his heel and walked downstairs. There was no whisky, so he settled for an ale.

He thought of Brenna, his intended. Had he given in to the yearning he felt for Devon, he might very well have found himself on the path Con had warned him about.

A century earlier, Con had urged him to let go of the promise he'd given Brenna. Con's argument was that she was long dead, and that Anson shouldn't hold onto something like that.

Though Con had a point, it wasn't Brenna's fault that he hadn't been able to fulfill his promise to take her as his mate. If he had performed the ceremony before the dragons were sent away, then he would've condemned her to an eternity alone without other dragons, never venturing away from Dreagan. Because a Dragon King's mate lived as long as they did.

And since a Dragon King could only be killed by another Dragon King, that literally meant all eternity.

Perhaps it was better that they hadn't been coupled. More so because if Brenna had truly been his mate, he wouldn't be thinking about Devon as much as he was.

All those years, he'd believed that Brenna was his one and only. Dragons mated for life, so when they entered such a union, both knew without a doubt of their love.

Is that why he had put off the ceremony with Brenna? Had he known then that she wasn't the one? While other Kings had looked to humans to occupy their beds, Anson had preferred to remain with dragons.

Mainly because a union between a Dragon King and a human had never brought forth a living child. At least with a dragon, Anson had known his line would continue.

That didn't seem to matter now that all the dragons were gone.

In an effort to move his thoughts from the past, he sent Kinsey and Esther a text, letting them know what Devon had found during her search of Kyvor. He then stared at the window, the next hour crawling by with excruciating slowness.

The flat was quiet. He didn't hear any noises coming from upstairs, so he assumed that Devon had gone to bed. Another long night was ahead of him. He lay out on the sofa and put one arm behind his head as he closed his eyes. He wouldn't sleep, but he could rest.

His thoughts drifted to the time before humans had arrived on the realm. Most of the other Dragon Kings called it a simpler time. That wasn't the case with him. It had been the worst kind of hell.

A dragon chosen to be a King wasn't given a choice. As soon as it became evident that a dragon had more magic and power than the current King, everyone wanted—and expected—a battle.

Anson had never asked for the gifts that put him in the position to become a Dragon King. He'd hidden his power for years until it became impossible to do so.

He wasn't the one to issue the fight, but he hadn't backed away from it either. When the King of the Browns had put out the challenge to him, Anson was ready to face whatever his fate might be.

Even now, he recalled Con and other Dragon Kings— Kellan, Rhys, and Banan—watching as the fight commenced. The battle had seemed to last for days. At one point, Anson thought for sure he would die.

Then his instincts took over, and before he knew it, he stood over the dead body of a dragon. Cheers went up from his browns as they looked upon their new King.

Except he hadn't celebrated. He'd had to kill for the position, a title he hadn't even wanted. He'd kept that to himself as Constantine came to talk to him. In the middle of that conversation, Anson had shifted to human form for the first time.

It was Banan who helped him navigate the new body and learn to shift back and forth at will. Through it all, he kept his true feelings about being a Dragon King to himself.

There were few times in the thousands of centuries since that he was glad of who he was. Now was one of them. Because only a Dragon King could protect Devon.

As if his thoughts had conjured her, he opened his eyes to find Devon standing beside him. He blinked, unsure if she were a figment of his imagination or real. Then she sat on the edge of the cushion.

He still wasn't convinced it was really her until she bent and placed her lips on his.

CHAPTER TWELVE

There was no denying it. She had well and truly lost her mind.

But it felt *heavenly*.

Devon could barely fill her lungs with air as she perched on the few inches of sofa cushion not taken up by Anson's powerfully built body.

It might be practical to say something, but for the life of her, she couldn't think of anything. Ever since he'd pressed that hard physique against her, she hadn't been able to think about anything but him.

Running her hands over those muscles.

Sliding her fingers into his black hair.

Feeling the weight of him atop her.

Having him inside her.

When he'd tried to kiss her in the hallway, she'd been so shocked that she looked away. *Looked away*! What kind of idiot does that?

Her, apparently.

She'd tried to read. She'd even tried to sleep. But he filled her mind completely. So she decided to do something she'd never done before—make a move.

Now, here she was, sitting beside him as he lay on the couch. His eyes watched her curiously—and with a touch of anticipation. The fact that he *wanted* her to kiss him gave her the boost of confidence to finish what she'd begun.

Her heart hammered against her ribs. But not in fear or even anxiety. In *eagerness*.

She leaned down and pressed her lips against his. There was a second where he didn't move. Then he let loose a groan that rumbled his chest.

A sigh escaped her when his fingers entwined with her hair once again. Her head tipped to the side as the kiss deepened. She could tell he was holding back, and after she had turned him away upstairs, she didn't blame him. But if she were going to do this, she wanted all of him.

Devon ended the kiss and straightened. Confusion filled his gaze. She smiled and got to her feet before unbelting her robe. There was a millisecond where it felt as if she had an out-of-body experience and was looking down upon the room.

Despite this being so out of the ordinary for her, it felt good. Right, even. There was a grin upon her lips as she pulled open the robe and let it fall to her feet to reveal that she had nothing on underneath.

His gaze heated her skin as he gradually looked her up and down. He slowly sat up and reached for her. Large hands were placed upon her hips as he pulled her toward him. Then he stood, lifting her as he did.

Her legs wrapped around his waist, and her arms around his neck. Their gazes clashed. Her stomach quivered with excitement when she saw the desire he didn't try to hide.

He held her easily as he made his way to the stairs. Before she knew it, they were inside her bedroom. He stopped in the middle of the room and set her down as if it physically pained him to do so.

She didn't want to release him. It felt good to be in his arms, and she wanted to return there. Reluctantly, she let go. As soon as she did, he began to undress.

His white shirt was the first to go. Her lips parted as she took in his finely sculpted chest to his stomach where she counted each and every one of his abs.

With arms that rippled with chiseled sinew, her hands itched to touch him. Before she got the chance, he removed his boots and pants.

When he straightened, she bit her lip at the absolute perfection that stood before her. It was the sight of his arousal that caused her sex to clench in need. Her desire blazed out of control—and she loved it.

In the next heartbeat, he had her against him, his mouth plundering hers. He kissed her hungrily, greedily. Ravenously.

She moaned, her hands clutching him as she fought to get closer. It wasn't until she felt something against her back that she realized he'd moved them against the wall.

His kiss stole her breath.

It gave her life.

As if she had been sleepwalking up until that moment. Everything became crystal clear. The more their tongues mated, the more she felt herself changing. Like a caterpillar becoming a butterfly.

He pulled on her hair, causing her to expose her neck. She gasped in pleasure as he kissed down the column of her throat to lick her pulse point.

Everything he did was erotic, sensual. Utterly carnal.

Her fingers slid into the cool locks of his hair as he continued to her breasts. She groaned when his lips grazed a nipple. Then those lips wrapped around the peak and sucked before his tongue teased it.

She was gasping for breath at the pleasure that filled her. All the while, his hands roamed over her leisurely, learning every inch of her and leaving a trail of heat in their wake.

"Anson," she whispered when he moved to her other breast and began to flick his tongue over the peak.

It wasn't long before she was rocking her hips in need. She relished the thought of being so thoroughly under his control. Helpless.

Ensnared by his skill.

He was better than any fantasy she'd ever had—or ever would have. With her head moving side to side, she waited—breathlessly—for more.

As his lips trailed down her stomach and lower, she moaned at what was to come. He then lifted one of her legs and placed it on his shoulder, exposing her sex. She kept expecting to feel his fingers or tongue on her. But there was nothing.

She opened her eyes and looked down to find him gazing up at her. The look of hunger, of need she saw there made her heart skip a beat.

But it was the unspoken promise that he wouldn't stop until she was fully satisfied that had her panting.

Still holding her gaze, he blew on her sex. Her head dropped back as her eyes slid closed at the first touch of his mouth against her clit.

His masterful tongue danced over her sensitive bundle of nerves until her knee buckled. Strong arms were there to keep her upright. As if the knowledge that he had her on the brink spurred him on, he doubled his efforts.

She could picture every motion of his tongue against her clit, of his lower lip against her entrance. Electric currents of ecstasy blazed through her as she rapidly succumbed to his expert teasing. He brought her to the pinnacle of pleasure, only to stop right before she climaxed.

She was so trapped in her need to orgasm that she couldn't form words. Then she felt his thick finger slip inside her, stroking slowly, confidently.

Going deep before using short thrusts that barely entered her. Every movement drawing her desire tighter and higher. She was shaking with need. A plea on her lips was never voiced because he kept her drowning in pleasure.

Once more, he brought her to the edge, only to refuse her release.

Her only thought was Anson. His touch, his taste. His body. She was trembling when he set her leg down, but not once did he relinquish his hold on her. He supported her even as he straightened.

She forced her eyes open to look at him. His jaw was clenched, showing he longed for release as much as she did. The knowledge that he was prolonging it for both of them made the flames of desire grow.

His hands cupped her butt before slipping beneath her and lifting her. He raised her high so that he had to look up at her. She gazed down at him, wondering at the attraction between them.

Her fingers lightly trailed down his cheek, feeling the stubble along his jaw. It was soon forgotten as he began to lower her so that she could wrap her legs around his waist. Her lips parted when she felt the head of his cock brush against her sex.

Then he was filling her inch by incredible inch. As her body stretched, she gloried in the feel of him inside her. Once he was fully seated, he nipped at her earlobe.

"Devon," he whispered, his hot breath fanning her neck.

Her name had never sounded so sexy. She wanted to ask him to say it again, every day for the rest of her life.

The first thrust of his hips halted any thoughts. She became centered on him, on their joined bodies. Time stood still in their bubble of ecstasy.

With the wall at her back, and his hands holding her, she was helpless to move as he plunged harder and deeper. No longer were they two people, but one.

One heartbeat.

One soul.

It frightened her, this connection she felt. But there was no way to stop it now—even if she wanted to. Everything about the past few days had been a roller coaster. The only thing that felt right, that felt good was him.

His strength, his masculinity brought out something primal within her. In his arms, she felt like the Amazon warrior she'd once pretended to be as a little girl.

"Look at me."

As if she could resist such a demand. She opened her eyes and gazed into the blackness of his gaze. His orbs were fathomless, bottomless. She could sink into the obsidian depths and happily give herself—body, heart, and soul—to him.

Who was he to be able to consume her in such a way? He had filled her body and mind as easily as if he wielded some type of . . . magic.

As she fell into his gaze, she caught a glimpse of something. It was so fleeting, so transient, that she couldn't put a name to it.

But one thing was for certain . . . he was much more than he claimed.

She could sense it within him. As their bodies joined, it flowed into her, as well. She was defenseless against the tide of power that flooded her and the satisfaction it gave her.

She delved her fingers into his long hair, and her body tightened right before pleasure erupted. Her lips parted, but the climax was so intense, the scream was locked in her throat. She was seized, captured by the force of it, before she fell into an abyss as dark as night. Surrounded by Anson.

He filled her every pore, every thought. Every reason, every wish. The only thing that mattered was the one thing she could hold onto—Anson.

Just as she was coming down from such an unbelievable orgasm, he thrust deep and held still. Her breath left her in a rush as the climax built once more. Defenseless against the onslaught of such wicked pleasure, she could do nothing but let it engulf her.

The scream finally found its voice when he began to move within her once more. He pounded her hard and fast, sending her winding down into a void where nothing but decadence and indulgence reigned.

Unable to even hold her head up anymore, she inwardly smiled when he walked to the bed. There, he carefully placed her on her back. Her legs widened of their own accord, wanting and needing more of him.

He braced his hands on either side of her head and pulled out of her, only to twist his hips as he slid back in. Her eyes rolled back in her head.

How could she still want more after such a fulfilling climax? She arched her back when he filled her deeply. For the first time, she understood what an addict felt like because she was quite simply obsessed with Anson.

His hips moved faster as his cock pounded her relentlessly. She watched desire darken his gaze before it gave way to pleasure as he drove inside her one last time and held still. With his arms shaking, and their gazes locked together, she felt his seed fill her.

Only the sound of their harsh breaths filled the room

until he lowered himself to his elbows before gathering her in his arms and rolling onto his back.

Even as he pulled out of her and the contentment of their joining enveloped her, she felt something nagging at the back of her mind.

It wasn't until she was drifting off to sleep that she realized what it was—they hadn't used any type of protection!

CHAPTER THIRTEEN

Sweden

V sat in the forest long after Ulrik had departed. The memories of a time long ago came to the surface, ones that V would rather forget altogether. But that wasn't to be.

It was the Dragon Kings' curse to remember.

Everything.

It was known that V hadn't been on board with welcoming the humans when they arrived on Earth. He'd argued against protecting them, but Con had given the final verdict. Though V wasn't one to back down from a fight, Con had the role of their leader for a reason.

In the end, he deferred to Con's decision. The peace that followed had been surprising. But it hadn't lasted. It seemed only a blink later that the betrayal by one human female had begun the war.

V willingly hunted down the bitch for wanting to betray Ulrik. Every reason he had to reject the humans came back with a vengeance. When Ulrik went after the mortals, V was by his side, slaughtering his way through the ungrateful wretches.

The dragons had accepted mankind. The dragons had

even moved away from their homes, from land that had been theirs since the beginning of time for them. How did the creatures repay such kindness?

By hunting small dragons for food and planning an attempt on Ulrik's life.

V didn't regret any of the mortal lives he took. They'd brought the wrath of the Dragon Kings down upon their heads. Yet as the months passed and more and more dragons were killed, V began to see the futility of it all.

It didn't matter how many humans died, nothing would bring back the dead dragons. He had helped Con convince many of those who followed Ulrik to return to Dreagan. Then his worst fears had come to pass—the dragons were sent away for their safety.

After Ulrik had been banished from Dreagan, and the Kings took to their mountains, V didn't think he would ever wake from dragon sleep again.

But he did. What he discovered of the world was far different than what he'd left behind. And just when he thought he could forgive the mortals, one of them stole his sword.

Every Dragon King was given three things: the ability to shift from dragon to human, a tattoo, and a sword.

Not having his sword haunted him, and he'd let his temper get the better of him, killing many of the villagers before he could get any answers.

Con had intervened, and V returned to his sleep. He didn't know how much time had passed before he woke the next time. His first thought had been finding his sword. It consumed him, that driving need to find what had been taken from him.

No matter how hard he searched, though, he couldn't find it. Every mortal he came across refused to even listen to his story or try to help. In his fury, he'd caused the Great Fire of Rome.

He slept again, waking hundreds of years later, intent on doing things differently. However, no matter what he did, things always ended the same. So when he'd found his mountain for the fourth time, it was with Con's vow that he wouldn't be woken unless the dragons were returning.

V looked around the forest. If only he could remember where he'd been when he lost his sword. Though it had been thousands of years since it was stolen, he had a feeling the sword hadn't moved far from its last location.

He wouldn't be whole again until the weapon was in his possession. It exasperated him that he might never know why it had been taken. He'd been good to the humans around him. Was it greed that had pushed them to take something that wasn't theirs?

When he'd left Dreagan this last time, V vowed not to return until he had his sword. As he'd spent the weeks traveling, he realized that he needed help to finish his quest. That help was at Dreagan. Returning didn't mean he was doing anything for Ulrik.

He'd spent so much time sleeping, that he had no idea what was really going on with the Dragon Kings, their war, Ulrik, the Fae, or the mortals.

It was time he got up to speed on everything before he chose a side. Because in a war between Dragon Kings, there wouldn't be a chance to change sides once the lines were drawn.

V might not know where he was, but he knew how to get home. He turned to the south and started walking. Once it was dark, he would take to the skies.

He passed many mortals on his trek. None stopped. Villages or cities, it didn't matter. They kept to themselves, their heads buried in their electronics.

Decadence lay all around him as the humans hoarded

things they didn't need to survive. Huge houses, various vehicles, fancy jewels. Yet they still coveted land, even though it was getting harder and harder to come by.

The mortals had the entire world after the dragons left, and all these thousands of years later, it still wasn't enough for them. He heard talk of space exploration to possibly colonize another planet.

Did they not remember their own beginnings? How could any species continue if they didn't know their origins? It boggled his mind, but then again, he'd come to expect nothing less from them.

He'd never been more thankful than when night finally descended. Though he'd covered a fair distance in his walk, he'd be able to reach Dreagan in dragon form long before the sun rose.

The onslaught of a thunderstorm made him smile. He shifted and let the coming storm cover his ascent into the clouds. He never felt more at home than when the wind was rushing over his scales as he flew. It wasn't right that the original inhabitants of the realm were forced to hide who they were, flying at night or not at all, simply because the humans couldn't accept them.

The actions of the mortals in the past and present were pushing him to side with Ulrik once more. V wanted to hear Con's side of things first, however. And since it had been nearly eight hundred years since he'd walked the world, he needed to learn what happened during that time.

He'd just reached Scotland when Con's voice filled his head. His first instinct was to ignore the King of Kings, but since he was returning to Dreagan, that wouldn't be a wise start.

V opened the link. *"Con."*

"I was beginning to wonder if you'd ever answer me."

The annoyance dripping from Con's words wasn't a good sign. *"You wanted me at Dreagan. I'm returning."*

"As much as that pleases me, you can no' do it as a dragon."

"Why?"

Con sighed. *"We're being watched. Mortals actively search the skies for dragons now."*

This must be part of the war with Ulrik. V ground his teeth together. *"Even in a storm?"*

"How far out are you?"

"I'll be there in less than thirty minutes."

"Stay high and in cloud cover until Arian can get a storm brewing."

The link was severed. V liked Con. He always had, even if he didn't agree with every decision the King of Kings made. And V loved Dreagan. The Kings were his family. He really didn't want to walk away from all of that, but so far, nothing was helping their cause in shifting his decision to them.

Ulrik must've known that's how he would feel. The King of Silvers was an amazing tactician. Ulrik didn't do anything he hadn't looked at from every angle.

The winds were blowing the rain sideways as Dreagan came into view. V dove from the clouds to the back entrance of the mountain connected to the manor. He landed and folded his wings as he spied Con and Kellan standing together. V shifted into human form and met Con's gaze.

"Ugh. Cover up," Darius said as he threw something at him and walked into the cavern.

V caught the jeans Darius tossed his way. No one spoke until he'd buttoned and zipped the pants into place. Then he met Con's black gaze.

"Why did you leave?" the King of Kings demanded.

V had expected this. "You know why."

"There's a lot going on," Kellan said. "We need you here."

"I'm here now."

Darius scratched his eyebrow. "What brought you back?"

V looked at each of them. He saw the wariness in their gazes. Ulrik must have done a lot of damage to create such an atmosphere within Dreagan. "As I'm sure each of you is aware, things have changed much in the mortal world. I still doona remember where I lost my sword. I grew tired of searching with nothing to show for it."

"So you returned for our help," Con concluded.

He gave a brief nod. "I did."

Kellan took a step toward him. "And during your time away, did you speak with Ulrik?"

"Aye." There was no need to lie. They would discover the truth soon enough anyway.

Both Darius and Kellan grew incensed at the news. Con was the only one who didn't so much as blink. In all the time that V had slept, Con hadn't changed at all.

"You might wonder why Darius and Kellan are acting in such a way," Con said.

V looked at Kellan and Darius. "Ulrik told me some of us have taken mates. I assume that includes both of you."

"Aye," Kellan said tightly. "Did Ulrik also tell you that he tried to have my woman killed?"

That part had been omitted. It was one of the reasons V hadn't made a rash decision. He liked to figure things out on his own with as many facts as he could piece together.

Darius's gaze flashed with fury. "He tried to turn Sophie against me. When that didna work, he went after her. Talk to any of the mates here. They'll tell you how Ulrik tried to kill them."

"Or was involved in their deaths," Kellan said. "Like Rhys's Lily."

Rhys mated? That wasn't possible, surely. V had been with Rhys on some of his womanizing forays. If Rhys had lost his mate, he would be inconsolable. "Lily died?"

"For some reason, Ulrik decided to bring her back to life," Con said as he crossed his arms over his chest.

That's when V knew it had been Mikkel, not Ulrik, who'd had Lily killed. Ulrik had said that the Kings blamed him for everything Mikkel did. That wasn't saying that Ulrik wasn't responsible for some of the attacks on the mates, but it did explain why he'd brought Lily back.

It also made V wonder if Ulrik was really over the betrayal of his woman. He'd thought her his mate. Even after all the centuries that had passed, Ulrik couldn't stand to have a King lose his mate. It was why he'd saved Lily.

Not for himself.

Not for Rhys.

Not even for Lily.

But for love.

Though V doubted Ulrik would admit that. Hate had turned Ulrik into something twisted and cruel, but the old Ulrik was still inside there somewhere. Which meant there might be hope for them yet.

"What did Ulrik tell you?" Kellan asked.

V looked into celadon eyes and wondered why Kellan didn't know. He was Keeper of History, which meant he saw things as they happened and wrote them down.

Those events were usually important ones. So either V's chat with Ulrik hadn't been significant enough for Kellan to *see* it. Or he was lying.

"He mentioned the mates. He also told me that there was a war and he intended to fight Con," V said. He intentionally left out the mention of Mikkel. For now.

Darius raised a blond brow. "He didna ask you to join him?"

"Of course, he did."

Con's gaze narrowed a fraction. "Have you returned to spy for him?"

"Apparently, Ulrik already has a spy. Nay, Con. I returned for the reason I told you. If you doona believe me, I'll leave."

Kellan shook his head as he looked to the ground. "I want to believe him, but we're already looking for—"

"I know," Con interrupted him. Then he glanced at Darius and Kellan. "Leave us."

V waited until the Kings were gone from the large cavern before he allowed himself to look around. While he'd slept the years away in his mountain, it was easy to forget how much he loved Dreagan until he saw it again. His gaze swept over the etchings and drawings of dragons around the spacious cavern.

"Can I trust you?" Con demanded.

He looked into Con's eyes and told him the truth. "I heard Ulrik's side. I want to hear yours."

"You've no' changed, V."

"Neither have you."

Con dropped his arms and pivoted, waving V to follow him. "Let's get a drink, and I'll fill you in."

CHAPTER FOURTEEN

Though Anson had his eyes closed, he didn't have to look at Devon to know that something was wrong. He could feel it in the way her body tensed in his arms.

"What is it, lass?"

"You didn't use a condom."

"I can no' get you pregnant."

There was a soft sigh from her. "Oh. But there're still diseases."

"You willna catch anything from me."

"Because of magic?"

He heard the dubious tone of her voice, but he didn't take offense. Instead of trying to explain immortality as magic, he opted not to reply at all.

Devon rose up on her elbow and looked down at him. Her blue eyes scrutinized him. "What happened between us was . . . beautiful."

"Aye. It was." Even he could admit that.

Having her in his arms had felt so absolutely perfect that it had taken his breath away. The way her body had responded to his touch, the way her eyes had held such wonder and passion, and the way she had given herself to him had been his undoing.

"No one has touched me like you," she said.

It was on the tip of his tongue to tell her that no man ever would again, but he stopped himself in time. He feared they might very well fall—and he wasn't sure just where they would land.

He'd lived most of his eons of time in the shadows. Yet with her, he wanted to be in the sunlight, basking in her beauty.

"Why am I drawn to you?" she whispered.

His fingers grazed her jaw before sliding into her thick hair and cupping her head. He rolled her onto her back, moving atop her and lowering his head until their lips were nearly touching.

"Sometimes, it's better no' to ask such questions."

She lifted a finger and traced his lips. "Because of the answer?"

"Because I doona have a reply."

"I should be terrified of this hunger I have for you. I'm not, though."

The pulse at her throat was erratic as her chest rose and fell rapidly. Her pupils dilated as desire filled her eyes once more. His cock responded instantly.

He ran his hand down her side to the indent of her waist and then over her hips to her long legs. His gaze lowered to look at her full breasts and the dusky nipples that strained for attention.

Hunger. Aye, that's exactly what he felt for her. That first taste had merely been a sample. He craved more. Even as it led him closer to the edge of this unnamable precipice, he wouldn't be denied what was so sensually offered.

"Anson."

He looked up at her parted lips still swollen from his kisses and groaned. Taking her to bed had complicated things, but he couldn't undo what had been done. Nor did he want to.

Just as he was lowering his head to kiss her, someone rang the doorbell. His head jerked around, and she stiffened beneath him.

"Expecting anyone?" he asked.

She shook her head. "No."

He jumped up and yanked on his jeans before hurrying downstairs. At the door, he looked through the peephole and saw Devon's assistant.

When he turned around, Devon stood behind him in a blue silk robe. "It's Stacy," he told her. "I'll be upstairs."

Devon walked behind him and placed her hand in the center of his back on his spine where his tattoo was. Warmth spread from her hand over every inch of the tat. He wanted to ask her what she thought of it.

The doorbell rang again, and her hand fell away. It was his cue to vanish from sight. He looked back as he reached the stairs and found her staring at him. He shot her a smile of encouragement.

She returned it before unlocking and opening the door. He heard the two women talking as he returned to the bedroom and the rumpled bed.

The night had turned out quite differently than he'd imagined. He hated that Stacy had interrupted them. Perhaps it was beneficial. He was there to protect Devon, not make love to her all night. With his attention on her in such a way, he couldn't guard her properly.

He heard something buzzing and bent over to find his mobile that had fallen under the bed. Once it was in his hand, he saw that he'd missed six texts from Kinsey and Esther. Now they were calling him.

"Aye?" he answered.

There was a grunt before Kinsey said, "About time. What were you doing? Shagging her?" The laughter on the other end of the line died when he didn't reply. "Anson?"

"Someone attempted to break into the second-floor window. I've used magic to prevent anyone from getting in. Same with the doors," he explained.

"Yeah. Okay. Um . . . is that all?"

"Her assistant just arrived."

Kinsey cleared her throat. "Well, I guess that's nice. In the days we watched Devon, no one came to her flat except those with deliveries."

"Stacy said it was to check on her since Devon had acted so weirdly this morning."

"How is Devon?"

Passionate. Warm. Beautiful. "She's beginning to comprehend how treacherous all of this is."

"Does she know that Stacy may be part of them?"

"She's smart enough to keep things to herself."

"Hmm. About my comment regarding you shagging her—"

He didn't want to talk about it, so he quickly interrupted her and said, "Leave it."

There was a beat of silence. "Just . . . be careful."

"I'm no' the one you should be telling that to."

"I'm out of my depth here. This is probably a conversation you should be having with Ryder. Or even Con."

He ran a hand down his face. "This is my business."

"Well, not technically. We're all in this together. We need Devon completely focused on her task."

"She will be."

"Next time, answer the phone so we don't worry," Kinsey said. "By the way, has she mentioned anything about returning to work tomorrow? The quicker we get this done, the better."

He thought back over the evening. "That subject hasna been broached."

"Well, bring it up. I'm finishing hacking into her phone and laptop that Kyvor infected. I should be done tonight and can return it to her in the morning."

"As soon as I know what her plans are for tomorrow, I'll let you know."

Kinsey paused for a moment. "Answer the texts next time, Anson. I hate worrying."

The line went dead. It made him grin that she was concerned about him. That could be because Kinsey knew exactly what a Dragon King went through when he found a woman who was their mate.

He desired Devon to a degree that seemed crazy, but he wasn't thinking she was his mate. That's what he needed to let Kinsey know. Just because a King took a mortal to their bed, didn't mean they were in love with them.

While Stacy lingered for the next hour, he remained upstairs, peeking through the blinds to see if anyone was watching the flat. Everything was going well until he spotted a Dark Fae strolling down the street.

The Dark didn't stop two women, even when they all but threw themselves at him. However, the Fae did look right at Devon's flat.

It was unnatural for a Dark not to take humans when they offered themselves. Something was very wrong. The Kings had been thankful the Dark Fae had grown quiet since their Halloween attacks on all the major UK cities.

Apprehension snaked down Anson's spine. Ryder watched the Dark while also searching the world for Ulrik and keeping an eye on the MI5 agents on Dreagan. However, the one who really knew what the Dark Fae were up to was Henry North.

He reached for his mobile and dialed Henry's number. This wasn't a matter that could wait until morning.

"Where are you?" Anson asked when Henry answered.

There was a short chuckle before the British accent came through the mobile. "Actually, I'm outside Devon's flat."

"What?" Anson wasn't sure if he was happy or not at that news.

"Did you really believe I'd allow my sister to spy on Kyvor and not be there to protect her? I let her down once. I won't do it again."

Anson briefly closed his eyes. "You had no idea she was even working with MI5. You can no' blame yourself for what happened."

"Maybe not, but I'm going to be here for her now."

"Does she know you're here?"

Henry made a sound in the back of his throat. "I only told Con before I made the trip. I wanted to get a look at the situation before I let any of you know."

"Is there anyone lurking about besides you?"

"I do a sweep of the area every thirty minutes, and I've not seen anyone yet."

"What about that Dark Fae?"

There was a string of curses that came through the phone. "Where?"

"Right out front just before I called."

"I gave Con a map of the Dark and their movements before I left. They've been strangely silent of late."

"Too silent," Anson murmured.

Henry blew out a breath. "Who did the Dark take?"

"No one. He ignored two women while keeping his attention on Devon's flat before continuing down the street."

"Something is definitely up."

Anson hadn't been sure about bringing a mortal into the fold at Dreagan, but Banan had vouched for Henry. Since the MI5 agent had taken up residence at Dreagan, Henry had been driven to keep track of the Dark to the point that it had become an obsession.

"Keep an eye out for any more Dark tonight while you're out there. Tomorrow, I'd like to see that map you gave Con."

"Agreed. I'd begun to believe the Dark realized they couldn't win against the Dragon Kings. That could prove to be a fatal mistake on my part."

"No one knows their movements better than you. We'll figure this out," Anson assured Henry.

Henry changed the subject. "How is Devon? Esther sent me a text earlier that said Devon agreed to help."

"She's frightened but also brave to undertake such an endeavor."

"You sound like you approve of her," Henry said, his smile evident in the inflection of his words.

Anson more than approved. "She'll get what we need."

"That's good news. It's too bad none of us can go inside Kyvor with her. Anything can happen within that building. Esther and Kinsey are proof of that."

Why hadn't he thought of that before? Anson was spending so much time protecting Devon now, but he would be powerless to do anything once she was inside.

Kyvor knew every Dragon King. If he entered the building, they would be alerted immediately. He wouldn't get to the lifts before they stopped him. And what would that do to help Devon? Nothing.

Even Esther and Kinsey were unable to help. Kinsey might be able to get inside, but Anson wasn't sure how much more she could do after that. That would also put her in harm's way, something that he had vowed to Ryder he would not allow.

Fuck!

"Anson?" Henry said.

"We've got to find a way to keep an eye on Devon inside Kyvor in case she needs us."

"Ah . . . yes, of course."

"Talk to the girls about it. I've got to go."

He hung up when he heard Devon walking Stacy to the door. As much as he wanted to take Devon back to bed for an uninterrupted night of love, her life was on the line. If his desires hadn't taken over, he would've remembered that earlier.

It was time he got himself under control. He put on his shirt and shoes. Then he started planning.

CHAPTER FIFTEEN

Something had changed with Anson since Stacy's arrival, but Devon couldn't put her finger on it. Before, she and Anson had been lost in a wonderful tangle of desire.

Now, he seemed to have put a wall between them. He constantly checked the flat. When he wasn't doing that, he stared off at nothing, deep in thought as he sat at her kitchen table.

"Does she visit often?"

Devon was so surprised that he'd spoken that it took her a second to realize the question was posed to her. She shifted on the sofa to look at him. "No. That's a first for Stacy."

"Do you trust her?"

"She's worked for me for several years, but I'm at the point now where I don't trust anyone but you, Kinsey, and Esther."

"Good. What are your plans for tomorrow?"

She glanced at the ceiling, thinking of her bedroom and the delicious, wonderful things Anson had done to her. Except she knew he wasn't referring to their amazing sex. "You mean about work?"

"Aye."

If she went in, then she could begin looking for whatever it was Kinsey searched for. It also meant that Devon could very well put herself in the middle of Kyvor's crosshairs.

"Take another day if you need it," Anson said.

She played with the edge of her robe, recalling how just a few hours before, she'd stood by the sofa and bared herself to Anson.

"It's better if I get this over with," she said. "All I have to do is look for anything on Dreagan, right?"

"We know what information they have. We want to know who is collecting it and where it's stored so we can destroy it."

"Of course." Kinsey had told her that. "I'll go in tomorrow and begin looking. If I'm lucky, I'll find what you need."

He nodded in approval. "I'll let the girls know."

Then, to her surprise, he rose and went to the kitchen and began washing the dishes. She smiled and sat at the table, her chin on her hand, completely enamored with him.

"I didn't know you did dishes, as well," she teased.

He threw a glance at her over his shoulder. "We're . . . private at Dreagan. We had someone clean the manor once a month, but in between, each of us has duties."

"Had? You no longer have a maid?"

He gave a shake of his head, his black locks moving against with the movement. "Several of us have taken ma . . . wives. They divvy up the work among themselves."

"What were you going to say just then instead of wives?" she pressed.

Shutting off the water, Anson kept his back to her as he said, "Mates."

"Magic. Mates. Druids. Whisky," she said as she sat back in the chair. "What a life you lead."

He turned to face her then. "Whisky is a business."

"A lucrative one if you're Dreagan Industries." She smiled at him then. "I'm having a hard time believing you do housework."

His lips curled and his eyes crinkled at the corners. "So you know one of my secrets. What's one of yours?"

"I don't do my own laundry." She laughed as his brows rose. "I detest laundry to the point that it makes me want to scream."

"That I wouldna have guessed."

She folded her hands on the table, suddenly curious to know all about him. "It sounds like there are a lot of you at Dreagan."

"There are workers we employ for the whisky, but I suspect you mean living at Dreagan. Aye, there are."

"All family?"

"Aye."

She wondered what Anson's parents were like, and she couldn't wait to meet them. Her smiled died when she thought of her own parents.

"And you?" he asked.

Devon shrugged but couldn't quite meet his gaze. "It's just me."

"It's late and has been a long day. You should get some rest."

She nodded and stood on wooden legs. Thinking of family always pulled her down into a pit of depression. Even after all these years.

When she climbed into bed, all she could smell was Anson on everything. She slid between the sheets, imagining them to be his arms, holding her, comforting her.

How she wished Stacy hadn't shown up. What might've happened between her and Anson? She'd never know now.

Though she could fantasize. She kept listening for him downstairs, hoping and wondering if he would return to bed with her, but she knew he wouldn't.

Somehow, she managed to doze for a few hours. At four, she woke, unable to go back to sleep. She rose and meditated before doing some yoga. That ate up another hour. Then she got into the shower to get ready for the day.

By six, she was dressed. She made her way downstairs to find Anson standing before her windows. The blinds were open, and the sunlight streaming in. He had his back to her as he finished fastening his jeans.

Her gaze landed on the massive tattoo on his back. It was of two dragons in a yin and yang formation. They had their mouths open as if roaring at each other. The edge of the circle seemed to be designed as if it were on fire with flames shooting up.

There were no other tats on his entire body. Weirder still was the color of ink. It wasn't black or red, but a curious blend of both. She wasn't an expert on tattoos, but she didn't think such a combination was possible, at least not with such consistency throughout.

He pulled on his shirt, cutting off her look at the artwork. Then he turned to her. She gazed into his midnight eyes, hoping to see the man she'd glimpsed last night when he'd been making love to her.

"Are you sure about this?" he asked as he nodded to her clothes.

She raised a brow and walked to the kitchen to brew some coffee. "Before you were doing everything you could to talk me into this. Now it feels as if you're talking me out of it."

"I am."

Her hands stilled. She set down the coffee and turned to him. "Why?"

"I know all too well what these people are capable of. I doona think you should go back there. Ever. Forget them and everything about the company."

"I know that by helping you I'll lose my job there. I'm fine with that. I don't want to work for such a company. But you need my help."

"We'll find another way."

"An insider. That's what Kinsey told me."

He ran a hand through his black hair. "Having help was the quickest option, but that doesna mean it's the best."

"Let me try."

She turned back to the coffee maker and proceeded to put in the filter. That's as far as she got before Anson spun her around, his grip tight on her shoulders.

"Doona do this," he implored.

His gaze was intense, as if he could will her to do as he wanted just by staring at her. She'd been scared last night, but knowing he was there helped to ease that. Now, she was full-blown terrified.

"What do you know that I don't?" she demanded.

He shrugged. "I just doona want to see you hurt."

"It's a chance I'm willing to take so all of this stops and no one else gets hurt."

"Getting us that information will hopefully lead to the downfall of Kyvor, but there're no guarantees."

Well, that just burst her bubble. She'd assumed Kyvor would crumble, but that was her own fault for getting to that assumption without clarifying it with the others.

"They could kill you. Or worse."

Worse meant the mind control they'd done on Kinsey and Esther. "I'd rather avoid either scenario."

"So would I. Doona go."

Her fear had grown to epic proportions. So it was easy for her to say, "I won't."

Anson sighed loudly, his shoulders dropping as if a

huge weight had been lifted from him. "I'll tell the girls so we can come up with another plan. Resign today."

He didn't promise to keep protecting her or watching over her. He didn't say that he would stick around to see the outcome of her leaving.

And she didn't ask him for any of it.

Not aloud, at least.

"Stay here. I'll be back after I check in with Kinsey and Esther," he said before walking out the back door.

Devon moved around the table and sat heavily in one of the chairs. Her gaze landed on the laptop Kinsey had given her. All the hours she'd searched Kyvor and come up with those poor people who had died after speaking out against the company.

There was no proof that Kyvor was responsible, but it wasn't a far stretch. For those souls who had been classified as suicides, their families were still fighting that ruling, saying that their loved ones had never exhibited any signs of depression.

For the ones who'd had the accidents, some of the families were questioning those, as well.

How could she sit sheltered and safe within her home when she knew such despicable acts were being committed? It wasn't just those dead people either. Kyvor had followed Kinsey. They were following her, as well.

They'd put cameras in her flat and spyware on her personal mobile phone and laptop. Where did it end? When did someone stand up and say it was enough?

Someone had to do it. If she stepped back and refused, how would she ever be able to look at herself in the mirror again? She'd already caused a horrible accident in the past that had nearly ruined her.

This would surely do it.

In order to overcome the past and the present, she had to do the one thing she feared: stand against Kyvor.

She got to her feet and walked to the door. She put on her coat, turned on her mobile, and grabbed her purse. Then, she walked out.

The taxi ride to Kyvor went by entirely too fast. Her heart pounded sickeningly in her chest as she paid and climbed out of the cab. She didn't hesitate before going inside Kyvor because if she did, she might back out.

Just as she was walking through the doors, she glanced to her right and spotted Anson running toward her. He slid to a halt when he spotted her.

Somehow, she would explain it all to him. That was if she lived through it.

The ride up in the lift was quiet. Even the twentieth floor seemed out of sorts, but maybe that was because she saw the company in a new light.

One that wasn't favorable in any way.

In her office, she hung up her coat and let her gaze wander over the space. Everything seemed to be as she'd left it, but she could've said the same for her house. Not once had she ever thought that someone had entered her home and placed cameras throughout.

If Kyvor could so easily do that in her own private, secure residence, what would stop them from putting them in their own building?

She looked out at the visible camera that hung in the corner over Stacy's desk and pointed at the doorway of her office.

A tech company as proficient as Kyvor could install hidden cameras all over the place so that they were never noticed. It was one of the products that she had been so vocal about supporting to clients.

How ironic that it was the equipment being used against her. The more she learned about Kyvor, the more she hated them. That fire helped to thaw the fear in her bones.

She hadn't gotten to her position within the company because she dressed nicely. She'd gotten there because she was smart enough to use everything at her disposal to get what she wanted—whether that was another client or a promotion.

Devon sat at her desk and turned on the computer. She had to remember that every stroke was being monitored. If she were going to find anything about Dreagan, she needed to be cunning while doing it.

Manipulation was something she'd learned at university. She hated using it, but sometimes, it was needed. It was a skill that she'd acquired and perfected. And it would probably come in handy in her current situation.

She looked through the calls she'd missed from the day before. Then she read reports.

She saw none of it. Her mind was on how to search Dreagan without being obvious. And she had to appear as if she were actually working while coming up with such a plan.

It was the camera on her computer that made her aware that they were probably watching her from there, as well. How many clients had she urged to put cameras above their employees so they could look down and see exactly what they were working on?

Which meant there was a camera above her. This only made her job that much harder, but she was up for the task. Because every time she questioned herself, an image of one of the sixty people killed popped up in her mind.

Suddenly, she paused, frowning. She set aside the report and went back through the missed calls. That's when she saw one from Blair Athol, a competitor of Dreagan.

The perfect reason to do a search of Dreagan to see if Kyvor had done any work for them, and learn what had been installed.

Although her hunt would need to go much deeper, it was a start. And that stepping stone was exactly the one she'd been looking for.

Devon saw Stacy come in and said, "I saw the missed call from Blair Athol and their interest in some security on their computers and the grounds. I want everything we have on any other whisky distilleries we've worked on."

"I'm on it," Stacy said.

Devon wanted to smile, but it was the first step up a mountain of obstacles. But, at least she was on the mountain.

And she would climb to the top!

CHAPTER SIXTEEN

Anson stood in complete shock as Devon entered the building. He took a step to follow when someone put a hand on his chest to block his way.

He looked down, ready to toss the bugger aside, only to find that it was Henry. Shoving Henry's hand away, Anson shouldered his way past the MI5 agent, but once more, the mortal stood in his way.

"Move," Anson demanded.

Henry shook his head of short brown hair. "I can't."

"You can. You will."

"No, he won't," Kinsey said from behind him.

Anson fisted his hands. Surely they hadn't forgotten that Kyvor had facial recognition going for a two-block radius around the building? They were taking a chance being spotted.

"She can do it," Esther said.

Out of the corner of his eye, Anson saw Henry motion for the girls to leave, but Anson didn't care. His entire focus was on Devon and what she had done. How long before Kyvor grasped what she was about?

How long until they tried to kill her?

Or worse?

He closed his eyes, unable to allow his thoughts to go further. All night, he'd gone over and over every situation and consequence of her alone inside Kyvor. Each had ended with Devon getting caught.

That couldn't happen. He refused to allow it. And he'd believed that he had things under control when he'd left her flat that morning. He'd barely reached the house where Kinsey and Esther were when Henry called him.

Anson hadn't cared who saw him as he ran down the sidewalk, barely leashing his speed in an effort to reach Kyvor before Devon—only to get there seconds too late.

"Kinsey didn't pick Devon on a whim," Henry said, breaking into Anson's thoughts.

Anson didn't want to hear any of this. Everything that would be said was to ease the tight knot of dread inside his chest that was growing by the second. But nothing could help Devon.

"Anson," Henry bit out in a low voice filled with a touch of anger and a heavy dose of insistence.

For the first time, he really looked at Henry. The mortal was growing more uncomfortable as the moments passed. Anson took a step back before turning on his heel and walking away.

A quick glance confirmed that he'd drawn attention. All he could do was pray that Kyvor hadn't witnessed anything because that scene on the sidewalk might just make things worse for Devon.

When they were about six blocks away, Henry tapped him on the arm and said, "This way."

He followed without question down the narrow alley. Less than a hundred yards away were Kinsey and Esther. Once they were together, Anson leaned back against the stone of a building and dropped his chin to his chest.

"If no one else will say it, I will. You've lost your mind," Esther announced.

Anson ran a hand down his face and looked at her. "Because I doona want Devon to die or have her mind controlled?"

Kinsey blew out a long breath. "I gather from the look she gave you before walking in that you tried to change her mind last night."

"This morning," he corrected. "There has to be another way to get what we need."

"It's easier with someone inside," Esther stated.

Anson pushed off the wall and glared at her, walking to her until she had to look up at him. "Do you care so fucking little for another's life that you're willing to sacrifice someone to get what you want?"

"You mean, what you want," Esther said calmly, almost daring him to let loose his anger.

Didn't she know how tightly he was holding onto his emotions? Didn't she realize the devastation he could cause if he lost control?

Because the one time he had let go of that control was the day he'd killed the previous King of Browns.

Henry said, "Stop it. Both of you."

"Henry's right," Kinsey said. "This is getting us nowhere."

Anson continued to glare at Esther, looking into her brown eyes. She had yet to argue against his statement, and he could see that she had no intention to. "I'm no' going to allow Devon to be harmed."

"There isn't much you can do now," Esther replied.

He spun around and walked several steps away before he gave in to the need to bellow his fury. It felt as if everything was set against him.

Henry called his sister's name. "You aren't helping matters."

"She's only speaking the truth," Kinsey said.

Anson looked around the alley and noted the few shop entrances. It was quiet with no cameras anywhere, which meant Kyvor couldn't see where they had gone.

It wasn't long before Kinsey walked to him. They simply stood in silence watching the people walk past the alley unaware of the wars they fought on multiple fronts.

"They didn't see it," Kinsey said.

He looked at her with a frown, unsure what she was referring to.

"You saw me in pain before the magic took over my mind," she reminded him.

Anson grimaced. It had been a horrible experience. He should have been guarding her, and yet he hadn't been able to stop her when the magic took over.

Was that what it was like when he used his power on others? He possessed their bodies, much like the Druid had done with Esther's and Kinsey's minds.

"I remember nothing of what I did," Kinsey continued. "Neither does Esther. But you witnessed it all. At first, I thought that was the reason you were so protective of Devon, but it's more than that, isn't it?"

He didn't want to talk about what had happened between him and Devon with anyone. Mostly because he wasn't sure how to classify it.

Kinsey glanced at the ground. "I like Devon."

"No matter how I look at it, there isna a way Kyvor willna catch her," he said.

"So you tried to stop her."

He nodded. "I thought I'd changed her mind. She waited until I was gone before she left."

"It was her decision. You need to understand that."

"She wouldna have made that decision had we no' entered her life," he said as he turned his head to Kinsey.

She looked regretfully at him. "I can't deny that.

Devon also did her own research, digging deeper. Ryder sent me the same info she found. A person can't look at something like that and not want to take action."

"I should be with her. I should be standing beside her as she confronts them."

"She's not confronting them. She's going to find what we need and sneak it out," Kinsey said.

He shook his head in frustration as he faced her. "Despite MI5 going to great lengths to hide Esther's true reason for being at Kyvor, they found her out. An MI5 agent with an entire force behind her who spies for a living. Can you honestly stand there and tell me you doona fear for Devon?"

"I do. A lot. Then I think of Ryder. I think of Dreagan, the Dragon Kings, and all the other mates. I'm doing this for them. That's what keeps me from altering the course I've set."

Staring into Kinsey's violet eyes, he recognized the steel within her as something Ryder had fallen for. "This isna the first time Dreagan and our way of life have been in jeopardy. It willna be the last. I can no'—and willna—put an innocent's life on the line to continue my own."

"What are you going to do?" Kinsey asked.

"Whatever it takes."

She lifted her chin. "Then I'll help."

"That includes us," Henry said as he and Esther joined them.

Esther's brown eyes slid to Anson. "I tend to get focused on a mission and forget other things," she said in way of apology.

"With two MI5 agents and a hacker, we'll be able to help Devon." Anson nodded to each of them. "Even in the middle of Kyvor, we should be with her."

Esther's eyes suddenly lit up. "Magic."

"What?" Henry asked with a frown.

"Dragon Magic. Why didn't you use it on Devon so the Druid couldn't harm her?" Esther asked.

Anson ground his teeth together. "I used my magic on her flat, but I didna think to protect her personally." Because he'd expected to be beside her the entire time.

"Do it tonight when she gets home," Henry said.

No one mentioned the "*if*" that hung unsaid.

Kinsey smiled suddenly. "Ryder and I got into Kyvor's system before. They've since updated their firewalls, and we probably can't communicate with Devon, but we should be able to see what Kyvor sees."

"Get it done," Anson urged.

"I need to be at the flat. And I need Ryder's help."

Esther said, "I'll go back with Kinsey."

"I'm staying with Anson," Henry stated before anyone could ask.

Kinsey met Anson's gaze. "Good luck."

"I'm here to watch over both of you. I'll walk you back to the flat," Anson said.

Esther raised a brow and smiled. "No need. Just give us some of that dragon magic."

He hesitated. They knew next to nothing about the Druid working with Kyvor. The fact that she had been able to manipulate their minds and bodies to such a degree suggested that she might very well be more powerful than any Druid they had come across before.

This Druid might even rival some of the Fae in power. It was a fact that nothing could best dragon magic. Yet. There was always a weakness somewhere, somehow. None of the Fae had ever found it, but that didn't mean this Druid—or another to come—wouldn't.

The Dragon Kings had never depended solely upon their magic for this reason. It would be folly to do so now. The Kings had won all of their battles because they used their skills and unity.

Times, however, were changing. And rapidly. The Kings were barely keeping up, but that was because they were playing by rules none of the others used. Perhaps it was time to put those guidelines aside.

"I doona like this idea." Esther rolled her eyes, but he continued before she could speak. "I'm going to do it even though it goes against everything I vowed to Ryder."

"We all know Devon needs you more than us," Esther said.

That might be true, but none of them could comprehend what Ryder would do if Kinsey were harmed in any way. And Anson would never forgive himself either.

He was being pulled in two different directions. It wasn't that long ago that he'd heard Warrick say something similar. He hadn't grasped then exactly what War had meant, but he certainly did now.

Anson put his hands on Kinsey's and Esther's shoulders. Then he gathered his magic and pushed it into them, encircling them in a protection spell that he hoped would keep even the unknown Druid from getting to them.

When he'd finished, he dropped his arms and nodded to the girls. "Stay away from the cameras as much as you can. Hurry to the flat and doona leave until I return."

"There won't be a need," Kinsey said with a grin. "We have everything we need at the flat, and it's protected. Do what you need to do for Devon. I'll let you know when we arrive."

Esther gave her brother a kiss on the cheek before winking at Anson. "We've got this. I know London. I'll get us quickly to the flat."

"She's not lying," Henry said as the girls walked away. "She knows this city better than I do."

Anson inhaled deeply before slowly letting it out. "Now comes the waiting."

"And planning."

He looked over at Henry to find the mortal grinning as he turned his mobile to the side to show specs for the Kyvor building. Anson smiled as they began figuring out the best ways in and out of the building.

CHAPTER SEVENTEEN

Ireland—middle of nowhere

Ulrik watched the pub for several hours. Graves was more than just a simple tavern. Fae—both Dark and Light—as well as Druids visited.

So did mortals.

The beat of music could be heard out on the street, but the locals in the small village didn't seem to mind. They went about their business as if other beings weren't walking among them. And the oddest part was that no Dark gave any of those humans a single glance.

It had taken very little to learn that no violent deaths had occurred in the sleepy town for over seven years. That was no fluke. Something—or someone—made sure the residents were left alone.

That would take a person with a healthy amount of magic and power enough to put even a Dark in their place. It had to be the Druid Mikkel was working with.

Anger sizzled through Ulrik at the thought of his uncle and the Druid in The Silver Dragon, conspiring to kill him. Mikkel knew that only a Dragon King could kill another Dragon King. Nothing he did was by chance.

That meant his uncle truly believed that this Druid could kill Ulrik.

Ulrik fisted his hands as he fought to control the tide of fury that gripped him. This must have been Mikkel's plan all along.

No wonder the man hadn't seemed worried about killing Ulrik once Con was dead. He had wanted to keep the Druid secret until the very end.

This was Ulrik's fault. He hadn't kept his hatred for Con a secret, and Mikkel had used it against him. All these months, Ulrik believed he'd outwitted his uncle. The truth was, he'd become too cocky and didn't look at all the developments or the consequences that could come from his uncle.

Because he'd believed he could take out Mikkel at any time.

That arrogance could very well be his downfall. All the centuries of planning, all the families that had worked for him, all his aliases, and all the deals he'd made could be for naught.

No. He wouldn't let that happen. He hadn't come back from insanity to let his retribution against Con slip through his fingers when he was so close.

It was time for him to put all his attention on his uncle. The first step was discovering more about his Druid. He sent a quick message under one of his aliases via his mobile to his technical team to dig deeper into Mikkel.

Ulrik might know about all his uncle's houses, cars, and business, but he wanted information beyond that. He wanted to know every nuance about Mikkel, and right now, he didn't have time to do the research himself.

With that done, he returned his gaze to the pub. Graves sat at the edge of town. The stone and brick of the three-story building looked to be at least four centuries old, but what would the inside hold?

It was time he found out.

Ulrik pushed away from his hiding spot and walked to the black door where two men stood guard. One a Dark Fae, the other a Light. Their gazes swung to him as soon as he started toward them. They opened the door without a word.

Was it his alliance with the Dark that got him in? Could it be his war with Con? Was it because he was a Dragon King? Or was it that the Druid knew he would come?

Not that any of it really mattered. He'd planned to get into the tavern one way or another. This was simpler. And cleaner. It would give him time to look around and observe what the Druid held dear.

That knowledge could benefit him. Everyone had a weakness. No matter what they said. She hadn't been pleased when Mikkel called her away from the pub, which meant that she preferred to be within the walls of what was hers.

Such information could be used against her once he learned if it was just personal preference or if she was more powerful within the pub's walls.

He'd discovered soon after being banished from Dreagan that the more he observed and learned about an individual, the better he could manipulate them.

As he walked through the doorway of the pub, darkness enveloped him. He was well versed in the shadows and felt at home in obscurity.

Magic pulsed within the building—and not just from the occupants. He slowly made his way through the crowd to discover that he wasn't on the main floor. Spotting a railing, he moved to it and saw that the level was open in the middle, showing a dance floor below.

The music thumped while the area below was filled to capacity with bodies moving sensuously, erotically with the beat as they ground against each other. Lasers of various colors bounced around the room in a fabulous light show.

He noticed that there wasn't just a mix of species within Graves but also of class. Wealth dripped from some, while others were counting change to buy drinks.

Everyone wanted in the pub. Why?

The place was decorated meticulously. The walls were painted black matte. The floor, tables, and chairs were shiny black with accents of chrome and white throughout that gave the space a contemporary vibe.

The main floor where he stood was nothing but half-moon shaped booths lining the walls so the occupants could look down at the dancers.

Ulrik looked up to find a high ceiling of mirrors. Yet he knew something was above him on the third floor. That could wait until later. For now, he would take a look at the level below.

He made his way to one of the two black, curving staircases with gold lights lining the edges. As he made his way down to the dance level, he spotted the bar on the far wall—a piece of art done in polished black.

Behind it were bartenders, who had their choice of every brand of liquor from around the world lined on glass shelves attached to a mirrored wall and lighted to show off the spectacular bottles.

The lighting was decadent, giving the atmosphere one of luxury, intrigue, and hidden treasures. It was bright enough to see but dim enough to lower inhibitions.

His attention shifted to the workers. The female employees wore leather—some full bodysuits, others little bits that covered their sex and nipples. The men were shirtless with leather pants. Some were Druids, some Fae, and some non-magical humans.

But all were beautiful.

All around him, Fae, Druids, and mortals laughed, drank, and danced as one. How had he not known the existence of such a place? Not once had a Dark made mention of Graves, which seemed odd in itself.

His gaze scanned the people as he walked among them. When he reached the bar, he turned to face the room, leaning his back along the wood. He studied the dancers for a long time. How free they looked, how limitless and uninhibited.

He'd felt that way at one time. It was several lifetimes ago, but it still haunted him. Never again would he enjoy such a feeling. Perhaps it had never meant to be his to begin with.

Ulrik pulled himself from the precipice of such thoughts and returned his attention to Graves. In any other place, the Dark would be draining the mortals of their souls with sex so wonderful the human wouldn't have any idea they were dying.

The Dark weren't using glamour to hide their red eyes or the silver in their black hair. The Light weren't attempting to hide their silver eyes.

It was more than that, however. Though the Dark and Light danced with the mortals, not a single human seemed to be throwing themselves at the Fae. Though all Fae could shut off the allure that pulled humans to them, leaving the Fae to keep control wasn't smart because they always gave in to their particular appetites. However, it would take a considerable amount of magic to keep the normal magnetism of the Fae at bay.

Another testament to the power of the Druid.

And since none of the Fae were trying to woo their human dance partners with sex, the Druid must have also contained them.

Ulrik was becoming more intrigued about her by the second. How he hated that Mikkel found her first. In his search for a Druid who could unlock his bound dragon magic, he hadn't even heard of one such as she. If he had, he would've sought her out immediately.

Now he understood why his uncle had demanded that Darcy be killed. Darcy had been powerful enough to touch his dragon magic and not die. Then she'd been able to break Con's spell binding Ulrik's magic.

In other words, Darcy might have been able to rival this Druid. It was too bad that Darcy had lost her magic while helping him. If Mikkel hadn't discovered her, and she hadn't become Warrick's mate, then she could've been of use to Ulrik.

Ulrik sensed he was being watched. He looked up, his gaze clashing with a woman of such lethal beauty that, for a heartbeat, he forgot why he was there.

Eilish.

The Druid was standing above him at the railing with her eyes locked on him. They stared at each other for a long minute before she turned to the stairs. He remained at the bar and waited as she gradually made her way to him. Despite her being human, he found her delightfully exquisite.

Long, dark waves of hair fell about her shoulders and down her back. Just like her employees, she was encased in all black from her stilettos to the tank that molded to her ample breasts.

He didn't take his gaze from her once as she came to stand beside him. Shifting toward her, he looked into her eyes that were a striking mix of green and gold with mocha skin that looked as if it were gilded.

One of the bartenders placed two glasses of whisky before them. Silently, they watched each other, sizing one another up.

She rested her left arm on the bar. He spotted the silver claws that fit to her second knuckle on four of her five fingers. The design was Celtic in nature and so elaborate that the historian in him wanted a closer look.

Finally, he said, "Since I missed you at my store, I thought I'd stop by to see what you wanted."

Her smile held no tenderness. "That was your second mistake."

Intrigued, he tossed back the whisky. Her American accent captivated him, but it was the hint of an Irish brogue that held him spellbound. So much so, that he set the glass down and found himself asking, "My second? What was the first?"

"Believing I'd want to hear anything you have to say."

"I doona think that was a mistake since you're standing here talking with me."

Her ire was evident in the way her green-gold gaze narrowed. "You think because I'm standing here that I give a rat's ass?"

"I do. I think my uncle has used you repeatedly, but I think you're curious about why he doesna want to take me on himself."

"Don't, for one minute, think I'm a fool." She drank her whisky in one swallow and motioned the bartender to fill both of the glasses again. "I know who you are, Dragon King."

He wasn't surprised. She didn't look like the type of woman who wouldn't learn everything she could about those who employed her particular talents—or those she was to use those talents on.

"Do you?"

Her eyes flashed as she cut him a look. "The banished King of Silvers who dared to begin a war with mortals."

"They began the war," he bit out, the old anger rising

quickly at the mention of the betrayal that had torn his life apart.

She raised a brow, a faint smile upon her lips. "Indeed."

This was usually the part where he found out how she was working for Mikkel and discovered if he could win her to his side. But after their brief exchange, he knew that wouldn't work. She was different.

So, he would take another approach.

"I'm going to kill Mikkel," he announced.

There wasn't the least bit of surprise on her face. "Why tell me?"

With those three words, he had the answer to his unspoken question. She assumed he'd do that very thing—and so did Mikkel. Which, of course, meant that his uncle had put precautions in place to prevent such a measure. Namely, Eilish.

Ulrik was going to have to fight her to get to Mikkel. The idea of killing a human didn't bother him one bit after everything they had done to ruin his life.

But . . . he would regret her death.

Strange. He'd never mourned a mortal death.

"So you can tell my uncle," he replied, realizing he hadn't answered her.

She turned the tumbler around, her claw rings clinking against the glass. "I didn't take you for someone who would do something so . . . foolish."

"I doona do anything without purpose."

"Is that a threat?"

He shrugged. "Take it as you want."

"You should've stayed away. You should've run."

"I doona run from anything."

"You've never encountered me."

CHAPTER EIGHTEEN

Desire and Regret

Devon's stomach was so wound with knots that she was nauseous. How did spies do it? How did they search someone's home or office and not break into a sweat or vomit from the fear of being caught?

It just proved that though she enjoyed a good spy movie, she wasn't cut out to even think about executing anything they did. Yet here she was, doing exactly that.

Any moment now, she expected to see Harriet or the security team arrive to escort her off the premises.

And she hadn't even *done* anything yet!

She swallowed and tried to remember what she did on any given day. Because normal was important. If she could recall what *normal* was. It was increasingly difficult with her new understanding of what Kyvor really was.

It was all she could do not to look at the camera on her computer or the one above her.

She read reports, made notes, and returned calls. Somehow, she managed to sound like her heart wasn't about to burst in her chest while talking on the phone, which was a feat unto itself. She was rather proud of that accomplishment.

By the time lunch rolled around, she wanted to bang her head on the desk at how slow the day was crawling by. Stacy still hadn't gathered all the information on the whisky distilleries. That meant it would be that much longer before Devon could dig into Dreagan.

"Ugh," she mumbled.

Stacy stood at the entrance to her office. "You want to get some lunch?"

Devon looked up, her brain seizing. It wasn't typical for her and Stacy to eat together, but then again, they had done it in the past. She didn't know if her assistant was trying to get close to find how if she knew anything or whether Stacy was just being nice.

By the end of the day, Devon was going to be dead from all the second-guessing and fear spikes. She opened her mouth as she searched for an excuse to bow out when movement through the glass caught her eye.

"A delivery for Ms. Abrams," said a young man with too-long hair and a bored expression.

Stacy accepted the package with a smile before bringing it into the office. "I see you ordered in."

The food smelled delicious. Devon only hoped she could eat it. She needed something to fortify her for the remaining hours. But she hadn't ordered anything. Could this be Kinsey or even Anson? "Yeah."

"I'll see you after lunch, then. The reports should be finished printing by then."

She waited until Stacy was gone before taking the food from the bag. It was her favorites from the Chinese restaurant not far from her flat.

As she reached for the chopsticks, she saw something written on the paper. "*We've got your back. Be strong.*"

It made her want to smile. She might be by herself inside Kyvor, but she wasn't alone dealing with all of it.

Kinsey, Esther, and Anson were there for her. And that made all the difference.

She tore the paper on the chopsticks and wadded it up. That simple message comforted her, allowing her to be able to eat. She took a few bites of fried rice before realizing she needed something to take her mind off things.

With a few clicks of her mouse, she returned to her favorite blog. There was a picture of a woman turned away from a mirror in shame with a sheet covering her body to start off the next post.

The title was: *Giving in to Desire . . . and the Regret that Follows*. It was something Devon was sadly familiar with. She leaned back in her chair and began reading.

Dating is hard. I know I say that in almost every post, but it's the God's honest truth, people. There is so much pressure!

A few of the things we have to worry about are:

1. *Choosing the right outfit. We want something that is sexy without being slutty, something elegant without looking like your grandmum, or something fun without looking like you're stuck in your teens.*
2. *Witty banter. Conversation can be a killer! Especially when it all seems to fall on you to keep things going. You need to be smart and up on current events or risk coming off looking insipid. Not to mention funny so that he laughs, which means knowing the right kind of jokes. Not everyone will get the sarcastic ones (my personal favs, btw).*
3. *Manners. Really, this comes down to making sure not to wear white. If I wear white, 9 times out of 10, I'm going to be wearing my food before the night's over. Seriously. I think the cosmos get a good laugh at my expense.*

4. *Your story. This really is to make sure you don't overshare (side note: I should do a post about this. I have tons of material). Telling everything wrong about your life, your job, your body, your family, or your past relationships is a surefire way to send your date packing.*

Now, do 1-4 while sounding intelligent, clever, and sensible.

Just look at that list and tell me that isn't enough to send many of us contentedly into the single corner for a bit longer. I know it does me.

So, why do I continue to put myself out there? Well, that's easy. I want to fall in love. I want to meet Mr. Forever, not Mr. Right Now.

Unfortunately, all I've been getting are Mr. Why-Did-I-Agree-To-This-Date or Mr. I-Lied-On-My-Profile.

There are a lot of those. A lot!

Let that sink in a moment. Does it make you shudder? Yeah. Me, too.

So, color me surprised when my date last night wasn't just handsome but also charming. He put me immediately at ease. There was no lull in the conversation at dinner. He made me laugh and kept me interested.

In general, I wasn't struggling to find something to say. It was a fun, fun date! (A first in a while)

As a plus, he appeared just as engrossed in everything I said. Let me say that this is a huge (HUGE!) plus for me.

When dinner finished, we had dessert and laughed some more. Then we went for a walk. That might sound boring, but it can be something special between two people who have a spark.

And there was definitely a spark, people!

He held my hand and turned the cold night into a very romantic one. I was completely won over. Then he *mentioned a second date, and I didn't hesitate to agree. I hate to admit it's been over a year and a half since I've gone on a second date (let's not dissect all the reasons that factor into that, please).*

Let's skip to the end of the date where I was surprised and pleased at the desire I felt. I knew it was wrong, but I gave in anyway. How many times have I slept with a guy after a first date and regretted it?

Well, lovelies, chalk this one up as a big checkmark in the "I Knew Better" category. The only positive is that I didn't bring him to my place. We went to his, and the prince turned into a frog in the morning light.

All the charm and romance I had been treated to during the night evaporated with the dawn. He couldn't get me out of the flat fast enough. When I asked about our second date—the bitch in me just leapt out!—he pretended as if he didn't know what I was talking about.

(I'll add a bit here—because I know you're going to ask. The sex was . . . well, it wasn't awful. But it wasn't great either.)

Just when I thought the dating gods had finally smiled upon me, I was shown more of the hard, ugly truth.

And to make matters worse, the first people I saw after that horrid experience were my best friend and the love of her life. As if I needed another reminder of what I'm missing—and longing for.

I hope my embarrassing retelling of this crap-tastic night helps one of you. I'm really considering compiling all of my dating experience into a book.

More to come on that. In the meantime, good luck out there! Most of us need as many well wishes as we can get.

Devon stared at the screen. Was it coincidence that she and this blogger seemed to be on the same date? The only difference was that Anson hadn't been an ass.

Detached, yes, but not mean. His concern had been for her safety above all else. Then there was him showing up at Kyvor to try and stop her from entering. If that didn't tell her that he cared—at least a little—then nothing would.

She stared out her window overlooking the city for the rest of her lunch. When she looked down at the food, she was surprised that she had nearly finished all of it. And she was in a much better frame of mind when Stacy returned.

In no time, the documents for all the whisky distilleries they had done work for were on her desk. She ran down the list, not hesitating when she spotted Dreagan's name.

One by one, she highlighted the top distilleries with the most brand recognition, Dreagan being one of them. Then she set about doing some research on her computer. Dreagan was the second company she searched.

None of what she was doing was out of the ordinary, so none of it should raise any red flags. Though everything she did, she did with the knowledge that someone was watching her because she knew about Kinsey and Esther.

She wanted to pretend that Kyvor was oblivious to who she spoke with, but in this technological age, that was highly doubtful. Not to mention, there were things in the prototype department she wasn't even aware of that could be used on and against her.

It made the world a very scary place. At this point, the idea of magic seemed something she'd rather embrace than what actually stared her in the face.

How many times had she argued with people that technology wasn't intrusive? The entire time she'd been lying. She hadn't known it, but that didn't ease her conscience any.

Every time she saw Dreagan's name, she thought of

Anson. She wondered what he was doing. It made her feel good that she would be helping him and the others affected by Kyvor's actions. She just hoped that, somehow, she made a difference.

Next came a second round of research that was more in-depth on the companies she'd put asterisks next to. This time, she made it look as if one of the distilleries were of more interest to her than any of the others.

She spent a good forty-five minutes on that one company before she moved to another. After another thirty minutes, she put in Dreagan.

As she was about to hit enter, Harriet sauntered into her office. And just like that, her fear returned tenfold.

"I'm glad to see you looking better," her boss said as she sat in one of the chairs before the desk.

Devon leaned back and smiled. She took in the heavily applied makeup, red lips, and perfectly styled blond hair. Her gaze then lowered to Harriet's red skirt and white shirt with red trim along the collar and cuffs.

"Me, too," Devon said. "I think I just needed a bit of a rest."

"You've been very wound up about the meeting. I know how much is riding on this for you. The Board was very disappointed that we had to reschedule."

"I feel awful about having to cancel it."

Harriet tsked. "As you should. People made room in their schedules for you. Your name was bandied about quite a bit, but any more such things, and it won't look favorably upon you."

"I overworked myself," Devon explained, trying to keep her voice calm. Then she thought back to what she would've said before Kinsey had come into her life. "My position here is important to me. I put my job before anything else. It was one hiccup that won't happen again."

Harriet tapped her long, fake nails painted a bright red on the arm of the chair. "Women are making a name for themselves in higher positions, but it's slow progress. If you play your cards right and do what I tell you, you'll get to the top. After me, of course."

"Of course," Devon replied with a tight smile.

"Unfortunately, the meeting has been pushed back for another three months."

That was her punishment for taking the day off, even though Harriet had insisted upon it. Devon's smile widened because she could see Harriet for who she really was—a jealous woman.

The funny thing was that Devon had never been after her job. However, the one she'd been going for would put her equal to Harriet, and that was the problem.

Devon opened her date book and flipped to April. "I hate to hear that, but I can only imagine how busy everyone's schedules are. I've got my calendar marked."

When she looked up, Harriet's blue gaze was locked on her, and there was nothing friendly in the stare. Then, in a blink, Harriet had her smile back in place.

"I look forward to hearing your presentation. Would you like me to look over it beforehand?"

Devon wasn't fooled by her offer. "I'm going to work on it a bit more now that I have the time. When it's finished, I'll send it your way."

Harriet pushed herself up and stood. "I need the quarterly reports on my desk tomorrow."

With those parting words, she walked out. Devon didn't roll her eyes and sigh as she wanted. Instead, she went back to her computer and hit enter.

There was a thread of excitement as information about Dreagan began filling the page.

CHAPTER NINETEEN

The waiting was killing Anson. He didn't care about all the technical terms Kinsey excitedly rambled off to him in their phone calls. He didn't even care that Ryder had hacked Kyvor once more and that Kinsey was "piggybacking" on him—whatever the hell that meant.

As soon as Kinsey began to talk in "tech-speak" as Anson had now dubbed it, he tuned her out. The specifics of what she and Ryder were doing mattered little. What Anson wanted to know was about Devon.

He grew interested again when Kinsey and Esther told him how they had sent Devon lunch with a hidden note. He should've thought to do something like that, but he was glad the girls at least had.

"I can see her," Kinsey said through the phone call connecting him and Henry to her and Esther.

Anson closed his eyes in relief. He and Henry had moved closer to the Kyvor building while still staying out of sight of cameras. It wasn't an easy feat because Kyvor had them everywhere around their building.

But a look at the schematics of the building—thanks

to Ryder—showed where there were two possible ways in and out if he needed to go in for Devon.

"Where?" he asked Kinsey.

There was a pause. Then she said, "Devon is at her desk. She's doing research on . . . Holy shit. She's looking up Dreagan."

Anson braced a hand on the side of a building and glared at the ground as he hung his head. "Can you talk to her?"

"No. I can only look at what she's doing."

"What are you no' telling me."

"Anson," she began.

He drew in a sharp breath. "Tell me."

"I can see what Kyvor can see."

Though he wasn't the type to go around punching things like Rhys did, Anson could've gladly put his fist through something at that moment. "They know what she's doing, then."

"They do," Kinsey replied. "But she's being smart about it. I'm looking up her past search history for today, and she's done research on several distilleries."

He felt a little better but not enough to wipe away all his anxiety. Everyone had known Kyvor would be watching her. It was the confirmation that solidified things.

"Does she look scared?"

"See for yourself," Kinsey said.

Anson looked over to find Henry staring at the screen of his mobile. When he turned his phone, Anson saw Devon, her gaze moving across the screen as if she were reading something. Anson touched her face, wishing it were skin and not the screen of a phone.

"You'll have the feed as long as we do," Kinsey said over the speaker.

Henry asked, "Has Ryder gotten any further in Kyvor's files?"

"It's something Ryder and I've been doing since we first hacked into Kyvor when I was sent to Dreagan. New firewalls went up and blocked some of the places Ryder wanted to go. He's gotten through them, but he barely begins searching the files when it starts all over again."

Anson blew out a breath in frustration.

"That's my long way of saying that we're both working on it," Kinsey said. "But it's slow going. Ryder is the best that I know. He'll get through eventually."

Esther's voice came over the speaker then. "Time is something none of us have. It's why Kinsey and I knew the best option was for us to go to the source."

"It's not something Kyvor would expect," Henry added.

"Either way, we doona have time to wait," Anson said.

Kinsey snorted. "You're going to have to make time. Right now, Kyvor doesn't know we're in their system. Ryder is that damn good. But the minute he blasts through their firewalls like a bull busting through a gate, they'll know. Then every hacker they employ will be tasked with keeping him out. So for now, we tiptoe around and watch Devon. She's not making a fuss, so all should be fine today."

"This was much simpler a hundred years ago," Anson grumbled.

Henry made a face, but nodded in agreement.

For the next hour, Anson watched Devon meticulously go through several searches of Kyvor's files of whisky distilleries. Just when he thought she was finished, she omitted companies, and continued researching, each time narrowing the search field.

Again and again, she did this, and Dreagan was in every search. Each time, she learned a little more. Though there was nothing that would help them.

It seemed a colossal waste of time that did nothing but put her in needless danger. With every hour that moved past, Anson found it increasingly more difficult not to go in after her.

If Henry hadn't been with him, he'd have already entered the building. The MI5 agent wasn't just there to keep him from doing something stupid, however.

While Anson watched Devon, Henry was messing with his mobile. Anson thought he was playing games. Then Henry called him over. When Anson saw the specs of the building and the route straight to Devon's office as well as another to the server room, he smiled.

Both courses showed where the cameras were and how to avoid them. Anson quickly put both paths to memory in case he had to go in after Devon.

Now he knew how to get in and out of Kyvor, as well as to Devon and the server room, where most likely everything pertaining to Dreagan was stored.

Anson was more than ready to sneak into the building to get what they needed if Ryder and Kinsey couldn't do it remotely. Matter of fact, he was hoping for just such a scenario. He'd love to wrap his hands around the necks of those who dared to mess with the world the Kings had carefully crafted—for themselves and the safety of the mortals.

"Just in case," Henry said with a crooked smile.

Anson grinned. "Better to be prepared."

He turned his attention back to Devon. She was skilled in how she went about her pursuit of information on Dreagan. Each search allowed her to dig a little deeper. His worry skyrocketed when she sent a note to someone named Cecil to speak to Kinsey Burns regarding the work order for Dreagan. That same email requested three other people for their work on other companies.

Devon was smooth. It alleviated some of his apprehension, but not nearly enough.

"Have you spoken to Rhi?"

Anson lifted his gaze from the screen before slowly turning his head to Henry. Every Dragon King knew that Henry had fallen in love with the Light Fae. And every King knew that Rhi didn't return the human's affections.

Rhi had told Henry as much, but the mortal hadn't listened. Nor would he now, Anson realized.

"No' since she helped interrogate Esther at Dreagan," Anson replied.

Henry's nostrils flared as he took in a breath. "I need to see her."

"I doona think that's a good idea."

"Because you don't believe I'm right for her," Henry said in a clipped tone.

Anson ran a hand down his face as he struggled to find the right words. "I doona believe she's right for *you*."

"Because I'm mortal," he replied with a sneer.

"That's part of it, aye. Fae turn the heads of every human. It's what makes them Fae. You're drawn to Rhi because she's Fae, no' because you have real feelings for her."

Henry's hazel eyes grew as cold as the arctic. "I love her."

"It's hard no' to. She's gone out of her way so many times to help the Kings, and—"

"You know that's not what I mean. I'm in love with her."

So much for him trying to prove that everyone loved Rhi. Anson didn't want to be cruel, but it seemed there was no other way. Henry had to know the truth. This thing between him and Rhi had gone on entirely too long.

Anson turned to face Henry and looked him in the eye. "You know the story of Rhi. You know how she and her Dragon King fell in love."

"And how he tossed her aside."

"No one can deny that. What you doona know, is how strong their love was. It was the kind of romance that lives throughout eternity. The kind that time will stand still for. The kind that doesna ever die—no matter what either of them might say."

Henry glanced away as he took all of that in. "You're saying the two are still in love?"

"Aye."

"Then why did the bastard let her go?"

"It's a question we repeatedly ask without any response. We may never know. My point is that Rhi would never be able to give her heart to you."

Henry nodded slowly. "I understand."

Finally, Anson thought. He couldn't wait to let the others know that the Rhi/Henry problem was now taken care of.

"I'll love her enough for both of us," Henry announced.

Anson turned and leaned against the building before dropping his head back to look up at the cloudy sky in defeat. Nothing he'd said made a difference, and he was beginning to think there was nothing anyone could say that would sway Henry enough to let go of Rhi.

Something would have to happen. Words weren't enough. It was time for action. The problem was, what kind? It wasn't as if Rhi and . . . well, they weren't going to get back together.

That left Henry falling in love with someone else. That was going to be a difficult feat given that the MI5 agent rarely left Dreagan since he'd started focusing on the Dark Fae. Dating in the middle of a war was impossible.

"You don't believe I love her enough," Henry said with a snort at the silence that stretched after his declaration.

Anson shook his head and looked at Henry. "I believe if anyone can, it's you. You're our friend. You work with us side by side and have become a strong ally. I doona want to see you hurt."

"Love is like walking a tightrope thirty thousand feet in the air. It's bloody terrifying. And it's amazing," Henry said with a bright smile. "You should try it sometime."

Anson was more than startled when his thoughts immediately turned to Devon. His reaction to her had been instant and engulfing.

Unaware of his thoughts, Henry kept talking. "Besides, it seems like more and more Dragon Kings are finding mates. Why shouldn't you be one of them?"

There was a moment of panic, but it passed quickly. What did that mean, exactly? That he was fine with finding a mate? Or that Devon wasn't meant to be his?

Then another problem occurred. Anson wasn't sure which reaction bothered him more. As he'd already concluded, his vow to Brenna was long since over. For years, he'd held onto that promise as a reason to keep his heart hidden.

That argument was no longer valid. There was nothing standing in his way. He could open himself up to the idea of finding the one woman he was meant to be with.

Would a Dragon King who'd once turned against humans with brutality and vengeance be able to love one? And would a mortal be able to accept everything about him, even the vicious parts?

It wasn't something he wanted to test, no matter how tempting Devon was. The Kings needed to concentrate on the war with Ulrik, the Dark Fae, and the humans, not worry about finding mates.

He couldn't believe he'd even considered such a thing.

No wonder Con became incensed each time a King brought a mate to Dreagan. Until the ceremony that bound the mortals and the Kings for life, the women were liabilities and could be killed.

They needed to put their attention back on protecting Dreagan and their secret, not add more pressure to everything by bringing humans onto their land.

So, no matter how badly his body might want to feel Devon against him again, he had other matters to attend to first. The secret of his existence, the safety of Kinsey and Esther, as well as Henry, and the protection of Devon.

There was a lot riding on his shoulders. He couldn't forget why he'd been chosen for the London mission. Ryder was counting on him. Hell, every Dragon King was.

Pressure generally didn't affect Anson, but this time, there were so many lives at stake—both immortal and mortal—that he'd doubted himself for a second. That brief moment was all the time he allowed himself.

Then he recalled who he was. He'd battled a great King to become Dragon King to the Browns. He'd fought against the humans and Dark Fae. He'd survived losing his dragons and had come out stronger for it.

He wouldn't be the cause of Ryder losing his mate. He would get Kinsey, Esther, and even Henry back to Dreagan when this was finished.

And they would get the information they needed from Kyvor, and hopefully, take down the company in the process. Which is exactly what the fuckers deserved.

Somehow, through it all, he would save Devon.

He looked at his mobile to find Devon's lips pinched and a frown in place as she read over another document.

Yes, Devon would be all right. He would make sure of it.

CHAPTER TWENTY

Devon stretched her neck first one way and then the other. The knots that had taken up residence were only partly due to the way she sat. Mostly, they were caused by the trepidation that had an iron grip on her.

Not once was she able to forget that she was being watched. Cyber vigilance was the term she used when speaking with clients. Now, she felt as if the neighborhood creep were peeking through her window to see if he could get a glimpse of her changing.

How in the world would she ever be able to work in the tech industry again? Vigilance was nothing more than spying. Oh, the tech gurus, top executives, and governments could give a million reasons why monitoring people through CCTV, mobile phones, computers, or any other secret gadget was imperative to everyone's safety.

She'd bought into it hook, link, and sinker. It made her want to gag at how idiotic she'd been.

In her mind, she could hear Anson's brogue as he said, "Naïve, no' idiotic."

But even that was a load of horseshit. She called herself

knowledgeable. She'd gone to great lengths doing all kinds of studies and inquiries into the companies she'd applied to. During that, she'd looked into their products.

With so many walking around like zombies with their faces buried in their mobiles or computers or the tele, she had believed someone needed to monitor them to keep them safe.

There wasn't a single time in her entire life where Devon had ever felt so foolish. Protecting the population might have been why the cyber surveillance had begun, but that wasn't the main purpose now.

Just like everything else, the true reason was buried under corruption, blackmail, and immorality.

As she turned her pencil over to tap the eraser on the paper she'd been writing on, she felt as if she'd been trampled by a herd of rhinoceroses.

The human race made her despondent. And worse, she was turning into a skeptic. She was going to be a cynic, someone who scoffed at everything while holding a pessimistic view of any and all topics.

Ugh.

All because one handsome Scot with a brogue that made her weak in the knees had walked into her life and told her the truth.

It took her a second to realize that he hadn't told her much. It had been Kinsey and Esther. Why then did she want to put the credit in his lap?

Well, that was because she couldn't stop thinking about him and their incredible night that would probably never be repeated no matter how much she wished it.

God, she was a depressing individual.

She released the pencil and propped her elbows on the desk before dropping her head into her hands. The things she'd learned made her believe she was tumbling down a path that would suffocate her.

Life had tried to smother her several times, and each time, she'd managed to claw her way out stronger than before. She would get through this, too. She had no other option.

When she looked at her watch, she saw that it was just thirty minutes until the end of the day. Her normal routine kept her there an hour after everyone else. No matter how badly she wanted to leave, she couldn't. She'd have to remain for at least another thirty minutes.

Not that her observers would stop what they were doing. That meant they would be in the building after everyone else had cleared out. It also meant that she would be alone with them.

She swallowed around the lump of dread in her throat and sat back in her chair. When she'd made the decision to find the information Anson needed, she hadn't thought about this part.

The best thing would be for her to dive back into the research. It would eat up time, and it would take her mind off her numerous—and growing—fears.

Well, that last bit was a lie. But it would be good to at least give it an attempt.

Devon sat up and grabbed the pencil again. She went back to comparing the job descriptions on the work orders as well as any extras the companies had bought once the equipment had been installed onsite.

Kinsey had been the top performer in her department. Her work was done quickly and thoroughly. Every one of her clients complimented her work, and often asked for her by name when they called back. All of this was noted in the files.

What Devon found weird was that distilleries around Scotland and Ireland would go to such extremes to not just safeguard their company but also everything on the their computers.

Though she might not be a big whisky drinker, it had never dawned on her that the industry could be as competitive as any other. But what really drew her attention was the distilleries themselves.

All but Dreagan had been clients of Kyvor for years, returning again and again for updated systems or new technology. Dreagan was a recent client.

More disturbing was that she couldn't find where Dreagan had gone for their tech needs before Kyvor. There should be a record somewhere of who had installed Dreagan's security system on the grounds, as well as the one internally in the business.

Yet there was nothing. It was as if Dreagan had just started doing business, or . . . they had someone internally who could do it themselves.

Ryder. Kinsey had said he was brilliant. It must be Ryder who kept Dreagan from getting hacked or broken into. If one man could do what a company of over a hundred thousand employees like Kyvor did, it explained a lot.

Why then hadn't Ryder been recruited by Kyvor or other tech companies? When Kyvor went after people like Ryder, they paid a fortune to acquire them.

Money turned people's heads. It changed lives. And she hadn't seen one case where a person had refused a raise in pay. What made Ryder different?

Maybe the question she should be asking was what made *Dreagan* different? Kyvor wasn't after Ryder specifically. They wanted Dreagan. But . . . why?

If Kyvor really wanted a distillery, they could buy up any one they wanted. Why gather information on Dreagan as if they were the Security Service? There was something big missing from what she knew, and Anson had all but confirmed it.

Several times as Kinsey and Esther told Devon their

stories, they had looked to Anson. Sometimes, he would reply. Other times, he would remain silent.

Apparently, he was the one who got to decide if she learned everything or not. That kinda stung. She was risking her life, and he couldn't even give her the full story?

When she handed him the names of those who were involved, she was going to ask for whatever it was he held back. And she really, really hoped he told her. She was going crazy wondering what it might be.

"Devon."

At the sound of Stacy's voice, she looked up. "Yes?"

"You've been working really hard today."

Devon shrugged and smiled. "I'm trying to make up for yesterday. You know how I hate to miss work."

"I know," Stacy said with a laugh. "Harriett's office just rang. She wants to see you."

The room began to spin. Devon grabbed her desk in an effort to right her world. It took a moment, but she was finally able to nod. "Thanks."

When she pushed back her chair and stood, her legs threatened to buckle. This summons wasn't coincidence. Neither was Harriett's visit earlier.

She'd been careful in her search of Dreagan, so that meant they had something else on her? Maybe questions regarding why she'd turned off her mobile and laptop?

Or did they know about Anson and Kinsey?

Devon squared her shoulders and kept the dread from her face as she walked out of her office and took the lift up five floors. The stairs were her usual choice, but with the way her body was responding, she might fall down.

It seemed only a heartbeat later that she walked out onto the twenty-fifth floor and toward the back right corner where Harriett's office sat overlooking the Thames.

"Oh, good," Harriett said when she spotted her. "Come in, Devon."

Devon thought she had herself under control until she stepped into the office and saw three Kyvor security guards.

"Come," Harriett said, motioning for Devon as well as the guards.

Devon had no choice but to follow as Harriett put her arm around her and moved her along to the lift. Devon's mind reeled with possibilities—none of them good.

Harriet chatted on about something, but Devon wasn't paying attention. Not once did Harriett loosen her hold. It was almost as if she thought Devon might try to run.

It was definitely something she considered.

If she thought she could get away, she might actually try. As it was, she was too frightened to do much of anything. Which only pissed her off.

Her gaze scanned the floor as the lift doors opened. It was the thirtieth floor. No one paid them any heed as their small group walked around desks to a conference room with a huge, white table and twenty-four white chairs.

This was no normal conference. The windows looking out were made of really thick glass, but it was the walls that caught her notice. As well as the door with its two locks.

Since when did a conference room have locks on the door?

Devon didn't think she could get any more terrified until that moment.

Until Harriett released her. That's when Devon saw one man sitting at the head of the table.

"Hello, Devon," Stanley Upton, CEO of Kyvor, said with a smile. He had dark blond hair with a touch of gray that was styled in the latest cut. His blue eyes were piercing as they pinned her. "I've heard a lot about you. Why don't you sit?"

Her first response was to refuse, but that wouldn't get her far. So she smiled, acting as if she had nothing to worry about, and pulled out the chair he'd indicated with his hand.

Harriett sat beside her, a smug look on her heavily made-up face. Devon fought the need to turn and vomit her lunch. The only thing that made her feel remotely better was imagining getting sick all over Harriett's white shirt.

"Do you know who I am?" Upton asked

Devon crossed one leg over the other and looked at his expensive suit, noting the way he held himself as if he were untouchable. "Of course. You're the CEO."

"From what Harriett has told me, you've blazed quite a trail through our fine company in the six years you've been here."

Devon glanced at Harriett. "I was lucky enough to have her mentor me."

"This is still very much a man's world," Stanley said. "Yet here are two women who have clawed their way up the corporate ladder. Both of you have gone about it different ways, but still managed the same type of success."

On any other day, Devon would've been over the moon to hear such praise heaped upon her. Except she knew it wasn't a compliment. Kyvor wanted something. They were buttering her up before swooping in for the kill.

"Thank you," she said, making her lips lift in a smile she hoped looked more genuine than it felt.

He ran his hand down his blue, striped tie, pressing his lips together. "It was a real disappointment that your meeting had to be cancelled yesterday."

"I feel horrible about that, sir," Devon said. "It's the

first time something like that has happened, and I swear it won't happen again."

His eyes shifted to the side toward Harriett before he looked back at Devon. "I'm glad to hear it."

The room grew quiet as she felt every eye on her. That's when she realized without a doubt that Kyvor knew what she'd been doing all day. It no longer mattered how they had discovered what she was up to.

She was now firmly caught in their web—and there was no escape.

CHAPTER TWENTY-ONE

"Anson? Anson! Answer me," Kinsey's voice yelled through the phone.

He stood glaring at the hated building, his thoughts on Devon. His heart had fallen to his feet when she'd risen from her desk and walked out of her office. They'd been able to track her through the office cameras, right up until she walked into the conference room.

"He's right here," Henry replied.

Kinsey blew out a frustrated breath. "Dammit. I thought he'd rushed into Kyvor."

Not yet, but he was about to. "Find her," Anson demanded.

"I'm trying," Kinsey said testily. "As soon as Devon entered the conference room and the door shut, I lost her. There doesn't appear to be cameras in that room."

Henry peered around the corner where he and Anson were hiding and glanced toward the Kyvor building. "That's not a good sign."

"Tell us something we don't know," Esther snapped over the line.

"They know what she was doing," Anson said. He was certain of it.

The camera feed from Kyvor suddenly vanished, replaced by Kinsey's and Esther's faces. Kinsey gave a shake of her head. "You don't know that."

"I do. And so do you."

Esther rubbed one of her temples. "Devon was so careful. She did exactly as I would have."

"Then that means something else triggered their attention," Henry said as he came to stand beside Anson and peered into the camera of the mobile.

Anson frowned at Henry's words because he'd been thinking the same thing. "I'll no' sit here and argue about this. Devon has to come out of that conference room. I want to know where she goes."

"What if she's not alone?" Kinsey asked.

Anson fisted one of his hands. "I hope she isna."

"What if it's worse than that?" Esther's face went white. "What if the Druid is there?"

"We doona know what she looks like, so for all we know, she is." Anson felt his fury rising. "Doona stop looking at those cameras. Henry and I are going to move closer to Kyvor."

Kinsey's eyes bulged. "That's not a good idea. Can you imagine if Kyvor got their hands on you."

Anson gave her a flat look. "I'd like to see them try."

"Fine," Kinsey said with a roll of her eyes. "But be careful."

He turned off his phone and pocketed it. Henry's hand on his arm stopped him before he could walk away.

"We're going to need these," he said and handed something small to him.

Anson held up the earpiece and inspected it with a frown. He put it in his ear. "Are you sure Kyvor can't hack these?"

"They're Ryder's design," Henry replied with a grin.

That was the kind of news Anson needed. With a nod, the two set off on their routes toward Kyvor. It would take him longer to dodge the CCTV cameras everywhere. Even when Kyvor was in sight, Anson couldn't get as close as he wanted because of their cameras.

He had sent Henry to the front of the building while he waited at the back. If Devon exited the front, then he could easily catch up with her.

If she left by the back, that meant things had taken a turn for the worse. And he was ready to do whatever it took to get her away from the company.

Of course, that would alert Kyvor that Dreagan was on to them. It would make getting the names and information they needed even more difficult. It would also mean that Anson would have to get inside the hated building.

He should've done that to begin with. All of this cloak and dagger shite was driving him mad. It was another reason Ulrik and the Dark were winning in the war. If Dreagan didn't hide who they were, Anson could've gotten what they needed on his own.

Using Kinsey and other innocents took too long and put too many in danger. If he'd gone inside, he would be the only one at risk.

And he'd like to see the mortals try and hold him.

He wouldn't think twice about shifting since the assholes already knew about him thanks to Ulrik. In his true form, Anson could do much more damage to the mortals who'd dared to meddle in the affairs of dragons.

"Anson," Kinsey said through the earpiece.

He flexed his fingers. "I'm here."

"The workday has ended. Everyone is beginning to leave Kyvor."

"Any sign of Devon?"

There was a long pause. "Not yet."

"Once she's back with us, I'm going inside Kyvor. Henry and I have already marked off a route that will get me to the server room. I'll get you connected from there, and you can find the files we need erased."

"With a little more time—"

"No," he cut her off. "The next one to go inside Kyvor will be me and only me."

Kinsey said no more on the matter. He understood her position, but he was the immortal one, the one with magic and powers and the ability to shift.

Kinsey, Esther, Henry, and Devon should've never been involved. He was furious with Ryder and Con for allowing such a thing.

What drove Kinsey and Esther was the need for revenge. Anson could understand that. Someone had gotten into their minds and altered them. It was even worse with Kinsey because they had followed her for years hoping for information on Ryder and Dreagan.

But this went beyond payback for mortals caught in their war. This was about Dreagan and the Dragon Kings. It had been from the beginning.

Ulrik might be fine pulling mortals into their war to sacrifice them, but Anson wasn't. He wouldn't be party to it anymore. Con had sent him for a task, and he was going to complete it how he saw fit.

In the end, Ryder would be happy that his mate would be returned unharmed to Dreagan. Esther and Henry would go back to Scotland without a scratch, and Con would get what he wanted.

A win for everyone.

Except for Devon.

The world as she knew it was forever altered. He'd seen it in her eyes that morning when she'd come down.

The stories they had told her, coupled with her own research had shown her a different side of a coin, and she didn't like it.

Taking down Kyvor would also be for her. She would be free of them forever. That was if he could get her out of their clutches now.

"Bloody hell. There are too many people," Henry ground out in his ear.

Seconds felt like an eternity as Anson kept his gaze on the back door, hoping Kinsey would spot Devon. It was nearly an hour later before he heard anything.

Kinsey said, "The conference door has opened. The three men who accompanied Devon and Harriet inside just walked out."

"Movement is good," Henry said.

"While we waited, I backed up the video to the top floor to see who might have been inside the conference room."

Anson asked Kinsey, "What did you find?"

"It was the CEO, Stanley Upton," she answered.

Henry snorted. "Blasted bugger. He wouldn't be involved if it wasn't serious."

"No," Esther chimed in. "He wouldn't. The fact that he's there isn't good, but at least we have two names. Upton and Harriet."

Suddenly Kinsey shouted excitedly, "I see Devon!"

"And?" Anson urged, hope tightening his chest.

"She looks . . . well, like she's walking to see the hangman," Kinsey said softly.

"Which direction?"

"Oh, shit," Kinsey said after she'd gasped. "They're taking her down a different elevator that leads to the back entrance."

Just what he wanted to hear.

He glared at the door, wishing he could evaporate it with a thought. This is when his power would come in handy. He would use his magic on the men around Devon so that they brought her straight to him. It was going to be the easiest thing he'd ever done.

"They'll reach the door in thirty seconds," Kinsey said tightly.

He was counting down the time and not paying attention to his surroundings. So Anson never saw the blast of magic before it hit him in the back.

His spine arched from the pain of the black magic searing through his clothes and into skin and muscle and bone. He dropped to his knees and fell forward on his hands with a grimace.

If he wanted to get to Devon, he had to move. He pushed aside the agony wracking him and tucked his head to roll. A bubble of magic landed right where he'd been.

He came to his feet and turned to face the Dark Fae who had attacked him. There were four of them, each holding large spheres of swirling magic in their hands meant to bring him down.

"Walk on," he told them. He wanted a fight, and he was getting one.

The Dark on the far left chuckled. Then he said in his thick Irish accent, "No."

"Then you die."

Anson rushed them with a furious growl. His hand punctured the chest of the one who'd mouthed off. Anson clamped his fingers around the evil bastard's heart, even as they pummeled him with Dark magic. He yanked out the organ and tossed it in the face of another of the Dark.

One down, three to go.

Behind him, Anson heard the door to Kyvor open and

the patter of several pairs of feet moving quickly over the concrete. He didn't have time to deal with the Dark.

He elbowed one in the face and ducked an orb as tires squealed and he heard the sound of an engine. His gaze swung toward the building, and he locked eyes with Devon for the barest second. Then she was shoved inside a black sedan and driven away.

"I'm on my way!" Henry bellowed in Anson's ear.

He didn't have time to warn Henry away before one of the Dark grabbed Anson from behind while the other two threw bubble after bubble of magic at him.

The Fae were so absorbed with defeating him that they never saw Henry coming. The MI5 agent didn't use any hand-to-hand combat nor did he use the pistol he always carried. Instead, Henry withdrew a long, serrated Fae knife from his jacket that he plunged into the spine of a Dark.

The Fae dropped lifelessly to his knees. It gave Anson the time he needed to toss his head back against the Dark holding him while Henry tried to get the upper hand on the third Fae.

Anson kicked the Dark's feet out from beneath him. Then he flipped him onto his back and stood over him. It felt satisfying when Anson wrenched out the Fae's spinal column.

He turned to Henry and the last Dark. With one look at Anson, the bastard teleported away.

Henry was breathing hard with blood sprayed over his face and chest. "You look like shit."

"Devon," Anson gritted through his teeth, the pain taking its toll.

Kinsey's response was immediate. "I'm tracking her through the CCTV cameras. They're taking her northeast."

He nodded and turned to follow. One of his legs gave

out, and he fell to a knee. He finally looked down to see his chest exposed. What remained of his shirt hung in tatters on his shoulders and by a thin strip at his side. He was mending, but too slowly for his tastes.

"You're not going anywhere, mate," Henry said and took one of Anson's arms and pulled it around his shoulders as he helped him up.

With Henry's help, he got to his feet. He made his legs move even as he struggled to remain upright. "I have to get to Devon."

"You won't do anyone any good in your present condition. You might be immortal, but it takes you longer to heal from the Darks' magic."

Henry pushed him against one of the buildings and quickly took off his jacket before draping it over Anson's front. It was all he could do to stay upright, so he didn't question Henry.

"That'll cover most of your chest while you heal. Now, stay here," Henry ordered. "I'm going to get us a ride."

"Blood."

Henry frowned then looked down at himself. He wiped his face on the sleeves of his shirt to remove a large portion of the blood as he sprinted away.

Anson closed his eyes as Henry ran off. "Kinsey," he said. "Please doona lose Devon."

"I won't," she promised, her voice low through the earpiece.

Esther then said, "More Dark could show up."

"Aye." They most likely would—with more reinforcements.

"I'm sorry," Kinsey said. "I should've seen them approach you."

His eyes opened when he heard the screech of tires as a dark gray Mercedes CLS pulled up alongside him.

He pushed off the building, and half fell inside the passenger seat of the car.

"You can make it up to me by telling us where Devon is," Anson said.

CHAPTER TWENTY-TWO

Devon was drowning in a pit of panic, shock, and—worst of all—fear. She'd honestly believed she could make it through. How . . . stupid.

Just when she thought she'd stopped being so foolish, she was right back in that boat again. And it well and truly sucked.

The first time her pride had taken a hit because she'd thought herself smart and experienced. This second time, however, she could lose her life.

As she sat in the conference room and stared into the cruel, blue eyes of Stanley Upton, she began to shake. His sneer was enough to make her wish to turn away. Somehow she kept her gaze locked with his.

"How did you do it?" Upton asked. The pleasantries were over. Now, they were going in for the kill.

Devon blinked. "Do what?"

"How did you bring a Dragon King to London?"

Was this a dream? She prayed it was because she felt as if she'd fallen down a rabbit hole much like Alice. And quite frankly, she wasn't having any fun.

She pinched her arm in the hopes that it would jerk

her out of this nightmare. But it was just her luck that nothing happened.

"Dragon King?" she asked in confusion.

Didn't these people know that dragons weren't real? She might have recently discovered that she worked for an immoral company, but she hadn't known they were also as daft as a loon.

Harriett laughed as she drummed her long, red nails on the white table. "She doesn't know."

"I think you're right," Upton said, his glee at the news making his eyes bulge. "How fascinating. We'll get to see a proper reaction."

These people were stark raving mad. And Devon wanted away from them as quickly as possible. It was time she made her exit. Unfortunately, it would be her last time at Kyvor. She wasn't going to chance another such meeting.

"It's been a long day," she said and scooted back her chair.

Harriett reacted instantly by shoving the seat forward so that the table slammed into Devon's midsection. She grunted as she leaned back and put her hand over the area hit.

Devon turned her head and glared at Harriett. "What the bloody hell was that?"

"You're not going anywhere," Harriet stated, her lips pinched in a cruel line.

Devon's gaze moved to each person in the conference room until she reached Stanley Upton. Her initial assessment had been correct—she was caught in a web.

And just like those poor insects, the more she fought, the more tangled she became. The spiders were coming in for the kill.

Upton set a mobile phone on the table and hit the record button. "I want to know everything about Anson."

Her stomach plummeted to her feet like a rock. How did they know about him? Kinsey had warned her that Kyvor's interest in Dreagan was extreme.

Devon might have done some stupid things for her career, but she wasn't going to give up anything about Anson to these crazy people no matter what they threatened.

"I don't know anyone named Anson," she said.

Upton's hand came slamming down on the table with a loud thud. "Don't lie to me!"

She jumped at his bellow. There was no reason for her to pretend to be afraid because it was the only emotion within her at the moment.

"I can see being polite isn't going to get us anywhere." Upton shoved back his chair and stood. He paced the long length of the windows facing London.

"I can't tell you what I don't know," Devon stated.

Harriett ignored her and spoke to Upton. "Perhaps she doesn't know his name. I could see him using another in an effort to keep us from learning who he was."

Stanley halted and turned his head to Devon. "The man outside the building this morning who ran toward you. What do you know of him?"

"Nothing." She should've known Kyvor would see him. Anson had been right next to the building. Dammit.

Stanley leaned his arms atop the chair he was standing behind. "He looked at you. You looked right at him. Shall I show you?"

Her attention went to the opposite end of the room and the large television screen that had flared to life. It showed where several cameras had picked up the event that morning. No longer could she deny that she hadn't seen Anson. But that didn't mean she had to admit to knowing him.

"Oh, him," she said with a nod. She swallowed, hoping to quell some of her distress. "I do recall that. He's gorgeous, but I don't know him."

"He's a Dragon King," Harriett announced in a biting tone.

Devon looked at her and frowned. "Is that a new band or something?"

"You know exactly who he is, you bitch," Harriett said, her eyes narrowing in hatred.

With brows raised, Devon shook her head and shrugged. "I don't listen to the radio anymore. Mostly, it's just playlists from my mobile. If these Dragon Kings are a new band, I had no idea."

While Harriett seethed in rage, Upton merely smiled. A chill went down Devon's spine.

"You're good," Stanley said to her. His lips twisted. "Not good enough, though. We've been monitoring everything you do on the computers here. You've done an interesting amount of research on Dreagan today."

She'd been prepared for this from the first moment she keyed Dreagan's name into the computer. "Of course. I looked up many of Scotland and Ireland's distilleries that we've done work for in order to find out what our new client might need."

"Wouldn't you give that to one of your employees?" Harriett asked, pinning Devon with a shrewd look.

Devon lifted one shoulder and kept her hands clasped in her lap in an effort to show that she wasn't upset. "For the important clients, I do a lot of the initial work myself. After that, I pair closely with whatever team I put in charge of the project. It's how I've always done my job."

"Perhaps." Upton walked back to his chair and sat. "It isn't a coincidence about Dreagan."

Devon tucked her hair behind her ear. "They're one of the most well-known distilleries in the world. Everyone wants to sell their Scotch, but they're also known for being very selective about who carries their whisky. Every distillery wants to do the kind of business Dreagan does."

"All that is true. How does that factor in to any cyber or security system we install?" Stanley asked.

"If I know what was sold to Dreagan, I can easily sell that to Blair Athol, as well as all our other clients in the same business."

Devon wanted to yell "ha!" afterward for being so calm as well as quick-thinking, but she kept it inside.

Upton stared at her for several moments. "As I've said, you're good. Tell me, Devon, do you know what Dreagan means in the Gaelic language?"

"No." And she wasn't sure she wanted to know.

"Dragon. Even their logo boasts two dragons."

She knew about the logo but declined to advertise that fact. "The owners must like dragons."

"Because they *are* dragons, you stupid girl," Harriett snapped.

Upton laughed and leaned back in his chair. "She really doesn't know."

"Or she's a good liar," Harriett replied.

Stanley shook his head at Harriet. "She doesn't know, just as I suspected. Yet there's no denying she knows Anson."

"*She's* right here," Devon retorted. "I don't know what's going on, but I don't want any part of this."

"It's too late for that," Harriett stated.

Upton gave a nonchalant shrug. "Harriet's right. You'll be leaving Kyvor, but it'll be with me."

"Thank you for the offer, but I have an appointment in half an hour," Devon said.

"You're going to miss it. And it wasn't an offer." Stanley's smile widened. "You see, Devon. You're going to give us what we've been trying to acquire for some time.

We put a lot of time and money into you. I should've known you'd help us capture a Dragon King. You practically dumped what we wanted right into our laps."

She shook her head. "No."

"Not your call." Upton motioned to the guards.

Devon watched as they rose and walked straight to her. The two men grabbed her arms and yanked her to her feet. She was led out of the room behind Stanley with Harriett following.

Out of the conference room, she looked around, hoping someone might help her—not that she was sure anyone would. But everyone had left the building.

Her gaze caught one of the cameras. Were Kinsey and Esther still watching her? Would they alert Anson that she was in trouble? Had they heard everything in the conference room?

She was escorted to a private elevator used only by the top executives. Every time she turned a corner, she hoped that Anson would be there, and each time, she was disappointed.

Then, the back door was opened, and she was roughly hauled outside. The cold hit her like being doused with ice water, but it was nothing compared to glancing over and seeing Anson.

Her excitement quickly evaporated when she spotted him fighting three men with another lying still on the ground. Her mouth fell open as a huge iridescent orb was thrown at Anson. His face contorted in pain.

She was shoved into the car, and though she tried to turn around to see through the back window, they kept her facing forward.

The car drove away, but all she could see each time she blinked were the red eyes of the men fighting Anson. And no matter how many times she tried, the image wouldn't go away.

With everything that had happened over the last couple of days, perhaps it was her imagination playing tricks. All the talk of dragons and Dragon Kings and magic must've had some kind of effect on her brain that turned everything into some fantastical element.

It was the silence inside the car that reminded her that she wasn't there by choice. Anson hadn't saved her. In fact, he was fighting for his life. The only one who could help now was her, and she wasn't even sure what to do.

Devon didn't need to see Harriett's smug smile or Upton's confident expression to know that they would do whatever they wanted. Would it mean using hypnosis to alter her mind? Or death?

After what felt like an eternity, the car finally slowed. She looked out the window to see that they were pulling up to a warehouse. They drove up a short ramp and through a large doorway right into the building.

None of this looked hopeful for her to walk away unscathed. The dread that filled her was so intense that she found it difficult to pull air into her lungs.

The car came to a stop, and the doors opened. Then she was roughly pulled out of the car. As she was dragged toward the right side of the warehouse, she saw two more vehicles where men draped in weapons hurriedly exited and took up positions in various places around the building.

Was this for Anson? She hoped not. Even if he could get away from the men he'd been fighting, he'd never find her.

That meant that all of this was for the Dragon King Upton and Harriett wanted. She didn't bother to tell them that they'd be waiting for eternity for such a creature. They'd find out soon enough.

Still, they had kidnapped her. It wasn't likely that either of them would allow her to leave. Any hope of an escape diminished at the sight of all the men with guns stationed everywhere.

Her only chance was if Kinsey had tracked them and was even now calling the authorities. Devon strained her ears to listen for sirens, but she heard nothing but Upton barking orders to the soldiers.

Devon was rushed into a small room where she was thrown inside. She fell to her hands and knees, scraping both on the rough, frigid concrete.

It was the sound of a lock being clicked in place that got her to her feet. She rushed to the door and tried to open it. When it didn't budge, she fought the urge to slam her fists against the slab because it wouldn't do any good.

She wrapped her arms around herself and moved back to the far corner. How long would she have to wait before she found out why she'd been brought to the warehouse?

CHAPTER TWENTY-THREE

Rome, Italy

For the past two hours, Rhi had sat on a bench outside of the Pantheon watching tourists *ooh* and *ahh* at the attractions. From their attire alone, she could pinpoint where each of them lived. It was always a fun way to take her mind off things that infuriated her.

Since she didn't want to start glowing and blow up the world, it was exactly where she needed to be.

She didn't veil herself. Part of the appeal was to be in the mix of things with the sightseers. She wanted to hear them, but also be a part of the scenery.

A laugh bubbled up inside her when an older woman on the plump side saw her husband ogle a female in a flowy skirt and skimpy shirt that walked past.

Rhi's smile died when her gaze landed on Inen standing across the way. She didn't want to talk to the captain of the Queen's Guard. Their last words hadn't exactly been pleasant. Then there was the fact that Inen couldn't see what Usaeil was turning into.

Unperturbed, he strode through the crowd toward her. Rhi stayed seated, mainly because it was such a shock to see him in the human world. Inen preferred the Light

Castle to mingling with the mortals. He called them trouble.

And she had to admit, the humans were certainly that.

"Rhi," Inen said as he came to stand before her.

She used her hand to block the sun from her eyes as she looked up at him. Then she noticed everyone staring at them. Neither had used glamour, and it was drawing more and more attention.

"I'd like a word," he continued.

She dropped her hand and stood, letting him see her annoyance as she glanced around. "Not here. Too many watchers." He waited without moving. With a sigh, she rolled her eyes. "Fine. Follow me."

The mortals parted, their gazes locked on the two Light Fae. If it wouldn't cause such a scene, Rhi would veil herself. She didn't slow or speak until they reached more deserted streets.

Before she could say anything, Inen said, "There's a problem."

Only one thing would send him into the human world. Usaeil. Rhi halted and kicked at a pebble. She'd told herself she wasn't going to get involved. It was better if she left it all behind. Usaeil wouldn't listen to reason, and the Light Fae were oblivious of any of the danger.

Except that was a lie. The Light knew something was amiss. The problem was, they blamed the wrong group. They thought the Reapers were after them when that wasn't the case at all.

She'd kept her knowledge of the Reapers to herself. After Death had gone to such lengths to erase her memories of everything to do with the Reapers, Rhi thought it better if she pretended she still knew nothing.

That was proving to be more difficult than she'd anticipated. First, because she knew her silent watcher who had been following her for months was a Reaper. Yet, she'd gotten rid of him.

Sort of.

The Reaper didn't get close to her anymore, but he still managed to find her. Just as he stood off in the distance, watching her now.

"Did you hear me?"

She looked up at Inen. "Yes."

"That's all you have to say?" he demanded, his face contorted with anger.

Rhi blew out a breath. "You didn't want my help earlier."

"That was before Usaeil went crazy."

"There are a lot of reasons that could be happening. Tell me what you think it is." She certainly wasn't going to open her mouth about anything if Inen didn't already know—which meant she'd stay quiet about Con and Usaeil's affair.

Inen ran a hand through his shoulder-length black hair. His silver gaze briefly looked around before he faced her. "Usaeil hasn't been to the castle in months. It's the longest she's been gone."

"I know. I was recently there."

"Why didn't you come see me?"

She raised a brow. "Why would I? I'm no longer part of the Queen's Guard."

"I keep forgetting that," he mumbled. He shook his head slowly. "Usaeil isn't the same queen."

"She hasn't been for a long time. You're just now seeing it. What happened?"

He moved to stand beside her and leaned his back against the building. "She wouldn't answer any of my calls for her to return to Ireland and our people. So I went to find her."

Rhi smiled at his initiative. Inen was acting like a Fae

more concerned with their people than the queen. It was about damn time. "And?"

"She was pissed I found her."

Rhi crossed her arms over her chest and leaned a shoulder against the brick as she faced Inen. "Sounds like her."

"Everyone is frightened of the Reapers, Rhi. The Everwoods are all dead. It's said that Reapers did it."

Since she couldn't tell him that she'd been a part of all of that, or that Neve was alive and well and now a Reaper, Rhi kept silent.

Inen held her gaze. "You know something."

"I know quite a lot, actually."

"Tell me," he begged.

She looked away. "I can't."

"Our people are in trouble, Rhi."

That was the one plea she could never ignore. She closed her eyes and took in a deep breath. As she released it, she looked at him. "Tell me everything that happened with Usaeil."

For the next twenty minutes, she listened as he went over the entire episode until the queen had left in her car. Rhi thought Usaeil had shocked her for the last time, but she was wrong again.

She dropped her arms and grinned at Inen. "You're the captain of the Guard. It's your duty to lead the people when Usaeil isn't there."

"I can't."

His declaration shocked her to the point that she took a step back.

Inen's bark of laughter held a note of hysteria. "I always thought I could, but it's obvious I can't. Things are beginning to unravel. We need Usaeil back."

"She's not going to return until she wants to. She's having fun, and right now, that's all that matters to her."

"There's something else. I didn't want to tell you. In fact, I'd hoped I'd never have to."

Rhi moved closer to him, curious. "What is it?"

"Usaeil . . . well . . . she's been seeing someone."

It touched her that Inen would know how painful such news would be. She put her hand on his arm. "It's all right. I know. I've seen the picture."

"It looks like Con."

She kept her smile in place. "It does."

"Rhi, I'm sorry."

Her gaze moved away as she shrugged. "What I had with my King is long over."

"I had no idea when she went to such lengths to break you and—"

"It's in the past," Rhi said at the same time. Then she stopped, anger churning in her gut. "Wait. Did you just say she broke us up?"

He nodded, his face contorted with regret. "I helped her because I believed her when she said that the Fae and Dragon Kings shouldn't mix. Then she aided Shara and Kiril. At first, I thought it was because Shara had left the Dark to come to the Light. Now, I know it was to help pave the way for her own affair with a King."

Rhi was going to be sick. She'd known Usaeil hadn't approved of her love for her Dragon King, but she hadn't known the queen might have actively helped destroy it.

"Did Usaeil's actions succeed in ending my relationship?" she asked tightly.

Inen took a step back, a look of unease rippling over his face. "Rhi. You're glowing."

"Answer me!"

He held up his hands. "Yes! Yes, she was part of it."

Everything in Rhi evaporated, leaving her deflated. All those centuries she'd turned to Usaeil as a friend, and the entire time, the bitch had been responsible for breaking apart the very thing that had given Rhi meaning.

"Say something," Inen pleaded anxiously.

Rhi looked away from him. She drew in a shaky breath, going over everything with Usaeil in her mind and seeing things with new eyes. "I should've known. It was right there the whole time. I was just too blind to see it."

"I believed it was for the best. I trusted Usaeil's order. She wanted you married to a prominent Light to keep you at the castle."

Her gaze jerked to his face. "Why?"

Inen shrugged helplessly. "She never shared the reason with me. I was always jealous of how you could walk into a room and have everyone's attention. You led without even trying. Imagine what the Queen's Guard could be if you were captain."

"Usaeil appointed you to that position because you deserved it. Never forget that. Remind our people who you are."

He threw up his arms in frustration. "How? I've tried to talk to them."

"Show them," she said. "Call in some of the army to station around the castle. That will quell some of their hysteria. You lead the Guard by respect and admiration. You can lead our people, as well."

"Come back with me," he urged. "Rejoin the Guard."

She flashed him a grin at the offer. "I can't be anywhere near Usaeil right now."

"Our people need you."

"No, Inen. They need *you*."

He pushed away from the wall and took her hands in his. "I'm sorry for being an arse to you all those years."

She laughed and lifted a shoulder. "I'm pretty sure I deserved it sometimes. I know how difficult I can be."

"I can talk to him."

She didn't have to ask who Inen was referring to. "No."

"He should know the truth."

"It doesn't matter anymore."

His silver eyes narrowed as he searched her face. "You lied just now. You never used to be able to do that. Does it no longer bring you pain to lie?"

"I've learned to control it." It felt like her insides were on fire, but it would pass soon enough.

"You've changed a great deal, but there's one thing that hasn't. You still love him."

She pulled her hands out of Inen's grip and stepped back. "I'm letting him go. I'm learning to stop loving him."

"That's not possible, and you know it."

"It has to be. I can't live like this anymore."

He rubbed the back of his neck. "Usaeil said it was just a fling. If I'd known—"

"It's not your fault," she interrupted. "Truly. You believed your queen. I shudder to think of the things I've done because Usaeil got me to accept what she said."

"You deserve to be happy."

"I'm going to get there. Right now you need to return to the castle and take charge."

He turned to leave but paused to look back at her. He shot her a crooked smile before he teleported away.

Rhi remained while trying to sort through the numerous and various emotions stirring. She didn't want to think about what she'd learned because if she did, she was likely to go nuclear and destroy Earth.

Then the Dragon Kings would really be pissed at her.

She started walking, meandering up and down streets until she found a deserted alley. From there, she teleported to Dreagan. It was the wrong thing to do. She knew it, and yet there wasn't anywhere else she wanted to be.

Veiled, she walked the mountain connected to the manor. She'd put her past with her King behind her. Hadn't she? Balladyn was now her lover and helping her move forward. It was a decision she didn't regret.

This new information regarding Usaeil set her back on her heels, however. Emotions returned with a vengeance she didn't want to feel—but was helpless to ignore.

Just this once, she was going to allow herself to think of her King and imagine how life might've been had their affair not been halted.

Would they be mated now?

She'd like to think so. Then again, perhaps not. The Dragon Kings had accepted Shara, but would they have done the same for her? Sure she'd gotten them out of binds and saved a few of their mates, but would it have been enough?

"No," she whispered to herself.

She refused to go down that road again. It led to more heartbreak, and she wasn't going to do that to herself anymore. Her King had left her behind.

Now, she was going to do the same to him.

CHAPTER TWENTY-FOUR

How could time stretch endlessly before him, but when Anson needed it, it was slipping through his fingers faster than grains of sand in a hurricane?

"You need more time," Henry said, glancing at him.

Anson kept his gaze riveted on the road as Henry weaved through traffic, causing him to brace a hand on the dashboard as he was jerked to the right. "I doona have it."

"How bad is he?" Kinsey asked Henry through the speaker of Henry's mobile.

Every second, Anson's body healed more of the damage the Dark had done, but it wasn't quick enough. Once more, time was his opponent. "I'm fine," Anson snapped.

"He's not," Henry stated in a matter-of-fact tone.

Anson sent a glare to the spy that went unnoticed. "Just get me to wherever Devon is."

"She's at a warehouse," Kinsey said. "I just hacked the GPS of the car you stole, Henry. The coordinates should pop up shortly."

Almost immediately, the screen on the dash switched, showing the route. The dot of their final destination caught Anson's attention. If the humans had any sense, they wouldn't harm Devon. Because if they did, he wouldn't be responsible for his actions.

"We're about four minutes out," Henry said.

Anson grabbed the handle above the window on the door and ground his teeth together. He had to be healed by the time they reached the warehouse. There was a chance more Dark Fae were there.

"We could use some help here," Henry said.

Anson shook his head. "That's exactly what Kyvor wants, and I'll no' give them that."

"We have no idea what we'll be walking into. Don't walk in there without more Dragon Kings with you."

Anson had already decided that he was going to ensure that he entered that warehouse alone. Henry didn't need to be a part of it.

It wasn't just that Henry was mortal or because he had family. The Dragon Kings needed him. And Anson couldn't stand to be responsible for a friend being killed.

Odd. He'd once hated humans to such an extent that he didn't think he could ever walk among them. Now, he called one friend.

So much had changed, but there was so much more that hadn't. In that warehouse was a group of mortals who wanted an up close and personal experience with a Dragon King. Well, they were about to get it.

Whether they survived or not was entirely up to them.

"I wish I were with you," Kinsey said, her voice breaking.

Henry's forehead creased as he glanced at Anson. "Where's my sister?"

"I . . . ah . . . I had to lock her in the closet," Kinsey replied hesitantly. "She tried to go help you two. And the look I saw in her eyes—"

"No need to say more." Henry shook his head. "Thank

you, Kinsey. Kyvor nearly killed Esther the first time. I don't want her near them again."

Anson looked down at his chest. He ripped away the remains of his shirt and saw the wounds healing nicely. The burn of Dark magic would last a long while inside his bone and muscle, but he barely felt it with his mind on Devon. He knew why Kyvor was leading him to a warehouse.

It was large enough to house a dragon.

He wanted nothing more than to show them exactly who he was—*what* he was—but he wouldn't. Too much was at stake already. The Dark had already filmed them shifting during a skirmish at Dreagan. That had brought all kinds of attention to them, so Con had commanded that no King shift.

Anson could handle the mortals in his present form. He was faster and stronger, with enhanced senses. Then there was his power and dragon magic. They didn't stand a chance against him.

He wondered if Ulrik would be there. In some ways, Anson hoped he would. But there wouldn't be time to talk to his old friend, not with Devon's life on the line.

"We're here," Henry said, breaking into his thoughts.

Anson stared at the warehouse ahead of him as Henry pulled over and shut off the engine. There were buildings around them, but none the size of the warehouse.

He looked at Henry. "There could be more Dark inside."

"I'm aware."

"It's a trap. For me."

Henry nodded. "Also aware of that."

Anson blew out a breath. "I need you to stay behind."

"Not going to happen, mate."

"I doona know how many mortals or Dark are inside that warehouse. I doona know if the Druid is there. What

I do know is that Devon is being held against her will. I'm going to find her and get her out. You ken?"

Henry glanced at the imposing structure. "You get her out, and I'll take her straight to the girls."

"We'll be waiting," Kinsey said. "Good luck, you two."

Henry smiled. "Go kick some ass."

Anson returned the mortal's grin before unfolding his frame from the car. That small movement caused a great amount of discomfort, but he shut his mind off to the pain. He then walked forward. Kyvor already knew he was there so there was no need to sneak around and attempt to surprise them.

He walked straight to the door that was propped open. Not once did he hesitate. He entered the warehouse and came to an immediate stop.

Before him, in the middle of the building, stood a man in a suit. To the right, and slightly behind him, was a woman. Anson knew both individuals, thanks to Ryder. Upton and Harriet.

It took everything Anson had not to allow his anger to rise to the surface. These humans made him sick. Their greed and entitlement allowed them to believe they could take whatever they wanted without consequences.

Well, he was the consequence. And things were about to get ugly.

Stanley Upton's conceited smile widened. "I knew you'd come."

Anson let his gaze slowly wander the expanse of the nearly empty warehouse. Though the armed men hid well, he still saw them. Twenty-five mortals with guns trained on him were spread out throughout the building. But so far, no Dark Fae or the Druid.

Or Ulrik.

"So," Stanley said as he clapped his hands together

and rubbed them. "Aren't you going to ask what it is we want?"

Anson kept silent. He didn't care what Upton or anyone at Kyvor wanted because they weren't going to get it.

Upton shrugged and said, "I knew it was only a matter of time before we found someone who could bring us a Dragon King. I never thought to use Devon. We were hoping to use her for something else until she began acting abnormally. Then we saw you this morning on our cameras."

Anson knew even if he'd stayed out of view that this exact moment would be taking place anyway. Upton wanted to place the blame on Anson's shoulders. He was fine with that because Stanley was about to get what was coming to him.

"The strong, silent type," Upton said to Harriett.

She smiled and crossed her arms over her chest as she cocked one hip out. "I know how to get him to talk."

"We'll get there," Stanley said, silencing her. Upton then turned his attention back to Anson. "Why Devon? What was it about her that drew your attention? Was it her pretty face? Or was it something else?"

Upton laughed and dropped his arms. "Kinsey was just as beautiful. When we learned that she was dating a Dragon King, we went to great extremes to get him. It was too bad Ryder left before we could put our trap in place."

The more Stanley talked, the more Anson wanted to kill him. How many lives had Upton destroyed? How many more would he wreck if he weren't taken down?

"Still nothing?" Stanley smiled, shrugging. "It's all right. We know all there is to know about you, Anson."

There was movement behind the duo as two men walked to a door and opened it. A moment later, they dragged Devon out between them.

As soon as she caught sight of him, Devon smiled. But it faded as she took in the situation. Anson wanted to tell her it was going to be all right, but he never liked making promises he wasn't sure he could keep.

Upton laughed as he looked between Devon and Anson. "You came for her, Anson. I thought it only fitting that Devon get to hear—and see—everything."

This was going to stop before it ever got underway. Anson used his power and got control of both the men's bodies holding Devon. He made them release her before he had one of them turn to her and whisper, "Run."

Devon started running right for him. She'd barely gotten ten feet before a bullet struck at her feet. Anson tried to use his power on the soldiers, but he couldn't get control of their bodies.

Upton began to clap. "I wanted to see your power in action. It's why I had our secret weapon ensure that only the two men guarding Devon were susceptible to you."

Anson tried to gain control of Upton's body, but once more he was blocked. So the Druid had struck again. Anson was really beginning to hate her. Heaven help her when they did come face-to-face because he was going to take great pleasure in ripping her apart.

"I think he's a bit annoyed," Harriett said.

The two laughed as Devon looked on in confusion. Anson wanted to motion her to him, but he wasn't sure she would be any safer at his side.

In fact, he was beginning to see that his options were dwindling rapidly.

Stanley sighed and stopped laughing. "Now, I bet you want to know what it is we brought you here for? Come on. Ask me."

"What do you want?" Anson bit out.

Upton frowned. "I just don't understand why so many women like that brogue."

"I don't. I think it sounds guttural," Harriett said with a disdainful sniff.

"I couldna give a flying fuck what either of you like or doona like," Anson said. "You got me here. Tell me what it is you want."

Upton held out his hands. "Why you, of course."

"I'll no' go anywhere with you."

"You have to say that," Stanley said with a roll of his eyes. "But you will. Why? Because we know everything about you. We know you're the King of the Browns, that your power is possession of bodies, and that you once aligned with Ulrik to rid this world of us humans."

Anson moved slowly toward the duo as he kept Devon in his peripheral. "You think because you know a few specifics about me that you know everything? You're wrong."

"I disagree. We know how the Dragon Kings are trying in vain to keep the rest of the mortals from discovering the truth about your kind."

"Truth?" Anson asked with a snort. "The truth is rarely what you think it is. You're delving into matters you can no' possibly understand. There's a war going on, and you've stepped in it."

Stanley shrugged. "Things look good from where I'm sitting."

"That can change in an instant. You're a fool to trust Ulrik when his goal is to wipe your kind from this realm once and for all."

Harriett began to laugh. "Ulrik? That's not—"

"Shut it," Upton bit out, cutting her off with a scathing look.

That made Anson wary. If it wasn't Ulrik they were working with, then who was it?

Stanley then faced him. "You think because you have magic and power that you can decide our fates. That's not going to happen."

"Your fate was decided the moment your kind arrived on this realm eons ago, and the dragons made room for you. We gave you land and peace, and how did humans repay us? They kept taking more and more, driving us out. They killed dragons for sport. But what tipped the scales was when a female tried to murder a Dragon King."

Upton's lip lifted in a sneer as he said, "They were doing exactly what I plan to do. It's time dragons really did turn to myth. Kill her!"

Anson scarcely had time to use his magic to put up a shield around Devon as bullets rained around her. She huddled with her arms around her head, screaming.

With a bellow of outrage, Anson raced toward Devon even as bullets pierced his body. He was ready to get her out when the Dark Fae appeared.

Without another thought, Anson shifted.

CHAPTER TWENTY-FIVE

There is a moment, a nanosecond that feels like a life-time, where your brain blanks and freezes when facing something you can't reconcile. Seeing an enormous animal standing just in front of you that isn't supposed to exist is just such an event.

A scream fell from Devon at the sight of the dragon that suddenly appeared. The appearance of the creature caused her to jerk back and fall hard on her butt. Panic then had her scrambling to the nearest wall, twisting her ankle in the process, thanks to tripping over a piece of wood in her high heels.

She couldn't take her eyes off the beast. He snarled, smoke billowing from his nostrils to snake up around his face. Metallic scales the color of chocolate shimmered even within the dim confines of the warehouse.

The next second, the soldiers began shooting, the bullets raining down upon the dragon. The sound was deafening, and she quickly covered her ears with her hands. The barrage of gunfire didn't faze the dragon. His onyx eyes were focused on Upton and Harriett.

The jaws of the dragon parted, showing dozens of

razor-sharp teeth. His head lowered, giving her a glimpse of two membranous frills that ran from the base of his skull and down his back to the tail that had a hook-like extension on it.

Devon shook her head. She couldn't believe that she'd seen Anson change into this monstrous creature. It couldn't be real. It couldn't.

And yet . . . it was.

She pressed herself against the wall when the dragon drew in a deep breath. Her eyes bulged when she saw more smoke coming from its nostrils. He was going to breathe fire and kill all of them!

"I thought Dragon Kings made a vow to protect humans," Upton shouted over the shooting, his face pale.

The dragon hesitated. Devon watched the CEO of Kyvor. Stanley wasn't faking the slight shaking of his hands that hung at his sides, or the sweat that trickled down his cheek despite the cold. He couldn't force his face to drain of color—unless it was all real.

She wanted to close her eyes and pretend that none of it was there, but she couldn't even look away.

The dragon's throat rumbled with a growl as he snapped open his massive wings that slammed into the soldiers up in the rafters. His tail took out four more of the armed men that rushed toward him.

In a matter of minutes, all twenty-five of Upton's men were no longer moving. Whether they were dead or un-conscious, she didn't know.

Devon saw the door. With everyone staring at the dragon, she might make it outside to freedom. Then she would run as far and as fast as she could to get away from all of this.

She used her hands to help her stand against the wall. A look in the direction of Stanley and Harriett showed that both were staring open-mouthed at the dragon, looks of part fear and part excitement on their faces.

Kicking off her shoes, Devon prepared to make a run for the door when two men suddenly appeared before her. She gasped when she saw their red eyes—just like the men she'd seen Anson fighting earlier.

It wasn't just their eyes that startled her but the thick stripes of silver within their black hair, as well. Not to mention the look of pure glee on their gorgeous faces at finding her.

She tried to step back, but the wall blocked her. What the hell kind of nightmare had she marched into, and why couldn't she leave?

"Halt!" Upton bellowed when the dragon took a step toward him.

One of the men grasped Devon, yanking her beside him as he turned to face the dragon. The man's hand wrapped tightly around her throat.

The second one held out his hand as an orb began to form. It was shimmery with ribbons of energy swirling through it, and it continued to get bigger.

Devon was tired of people manhandling her. She was sick of being terrified. It was time she did something. She elbowed the man holding her in the ribs. As soon as she felt his hold loosen, she made a break for it.

She only got a few steps before the second man was suddenly standing in her way, still holding the orb. He grabbed her, turning her so that her back was against his chest.

Then he brought the ball closer to her. She didn't know what it was, but she knew that she didn't want it touching her. The more she fought him, the stronger his hold became. Until he swiped the orb against her arm.

The pain was instantaneous and debilitating. She let

out a scream, and thankfully, blessedly, the ball didn't touch her again.

When she was finally able to open her eyes, she found the dragon staring at her. She met those black eyes of his, and her heart missed a beat.

She knew those eyes. It was Anson—even as her mind refused to believe it.

"If you want her to live, you'll come with us," Upton said, breaking the silence. "Shift back."

Devon was so wracked by agony that her legs gave out. The man holding her forcefully kept her upright. She couldn't move her injured arm, nor did she want to. It might make the agony even worse.

Upton motioned toward her as he spoke to Anson. "You know what the Dark will do to Devon. Look at her. She's in pain. Do you want her to experience more of it?"

The dragon swung its head and glared at Upton for a long minute. Then the creature was gone, leaving Anson standing naked in the middle of the warehouse.

Anson's hands were fisted at his sides, and his gaze didn't move away from Upton. "Release her," he demanded.

Stanley barked with laughter. "With Devon in our grasp, you'll do exactly as we say."

"I could kill you all in the next second."

Upton shrugged indifferently. "Do that, and the Dark Fae will take Devon away. If you manage to find her again, it'll be too late."

Devon blinked. Had Upton just said *Dark Fae*? Is that what he was calling the men with the red eyes? Was everyone crazy? Magic, Dragon Kings, Dark Fae—none of it could be real.

Anson took a step toward Upton. "If you harm her again, I'll—"

"What?" Stanley interrupted. "Kill me? I get that threat every day. So stand in line."

She might not know Anson well, but Devon could practically see the fury surrounding him. She was there to keep him in line, to make sure that he did whatever it was Stanley and Harriet wanted. Though she knew without a doubt that Upton would gladly hurt her just for the hell of it.

The Dark holding Devon lifted her in his arms. The motion was so unexpected that the throbbing in her arm intensified, consuming her with such anguish that she welcomed the blackness that took her. Even then, she thought she heard someone shout her name.

When she opened her eyes, the warehouse was gone. There was a light on above her, casting shadows across everything. She had no idea how long she'd been unconscious.

A coarse blanket rubbed against her good arm. She turned her head to discover that she was in what looked like a jail cell with thick bars caging her inside.

She kept her injured arm against her as she threw off the blanket and sat up, swinging her legs over the side of the narrow cot. No longer was she cold, and the pain seemed to have disappeared.

When she looked down at her arm, there was no injury. Had it all just been a dream? She must have lost her mind, a product of being overworked. Though she'd like to know what she did to have the police lock her up.

She leaned forward and tried to see other cells, but there was nothing except blackness all around her. Her prison was roomy, but she got the sense that she was within a much larger space.

Another few lights lit a path. Upon closer inspection, she was able to make out the outline of a door. Seeing that didn't make her feel better. In fact, she was more scared than before.

"I'm sorry."

Her head jerked to where she heard Anson's voice. "Where am I?"

"I doona know where the Dark took us."

Dark. Shit. She was still inside her nightmare.

"I'll get you out somehow," Anson said.

She shook her head. "I let you in my house, in my bed."

"I was there to protect you."

"Right. You just left out the part where you could change into a dragon."

There was a slight pause. "You wouldna have believed me."

Of course, she wouldn't have believed him. Who would? "You knew what you were pulling me into, and you did it anyway."

"My family and our verra way of life are being threatened. What would you do for your family?"

She chose not to answer that question—or think about her family. "I had a right to know. I told you to tell me everything."

"This from a lass who didna believe us when we told you about the Druid. As if you'd have listened," he replied testily.

He had a point. Damn him.

She thought of the dragon and shuddered. He'd nearly breathed fire on all of them. Anson was dangerous, that much was obvious. She'd never been more thankful to be within the confines of a cell before.

Except she didn't know if it could withstand a dragon's strength. Or his fire.

Devon braced her hands on the edge of the thin

mattress. Upton had used her for bait just as he'd tried to use Kinsey. Kinsey!

She started to ask Anson about her but stopped. Anyone could be listening and probably was. Kinsey might be in league with Anson, but she and Esther were also Devon's way out. The less Stanley knew about them, the better.

"Devon."

She jerked around and fell off the bed when Anson approached the cell. She hadn't heard him moving. In fear, she scooted as far from him as possible as she took in his shirtless and shoeless form.

He stood silently, staring at her for a moment, then his lips curved, but the smile held only scorn. "You're afraid of me. How typical of a mortal when I've done nothing but protect you. It's your own kind who betrayed you."

"How do you expect me to react? I saw you change into a dragon!"

"I expected you to be smarter than most. I expected you to realize who I am, and yet that seems to be impossible for your kind. You see the worst in most and overlook evil in the rest." He turned on his heel and walked away.

She caught a glimpse of the dragon tattoo on his back before he faded into the darkness. Was he right? She had been blind to the maliciousness of Kyvor.

While Anson, Kinsey, and Esther had done nothing but open her eyes to the truth and try to safeguard her. Anson had put himself on Kyvor's radar by attempting to stop her from going into work that morning.

Yet her mind couldn't fathom him being a dragon. How did he exist? How was he still around? And how the bloody hell didn't anyone know of him?

Dreagan.

Now it all made sense. Dreagan wasn't just his business, it was his home. How many other dragons lived there?

She walked to the corner of the cell near her cot and slid to the concrete floor. "Will you tell me your story now?"

"You doona want to hear it."

"I do."

"Give me one good reason," he demanded harshly.

She leaned her head back against one of the bars. "I don't want to be surprised again. I want to know if there is something I can do against the Dark or . . . even your kind."

There was movement out of the corner of her eye. She turned her head and saw Anson's face within the darkness. In another step, he appeared.

"You still fear me."

She nodded, not bothering to lie. "I need some time to digest this. I can't see something for the first time that isn't supposed to exist and be all right with it."

"Did I harm you?"

"You were going to burn us all."

He snorted loudly. "I'm as old as time itself, Devon. I know where to direct my dragon fire. You were never in danger."

"I'm sorry," she said in shock, her brain trying to keep up with the information he'd just dropped. "How old did you say you were?"

"Dragons have been around since the dawn of time. This planet was our home."

"How is it there is no record of dragons?"

His chest expanded as he inhaled. "Because we made sure there was no evidence of us."

CHAPTER TWENTY-SIX

Anson knew he and Devon were being spied upon. Upton wanted any little tidbit he could acquire, but Anson wasn't going to give it to him. He used his magic to cocoon him and Devin so their conversation would be private.

To Stanley and anyone watching, it would appear as if he and Devon were ignoring each other.

"You . . . you did what?" Devon asked.

Anson watched a lock of her brunette hair fall between the bars. "We made sure there was nothing humans could find that would suggest dragons were real or had once inhabited this realm."

"Realm," she repeated. "Perhaps you'd better start at the beginning."

He looked around the sparse and vast room that held no comforts for either a dragon or human. It was going to be near impossible for him not to kill Stanley or Harriett after what they'd done to Devon, Kinsey, and Esther.

His gaze swiveled to Devon to find her blue eyes locked on him. There was no reason not to tell her the history of the Dragon Kings now, but he wasn't sure it would do any good. Her mind was made up.

"From the beginning, this world was ours. In all the realms, this was the only one where dragons existed. For millions of years, we lived, loved, and fought here.

"There were billions of dragons in every color and size that called Earth home. Each group of dragons was designated by a color. Within each clan was the one chosen to be the Dragon King because they were the strongest among them, the one with the most magic."

Her gaze didn't waiver, and he took some comfort in that. "The Dragon Kings ruled their dragons. Among the Kings was one with even greater power and magic—the King of Kings."

"Were you a King?" she asked.

Anson slowly nodded and moved closer to the cage. "I was King of the Browns."

"So when you came to power, did the other King of Browns step aside?"

"Nay. Once a King, always a King. It's part of our blood to protect our dragons and land."

Devon wrapped a hand around one of the thick bars. "So you had to fight?"

"Aye. There was a battle."

"But you won. That's good, right?"

He turned his head away. "For years, I hid my growing power. I knew there would come a day that I'd have to challenge the King for the position."

"Did you not want it?"

"It was my destiny. And, aye, I wanted to be a Dragon King."

"I don't understand," she said with a frown.

Anson looked at her. "In order to become the next King, I had to fight—and kill—my own father."

"Oh. I see," she said, her voice tinged with sadness.

"It was both the worst day of my life and the best." And one he'd never forget. "My father was a great King.

He protected our people and was fair and wise. It's why I hid my power and magic for as long as I could. But the day came when I couldna keep it from him any longer. I didna want to fight him because I knew one of us had to lose. His last words were that he was proud that it was I who would be taking his place."

Devon gave a shake of her head, her blue gaze filled with sorrow. "I can't imagine what that was like."

"It's our way," he said as an explanation. "Mortals had only recently arrived on this realm. As soon as they showed up, the Dragon Kings shifted into human forms. It's how we were able to communicate.

"We realized that the mortals had no magic and needed our protection, so we vowed to defend them. Each Dragon King gave up a portion of land for the humans. The dragons mostly kept away from the mortals, but there were Kings who helped them build villages and interacted with them often."

Devon asked, "Were you one of those?"

"Nay. I chose to keep my distance."

"Go on," she urged.

He swallowed and came to stand beside the cage. Leaning back against it, he said, "Before we knew it, the humans had outgrown the land we'd given them. They kept asking for more, pushing dragons farther and farther from their lands. Then the mortals began to hunt some of the smaller dragons for food."

"Wasn't there other food for them?"

"Oh, aye," he replied, turning his head to the side to see her. "There was plenty. Every once in a while, a dragon would eat a human. The Kings managed to keep the peace. Con did most of it."

"Con?" she asked.

He turned his head to her. "Constantine. The King of Kings. He diffused tense situations and kept everything calm until the day came when it was out of his hands."

She moved closer to the bars. "How? What happened?"

"During that time, it wasna uncommon for a King to have a house in the villages. Some of the humans flocked to these Kings because they knew they would be protected. Because of this, the Kings would often take mortal women as their lovers."

"I can see how that would happen."

He shrugged and lowered himself to the floor. "There were drawbacks. None of the humans were able to carry a child conceived by a King to term. Most of the pregnancies ended after a few weeks. On the rare occasion that the woman was able to bring the pregnancy to term, the bairn was stillborn."

"All of them?" she asked in surprise.

"All. It was for that reason that most of the Kings decided no' to take humans as mates. You see, Devon, dragons bind themselves for life to their mates. If a King chose a mortal as his mate, then he was effectively ending his bloodline.

"Even with that knowledge, a handful of Kings fell in love with humans. Ulrik was just such a King. He and Con were as close as brothers, and everyone knew he could've challenged Con to be King of Kings."

Devon's brow furrowed. "Why didn't he?"

"Ulrik was happy leading his Silvers. He was a good King, one who enjoyed the simple things. He played jests on us constantly," Anson said with a smile as memories surfaced. "Everyone liked him."

"But something happened," she said.

Anson's grin faded. "Somehow, Con found out that the woman Ulrik had chosen as his mate was going to betray Ulrik. She intended to kill him the night before the ceremony that would've bound them for eternity."

"Why?" Devon asked. "Didn't this woman love Ulrik?"

"We thought so. For all the time she spent within the walls of Ulrik's house as he fed, clothed, and protected her and all of her family, she didna learn anything. A human can no' kill a Dragon King. Only a Dragon King can kill a King. But she also gave up immortality."

Devon's blue eyes widened. "How do you mean?"

"A Dragon King is immortal. When we take a mate, they live as long as we do."

"I see," she mumbled, a frown forming. "So why did she want to betray Ulrik?"

He shrugged. "I doona know. Con gathered us and told us what he'd learned after sending Ulrik away on some business. All the Kings hunted down his intended mate and killed her for what she'd planned to do to Ulrik. I knew it wouldna solve anything, but I was angry on behalf of my brother. And we knew he'd never be able to take her life because of his love. That's why we stepped in. Except we unknowingly set in motion a war that would eventually destroy us."

She released a breath. "Will you tell me more?"

He turned and met her gaze. "Ulrik returned to discover what we'd done. His anger was volatile, and he unleashed his fury. Right before our eyes, he changed. He immediately set out to destroy the humans—and he began in the verra village he'd helped to build.

"He engulfed his home in dragon fire. His Silvers joined him. When there was nothing left, they moved on to the next. In retaliation, the humans slaughtered the smallest of the dragons, wiping out entire clans. That's when I joined Ulrik.

"Some of the Kings remained with Con as they tried to bring about a truce, but many of us went with Ulrik to rid our world of the beings who had caused nothing but harm.

"The Kings fighting with Con set up dragons to guard the humans, and those verra people turned and killed the dragons. I watched in horror as the dragons failed to defend themselves because they'd been sent to shield the mortals. I knew then the war would only end when one of our species ceased to exist."

He stopped and closed his eyes as memories flooded his mind. The screams of dying dragons, the roars of others who watched the massacre. The fire, the blood.

The death.

A soft hand rested on his arm. His gaze snapped open to look at Devon. Her blue eyes were filled with a wealth of sadness.

He inhaled deeply and continued. "It didna matter how many humans we killed, it seemed more appeared. During all of this, more and more dragons died. That's when I went to Con. Eventually, all the Kings but Ulrik returned to Con. Together, we called the dragons and used our magic to create a dragon bridge that allowed them to escape this world and go to another. It was the most horrific day of my life.

"No' even the dragons leaving appeased the mortals, though. Ulrik and four of his largest Silvers ignored Con's call. They continued to wreak havoc on the mortals so that we had no choice but to make the Silvers sleep. That incensed Ulrik. After we'd moved the Silvers inside a mountain on Dreagan, we were able to corner Ulrik.

"He wouldna listen to reason. His anger hardened him to everything. Con commanded us to unite our magic to bind Ulrik's. Con then made sure Ulrik walked this world in the verra form he detested—human. And to seal everything, he banished Ulrik from Dreagan.

"We had little time to come to terms with what had happened to Ulrik, because the humans were still hunting us. It didna matter that they couldna kill us, or that we could've wiped them out with ease. We retreated to Dreagan and our mountains to sleep away centuries, only to emerge when tales of dragons were only myth. We've been living among you ever since, hiding who we are and fighting wars to protect you."

Devon's lips were parted. She blinked twice. "I don't really know what to say. That's quite a story. I have some questions."

"Ask them," he bade.

"How did you keep humans off Dreagan while you slept?"

He shifted against the metal. "Magic. Those barriers are still up to this day. They make the mortals uneasy, causing them to turn back before crossing onto our land. It's the only way we can guard sixty thousand acres. We altered it to allow visitors to the distillery, but only in certain buildings.

"The Silvers?"

"Still sleeping on Dreagan. Our magic keeps them there, caged."

She licked her lips. "All right. What about Ulrik?"

"His hatred for what we did has driven him for thousands of years. His goal is to take down Con and become King of Kings."

"Which means what for us humans?" she asked.

"Death. His loathing of you has only grown over the years. If he defeats Con, he'll wipe the realm of all mortals."

She twisted her lips. "What's preventing him from doing that now?"

"His magic being bound. Unfortunately, he found a Druid who was able to touch dragon magic and unbind some of his power. When his magic is fully returned, he can wake the Silvers and plunge the world back into war."

"Well. That doesn't sound like fun. What does any of that have to do with Kyvor, though?"

"Ulrik is working with the Dark Fae to expose the Dragon Kings to everyone. It's part of his plan to tear the Kings apart and mess with Con. By bringing in mortals, Ulrik is making it more difficult for us to fight him."

She scrunched up her face. "How?"

"Neither he nor the Dark Fae care about your kind seeing them, but the Dragon Kings go to great lengths so that mortals doona see us."

"I can understand how that might be problematic. However, that's twice now you've mentioned Dark Fae."

He smiled sadly. "We're no' the only beings with magic on this earth, Devon. We already told you about the Druids."

"This can't be real."

"It is. Denying it willna change anything."

She closed her eyes and nodded. "I'm finding that's truer than I ever realized."

CHAPTER TWENTY-SEVEN

MacLeod Castle

There was a restlessness about the castle, an uneasiness that seeped into the very stones and touched every person within the walls.

For Isla, it was even worse. She had been jerked awake by the sound of the Ancients screaming her name. Hayden asked her repeatedly what the Ancients were saying, but she couldn't make it out. She only knew it was imperative that she get inside the walls of MacLeod Castle and summon the other Druids. Hayden hadn't hesitated to dress and go with her from their home on MacLeod land.

She hadn't needed to worry about gathering the other MacLeod Druids, for the Ancients had woken them as well with shouts and screams. The only difference was that the Ancients only seemed to want to talk to Isla.

Isla now stood on the battlements of the castle next to Sonya, their gazes pointed west. Isla watched as her husband stood below with the other Warriors, talking amongst themselves. The fourteen men had scoured MacLeod land, looking for anything that might cause such a disruption, but they found nothing.

If that weren't disturbing enough, there was a growing apprehension within her. It's why she'd sought out Sonya. Except the flame-haired Druid was too intent on listening to the trees to even know Isla was beside her.

Something was wrong. Very wrong.

There was a whooshing sound above. Isla raised her gaze to see Broc stretch his dark blue, leathery wings as he glided over them, his gaze locked on Sonya. With a tip of his large appendage, he turned and landed beside his wife, folding his wings behind him.

Isla watched the dark blue fade from his skin as Broc tamped down the primeval god within him. His wings disappeared, as did the fangs and claws. The dark blue that filled his eyes from corner to corner diminished to reveal brown irises.

Sonya closed her lids and spread her arms as the trees bent this way and that as they moved, dislodging snow in their effort to speak to her.

Isla turned her head and looked down, her gaze locking with Hayden's. He'd released his god as well by the red of his skin and the horns sticking up through his long, blond hair.

She'd never thought she could love anyone as much as she loved him. Hayden was her life. He'd saved her, and shown her a world of love and contentment.

After all the battles each of them at MacLeod Castle had fought with *droughs*, this was their time of peace. So many times, they'd come close to death. Yet they'd banded together and become a family, overcoming all obstacles.

That was how they'd destroyed Deirdre, Declan, and Jason—*droughs* who had sought to take over the world with magic.

The Dragon Kings had come to their aid, and they, in turn, had helped the Kings. Was this new disturbance about the Kings?

Or had another *drough* appeared?

"Rhi is coming," Sonya suddenly said.

Isla looked to her friend to find the Druid's gaze on her. "When?"

"Now."

Isla glanced at the trees to discover them still once more. By the troubled expression on Sonya's face, the Light Fae's visit wasn't a social call.

Sonya turned and walked inside the castle with Broc at her side. As soon as the door opened, Isla heard a commotion within. It wasn't long before the Warriors also began to make their way within the castle walls, though Hayden lagged behind.

Isla huddled beneath her coat, bracing against the cold. Hayden took a few running steps before he jumped to the top of the battlements. He landed beside her and tamped down his god.

Without a word, she turned to her husband. His strong arms wrapped around her, holding her tightly. He stood in the elements with no shirt, completely unaffected by the chilly weather.

"What is it, love?" he murmured.

"If we go inside, we'll learn what woke me."

His chest expanded as he inhaled. "That wouldna be good, why?"

"Another fight is headed our way."

"Are you sure?"

She leaned back and looked into his dark eyes. "Yes."

"I've never backed down from a fight before. I willna now."

"Haven't we done enough? Haven't we given enough?"

His fingers skimmed down her cheek tenderly. "This is who we are."

"I know." She sighed and sank her fingers into his blond hair. "I thought we were done risking our lives."

He gave her one of his crooked smiles that she loved so much. "I'm a Warrior, and you're a Druid. We get to stop the day our hearts stop beating."

"I know. It's just . . . the Ancients feel scared. And that terrifies me."

"You're the strongest woman I know. If anyone can do this, it's you. And I'll be standing with you the entire time."

He always knew what to say. She felt her lips lift in a grin. "Promise?"

"There isna a being on this planet or elsewhere that could keep me from you. Shall we go and see what Rhi wants?"

She gave a nod. With their fingers entwined, they made their way inside the castle. As they descended the stairs to the great hall, they could hear the various conversations.

Isla's gaze moved around the hall to the couples sitting at the table. Only one person stood apart: Rhi. The Fae's gaze jerked to Isla.

Hayden's fingers tightened around Isla's as he led her from the stairs to the last two remaining seats at the table. Her heart was pounding. She didn't know what was wrong with her, but every instinct she had told her to run as fast and as far as she could.

The room quieted as everyone turned to Rhi. She pushed away from the wall she had been leaning against, her gaze never leaving Isla.

"What brings you to our home?" Fallon MacLeod asked.

Rhi shot a quick look at the leader of the Warriors. "Trouble."

Isla felt a shiver run down her spine. It was only Hayden's hold on her that kept her in her seat while Rhi slowly made her way to the middle of the great hall.

"What's going on, Rhi?" Phelan asked.

If anyone could get the Fae to talk, it was Phelan. He was half-Fae himself, and like a brother to Rhi. But to Isla's surprise, Rhi ignored the Warrior's question.

"Something called you Druids together," Rhi said, the statement directed at Isla.

No matter how she tried, Isla couldn't look away from the Light Fae.

"What did you hear?" Rhi probed.

Isla grimaced as the Ancients' voices suddenly rose up together in a tidal wave of shouts and screams in reply, a sound that had her clutching her head between her hands.

The voices ran over each other, making it impossible to distinguish even one word. Her head began to pound the longer the voices continued.

It was only Hayden's hands and his voice soothing her that kept her calm. Isla fought against the voices, wanting to get away from them.

"Concentrate, Isla," Rhi demanded. "Listen to them."

She shook her head. "No!"

"They're only talking to you. You have to listen!" Rhi bellowed.

Only talking? That couldn't be right. Isla opened her eyes and looked across the table to Laura, who sat with worry filling her gaze.

Isla clenched her teeth as the ache doubled. "I can't."

There was a scuffle of some kind, and she heard Hayden growl dangerously. Hands roughly grabbed her and gave her a little jerk.

"Dammit, Isla, concentrate," Rhi ordered. "They're trying to tell you something."

How did Rhi know about any of this? Isla couldn't understand what any of it meant. She only knew there was danger, so much danger.

"Focus on the voices. Push everything else out of your mind," Hayden whispered in her ear.

The sound of his voice gave her a dose of composure. She felt his hands on her, lending her his strength. She did as he asked, and immediately, the pain diminished.

The Ancients were still loud, but the sounds of those in the great hall were interfering. Isla gripped Hayden's hand tightly as she shut herself off from everything around her. With the outside noise removed, she was able to lose herself to the Ancients.

The longer she listened, the clearer the voices became. The first thing she noticed was the dread and distress she heard in their tones.

"I'm here," she told them.

"*Isla. Danger!*"

She'd been right. "Tell me."

"*The past is returning.*"

"What does that mean?"

"*They want payback.*"

She was growing more confused as they spoke. "Who?"

"*You'll not be able to stop them alone. You'll need the Light Fae. She has the answers you seek.*"

And just like that, the Ancients left. "Wait!" Isla shouted, reaching toward them.

Her body pitched forward only to be caught by strong arms she knew well. She looked up into Hayden's face and wanted to scream in frustration. But she couldn't. Not when the rest of them waited to hear what the Ancients had told her.

Isla drew in a shuddering breath. Her gaze clashed with Rhi's. The Ancients wanted her to work with Rhi. It was an odd request since the Druids tended to keep apart from the Fae.

She stepped out of Hayden's arms and walked to Rhi. "How did you know?"

"There was an incident," Rhi said loud enough for everyone to hear. "On Fair Isle."

"Oh, God. Faith," Ronnie said in alarm.

Isla vaguely recalled Ronnie mentioning something about one of her colleagues finding a dragon skeleton on an isle.

"Faith is fine," Rhi assured Ronnie. "We made sure of that."

Lucan MacLeod said, "I think you'd better fill us all in on everything."

"Of course." Rhi swallowed and faced them. "Faith did indeed find dragon bones—an entire skeleton. It had somehow been concealed with magic when Dmitri destroyed the bodies of the Whites who died on his isles. We thought the worst was the fact that a skeleton had been left behind."

Isla wrapped her arms around herself. As Rhi spoke, she could see the events unfold in her mind as if she'd been there with Dmitri and Faith.

"Dmitri brought the bones to Dreagan. When he removed them from the cave, Faith found something. It was a small, wooden dragon."

Isla took a step back from Rhi, her knees threatening to buckle—because, at that moment, the Ancients showed her the wooden piece. "A dragon carved to look like Con."

Rhi nodded. "Yes. When it was brought near any of the Kings, they had an overwhelming desire to kill all mortals. In Faith's hands, I saw a blade come out of it as she stabbed Dmitri. She kept saying that she wouldn't be the Kings' first kill, starting the war all over again."

"Did you touch it?" Phelan asked Rhi.

The Light Fae shook her head. "Shara, however, did. She passed out as rage consumed her."

"Why are you here?" Larena asked from her seat beside her husband, Fallon.

Isla backed up another step when Rhi glanced her way. She couldn't speak as the Ancients allowed her to hear the vicious, vile things the wooden dragon had caused the Dragon Kings and Faith to say.

"Because of what I felt when I examined the dragon," Rhi said.

Ramsey rose to his feet. He was the only Warrior who was also part Druid—a deadly combination that had saved them on countless occasions. "I want to see this object."

"I'm not sure that's a good idea, sunshine," Rhi cautioned.

Ramsey merely raised a black brow.

Rhi blew out a breath, and then there was a large sphere hovering over her shoulder. Without a word, the Fae put her hands on either side of the orb, not quite touching it, and focused on the wooden dragon.

Little bolts of lightning ran from the wooden dragon to the globe. It wasn't until a pale yellow light began to surround Rhi that Phelan rushed to her. Isla grabbed his arm before he could touch the Fae.

"I'm fine," Rhi said to Phelan.

His lips flattened. "Then stop glowing."

Everyone knew that Rhi glowing was never a good thing. So, at Phelan's request, she dropped her hands. Isla breathed a sigh of relief when the glow faded.

"I feel Fae magic within it," Rhi told them. "Both Light and Dark."

Hayden crossed his arms over his thick chest. "What else do you feel? Because you wouldna be here talking to my woman if there wasna more."

Rhi's gaze slid to Isla. "I feel Druid magic. Both *mie* and *drough*."

"Damn," Fallon muttered.

Rhi gave a pointed look Isla's way. "What did the Ancients tell you?"

"That there's danger." Isla looked at Hayden, knowing that he would stand with her no matter what. "And that the past is returning."

Ramsey frowned. "What the hell does that mean?"

Isla turned to Rhi. "They said I should work with you against those who want payback."

"Well, sister," Rhi said with a wry grin. "Let's get started."

CHAPTER TWENTY-EIGHT

Devon wasn't nearly done asking questions. "Will you tell me about the Fae?"

Anson's midnight eyes watched her for a long moment. "Do you believe what I've told you?"

"I believe that you believe it."

He raised a brow. "You saw it."

"Did I? You want me to accept that magic exists when I've never seen it, not in my entire life. To me, magic is dragging a rabbit out of a hat or pulling a coin from thin air."

"If you doona believe, why do you want to know more?"

She'd hoped he wouldn't ask that. Mostly because she wasn't yet prepared to allow herself to think about it, much less say it aloud.

"Devon," he urged.

"Because even though you scared me when you shifted, you're gorgeous in dragon form. Because your world is fascinating. It's beautiful and scary and enthralling, and I want to know everything."

His gaze shifted upward briefly before he slowly

nodded. "The Fae are from another realm. They came here centuries ago because of civil war and settled in Ireland. There are two kinds of Fae—Light and Dark."

She leaned her head against the bars and watched him. He wanted her to accept everything he shared, but he had no idea how difficult it was for her.

"The Fae are extremely beautiful," he continued. "Humans are drawn to them without even realizing it. The Light have silver eyes and black hair. They mingle with mortals, though it's frowned upon."

"Why?" she asked with a scowl.

"Because once you have sex with a Fae, no mortal will ever be able to satisfy you again."

Devon wrinkled her nose. "I see."

"There is something about your race that appeals to the Fae. Perhaps it's how easily you fall under their spell, but the occasional dalliance sometimes results in a child. There are thousands of Halflings walking this earth."

She took that in, thinking of all the beautiful people in the movies that seemed almost too gorgeous to be real. Charlize Theron for one. Devon was now sure she was a Halfling. "And the Dark?"

"You saw them today," Anson stated. "A Light Fae can turn Dark, but many of the most powerful Dark have family connections that go back millions of years. If a Fae is born into a Dark family, they will be Dark."

"Do any ever turn Light?"

"It rarely happens. It's the seductive power of their magic that holds them. Their magic is greater as a Dark, but it turns them evil. While a Light might give in and take a mortal for a single time, the Dark have other ideas. They feed on humans."

She jerked back at the thought. "You mean, they eat us?"

"No' in the way you're thinking. Mortals flock to them, their bodies uninhibited. They freely yield themselves to the Dark, who gives them the best sex of their lives. But each time a Dark couples with a human, they drain a bit of their soul."

Devon was repulsed by the thought. "Are you telling me that a woman will lie there in the throes of passion without knowing she's dying?"

"That's exactly what I'm saying. I've seen it. The first time a Dark takes a life, their eyes turn red. Every evil deed after that begins to turn more of their hair silver."

"They'd be easy to recognize," she said with distaste.

Anson shook his head. "The Fae have magic, remember. They can teleport. They can also craft Fae doorways only they can see. And they can use glamour to change their appearance."

"I think I might be sick."

"When the Fae first came to this realm, we told them to leave, but they took one look at you humans and saw a feast. It wasna long after that the Fae Wars began. At first, it was the Dragon Kings against both the Light and Dark, but Con managed to convince the Light Queen, Usaeil, that if she sided with us, it could also end their civil war.

"Since their wars all but destroyed their world, she accepted his offer. The Light joined us, and we were able to defeat the Dark."

Devon shifted, her hand sliding down one of the bars and coming in contact with his. A crackle of awareness rushed through her that she promptly ignored. "So you won because the Light helped you."

"We could've bested the Dark on our own, but we were fighting a war while keeping humans from witnessing any of it. And Con thought an alliance with the Light could only benefit us."

"Smart move," she admitted. "If you won, why didn't you push the Fae out?"

His expression hardened. "It's something we all regret. We signed a treaty. The Dark were meant to stay in Ireland and never venture into Scotland, and were not supposed to take a single human life. But the longer they remained, the more they pushed against those boundaries until they broke the bonds altogether."

"Are you at war with them again?"

"Aye. And doing our best no' to bring it to the attention of the mortals. The Dark doona care who sees them, so it makes it more difficult for us."

She blew out a breath. "None of this would be an issue if you didn't have to hide who you are."

"Nay."

"Are the Light still your allies?"

He hesitated a bit too long. "I think so. There is one Light. Her name is Rhi. She has done much for us over the centuries."

"Why? What ties her to the Kings?"

"The fact that she had a Dragon King as a lover."

Devon smiled at the thought. "Are they still together?"

"Nay, though none of us know why he ended the affair. They belong together. All of us knew it then, and we know it now."

"That's sad. And even though he ended it, Rhi still helps you?"

"She's risked her life to aid us on several occasions."

"So the Fae aren't immortal?"

He shrugged offhandedly. "No' in the sense that we are. They live verra long lives, but one of their specially made blades forged in the Fires of Erwar can kill them."

"Any chance I can get one of those blades?" she asked with a grin.

His lips tilted up in a breathtaking smile. "Does that mean you accept what I've told you?"

Instead of answering him, she cleared her throat. "What about Druids? Are they the Halflings you spoke about?"

"Druids are humans who are able to feel the magic that makes up this realm. Sensing and feeling the magic were the first steps. Magic then melded with them, becoming part of them. That's how the Druids came to be. There isna much magic left on this world anymore. Mortals' disregard of it has pushed the magic deep within the ground, but there are still some places it can be felt. Dreagan, of course, because we're there. For Druids, it's the Isle of Skye."

She lifted her brows. "Really? So close? I've heard of the beauty of Skye."

"Mortals think it's the splendor of the land that brings them, and though Skye is magnificent, it's the magic they feel."

"You make me want to go."

His black gaze was intense. "You should."

Unable to hold his stare, she hastily looked away. "Are there many Druids?"

"The more they procreate with non-magical humans, the more the magic fades from them. The Druids are a dying breed. There are a group of them who saved your kind several times against *droughs*—the evil Druids intent on taking over the world."

"*Droughs*," she said, testing out the word. It sounded foreign and difficult to say.

"It's Gaelic. The virtuous Druids are *mies*."

She turned her gaze to him. "How does a Druid's magic compare to a Fae's?"

"A Druid can be immensely powerful but no' come

close to a Fae. While Druids walk two worlds—their own and that of the humans—the Fae and magic are as one."

"Just like you?"

There was a slight frown on his forehead at her question. "We are magic. Magic is us. So, aye, like us."

What went unsaid was that the Dragon Kings were the most powerful of all. She didn't need to ask. He'd confirmed it with his stories. "A Dragon King."

"Without dragons," he said, looking away.

She put her hand on his arm. "I'm so sorry, Anson. I don't know why you still wish to help us after everything you've told me. I wouldn't. But what I really don't understand is why you freely tell me all of this, knowing that Stanley and Harriett have to be listening."

"You forget," he said with a grin as he turned his head back to her. "I have magic. I created a bubble around us to silence our words. They think you're there, but that I'm in one of the dark corners."

"So they didn't hear anything we've said?"

"No' a word," he replied with a grin.

Though she still wasn't sure about the whole magic thing, she decided it was better to hedge her bets. "And the Druid Kinsey and Esther spoke of?"

"She's powerful, but she willna be able to touch my magic."

That made Devon feel better. Then she recalled something that had happened at the warehouse. "Why did the men holding me suddenly let me go?"

"Because I made them. Each King has their own power. Mine is being able to possess someone's body."

"And their minds?"

He gave a shake of his head. "Unfortunately no'."

"Upton said something about the Druid preventing you from doing that to him."

Anson's lips flattened for a second. "That was my

mistake. I should've foreseen that Upton would take such precautions. I could've broken through the Druid's spells, but that would've put you in more danger."

"Next time, don't worry about me."

"Do you no' understand?"

She tilted her head. "Understand what?"

"They're going to use you to make sure I do whatever it is they want."

"No," she said louder than intended. "Don't let them."

He leaned toward the bars so their faces were close. "I'll no' let them harm a single hair on your head."

"They're counting on that. I saw the look in Stanley's eyes earlier. He's insane with the need to have you at his beck and call."

"It's his mistake," Anson stated in a cold voice. "He'll learn soon enough that I'm no' his toy."

She gripped Anson's arm tighter and leaned in closer. "Let him know that right from the beginning."

"And if they threaten your life?"

It wasn't as if she wanted to die. In fact, she very much wanted to live. Maybe it was the fact that she'd been taken by a psychopath, but she was finding it harder and harder to come up with reasons not to believe Anson.

"I'm one person," she replied.

He shook his head. "I can no' allow anything to happen to you."

"Look at the big picture. Without me, you can break away from here and get the information you and Kinsey came for."

"It's no' worth it."

She rolled her eyes and sighed loudly. "Why are you being so difficult?"

"Because I care about you. Because it physically hurts me to think about you harmed."

Devon's heart skipped a beat. How could he be real?

He was gentle and kind but also protective and authoritative. He was strong and commanding, and impossibly gorgeous.

"I want you," he murmured.

With three words, she accepted everything about him—Dragon King, magic, immortality—the whole package.

She swallowed as her blood raced with desire. "I'm yours."

When he took her lips in a hungry kiss, she forgot about the metal bars between them, Upton and his mad schemes, and the fact that she could die.

Because she was being kissed by a Dragon King.

Who had chosen her.

CHAPTER TWENTY-NINE

It took little for Anson's body to ignite into a blaze of desire. He detested the bars that kept him apart from Devon, but more than that, he loathed the people who dared to put her in harm's way.

They would pay.

Painfully.

There was nothing Con or anyone else could say that would change his mind. Worst of all, he knew he was the one responsible for Devon being in the entire predicament.

But that would change. He would see to it.

By all that was magical, he loved kissing her. His body ached with the need to be inside her again, to feel her tight, slick walls holding him.

Reluctantly, he ended the kiss and rested his forehead against hers. He remained calm, keeping control of his rising anger, when all he wanted to do was shift and tear down the building before taking her to Dreagan and to safety.

Then return and destroy anyone involved in their kidnapping.

"I don't have any family," Devon said.

Anson didn't reply. That tidbit had already been revealed by Kinsey. The fact that Devon said it with such sad eyes alerted him that the story behind it would be of the horrible kind.

"You already knew, didn't you?"

He smoothed hair away from Devon's face as he leaned back to look at her. "Aye."

"I've not said those words in a long time." She then shifted so that she rested her head on his shoulder through the bars.

Anson held her, smoothing his hand over her brunette locks as he waited for her to talk.

"My mum died when I was three. I don't remember her. My father didn't handle her sudden death well, and I didn't fit into the mix at all. He was in the Royal Navy, so when he shipped out, I went to stay with his brother.

"My aunt and uncle were good people and treated me as theirs. When I was four, they had their own daughter, and I lived with them permanently. My cousin and I were very close. Life was good. Really good." Her smile faded then. "A month before my thirteenth birthday, I learned my father had been killed."

Anson held her tighter, wishing he could take away the pain. She wasn't the only one to lose both parents so young, but that didn't make her suffering any less horrific.

"I'd always thought my father would come back for me." She snorted. "It was silly really. In the ten years following him leaving me with his brother, I only saw him twice. I think I always knew in the back of my mind that he didn't want me in his life.

"When I was younger, I learned all I could about my dad. Then one day, I put it all in a chest and forgot about it. With his death, I pulled out that chest where I'd stored pictures and anything my uncle had given me of my father. I became obsessed with all of it, including the magic tricks he'd apparently mastered at a young age."

Anson never stopped stroking her hair, giving her comfort as she spoke.

"For four years, everything I did revolved around magic. I was horrible at it, but I loved it. If a magician came to town, I made sure I was there. My aunt, uncle, and cousin bore it all with smiles."

"Because they loved you," Anson said.

Devon nodded, sniffing. "My uncle had been feeling poorly for weeks when the day came for us to go and see the newest magician. I don't even remember who it was, but I felt as if the world would come to an end if I didn't go. My cousin and I were on the way back to the house from a run to the store. Whatever had made my uncle sick had passed to my aunt. My cousin wasn't feeling well either, so I was driving. It was raining so badly, the windshield wipers couldn't keep up. I remember that clearly. That, and my fury."

He stared at her face, watching the play of emotions.

She shrugged, a rueful tilt to her lips. "I was so angry. I don't recall what my cousin said exactly. She was supposed to go with me. Otherwise, I couldn't go to see the show. When she said she didn't feel like going, I started yelling. The tires hit a puddle, and we hydroplaned right into oncoming traffic."

Anson closed his eyes. "You felt magic was your connection to your father."

"A man who didn't want me."

"He probably saw that you were better off with his brother and decided to leave you."

Devon sighed loudly. "I'll never know, will I? But that doesn't justify my anger."

"We can no' help how we feel."

"My cousin died that night." She sniffed loudly. "I thought I was going to have to tell my aunt and uncle, but I was taken to the hospital instead. They'd both gotten so sick, they had been admitted a half-hour earlier with lung infections. It was so bad that we held off the funeral for as long as we could until they were well enough to attend."

He could only imagine how her aunt and uncle had felt about losing their daughter, and he prayed they didn't take it out on Devon.

Devon picked dirt from her ruined skirt. "At the funeral, it was all I could do to stand there while others patted my arm and told me that sometimes awful things happened. No one knew that if I'd been driving slower, if I hadn't been yelling, and if I'd kept my eyes on the road, my cousin wouldn't have died."

Anson kissed the top of her head. "You can no' know that for sure."

"I had to tell my aunt and uncle the truth. They were so distraught over the loss of their only child, and I couldn't look at them every day and keep that secret to myself. You should've seen their faces when I confessed what had happened. Whatever love they'd held for me vanished."

He shook his head. "Surely no'."

"They told me that accidents happen, but that they still loved me. I believed them. I was so relieved. Days later when I brought them home, I saw the truth. They stopped looking at me and rarely spoke to me. I thought they needed time, but things never changed. Nothing I did, no amount of apologies helped. We endured that way until I turned eighteen. When I woke up that morning, there was a note taped to my door."

"What did it say?" he asked when she grew silent.

"Just six words. *Please be moved out by dinner.*"

He searched for something to say that would help take away her heartache, but there was nothing. "I'm sorry."

"I went to university, where I partied my way through the first three years. I'd been lost since my cousin's death, and it was only getting worse. But I didn't care. Nothing made sense to me, and I didn't want to figure any of it out. I was content to let my life slowly crumble. I thought I deserved it."

"You didna," he said.

She shot him a small smile. "It was the summer before my senior year that I received a letter from an attorney, telling me that my aunt and uncle had died in a car accident. Part of me was relieved. I hated myself for that, but I mourned them. They were my only family."

"And the other part?"

Tucking her hair behind her ear, she said, "It was like a wake-up call."

"Then you buckled down and looked to the future, aye?" he guessed.

There was a smile in her voice when she replied, "Yes."

"That's why you doona believe in magic."

She lifted her head, her blue eyes meeting his. "With my cousin's death, I realized that I was fixated on something that wasn't only bogus but didn't matter because my father was gone. It cost me my family."

"You're no' alone now. I'm here. Kinsey, Esther, and Henry are out there looking for us. And then there are the other Dragon Kings."

Her forehead puckered. "Henry?"

"Esther's brother. He's also an MI5 agent. He's the one who drove me to the warehouse to find you."

"Did they follow us?"

"I doona need them. I can contact the Kings anytime I want."

She turned her head slightly and gave him an odd look. "Why haven't you?"

"I need to know what Upton wants. I'll no' bring more Kings here if I can get us out on my own."

"Did Stanley say anything to you about what he wants?"

"No' yet." And that was one of the things that worried Anson. "Men like Upton enjoy telling everyone what they intend. He's no' said a word."

Devon wrinkled her nose. "That doesn't bode well for us. What do we do?"

"Pretend that you hate me."

"Why?" she asked.

He ran a thumb over her bottom lip. "Because if he thinks you care even the tiniest bit, they'll use it. He saw your reaction when I shifted. He knows you had no idea before today who I am—*what* I am. Let him believe you're terrified of me."

"I don't—"

Anson jerked when he heard approaching footsteps. He gave her a quick kiss and quickly stood, melding back into the shadows. "Stand up and pace. When they enter, don't look my way. Ever. Remember that."

She sat there for a second before rising to her feet and beginning to pace. He slowly dropped his magic so everything appeared as it should be.

His gaze was on the door when it opened, and Upton walked in alone. Anson briefly thought about attacking him, but that would be too easy. It's what they expected him to do—and what he longed to do.

Did they wish to find out if the Dragon Kings were more beast than man? If so, they were going to be disappointed. Because the Kings were all dragon.

Upton strolled into the room with the door closing behind him as if he didn't have a care in the world. He walked straight to the cage in the middle of the area and smiled at Devon.

She stopped in front of him and crossed her arms over her chest. Then she raised her chin and demanded, "Let me out."

"I'm sorry, dear. That isn't going to happen."

"Why?"

Upton's gaze scanned the darkness. "We need you."

Devon dropped her arms and took a step back. "Is he in here? With me? Now?" she asked in a voice filled with terror.

It was so convincing that Anson believed it himself for a moment.

"Yes, he is," Stanley said.

Her eyes grew round. "How are you standing there so nonchalantly?"

"Because he can't touch me."

Anson wanted to give a loud snort. Ever since Upton had walked into the room, he'd been scanning the area with his dragon magic.

The Druid was impressive with her work. She'd layered spells in such a way that it would take other Druids weeks to crack through it. But he wasn't a Druid.

With one thought, he used just enough magic to put the tiniest crack in the Druid's spells. He didn't want the enchantment removed now because then they would be alerted to his plan. But if the Druid checked, she'd never notice the fracture in the spells.

Yet it was all that he needed for when he decided to take down Upton. Whether Anson liked it or not, this was where he and Devon needed to be.

The mortals wouldn't lay a finger on her as long as Anson did as they asked. And the longer he was with them, the more he could find out what their ultimate goal was—and be able to put a stop to all of it.

"How is that possible?" Devon asked Upton.

Stanley's smile widened. "My little secret, dear."

"Please don't leave me in here with that . . . thing."

"Dragon King," Upton corrected her.

Devon waved away his words. "I don't care what he calls himself. He's not human."

"I did try to tell you that in my office. You really should've paid attention." Stanley turned his head toward Anson. "There's no need to hide in the shadows. Not any longer."

Anson remained silent.

Devon took a step closer to the bars. "Mr. Upton, I'm begging you. I didn't know who . . . I mean, what he was. You can't seriously be thinking of leaving me with him."

"I'm not thinking it. I'm doing it."

"He'll eat me!" she protested loudly.

Stanley laughed and put his hands in his pockets. "No, I don't think so. You see, Devon, for some reason, the Dragon Kings want to protect us mortals. That means we can do whatever we want to them and they won't retaliate. Ever."

"How do you know this?" she asked.

Upton grinned arrogantly. "A man who knows all about the Dragon Kings told me."

CHAPTER THIRTY

Devon's stomach clenched at Upton's statement. She wanted to look at Anson to see his reaction, but she kept her gaze on Stanley. She wanted to wipe the cocky smile from the insufferable baboon's face.

The fear that gripped her wasn't faked. It was all too real. But it wasn't directed at Anson. No, it was solely because of the worm that called himself a human—Stanley Upton.

By the way Upton continued to smile, his blue eyes shining, Devon realized that Stanley wanted her to ask for more information. So, she gave him exactly what he wanted.

"Who is this man?"

Upton inhaled deeply. "Only a Dragon King himself."

"And you trust him?"

The smile slipped as displeasure colored his face. "Why wouldn't I? He came to us."

"And you believe him?" Once more, she didn't have to fake her shock. It was very real.

Stanley shrugged. "Not at first, but he's convincing. He's the one who's been supplying all of our information."

"Yes, but . . . he's not human either," she said, goading Upton.

"My eyes were opened when the King came to me. He gave us all the names of the Dragon Kings on Dreagan."

"Did you look into him, as well?"

Stanley let his aggravation be known by the look he threw her. "He's an ally."

"He's a dragon."

"What's your problem?" Upton snapped.

Devon wrapped her arms around her middle. "I won't easily accept them. Ever. How could I? Nor will I ever trust one. The fact that you can put all of us in danger on the word of a-a-a dragon is preposterous. You've no idea if he's lying or not."

"He's not," came the terse reply.

"Then what does he want? If he's a Dragon King, why does he need our help?"

Stanley's crossed his arms over his chest and glared. "I'd never slap the hand of our queen away. I certainly won't do it with a Dragon King."

"Yes, but the queen is human. That . . . thing," she said, waving her hand about, "isn't."

"This man wants the humans to show the Dragon Kings that we don't need them. I plan to do just that."

It was worse than she'd expected. Devon swallowed past the lump in her throat. "How?"

Preening, Upton dropped his arms, a smug grin in place. "Anson will do whatever I want because not only will he refrain from harming me, but he'll do anything to ensure that nothing happens to you."

"That's absurd. He barely knows me."

"My friend said the Kings tend to be very compassionate when it comes to females, especially those they're attracted to."

Devon tucked her hair behind her ear. "This could all be a trap."

"No," Stanley said with a shake of his head. "He brought me a Druid. How do you think I'm holding the Dragon King here?"

"A Druid?" she repeated, lacing her words with skepticism.

Upton gave her a bored look. "You saw a man change into a dragon, and you have an issue believing there are Druids? Wait until I tell you about the Fae."

"Why are you telling me all of this?"

His smile was slow and cold as the Arctic. "Once you see my allies and the power I wield through them, you'll come to see how right I am."

"Why do you care if I agree with you?" Something was very wrong, and she didn't like the growing apprehension that was consuming her. It was too easy to fool Upton, but more than that, he was confident—very confident.

"You'll find out soon enough." Stanley turned on his heel and began to walk away. As he reached the door, he said over his shoulder, "You might want to make nice with Anson."

Devon didn't move long after Upton was gone. His words chilled her in ways that Anson's story never could. She felt as if everyone had lost his or her mind.

No. That wasn't quite right. There was Anson. He'd been kind, gentle, and caring. He'd told her his story, even though he knew she didn't believe it.

Instead of becoming angry over that, he'd simply accepted it. He didn't try to change her mind or argue.

Sometime in the sharing of their stories and while she'd told him her darkest secret, she'd subconsciously realized that. Perhaps that's when she began to slowly acknowledge that his words were . . . true.

She put her hand over her mouth and closed her eyes. Magic was real. Not the imitation kind, but the real, genuine—and tangible—type.

Her eyes snapped open. Why hadn't Anson said anything since Stanley left? She turned and let her gaze move through the darkness. Where was he?

She wanted to call out to him, to feel his hands on her once more. With him near, she knew she could survive this. Because there was one thing Upton had gotten right—Anson would shield her.

The weight of all she'd learned pressed upon her heavily. She walked to the cot and sat. If only she could help, but what could she do? She wasn't immortal, nor did she have any magic. She would only be in the way. How she hated being a liability instead of an asset.

"I'm here," Anson's voice came from behind her.

He wasn't close, but his whispered words did much to comfort her. She released a breath. "You know I didn't mean anything I said, right?"

"You were verra convincing."

She winced, wishing she could see him. "I did as you asked."

"I know. You did good."

"Is it Ulrik helping Upton?"

"I'm no' sure."

She stopped herself from turning around and gawking at him just in time. Dropping her chin to her chest to hide her face from any cameras, she asked, "What do you mean?"

"I know Ulrik. His hatred for mortals runs deep. He might use humans to some extent, but no' like this."

"It's been a long time since Ulrik has been the King you knew."

"That's verra true, but there are some things that doona change."

"Is there another Dragon King who could be doing this?"

Anson sighed loudly. "Nay."

"Then it's Ulrik."

"Perhaps."

She couldn't imagine how this news must affect Anson. "What do I do?"

"Nothing. I need to alert Con and Ryder."

She parted her lips to ask how but never got the chance.

"Our minds are linked, remember," he said, a smile in his voice.

She rolled her eyes. "Convenient."

The more she thought about it, the more she wished she had that ability. No more lugging around a mobile phone or trying to find where she'd put it during the numerous times throughout the day that she set it down and forget where. No more paying for the use of the cellular service or for the device itself.

It made her wish she had that bit of magic.

As soon as the thought went through her mind, she once again felt sadness at the loss of her parents, cousin, aunt, and uncle. All of them, in some form or another, were connected to magic.

Now the real thing was all around her, and it was changing her life. Much like the false kind had. The irony wasn't lost on her.

Was it Fate? Destiny? Or merely coincidence?

The longer she was around Anson, the more she came to realize that nothing was just happenstance or luck. The universe had a plan for everyone.

What was her part? Would she simply play a minor role? Or would she be more of a lead character? Because she really wanted the lead.

She lay back on the cot and threw an arm over her

eyes. There was much she wanted to talk to Anson about, and doing it while trying not to make her lips move was difficult. Plus, there were the audio recorders.

Then she realized she was silly to worry. Anson had already made sure they couldn't see her lips or hear her words. It seemed that magic was more than handy.

That made her smile.

"Ryder is stopping Kinsey, Esther, and Henry from coming to us," Anson said.

"Good. Kyvor has done enough to them."

"I agree. I've also told Con that I have things under control here."

"Did he buy that?" she asked.

A sound much like a grunt came from Anson. "Of course, no', but he knows additional Kings in London will only cause more harm than good. I'll get us out of this."

"I know." And she did. Because that was the type of man—dragon—Anson was.

He didn't say something unless he meant it, and he certainly wouldn't make such a vow unless he intended to keep it.

"Do whatever Upton wants of you," Anson told her. "Get him to believe that he's your savior."

She looked at the bars above her. "What if I encounter the Druid? Or the Dark?"

"The Dark he'll save for me. The Druid, well, I'm no' sure about her. I doona know what she looks like so she could be anyone."

"Harriett?"

"Nay. I didna feel any magic coming from her."

Now that shocked Devon. "You can feel another's magic?"

"Aye."

She drew in a fortifying breath. "Then I'll assume any

other woman Upton brings around me could be the Druid."

"If he has the Druid here, she'll make herself known soon."

"What do you mean *if*?"

There was a slight pause. "The Druid is helping Upton, but she doesna work for them. That means she decides when and where she goes."

"Unless she's working with Ulrik."

"I'm assuming she is. He's already proven that he knows how to find Druids and can use them to his advantage."

Devon crossed her ankles. "How long are we going to have to wait to see what Upton is really up to?"

No sooner had the words left her mouth than she heard a deep, guttural growl come from Anson. Her head jerked his way. When she saw the four men with varying lengths of black and silver hair, she jumped to her feet.

Her heart slammed against her ribs as she hastily backed away until the cage stopped her progress. The Dark had their red gazes locked on a spot in the shadows.

Lights suddenly flicked on, bathing the vast area in bright light. For the first time, she got to see where they were being held.

It was as large as the warehouse with soaring ceilings that could easily fit a dragon inside. Dread filled her. There was nothing Upton had that could be worth Anson subjecting himself to whatever awaited them. He should leave while he could.

Anson was on his feet, slowly stalking to the Dark. He leaned to the side as one of those iridescent balls formed by the Fae was thrown at him.

He easily dodged it, as well as the second one. It was the third that made contact and grazed off his hip. Devon gasped when she saw how his jeans burned away in a blink.

It wasn't until he went down on one knee and turned that she saw the hip—and the scorched flesh. The realization that the Dark were throwing magic at him hit her with the force of a sonic boom.

Though it must be agonizing, Anson fought as if he didn't feel it. Or the second orb that slammed into his left shoulder.

All she could do was watch the fight unfold before her. Her gaze was locked on Anson as he moved elegantly and lethally, dodging and blocking the orbs.

When he reached the first of them, he bared his teeth and punched through the Fae's chest to yank out the Dark's heart.

And it was all she could do not to clap and cheer him on.

CHAPTER THIRTY-ONE

Wrath. It consumed Anson. It blurred the agony of the Dark magic as the orbs found their marks. It focused him on the ones he could kill.

Even as he slew first one and then a second Dark, he was cognizant of Devon. She had made nary a sound, but he felt her gaze on him.

Hers, however, wasn't the only one he felt. Others watched him. Upton and his cronies. That only increased Anson's anger. Because of Upton's need to see with his own eyes what a Dragon King could do, he'd put Devon in the line of fire.

And that couldn't be forgiven.

Anson released the rage he'd been holding back on the last two Fae. Within seconds, he stood over four dead Dark, his body covered in their blood and burns from their magic.

He fought to stay on his feet even as the last bit of Fae magic twisted its way through his back and into his spine. Tilting his head to look through the locks of hair that had fallen over his face, Anson glanced in Devon's direction.

Her eyes were wide with shock, the devastation of

what she'd just witnessed visible by her pale features. First she'd seen him in his true form, then she'd witnessed him in battle. This was who he was. He wanted her to accept him—but he wouldn't push her.

There was a click, and the door opened. Anson's gaze locked on Upton as a feral need rose within him to end the mortal's life in the most gruesome way possible.

Stanley began to clap slowly. "Very good. My friend mentioned the skills of the Dragon Kings when it came to battle."

"So you wanted to observe it yourself," Anson said.

Upton grinned. "Precisely."

"Come here," Anson beckoned. "I'll show you firsthand."

The bastard didn't move, but Anson got some enjoyment out of Upton's nervous laugh that followed.

"Now," Stanley said after he'd cleared his throat. "After that little display, I'm sure you need recovery time."

Anson didn't bother to reply. Let the idiot come to his own conclusions. Apparently, Ulrik—or someone pretending to be him—was imparting all kinds of knowledge regarding the Kings.

Anson kept thinking about the man he'd seen in London that looked so much like Ulrik. Stanley had said it wasn't Ulrik helping him, but that didn't mean Ulrik wasn't involved in some way. And that disappointed him greatly.

"I'm also sure you realize by now that you can't escape," Upton said with a bright smile. "That is the work of our Druid. She's quite spectacular."

"Bring her in. I'd like to meet her," Anson insisted.

Stanley wiggled his index finger back and forth. "You'll meet her soon enough. Until then, get used to your accommodations. You and Devon will be here for a long while yet."

"What?" Devon cried out.

With that bit conveyed, Upton walked out the door. Moments later, the lights turned off except for the one over Devon's cell and the path from the door to Devon.

Anson walked to the nearest wall and leaned back against it before sliding to the floor. He watched Devon walk the confines of her prison with her arms crossed over her chest and her head down.

His decision to remain had been a hasty one. Mainly because he thought he could best whatever was thrown at him, stop Kyvor, and keep Devon safe.

It was his pride that had allowed him to believe that. Now, he wasn't so sure. Fighting the Dark had made it clear how easily they could've gone after Devon while he was in battle.

He wasn't concerned about the Druid. She might be powerful, but there had yet to be one who was stronger than even a Fae. The real issue was what the Druid could do to Devon.

That's what stopped him cold.

He recalled the vow he'd made to protect the mortals when they appeared on Earth. If he continued on this course, he would be breaking that oath because he'd be putting Devon in danger.

"*Con,*" he said, using their mental link.

The King of Kings answered immediately. "*I'm here.*"

"*Have Kinsey and Ryder located where we're being held?*"

"*You're about an hour outside of London beneath a large complex of buildings.*"

Anson sighed. "*That explains a lot.*"

"*Ryder is still digging through all the paperwork to see who the building belongs to. There really isna a need. I know it's Ulrik.*"

"*About that. We might no' be quite right.*"

"*What do you mean? Of course, it's Ulrik.*"

The bite in Con's words didn't bother Anson. *"Upton came in earlier to talk to Devon. He brought up the fact that a Dragon King was helping him."*

"Your point?" Con asked tersely.

"My point is that this doesna sound like something Ulrik would do. Can you no' admit that it seems odd that he would start doing that now while handing over every detail about the Dragon Kings to humans?"

"You believe that despite thousands of years of having his magic bound and being banished from Dreagan, that Ulrik is still the same King that he was?"

Anson hesitated only because he heard the doubt in Con's words. *"I do. This doesna make sense. Then there is the man I saw outside of Kyvor. Ryder spotted him on CCTV. It was Ulrik, but different."*

"Are you telling me that you think someone is impersonating Ulrik?"

"It's a possibility."

Con was silent for so long that Anson began to worry he'd severed the link. Then Con released a frustrated breath. *"Need I remind you of the Kings who have spoken to Ulrik? How about the talk, and subsequent clash, I had with him in Edinburgh no' that long ago? Then there are the mates he's attempted to kill, have killed, or turn to his side."*

"I'm no' saying Ulrik isna doing those things. I'm saying he may no' be involved in this."

"The only way we'll know that is if you can confront him."

Anson closed his eyes. *"I was easily able to crack the magic protecting Upton. Same with the magic around the building."*

"That's good. What's the problem, then? Because I can hear it in your voice."

"I just fought four Dark."

"*That should make you feel better,*" Con said with a chuckle.

Anson lifted his lids to see that Devon had resumed her position on the narrow cot. "*It did. For a moment. Then I realized they'll soon allow the Dark to go after Devon. I'll no' be able to keep up this guise of being held if that happens. I'll gladly face whatever the Dark, Upton, Ulrik, or the Druid throws my way.*"

"*But no' with Devon there,*" Con concluded.

Anson glanced at his healing hip and shifted position to alleviate the pain in his back while it mended. "*Aye. She's . . . special to me.*"

"*I can be there shortly.*"

"*I know that's a lie. Ryder didna tell me everything, but I know there is shite going on that you need to remain at Dreagan for.*"

"*There's quite a bit. I've called a meeting. You need to be here.*"

That wasn't going to happen. "*Fill me in later.*"

"*You can no' do anything alone. All you have are mortals with you.*"

He wasn't telling Anson anything he didn't already know. "*Bring Kinsey and Esther home. Have Henry remain behind because I'm going to need help getting Devon away.*"

"*Anson—*" Con began.

"*Upton has to die. So does the Druid.*"

"*Agreed. Though the Druids on Skye and at MacLeod Castle willna approve.*"

Anson fisted his hands as longing to go to Devon filled him. "*That matters no' to me, and it shouldna matter to you.*"

"*It should, and it does. We need allies.*"

"*We doona. We can end this current war in less than thirty minutes. We just have to stop hiding.*"

Con let out a slow breath. *"Whether you believe it or no', I've looked at that option from every angle. It wouldna be wise."*

"If we continue to hide, we continue to lose in this war. You continue to lose against Ulrik. We have the strongest magic, the most power. This realm is ours. The others are here only because we allow it."

"So you want to kick them out?"

"I want to stop hiding. I want to stand up against anyone who comes against us without worry if the humans see what we are. I've long come to terms with the fact that our dragons will never return. I'm talking about our lives, Con. Our future. Have we no' suffered enough?"

Con's voice was barely a whisper when he said, *"Entirely too long."*

"Get Kinsey and Esther away immediately. Ryder should have his mate with him, and Henry deserves to have his sister protected under our roof."

"I'll see it done."

The link was severed. Anson wasn't sure anything had been accomplished by his plea to Con about letting the humans know about them. But why fight the inevitable?

If they showed the world, then it would be one less thing Ulrik and the Dark could hold over them. Which was a positive in his book.

Now he just had to figure out a way to get Devon out. The best way would be for him to do it, but he needed to be the diversion that allowed her to escape.

There was a shimmer in the air to his left. Anson watched as it morphed into the outline of a person that soon became a female.

He saw the silhouette of her hair, but couldn't discern the color. The only thing he could tell about her was that she was tall and slender.

"And here you are," she said.

Anson was intrigued by the American accent tinged with Irish—and the fact that he could see through her. "Have I finally been blessed with the presence of the infamous Druid I keep hearing about?"

Her lips lifted in a smile, but there was no mirth there. "You think you know much about Druids."

"Because I do."

"You don't know me," she stated.

There was something in her voice that demanded he recognize the truth of her statement. Anson got to his feet and came to stand before her, hoping that would allow him to see her face. "And you doona know me."

"I know you, Anson. I know all the Dragon Kings."

"Because Ulrik told you?" he asked with a snort.

There was a small frown before she shrugged and said, "Sure."

He didn't miss that she hadn't agreed or disagreed. "So I gather you and Ulrik are close? He has a habit of using Druids."

"For someone you banished, you know a lot about him."

"He was my friend."

"Was. That's the key word in that sentence."

Anson narrowed his gaze on her. "What is it you want, Druid?"

"You've been testing the strength of my magic."

"As you've been challenging mine by having me put here."

She dropped her arms and glanced over her shoulder at the cage and Devon, who stared at them in confusion. "If you want her to remain alive without her mind being altered, you'll stop trying to crack through my magic."

Trying? He'd succeeded. Yet it was the Druid's arrogance that worried him. No one with that kind of attitude got it by chance. She knew how powerful she was, and she wasn't afraid to go up against a Dragon King.

"Let her go, and I'll do whatever you want," Anson said.

The Druid shook her head slowly. "It doesn't work that way. I make the rules. You follow."

"Well, let's be clear. It doesna really work that way either, does it? You're no' making any rules. You're following them."

She took a step closer to him. "Push me again, and I'll kill her with a thought."

"You're no' the first *drough* to think they had the power to take over the world."

"I think nothing, Dragon King. I know."

CHAPTER THIRTY-TWO

MacLeod Castle

Would there ever be a time when there wasn't a war? Rhi was beginning to think that there were forces at work creating such dissension.

Thank goodness the Druids of MacLeod Castle were going to help. Rhi was relieved they were going to help her with discovering how Druids and Fae had worked together. It bothered her that such an occurrence had happened without any sort of ripple to alert anyone. Or perhaps, someone did know.

Usaeil.

She thought of the queen, distaste filling her mouth. There was no use seeking out Usaeil because she wouldn't give Rhi any information. With the queen's current mood, she wouldn't likely talk to anyone.

If only Usaeil would act like the queen she should be, perhaps none of this would be happening.

"Rhi."

She blinked and looked into the turquoise eyes of Marcail. The Druid was married to the youngest MacLeod brother, Quinn. "What is it?"

"We've been calling your name," Marcail said with a frown.

Rhi looked at the other Druids, all of whom stared at her. She leaned back in the chair and quickly put a smile in place. "Sorry, chicas. I was wondering how a Light and Dark combined their magic with Druids' and no one knew."

"That's troubled me, as well," Gwynn said.

Gwynn was descended from a long line of Druids from the Isle of Eigg. Every Druid at the castle was powerful in her own right, but none—not even Aisley, who was a Phoenix—could compare to Isla.

Isla sat on Rhi's right, staring at the globe that hovered in the center of their group. Each of the Druids and Warriors had taken a closer look and inspected the wooden dragon, but none had any answers.

After battling mighty *droughs* such as Deirdre, Declan, and Jason, the occupants of the castle weren't leaving anything to chance.

The Warriors weren't far from their women. Ramsey had taken half the Druids around MacLeod land to fortify the spells that kept the castle hidden and unwanted visitors away.

Isla's ice blue gaze suddenly turned to Rhi. "What haven't you told us?"

Damn. Rhi hadn't wanted to mention anything about the Druid working with Ulrik just yet. Was it the Ancients that had let Isla know? It really didn't matter now. It was time for the truth to come out.

"I know some of you spoke with Darcy after Ulrik used her to unbind some of his magic," Rhi said. "It seems Ulrik sought out Druids for more than helping him regain his power."

Laura's brows furrowed, her moss green eyes locked on Rhi. "What exactly?"

"He looked for the most powerful of you."

Tara laughed dryly. "That's not possible. Otherwise, he'd have gotten to Deirdre before she died."

Rhi inwardly winced, thankful that Ulrik and Deirdre hadn't teamed up. "This is very recent."

"Just tell us," Aisley demanded.

Rhi looked down at her nails. The glittery plum shade—Muir Muir On The Wall—accented with an opaque crème—Be There in a Prosecco—in a swirling design was one of her favorites. "This Druid was able to get into the minds of two women with magic, controlling them. She did it to get more information about the Dragon Kings."

"Like Deirdre controlled Isla's mind?" Marcail asked.

Rhi lifted her eyes to Isla. "Did you lose time? Not remember doing things?"

Isla crossed one leg over the other. "Yes. But I don't think Deirdre had control of my mind. She was able to manipulate my body and shut down my mind."

"Which is more powerful?" Laura asked.

Rhi snorted. "Either. Both."

"The mind," Aisley stated.

All eyes turned to her, waiting for her to elaborate.

Aisley shifted in her chair. "If this Druid can get into a person's mind, who's to say she can't access their memories, as well?"

"Bloody hell," Rhi said as she got to her feet and paced. "The Druid locked Kinsey away deep in her mind. It was Tristan . . . um, Duncan, I mean, who was able to use his dragon power and call to her."

Rhi winced as she looked at Isla and Marcail, both ladies having known Tristan when he was still Duncan, twin to the Warrior, Ian—before Duncan had been killed and somehow transformed into a Dragon King. Rhi always forgot that little tidbit until it was too late.

"Thank God for Tristan," Laura said. "Otherwise, Kinsey might be lost forever."

Rhi stopped and looked out one of the windows of the castle. "It would've hit Dreagan even harder. She's Ryder's mate, but they've not done the ceremony yet."

"Leaving her mortal," Marcail said with a nod.

"She worked for Kyvor. The other one looking into things is Esther. She's an MI5 agent who was undercover. That's how Ryder found out they were watching Kinsey and taking photos. They wanted to get to him. The Kings outsmarted them, however."

Isla shook her head, her breathing quickening. "Something is wrong."

"What is it?" Laura asked from beside her.

Sweat beaded Isla's brow as she struggled to breathe. "I . . . I don't know."

"Have Kyvor and the Druid given up?" Aisley asked.

Rhi felt sick to her stomach. "No. Kinsey and Esther convinced the Kings to let them go back to London to procure the names of those involved in all of this. Once they found that out, they planned to wipe away anything to do with Dreagan."

"Get them out!" Isla shouted.

At her scream, Hayden, followed by Phelan and Fallon, came rushing into the room. Hayden fell to his knees and lifted Isla into his arms, cradling her gently against him as he said her name over and over. But Isla didn't hear him. She was talking incoherently, her head moving side to side as she squeezed her eyes closed.

"What's going on?" Fallon demanded.

The Druids stood and circled around Isla with joined hands. Their magic filled the room as they sought to figure out what was wrong. Rhi didn't attempt to join them. Her magic was different and might not be welcomed by the Ancients.

"Rhi," Phelan said as he stood in front of her. "What happened?"

As succinctly as possible, she filled the Warriors in on the Druid. Phelan's face crumpled in anger as he took a step back. Without another word, he turned on his heel and went to stand behind Aisley.

"She's there!" Isla cried out.

Rhi was about to teleport to Dreagan to see what Con knew, when Larena, the only female Warrior, strolled into the room with a mobile to her ear. She walked directly to her husband and handed Fallon the phone.

Larena waited for Fallon to walk out before she leaned close to Rhi and whispered, "It was Con." They were silent for a moment as they watched the Druids. "I've seen their magic do incredible things. I've also seen Druid magic do horrible things."

"It's the same with the Fae," Rhi replied.

"The Druids who used their magic for that wooden dragon can't possibly still be alive."

Rhi raised a brow. "Why not? All of the Druids here are."

"And this new Druid?"

"Who's to say she's new. We need to identify her."

"Quickly," Larena added.

As Rhi watched the frantic way Hayden talked to his wife, it caused a memory of her and her Dragon King to fill her.

The stars dotted the inky sky, while the moon hid behind clouds. Atop the tallest mountain on Dreagan, he gently undressed her, kissing her skin as it was exposed.

She sank her fingers into his long hair. In all her years she'd never been so happy as she was wrapped in his arms. Their passion ran high and swift, enveloping them in ecstasy.

*His breath fanned her neck, his lips skimming her ear.
Then his husky voice reached her. "I love you. With all
that I am, with all that I'll ever be. I'll never let you go,
Rhiannon. You're mine for all eternity."*

*She cupped his cheek, her heart exploding with con-
tentment. It wasn't lost on her that it was as though they
were exchanging vows. And since she knew she would
love him until the end of time, it made her smile.*

*"I love you," she replied softly. "With all that I am,
with all that I'll ever be. I'll never let you go. You're mine
for all eternity."*

*His eyes sparkled in the night before he took her
mouth in a sizzling kiss that made her toes curl.*

Rhi closed her eyes against the onslaught of love and
longing—and heartache. She relaxed her toes as the
memory of the kiss faded. She was supposed to be over
him. For good. She'd moved on with Balladyn.

"Isla," Hayden said, his voice breaking.

Rhi opened her eyes to see Isla smiling up at Hayden.

"I'm here, my love," Isla said. Then her gaze moved
past her husband and landed on Rhi. "We have to know
who this Druid is."

Dread filled Rhi. "Why?"

Hayden tenderly set Isla on her feet before she said,
"I saw a Dragon King and a woman being held."

"Held?" That wasn't possible unless it was the Dark.
And Con would've told Rhi that.

"Yes. I saw the woman standing in a cell in the middle
of a huge, locked room with the King."

Rhi tapped her foot, her mind running through everything. "Anson went with Kinsey and Esther to watch
over them."

"Why no' Ryder?" Phelan asked.

"Oh, he wanted to go, but he had to work his magic
with his computers," Rhi said.

Isla smoothed hair out of her face. "So it was Anson I saw. And the woman?"

"Devon Abrams," Fallon said as he walked into the room. "That was Con. Kinsey, Esther, and Anson convinced Devon to help them uncover information at Kyvor. Since Devon was rather high up in the company, they thought it was a good ruse."

Hayden's lips twisted. "Kyvor discovered the plot, I'm guessing."

"Yes." Fallon looked at Larena. "Anson was adamant about no other Kings coming to London for Kyvor to find, and Con says that if Devon isn't rescued soon, Anson might lose control. Though Con didn't say it, I suspect that would be verra bad."

Rhi wanted to smile. So Anson had found his mate. Good for him. They would need to celebrate, but first, all of them had to get out of London and back to Dreagan safely.

"The Druid was there," Isla said.

Rhi's thoughts halted as she gaped at Isla. "So Anson got a look at her."

"Not exactly." Isla licked her lips nervously as if her mind couldn't grasp what she'd seen. "The Druid was there, but . . . not really."

Rhi felt a pain in her temple. "You're not making any sense. And how did you know where Anson was anyway?"

"The Ancients. They showed me."

Rhi really wished she could talk to these Ancients since they seemed to know so much. "What happened?"

"The Druid wasn't in the room with Anson. Not physically. She projected herself there," Isla announced.

Aisley was the first to talk. "Is that even possible?"

"I've never heard of a Druid being able to do that," Marcail said.

Isla walked to Rhi. "This Druid could have more magic than Deirdre ever had. She didn't just project herself into the room, she spoke to Anson."

"Did you hear what she said?" Rhi asked.

"She knows all the Dragon Kings. She also told Anson that she knows he's been testing her magic. That's when she ordered him to stop and threatened to alter Devon's mind if he didn't."

"That couldna have gone over well," Hadyen murmured.

Isla shook her head. "Anson was furious and antagonized her. She didn't take the bait, however."

"Not this time," Rhi said. "I need to know every detail about this Druid."

For the first time in hours, there was the hint of a smile on Isla's face. "She's American. And I can give you specific details about her appearance."

CHAPTER THIRTY-THREE

With her heart in her throat, Devon stared at the spot where the woman had been. A woman who—for all intents and purposes—looked like a freaking ghost. A ghost!

"What was that?" she asked Anson.

"Upton's Druid."

Anson said those two simple words as if he were talking about the weather, as if a magical being hadn't just . . . well, appeared. Then disappeared.

Devon had never been claustrophobic, but the new fear was settling in nicely with a large freak-out set to occur shortly, making her feel trapped.

Her mind kept stumbling over things like magic, dragons, Fae, and Druids. It seemed her entire world—everyone's world—involved magic. How had she missed that?

How did nobody see what was right before them?

She leaned back against the bars, shaking her head. Technology. That's what did it. Everyone had their faces glued to their tablets, computers, mobile phones, or even the tele. They didn't see the people around them or even communicate properly. They certainly weren't going to notice beings not of this world—or even beings that were of this world.

It was so damn complicated. She put her hand to her forehead. She wanted to accept everything she'd learned, and she supposed she was. Just not as easily as others.

"Why?" she asked.

There was movement as Anson came to the bars of her cell. "Why what?"

"Why did she do that?" she asked, lowering her hand to look at him.

His black eyes were calm, holding none of the distress that gripped her. "She wanted to show her power."

"Well, she certainly did that."

"Did she?" he asked offhandedly.

Devon raised a brow. "From my perspective, definitely."

"Hmm."

She gawked at Anson. *Hmm?* That was all she was going to get? It was all so very difficult for her to take. Every time she thought she had a handle on things, she got another jolt of reality. And the reality wasn't kind.

In fact, it was pretty freaking horrible.

She turned her head away from him. Deep, calm breaths. That's how she would get through it. Deep. Calm. Yes, she could already feel her heartbeat beginning to return to normal.

"What's your favorite thing to do on a lazy day?"

She was so startled by Anson's question that she spun around to look at him. "I like to walk. I go a different direction each time, meandering down streets I've never been on before. Sometimes, I find a new shop to browse. Other times, I find a new place to eat."

"Do you walk in the rain?"

"Yes," she replied with a smile. His questions were taking her mind off the situation. "Few people are out then. It makes me feel as if I have the entire city to myself."

"Sounds nice."

She sat on the cot. "It is. And you? Do you even have lazy days?"

He chuckled softly. "I doona have a normal life, but when there were days I could take to myself, I would fly from one end of Dreagan to the other."

"You make it sound as if you've not done that in a while."

"I haven't. The release of that video has brought too much attention to Dreagan, so Con has forbidden any of us to fly."

She couldn't imagine the anger the Kings must feel at that. And once more, mortals were responsible. Maybe not directly, but it was because of the attention that the order had to be given. "I'm sorry."

"I'll fly again soon."

"Do you like being a dragon?"

His smile was genuine as it lifted the corners of his mouth. "More than anything. How do you feel about knowing a dragon?"

"I'm coming to like it very much."

She saw the desire in his eyes and wished she could go to him. More than anything, she wanted to feel his arms around her and kiss him. But for now, they had a show to put on for those with Upton.

They fell into silence, each lost in their own thoughts. Minutes stretched to hours. Devon kept reaching for her mobile to check messages or play a game, only to realize she didn't have it. Boredom did crazy things to a person's mind.

As she counted the bars—for the millionth time—she thought of her father and her brief interactions with him. She thought of her aunt and uncle. And she thought of her cousin.

When her family had been alive, they were her anchors, the things that kept her grounded and feeling needed. Loved. They'd been a huge part of her life, especially when it came to making decisions.

After her cousin's death, when her aunt and uncle had kicked her out, Devon had never felt more alone. Her tether had been cut, and she'd needed to navigate waters that were treacherous and deadly all on her own.

It had been terrifying—and exciting.

Every decision she made was hers. If something went wrong, she had only one person to blame. Herself. If something went right, well, the celebration was huge.

All these years, she'd truly liked being on her own. It gave her a certain freedom that was hard to give up. Not that she didn't miss her family, but she wasn't the same person as before.

Being alone had been her choice because she hadn't found anyone worth making room in her life for. That is, until Anson.

Her gaze landed on him as he slowly walked around her prison in a large circle, coming in and out of the light. He was part of a family—one that had suffered more than was imaginable.

They stayed together, their bond stronger for all the mishaps, disasters, and tragedies. What made some families resilient and others fall apart?

His gaze met hers. She wanted to reach out to him, to have his skin against hers. She needed—no, she wanted—another anchor, because the seas were getting rougher than ever before.

He gave her a nod so small that only she saw. It made

her smile. She lay back on the cot and closed her eyes. Though she had no idea what time it was, she needed to keep her wits about her, and that meant getting some rest for her exhausted brain.

Anson's nearness, his promise of protection, allowed her to slowly turn her mind off and rest. She closed her eyes and kept picturing Anson in dragon form.

She smiled, thinking how incredible he was. *A Dragon King.* It was her last thought.

The bellow that ripped through the room jarred her from sleep. She jerked upright to find an eerie blue light everywhere. Then she spotted the Dark. They had Anson pinned to the ground with one of them standing over him.

Devon stumbled backward to get away from the Fae, but her prison didn't allow her to get far. No sooner had she backed against the metal, than hands grabbed her.

She screamed and tried to get away, but their hold was like iron. Her eyes landed on Anson, who was struggling to throw off the Dark, but the one standing over him kept throwing magic ball after magic ball into Anson's chest.

"Oh, you're a pretty one," said a man from behind her with an Irish accent.

She turned her head away from him, only to have someone grab a fistful of her hair and hold her still while they ran their tongue along her cheek.

Gritting her teeth, she fought with everything she had against them. But she got nowhere.

There was an angry hiss, then another Irish voice said, "She's fighting us. She's been with the fekker."

"It doesn't matter," said another. "We can make her climax."

At those words, her heart skipped a beat. She tried not to look at Anson, tried to hold back her alarm.

Their gazes clashed. He was trying to give her strength

without words, and oddly, it worked. She was a fighter. She would survive whatever they threw her way.

Dreagan

Con tapped his desktop with his fingers. His mind was eased, knowing that Rhi was with the Warriors and Druids, but he suspected that path would lead all of them down a road more perfidious than any other.

On top of that, Asher had returned to Dreagan with Rachel—and a story that boggled Con's mind.

The fiasco with Dmitri, Faith, and the wooden dragon was only getting started. It was the beginning of a storm that might well settle over Dreagan for an extended time.

The man that Anson and Ryder said looked like Ulrik was another matter that would need to be dealt with quickly.

He ran a hand down his face. At least the Kings now knew of his affair with Usaeil. That was something off his plate, at least partly. There would come a time when he'd have to confront Usaeil. With Rhi.

On a good note, Vaughn had managed to get MI5 to leave Dreagan. And V had returned.

It was some consolation to the fact that humans held Anson. Con didn't even care that Anson had most likely found his mate in Devon, which was why the King wouldn't leave her.

Nor would Henry, Esther, or Kinsey return to Dreagan, no matter how much he and Ryder talked to them. The mortals wanted to be there to help Anson and Devon.

From the start, Con had wondered if sending the group to London was a mistake. Yet Elena had managed to make such a plan work against PureGems when they had information on Dreagan.

The difference was that Kyvor had a Druid. A powerful one at that.

All of this rolled around in his mind without any resolution, which only added to his frustration.

There was a split second of warning before Fallon appeared in his office. Con stared at the leader of the Warriors with his dark brown hair and deep green eyes. Fallon still wore the golden torc of his ancestors around his neck with the boars' heads.

"Isla saw the Druid," Fallon stated.

Con stilled, the potential of promise in those four words making him feel elated. "How? When?"

"The Druid used magic to talk to Anson by projecting herself into the room."

"I see." His delight dimmed. The Druid's show of power had been . . . extreme.

"What are we dealing with here, Con? Even Ramsey is unsettled by such a display."

Con rose to his feet. "We're going to find this Druid, and we're going to put a stop to her. One way or another."

"You say 'we' meaning the Kings, Warriors, and Druids, aye?"

"Of course," he replied.

The look of wariness in Fallon's gaze said he didn't quite believe him. "Good."

"We'll do this together, Fallon. That I vow."

The Warrior nodded. "I need to know every detail of where Devon and Anson are being held."

"Follow me," Con said as he got to his feet and walked from the office.

He took Fallon to the computer room where Ryder already had the specs up for the area where Kyvor held Anson. Fallon walked to one of the monitors and looked at the blueprints Ryder had uncovered.

"This facility is complex," Fallon said.

Ryder leaned back in his chair, a box of donuts untouched beside him. "More than you know. The security is multifaceted and more intricate than the Kyvor building in London."

"What are they doing there?" Con asked.

Ryder linked his hands behind his head. "Nothing good, I imagine. There is no list of workers, but I was able to go through all of the companies owned by Kyvor and found a link that showed me there are over three hundred people working at this facility."

Fallon whistled softly as he faced Ryder. "That's a lot of employees."

"That's no' even counting the ex-military they have patrolling the grounds."

Con frowned, hearing this for the first time. "How many?"

"Over a hundred," Ryder replied.

Fallon asked, "How did you find them?"

"By chance. A company such as Kyvor that goes to this much trouble to hide their employees and whatever is going on at the facility would want armed protection. So I went looking. It didna take me long to find some of the best from militaries all over the world vanishing from record."

Con put his hands in his pant's pockets. "I'm no' worried about the humans with their guns."

"What if they're waiting for us?" Fallon asked.

Ryder sat up, and instantly, a translucent display of 3D holograms appeared before him. Con watched as Ryder swiped, pinched, and pulled at the display to access the data.

Fallon said, "They could be working with the Dark."

"The Dark doona share their magic," Con reminded them.

Ryder halted his movements and looked up. "And until Ulrik, they'd never joined forces with a Dragon King."

Con clenched his teeth. "Let's focus on getting Devon out of there before Anson loses his control."

"That's probably exactly what they want," Fallon said.

Ryder blew out a breath. "Another video capturing a man shifting into a dragon. We doona need that."

"At least it wouldna be on Dreagan," Fallon pointed out.

Con turned the golden dragon head cufflink on his left wrist. Whether the video was shot on Dreagan or not wouldn't matter. It would be another item they had to deal with.

And if Devon were Anson's mate, then nothing would stop him from saving her. Nothing.

And that meant Anson would do whatever it took— even if it meant shifting in front of the entire world.

"Then I need to get in there," Fallon said into the silence.

Con gave him a nod. "I'm going with you."

"Ah," Ryder hedged. "I'm no' sure that's a good idea."

"It's no' up for debate," Con stated. "I'm going."

Fallon's nod of agreement was all he needed.

CHAPTER THIRTY-FOUR

Anson had expected some kind of assault. In fact, he'd been waiting for it. And he wasn't surprised that it had come from the Dark. What he hadn't predicted was the Fae going after Devon so quickly.

Up until then, the Dark's focus had been trained upon him. What had changed so suddenly?

And then he knew. The Druid.

He was going to kill her with his bare hands. Rip her limb from limb. Then scorch her with dragon fire.

Twice.

He didn't care that she was human. It wouldn't matter how much she begged—because she would, they all did— he was going to take great joy in making her hurt.

Because she was causing Devon pain.

"Get off me you useless, bumbling fuckwit," Devon ground out.

Anson tried to tell her to stop talking, to stop fighting them. The more she fought, the more enjoyment they got out of bringing her to heel.

But when he opened his mouth, the Dark above him— a fucktard of epic proportions with long, black and silver hair and a penchant for silk shirts—threw two large bubbles of magic into his chest.

Anson ground his teeth together as the magic went through his lungs. Even though his immortality and magic began the healing process immediately, there were seemingly endless seconds where his lungs stopped working.

The Dark grinned maliciously. "Does that hurt, dragon?"

Anson tried to jerk one of his arms off the ground, but the Fae holding his limbs was using magic to keep him still and pinned. Which wouldn't normally be an issue, but that was before his entire abdomen had been obliterated by Dark magic.

The Fae above him pressed one of his knees down on Anson's chest and glanced at Devon. "She's quite pretty. Not something I normally say about a mortal. I can't wait to give her a try."

"I'm going to kill you," Anson stated.

The Dark merely grinned, his red eyes filled with evil. "One of your kind told me that before. As you can see, I'm still here. He isn't."

No! Anson didn't want to think about what the Fae meant, but his mind had already made the connection.

"Yes," the Dark said with a laugh. "We took two Dragon Kings. I thought I'd have at least a millennium to play with them, but you dragons aren't as strong as you like to think. They went coo-coo for Cocoa Puffs much quicker than I anticipated. I wonder if you will?"

Anson bared his teeth and managed to get one arm free. He wrapped his fingers around the Dark's neck and squeezed. For that small amount of time, the fucker's smile disappeared. But all too soon, the two Fae had Anson's arm pinned once more.

The Dark above him rubbed his neck, a look of utter contempt on his face. "I wonder which of the Kings will kill you? Will it be Con? Or Kellan? They were the two who stepped up during the Fae Wars."

Anson thought he'd known what true hate felt like, but he'd only gotten a brief taste of it with the humans. It was nothing compared to the rush of loathing, of hostility and rancor that engulfed him now.

The Dark put more weight on the knee on Anson's chest, pressing right into the large wound. Then the Fae leaned close. "She's going to watch you. I'm going to keep her alive for however long it takes. She's going to see every second of you going insane.

"And you're going to watch me bring her pleasure again and again. I've waited thousands of years for just such an opportunity again. I'm dying to get started."

Anson headbutted the Fae. He grinned when the Dark grabbed his forehead and fell sideways. "I'm going to kill you," he promised.

The Fae responded with several more blasts of magic into Anson's chest as he yelled his fury.

Through all of it, while desperately trying to stay conscious, Anson heard Devon's voice shouting his name. He tried to turn his head her way, to look at her. It cost him much to execute that small movement, only to find something blocking his view.

"Hear her scream, dragon," the Dark whispered in his ear. "She'll be moaning for me soon."

The only thing that could kill a Dragon King was another Dragon King. The Dark had tried many times in numerous ways to slay them, but had never succeeded. The pain of the Dark's magic was excruciating as it wound its way agonizingly through Anson's body. But he wouldn't die from it. That was both a blessing and a curse.

A blessing because he would recover to save Devon.

A curse because the Fae knew just what Dark magic

did to a King, and they could keep him in a weakened state for however long they wished.

"*Con*," Anson called through their mental link.

He waited for an answer, but minutes ticked by slowly. Anson called for each of the Dragon Kings. No one answered. His eyes slid shut with frustration because he knew the Druid was somehow responsible.

"Leave me alone."

Devon's voice reached him through his haze of pain. Her words were laced with anger, revulsion, and a wobble of fear. Anson opened his eyes to see the Dark who had been talking to him standing before her.

Two more Fae held her from the outside of the cell, making sure she couldn't move. The Dark touched her face, and she jerked her head away.

Her blue eyes met his. Anson had to help her. She was waiting for him, silently begging him to do something. Right then, at that very instant, he recognized what he'd known from the moment he first kissed Devon—she was his mate.

And she was counting on him. He wasn't about to let her down. Not now. Not ever.

He released the hold he had on his anger. Then he gathered his magic and pushed his power into the bodies of the Dark holding him. Maybe it was because he was so livid. Perhaps it was because the Dark were preoccupied and not expecting anything. But it was almost too easy to gain control of them.

Once there, he made all four attack each other. Without so much as a sound, they did just that.

In the next heartbeat, Anson shifted. There was a moment of pain from the Dark magic, but it passed. He let out a roar that shook the building and had the remaining three Dark turning his way. The two holding Devon loosened their holds enough that she was able to break free.

She dashed around the Fae standing before her and out the cell door. As she made her way to the exit, Anson let loose dragon fire.

The lead Fae teleported before he got burned, but the other two weren't so lucky. Their screams died quickly. Too quickly to soothe Anson's wrath.

At the door, Devon stopped and turned to him. She began slowly walking back to him before running his way. He held out his claw for her to climb on so he could fly them out.

She was just two steps away, a smile on her face, when the Dark Fae appeared behind her. Anson had no way to warn her. He quickly grabbed her, moving her as far from the Fae as he could. Because there was no way the Dark was getting ahold of her.

It wasn't until he faced the arse again and saw the Dark's cold smile that Anson realized he'd mistaken who the Dark wanted. The Fae had gone after several women the Kings had shown interest in, so Anson had naturally assumed it would be the same this time.

It wasn't.

He released a blast of dragon fire the same time the Dark sent the spell that shifted Anson back to human form. Anson jumped to his feet and charged the Fae but didn't get far before he was hit with a peculiar magic that knocked him unconscious.

Devon was still standing, staring wide-eyed at the last place she'd seen Anson when the door burst open and Upton walked in. By the smile on his face, he wasn't at all surprised by anything that had just occurred.

How she wished she had magic, because she'd dearly love to level some at the smug tosspot. She wanted to see him on his knees, begging for his life. More than anything, she wanted that smile gone from his narrow face.

She stormed toward him, her hands clenched into fists. "Where is he? Tell me right now or I swear I'll—"

"What?" Upton interrupted her. "Continue to hurl words at me? You can't do anything else."

Devon blinked when two men appeared behind Upton. Both were tall and gorgeous, but one wore a pair of jeans and a beige tee, while the other had on black slacks and a white dress shirt with dragon head cufflinks.

Her gaze lingered on the second man with his blonde hair and pitch-black eyes. He was glaring at Upton with such contempt that she wondered how Stanley was still on his feet.

"I can do something to you," said the man in the jeans.

It was then that she noticed the gold torc around his neck. He spoke with a Scottish brogue that immediately made her heart hurt with longing for Anson.

Upton whirled around to face the men. The dark-haired one vanished, leaving Stanley with the golden-haired god that looked ready to level every brick of the structure.

Stanley must have recognized the man, because he stumbled back a few steps, his eyes wide with panic. "Devon," he called, glancing her way. "Help me."

"Help you?" she repeated and crossed her arms over her chest. "Why should I? I can't do anything, remember?"

"I-I can tell you where Anson is," Upton stuttered.

The golden god peeled back his lips in a snarl. "I already know where he is. I doona need you for anything, mortal."

Stanley promptly fell to his knees. "I can—"

"Shut your mouth," the blond said angrily.

Devon's arms fell to her sides. Upton hadn't shown this kind of fear to Anson, which meant that whoever this man was, Stanley was terrified of him.

That could only mean the golden god was none other than Constantine, King of Dragon Kings.

She looked to Con to find his gaze on her. They'd come for Anson, but it was too late.

"You'll get to decide his fate," Con told her of Upton.

Stanley looked at her, then turned on his knees to cower before her. "Please, Devon. I want to live."

"Didn't you think others felt the same?" she demanded.

"What I did, I did for the world."

She recoiled from his words. "That's a lie. You did it because you stupidly thought you had some power over the Dragon Kings. You were wrong. And you're going to live to regret it."

"I have the perfect place for him," Con said with a smile that didn't hold any mirth.

Upton began to cry, snot falling from his nose. Devon couldn't even stand to look at him. But she wasn't sure what to do. Did she leave? Did she stay?

She lifted her chin and walked to stand before Con. "I want to find Anson. I need to find him."

"I ken, lass," he said softly. "You'll come with me."

Tears of relief filled her eyes, but she hastily blinked them away. She'd kept her composure through everything else. She wouldn't break now.

Con held out his arm to her. She hooked her arm through his, but they didn't leave. They remained for several more minutes as Upton continued to cry.

"What are we waiting for?" she finally asked Con.

He blew out a breath. "Fallon is taking care of a . . . few things."

"You mean the others here."

"Aye.

"And Fallon is?"

Con's smile was kind. "A Warrior. Fallon MacLeod leads the others with primeval gods inside them."

This time, when she learned of a magical being, she didn't even blink. Primeval gods, huh? "I see."

"The gods allow the Warriors to have exceptional strength and powers. They shift by turning the color their god favors along with gaining fangs and claws."

A woman with iridescent skin and eyes along with fangs and long claws walked into the room. She looked from Devon to Con. Devon thought she kept her shock to a minimum when the colored skin, claws, and fangs disappeared to reveal a woman of exceptional beauty with long, golden blond hair and smoky blue eyes.

"This is Larena," Con explained. "She's the only female Warrior."

Larena smiled and stepped aside so that Fallon, now with black skin, eyes, and claws, could enter the room.

"The armed men are taken care of," Fallon said.

Con gave a nod. "Come, Devon. It's time you met some Druids."

She kept in step beside Con, now completely comfortable with the turn her life had taken. Dragon Kings, Fae, Druids, and Warriors. What more could a girl want?

CHAPTER THIRTY-FIVE

Dark Palace
Ireland

Thousands of years of preparation had finally gotten him exactly what he wanted. Amdir walked around the unconscious Dragon King who lay naked on his side. Thick manacles were locked around Anson's wrists, the chains bolted to the wall of stone.

He'd waited centuries to have another King to torture. In that time, he'd dreamed of all the ways he'd break another of the legendary dragons.

A smile lifted his lips as he heard footsteps approaching. Few ever ventured to his lab, but it wouldn't have taken long for word to reach Taraeth.

Amdir turned to face his king. Taraeth brushed past as he went to stand over Anson. But it was the Dark behind his king that rankled Amdir.

Balladyn.

Once a renowned warrior for the Light, Balladyn had somehow acquired the coveted position of the king's right hand. And Amdir loathed him for it.

"You deviated from the plan," Balladyn stated.

Amdir glared at him. "I saw an opportunity and took it. We're Dark. We do as we want."

"That's true enough," Taraeth said before an all-out argument could ensue between the two. "However, that wasn't the plan Mikkel and I agreed on."

Amdir turned and stared at Taraeth in shock. "Mikkel is no one. He's not even a Dragon King."

"He plans on being the next King of Kings."

Amdir fought not to roll his eyes. "With help. From a Druid. He's not the rightful King."

Balladyn issued a loud snort. "Now you're an expert on the Dragon Kings?"

"No more so than you," Amdir retorted. He then turned to Taraeth. "We have a chance of discovering what the weapon is. We came so close during the Fae Wars. I can get you the information this time."

Balladyn crossed his arms over his chest with a look of aggravation. "We had Kellan, the Keeper of History, and couldn't get him to tell us what it was. You'll not get it from Anson."

"I stake my life on the fact that I can," Amdir stated, making sure to lace his words with conviction.

Taraeth kicked Anson's arm. "I'm going to hold you to that, Amdir." He slid his gaze to him. "I'll handle Mikkel. You get to work on the dragon."

Amdir didn't hold back his smile as Taraeth walked out. Balladyn remained, their gazes locked in a battle of wills. Everyone knew how dangerous Balladyn was, but Amdir didn't fear him.

Balladyn was self-righteous and had grown complacent. He wielded power like Taraeth, and it was time Balladyn lost his station—the position that had rightly been Amdir's.

"You're going to fail," Balladyn stated.

"We'll see." No one needed to know that he was using more than Fae magic.

It didn't matter how he got the results, as long as he

got them. Soon enough, the weapon the Kings had hidden for untold eons would be used against them. Once the Dragon Kings were no more, Earth would be the new home of the Fae.

And it would all be because of him.

After that, his sights were set on an even bigger goal—the throne.

One step at a time. Amdir would break Anson and watch as Con had to behead another Dragon King. Then Amdir would find the weapon and use it on the Kings. As for Balladyn, he would die shortly after Anson.

Balladyn's red eyes narrowed as he dropped his arms and took a menacing step closer. "When this plan of yours takes a nosedive, and it will, I'm going to be the one to take your life."

"We'll see about that."

"You hide down here in your laboratory and miss what's going on out in our world. You don't know the alliances our king has made or his plans."

Amdir waved away such words. "I don't care about any of that."

"You should. Your actions today have disrupted things."

"Good!" Amdir shouted. "I see Mikkel strutting around here as if he owns us. He needs to remember who we are."

Balladyn gave a bark of laughter. "Mikkel needs us. As long as he does, we get information."

"Not the kind we need." Amdir pointed to Anson. "What we need comes from a Dragon King."

"You're thick," Balladyn said and jabbed his finger against his temple. "Did you miss the part where we had Kellan? There are only two Kings who have the location of the weapon—Kellan and Constantine."

Amdir was smiling the entire time Balladyn spoke.

The Dark made a face and scowled. "What the fuck are you grinning about?"

"I didn't sit down here in my lab all these decades for nothing. I've been planning this for a long time. It didn't matter what Dragon King I captured. Any of them would do," he said, hardly able to hide his glee.

A muscle jumped in Balladyn's jaw. "Why?"

"Con knows what I can do to his Kings. He knows the longer one of them is tortured, the quicker they'll lose their minds."

"It took centuries last time to make them go mad."

"I won't have to do a thing," Amdir said, gloating.

Balladyn looked at Anson's unconscious form. "Because you think Con won't allow another of his Kings to go insane."

"Precisely. He'll give me whatever I want in exchange for Anson."

"So you're going to hand Anson over to Con?"

Amdir laughed. "Never. The Kings are so much fun to play with."

"You're deranged if you think that will actually work."

He shrugged, uncaring if Balladyn agreed with the plan or not.

"Mikkel is going to want Anson."

Amdir turned his back to Balladyn and walked to his desk. "Someone should just kill him already. He had a few seconds of being a Dragon King. Now, he's nothing."

Anson came awake with a jolt, but he kept perfectly still. The floor he was lying on was cold and damp. He could hear water dripping somewhere behind him.

And there were two Dark in the room with him. One had just spoken. What had been said?

"He had a few seconds of being a Dragon King. Now, he's nothing."

Who the hell were they talking about? The youngest King was Tristan, but he was still a Dragon King. So who could this Dark be referring to?

"You push Taraeth into a corner, and our king will feed you to Mikkel."

Anson knew that voice. He'd heard it before. Months ago. Faces of Dark Fae scrolled through his head as he replayed the voice again and again until it came to him: Balladyn.

Somehow, Anson wasn't surprised to find him involved. But who was the other prick?

"We'll see about that," said the other Dark, the same one Anson had fought in the warehouse.

He didn't need to open his eyes to know he'd been taken to the Dark Palace, but Anson did enjoy hearing two such prominent Fae bickering.

It was evident in their words laced with such hatred and animosity, that the two would gladly kill each other if they could.

All of which was good to know, but there was something else Anson wanted above everything—Devon. Did the Dark have her? Was she safe? Hurt? No matter how he strained, he couldn't hear her.

He hoped they'd only taken him, but the odds weren't in his favor. Why would a Dark leave behind something that could force him to comply with whatever they wanted?

"Mikkel will be here soon," Balladyn said. "I suggest you be ready for a summons from Taraeth."

Mikkel? Who was that? Anson filed that name away for later as the conversation continued.

"I'm always ready."

Balladyn made a sound in the back of his throat. "Right."

"And Ulrik?" the Dark asked.

"What of him?"

"Will he be dropping by, as well?"

There was a moment of silence before Balladyn replied, "I'm not his keeper. Be warned, Amdir. You're walking on thin ice."

Amdir. At least now Anson knew the bastard's name. He'd also learned that it wasn't odd for Ulrik to be at the palace. Amdir implying that Ulrik and Balladyn were working together was interesting.

It seemed the only one who should have a connection to Ulrik was Taraeth. Not that it really mattered. It was bad enough that a Dragon King—even a banished one—had stooped so low as to align with the Dark.

"Get out," Amdir stated.

Balladyn tsked. "Did I make you angry?" he asked, a smile in his voice.

Could Anson get lucky enough for the two to begin fighting?

"Tell me, Balladyn, have you found that pretty Light Fae you kidnapped? What was her name? Oh, yes. Rhi. Taraeth is still upset about you losing such a gem. And you've not found her in all this time."

The sound of boot heels grew closer, and a moment later, so did Balladyn's voice. "Trying to move the focus away from your fekking disaster proves how unworthy you are. Take responsibility."

"Have you?"

"I have. Yours, however, is coming shortly."

There was the briefest moment of hesitation. "Taraeth is pleased with my acquisition."

Anson heard the question within the statement. Amdir was suddenly nervous. Why? Hadn't they always intended to capture him? If not . . . then what had been the plan?

Something was definitely off. He might've found

out more had he not been knocked out. He frowned as he recalled the feeling of that magic. It had been Dark, but there was something else in it, as well.

It took a moment before he figured it out. It was Druid magic. The combination had held a powerful punch that Anson hadn't expected—and never wanted to feel again.

"We'll see," Balladyn answered Amdir.

The sound of retreating steps alerted Anson that he was now alone with Amdir. At least now he knew what to expect when he fought the Dark again, but it was only a matter of time before he and Amdir clashed once more.

The wounds from the Dark magic were now healed. But that was the least of his worries. The sensation of metal against his wrists was a bad sign.

A small test of the manacles revealed that they were practically dripping with Dark magic. It wouldn't be easy to break through them, but Anson would do it.

Then he would find Devon.

His thoughts halted when Amdir drew near and squatted beside him. The Dark shoved at his shoulder, but Anson didn't so much as twitch.

"Can't take your magic, can you?" Amdir asked with a laugh. "The mighty Dragon Kings aren't so impressive, after all. And here I thought you might give me a challenge. I have to admit, I'm disappointed."

It was all Anson could do not to groan. Amdir was one of those who liked to talk to himself. That, combined with his huge ego, was enough to make anyone cringe.

"You're going to be my greatest achievement. Do you know that?" Amdir asked. "As soon as Con finds out I have you, he'll turn over the weapon in exchange for you."

If that's what Amdir thought, then clearly he didn't know Con. Anson kept that to himself, however. Let the Dark discover that on his own.

Though only Con and Kellan knew what the weapon was—or where it was hidden—every Dragon King knew that for it to be handed over to the Dark meant the destruction of the Kings.

And Con would never let that happen.

Neither would Anson.

CHAPTER THIRTY-SIX

Worried. That's what Devon was. She tried to hide it, but she couldn't.

"Where is he? Where's Anson?" she asked Con for the umpteenth time.

Finally, he stopped just as they entered a room where several women and one man stood together. Con turned and said, "Knowing willna help."

"Because I can't get to him, I know," she replied with a nod. "But I need to have the location."

Con drew in a breath and slowly released it. He'd been kind to her in the little time she'd been with him, but he was aloof, detached.

Not in a cold, unfriendly way. Instead, she attributed it to being the man—dragon—who shouldered everything. Mentally, he was in the thick of things, but emotionally, he was distant.

She suspected if she were in his position, she'd be the same. In order to make proper decisions, one had to remove emotion, and that was a near impossible task. Though it seemed Con had mastered it.

"The Dark took him. I suspect to their palace in Ireland."

She'd known that was a possibility, but to hear it fall form Con's lips was like being run over by a speeding train. "What will they do to him?"

"Nothing he can no' handle."

"I saw his wounds," she said, her mind flashing back to the horrible sight. "It looked agonizing."

Con turned her to face him. He bent his head to look at her. "I'll no' lie to you. What Dark magic does is painful. Terribly so. But it willna kill us."

"It weakened him."

"That it'll do. Killing him is another matter entirely."

She glanced at the group, who were now looking her way. "I know only a Dragon King can kill him, but suffering through such agony can't be good for anyone's mind. Not even beings such as yourselves."

"It isna." Con's face hardened. Then he turned to the group. "Devon, these are the Druids from MacLeod Castle."

In moments, she was surrounded. The one male took her hand and shook it with a smile. "I'm Ramsey. I doona know how much you know about us, but I'm part Druid, part Warrior."

"A badass," said a woman with wavy, light brown hair and a soft Scottish accent. She then looped an arm around Ramsey. "I'm Tara."

"My wife," Ramsey said with such devotion shining in his gaze that when he looked at Tara, Devon felt as if she were intruding.

Another woman with silvery blond hair smiled and held out her hand. "Don't mind them. I'm Danielle, though everyone calls me Dani. It's lovely to meet you. I just hate that it has to be under such circumstances."

"Yes," Devon said. She was never going to remember everyone's name. Each one introduced themselves to her, and she said their names after, logging their accents, but her mind was too focused on everything that had happened and finding Anson.

The last to introduce herself was a petite woman with ice blue eyes and black hair. "Hello, Devon. I'm Isla. We're here to help."

"Um . . . I should probably tell you that I just learned about Dragon Kings, Fae, and Druids a short time ago. And the Warriors about five minutes ago," she told them.

It was the redhead—Sonya—who replied in a Scottish accent, "Take your time. We'll answer any questions you have. Please know that we've knocked out all the magic from the other Druid."

The other Druid. Devon looked around her, searching for Con. She feared he would leave to get Anson without her, and to be honest, she wasn't so sure she wanted to venture into a place full of Dark Fae. They scared the shit out of her.

"Con is talking to Fallon and the other Warriors," Ramsey said.

Devon smiled her thanks. "Why are we still here? Why haven't we left?"

A Scotswoman with curly, chestnut hair and mahogany eyes said to the others, "Let's give Devon some room. There are a few other areas Lucan mentioned he wanted us to visit in the facility."

Devon could only watch as the Druids filed out—all except for Isla and Ramsey. A Druid and a Warrior. She felt inferior next to all these magical beings. It was like reverting to an infant and needing others to care for her.

That irritated Devon. She liked taking care of herself, but the fact was that she couldn't in this instance. Not in this world of magic. She was powerless. Literally.

"It's a lot to take in," Isla said.

Devon looked at them and shrugged. "It is, but I'd rather find Anson."

"Con and the other Kings will see that is done," Ramsey replied.

She looked at the half-Druid, half-Warrior. "You're not helping them?"

Isla hurriedly said, "The Dark aren't focused on us. We aid the Kings when we can, but most of us have children at the castle, and we'd rather not bring a war there."

"Of course," Devon said.

Ramsey walked her to a set of chairs and motioned for her to take one. He sat on one side of her, and Isla the other. Then Ramsey said, "You're looking to find your place, but you doona need to do that, lass. You already have one. This is your world."

"How do I have a place?" she asked, the anger coming out. "I don't have magic. I'm not immortal. I can't shift."

Isla laid a hand on her arm. "You caught the eye of a Dragon King. It doesn't matter if you have magic or not. This is your world now."

"I feel powerless," she admitted.

Ramsey touched his head. "You have power here. And here," he said, pointing to his chest where his heart was. "Use it for Anson."

He was right. She wasn't completely useless. It was time she stopped feeling sorry for herself and picked her arse up off the floor. She straightened her shoulders. "This Druid we sort of saw. Who is she?"

"We don't know," Isla said. "Someone with that kind of power we should know about, but we don't."

Ramsey leaned back in the chair and crossed his arms over his chest. "It's something I'd like remedied verra soon. What can you tell us about her?"

"She's terrifying. The way she spoke to Anson as if she thought she could end him with just a flick of her finger. . . ." Devon wrapped her arms around herself to hold back the shiver.

When she was alone, everything that had happened would truly hit her. Until then, she would hold it all together and concentrate on doing what she could to help.

"I know," Isla said.

Devon looked at her, unsure if she heard Isla correctly. "I'm sorry?"

Isla clasped her hands together while perched on the edge of the seat. "Druids have a connection to the Ancients. These Ancients are Druids who have passed into death, but their magic keeps their souls together. They see everything. And while they're not exactly forthcoming with information, they can alert us to things."

"You're saying the Ancients told you about this Druid?" Devon glanced at Ramsey to find him nodding along with Isla.

"In the wee hours of the morning, I was woken by them," Isla said. "They told me danger was coming. They warned me about this Druid, but told me nothing else."

Devon ran her hand through her hair. "This would be easier if they'd just tell you what you need to know."

"Ah, but the Ancients doona work that way," Ramsey said.

Devon was beginning to see that. At least, they'd given a warning.

Isla suddenly rose and began to pace slowly. "For some reason, they have connected me to this Druid. When she appeared here before you and Anson, I saw her. I heard her."

"So you saw that she was shimmery? Like a ghost?"

"Yes, but I saw her clearly through her projection. The fact that she was able to project herself at all is very troubling. No other Druid we know of has been able to do that."

"Surely, there have been other Druids that could do that."

It was Ramsey who replied, "The main faction of Druids resides on the Isle of Skye now. They've always had a large force. They keep records of the powers all Druids have."

Devon wasn't buying this. "So a Druid doesn't send in their powers to be recorded. There are a lot of people in this world."

"The Ancients tell the Skye Druids," Isla said.

Well. That certainly put a damper on things. "I think the Ancients forgot to notify the Skye Druids. There have to be others who can project as this woman did."

Isla stopped her pacing and faced Isla. "No. Not a one. At least, not that we've heard of. To make matters worse, we have no knowledge of what all this Druid can do."

"Have the Ancients not told the Skye Druids?" Devon asked.

Ramsey blew out a long breath. "The Skye Druids know nothing of this woman."

They were telling her absolutely zilch that could make the situation better. In fact, Devon felt even worse. "If you saw the Druid, then you don't need me."

"Not true," Isla said. "I saw it in my mind. You experienced it. There's a difference."

Devon swallowed as she recalled how Anson had approached the Druid without a thread of caution. "What do you want to know? My feelings? How I sat trembling on the cot while Anson strolled up to her without a care? You want me to say how I was too terrified to move but Anson all but threatened her? You want me to tell you how he reassured me after she left, even though I could see he was worried?

"How about when the Dark appeared after that and had him pinned, throwing those orbs of magic into his chest one after the other so he couldn't move? Or when two more held me against the bars of my cage while the one who hurt Anson promised to give me pleasure whether I wanted it or not?"

Now that she was on a roll, she couldn't stop. "What about when I tried to hold back my scream when that bastard touched me? And how Anson reacted by shifting into a dragon. Should I tell you that I shouted with joy when he killed those Dark? Or how about when I was walking toward Anson so we could fly off, and the leader of the group appeared. Without hesitating, Anson moved to protect me."

Her voice cracked, but she was determined to go on. "The Dark said something that made Anson shift back into human form. Then he took Anson. Took him! And I couldn't do a goddamn thing."

Something fell onto the back of her hand. She looked down and saw the drop of water right before the tears clouded her vision. She didn't even try to stop them. Devon covered her face with her hands and allowed herself to cry for her fear, her anxiety, and her anger.

A large hand rested on her shoulder. It wasn't a lot in the way of comfort, but at that moment, she wasn't sure she could handle anything more.

When she was able, she looked up to find it was Con who stood beside her. He gave her a nod. Somehow, she knew that his reaction was more than he would typically display.

"We're going to find Anson," Con vowed. "Right now, we're going to get you to Dreagan. Anson was adamant that you be taken to safety."

"Devon!" someone shouted from a distance.

There was the sound of running footsteps, and then

Kinsey, Esther, and Henry rounded the corner. And Devon's tears started all over again when Kinsey rushed to her, wrapping her arms around her. A moment later, Esther joined in.

No longer was Con's hand on her shoulder, but Devon knew he was near. Dreagan. She was going to see Anson's home. Only Anson wouldn't be showing it to her.

When she had collected herself, she rose to her feet and looked around the room at the humans, Druids, Warriors, and the King of Dragon Kings. She lifted her chin. "I'll go wherever you need me to go, talk to whoever you need me to talk to, and do whatever you need me to do. For Anson."

"We go to Dreagan," Con declared.

Devon barely had time to hear the words before Fallon took her arm. In the next blink, she was in the middle of a manor so grand it took her breath away.

And one look at the dragon décor everywhere confirmed that she was at Dreagan.

CHAPTER THIRTY-SEVEN

Eons of time learning to control his rage was what got Anson through Amdir's mind-numbing prattle about how he hated Balladyn and was going to claim what was his.

Fortunately, it wasn't long before Amdir finally left the room. Still, Anson waited until there was no doubt that he was alone. Only then did he sit up and look around.

The space wasn't what one would expect of a lab or a torture chamber. There were no instruments or racks. The only thing in the room was a long, wooden table.

Upon it were stacks of books. One was open. Anson climbed to his feet and got as close to the table as the chains allowed. He was able to get near enough to peer at the book.

Writing. The books were Amdir's journals. And at the top of this new page was Anson's name. He held back his snort of anger. So, Amdir wanted to jot notes during the torture. That wasn't going to happen.

The Dark weren't enemies of the Kings simply because the Fae slaughtered humans without regard, revered malevolence, or embraced everything wicked.

The Dragon Kings eagerly and enthusiastically killed

any Dark as retribution for the capture and subsequent torture of two Kings. The centuries of unrelenting torment had broken those Kings' minds. That's when the Dark had released one out into the world.

That day would live forever in every King's memory. The horror of seeing one of their brethren so . . . destroyed. They were the most powerful beings in the realm, yet the Dark had managed to get the upper hand—briefly.

Every King had stared in helpless dismay at their fellow King. They'd all wanted it to be an illusion, some deception that their brother would throw off and turn the tables on the Dark. But it wasn't to be.

That had left Con no choice but to put the King out of his misery. Yet, it hadn't been an easy task. It was a major event when a Dragon King killed another, which was why Con, as King of Kings, had shifted and stepped up to do what none of them could.

There had been a moment of quiet as Con stood over their dead comrade. Con then lifted his head, his dragon eyes locking on to the Dark. And in one of those rare instances, Con released his wrath upon the Fae.

For days after, Con had closed himself in his rooms, refusing to speak to any of them. None of them had expected to see it affect Con so. But each of them recalled the day when the Dark had freed the second Dragon King. Before any of the others could step up, Kellan took the second King's life.

Both Kings' deaths had been unnecessary. Yet it showed the Dragon Kings that they weren't untouchable and that sometimes being immortal was a hindrance.

Anson refused to be the third King driven mad—and killed by his own. He wouldn't make any of his brethren perform that horrible task. No matter what kind of torture Amdir administered, Anson wouldn't break.

He couldn't.

Not just for his brothers, or himself. But because of Devon.

He had to find her. Without a doubt, the Dark had taken her, as well. She was somewhere in the horrid Dark Palace. And Anson would find her.

Turning his back to the books, he looked at the wall where the chains were affixed. He yanked at them, expecting to feel some give. Unfortunately, there was nothing.

The chains were old. The wear upon the metal was evident by the scuffs and scratches. Then there was the dried blood. No doubt Amdir added magic to the chains with each use, building the Dark magic so that even a mortal would be able to sense it.

Anson tried to shift, and just as he'd expected, the chains prevented it. That didn't deter him from finding a way to break free, however.

"So the rumors are true," came a female voice behind him.

Anson spun around and looked at the Dark female. She wore a sleeveless, silver dress that skimmed the top of her thighs, showcasing black boots that laced up over her knees, and the bodice plunged down her chest, showing the swells of her breasts.

Never taking her red gaze from him, she slowly walked into the room and let her finger run along the table. Turning so that she looked at him over her shoulder, she bent at the waist to look at one of the books, revealing her bare ass. Her smile widened, and she straightened to face him.

"Most males would be on their knees begging to let them have me by now," she said.

"I'm no' most."

She gave a small pout. "I'm beginning to see that. What a pity. I like what I see."

He ignored her gaze that ran over his naked form. There was nothing about the female that appealed to him. Not after having Devon in his arms.

"I suspect more Fae will come to see the Dragon King that Amdir caught," she said with a smirk.

Anson held up his hands, the chains clinking. "Unlock me, and I'll give you and every Dark in this pit a show when I go after Amdir."

"I'm almost tempted to do just that." Her smile seemed genuine as she looked at him. "Almost."

"If you release me now, I'll no' kill you."

Her smile faded slowly. She flicked her long, black and silver hair over her shoulder and glanced at the door. "We all have a part to play. Yours is to be right where you are."

"And yours?" he asked, lowering his arms.

"More important than you could imagine. You might actually thank me later."

That intrigued him. "Your name, Dark?"

"Muriel."

Though the Dark Fae usually wore red or black, they were also known to wear silver. He disregarded it at first, but now he took another look at her.

On her wrist was a slim, silver cuff. He couldn't see the design upon it, but that along with the dress and her words told him what the connection was—Ulrik.

And for some reason, that infuriated him.

"Tell Ulrik if he wants to fight me, he fights me as a Dragon King. Tell him if he gets the Dark to do his dirty work, then he isna fit to be King of Kings."

Muriel walked closer to him but kept out of reach. "He had nothing to do with this."

"And why should I believe you?"

"It's not his way."

Damn her, but she was right. Anson had had that same thought earlier, but that didn't mean that Ulrik wasn't involved. "I want to talk to Ulrik."

"He doesn't know you're here. I'm trying to get ahold of him."

"Why should I believe you? This could be part of Amdir's torture."

She rolled her red eyes and put a hand on her hip. "You'll know when he's begun his torture."

Even if Anson wanted to believe her, he didn't. One look reminded him where he was. The Dark couldn't be trusted. So he would take her words with a grain of salt.

"You don't believe me," she retorted.

Anson shrugged.

She dropped her arm to her side and gave him a side look. "You'll find out everything soon enough. I'll return at that time, and maybe then you'll listen to what I have to say."

"Why does it matter so much if I believe you?" The irony didn't go unnoticed that Devon had uttered the same words to him once.

The Fae's red gaze briefly lowered to the floor as if she were thinking about something or someone. "It just does."

"You care about him," Anson said, suddenly realizing why Muriel acted so strangely. "You're in love with Ulrik."

She snapped her gaze to him and bared her teeth as she advanced on him. Quickly, she regained her composure and put her finger to her lips, telling him to hush. "You don't know what you're saying," she whispered.

"I can see it," he replied, keeping his voice low.

"Saying such things can get me killed."

"And having those feelings willna?"

Her gaze darted away. "I've been a slave to Taraeth nearly my entire life. Thousands of years, I've bent to his will, having sex with whoever he gave me to for the night. Ulrik was the first who looked at me like a person and not an object."

Anson wondered what Con would say if given such information. If Muriel could be trusted, then that meant the old Ulrik was still inside him somewhere.

"He cares about me," Muriel continued. "His soul is wounded deeply. I don't think he can love because the scars run too deep. But what he's given me is enough."

Anson looked at the Dark with new eyes. He wanted to call her a liar, but the truth was in her eyes and in her words. "You're taking a huge chance being here."

"I can handle things."

"There was a human woman taken with me. Can you find her?"

It was a long shot asking the Dark for help, but what other choice did he have? He had to know where Devon was so he could reach her when he finally broke the chains.

"I'll look into it." Muriel backed away before turning to the doorway. She walked through it without another word.

Anson moved to the wall and sat, leaning back against it. There was a chance, a small one, but still a chance, that he would get to talk to Ulrik. He didn't know what he'd say to his old friend, but he wanted to look into Ulrik's eyes.

No part of him approved of anything Ulrik had done in his quest for revenge. However, he did understand why his friend had taken such a road. Although, it didn't excuse any of the horrendous acts.

Sometimes, the need to retaliate outweighed good judgment. The anger that oftentimes consorted with vengeance eroded a person's soul, leaving nothing but hate, anger, and resentment behind.

Was Ulrik little more than a shell of who he'd once been? Or was there still a glimmer of hope? Anson had to know. For himself and all the Dragon Kings.

While he was left alone, Anson studied the room. It had high ceilings and arches around the door and the two windows. There was nothing of comfort or luxury in the lab. Besides the table, there were two stools.

It said a lot about Amdir.

With so little to look over, it didn't take Anson long to determine just what kind of Fae Amdir was. Motivated, dedicated, and determined.

He was single-minded in wanting to break another Dragon King. In his mutterings as Anson had pretended to be unconscious, Amdir mentioned the weapon Con kept hidden, but it was a ruse. All the Dark wanted was a test subject to experiment on.

Amdir was certifiable, deranged, demented. In a word—insane.

He was a mad scientist with no rules or governing body to stop him. The fact that Amdir had somehow made two prior Dragon Kings go crazy was enough to worry anyone.

And Anson was more than a tad concerned. He was determined to hold out however long it took. No matter what anyone told him, he knew Con and the others wouldn't rest until he was rescued.

The sound of approaching footsteps drew his gaze to the doorway. The door opened, and Amdir smiled at him as he strode into the lab, his red eyes twinkling with glee.

Yes, the Dark was definitely unhinged. And Anson

was about to find out just how far off the deep end the Fae had gone.

"I'm glad you're awake," Amdir said as he walked to the table. "I apologize for keeping you waiting. I had an audience with my king."

Anson followed the Dark with his eyes. "And what did Taraeth want?"

"To praise me, of course. I did capture another Dragon King."

"So you did." Then, just to play Devil's Advocate, Anson asked, "Why did none of the Dark try to take one of us during Halloween when they were out killing all the humans? There were plenty of opportunities. Could it be because capturing one of us wasna as important as it used to be?"

Amdir laid down the pen he'd picked up and turned to face Anson. "You seem to think you know a lot."

"I asked a question. If I knew the answer, I wouldna have asked."

"Hmm. I see something else entirely." Amdir began, walking toward him slowly. "I see a Dragon King who wants to gain some kind of edge by attempting to make me doubt my actions. That's not going to happen. Do you want to know why?"

"Enlighten me."

Amdir stopped before him and sneered. "Because I know the steps needed in order to win. You Kings had the advantage once, but you didn't follow through."

Unfortunately, the arse had a point. When the Kings won the Fae Wars, they should've rid the world of the Fae once and for all. But the alliance with the Light had put a crimp in that plan.

"You think you're better than everyone," Amdir continued. "But I'm not the one in chains. We're not the ones hiding. We go out in this horrible world you call home as we are. In doing that, we've gained the upper hand. We're going to win. And your capture is just one step towards accomplishing that."

"I'm really going to enjoy killing you," Anson replied.

Amdir raised a brow. "Good luck," he said right before he launched a ball of magic into Anson's chest.

CHAPTER THIRTY-EIGHT

Devon stayed in the shower far longer than usual. She hated the tears she couldn't seem to stop. But most of all, she hated that Anson was gone, and she didn't know how to help.

When she finished drying off, she put on the clean clothes that Kinsey, Esther, and Henry had gathered from her flat. She brushed out her wet hair but didn't bother to do anything else.

The room she'd been given was spacious and beautiful. The white, wrought iron bed combined with the white bedding contrasted beautifully with the blue walls that were a few shades lighter than navy.

The large rug covering the wooden floors had stripes of various shades of blue that mixed well with the lighter tones around the rooms as accents.

The colors were calming, the space soothing. Just what she needed. But what made her smile was the fact that, even in that room, there were depictions of dragons.

Hanging above the bed was a large tapestry with dragons. One of every color and size. She saw a Brown dragon and felt her heart twinge as she thought of Anson.

"Hold on," she whispered and touched the dragon. "We're coming for you."

Then she walked from the room to find Henry waiting for her. His smile was kind, but she saw the worry in his hazel eyes that he didn't hide.

"How are you holding up?" he asked.

"Don't worry about me. I'm fine."

He gave a nod, approval in his gaze. "Of course you are. The others are waiting in the library."

She walked down the stairs, her hand trailing along the wood banister with a dragon at the finial. With all the dragons about—some obvious, some not—she could spend a month investigating the house in search of all of them.

The library was huge, but then again, she expected nothing less in such a house. The books were shelved from floor to ceiling with a rolling ladder to allow someone to reach the top of the twenty-foot height.

The windows were placed in a way that gave optimum light. The glass looked different, thicker. Most likely it was specially made so as not to allow the rays of the sun to degrade the books.

There was a large fireplace with a supple, dark leather Chesterfield sofa before it. On either side were two Chesterfield armchairs.

And all around the room, there were oversized chairs, chaise lounges, and loveseats set about for anyone to curl up on and read. The dark paneling matched the wood of the bookcases, while the colorful rugs brightened the space.

The warmth of the fire helped to make the lovely library even more welcoming. Kinsey rose when she spotted them and held out her hand to Devon. When she took it, Kinsey pulled her down onto the sofa beside her.

"Would you like something to eat?" Con asked from

his position by the hearth. He had one hand on the mantel and a drink in the other.

Devon shook her head. "I think I'd like whatever you're having."

In the next heartbeat, someone held out a glass before her. She took it and looked up into azure eyes. "Thank you."

"I'm Dmitri," he said with a nod.

Devon didn't need to ask if he was a Dragon King. Though she didn't know how, she was able to tell who was a King and who was a Warrior of the men in the room. She took a sip of the whisky and let it slide down her throat.

The warmth spread to her stomach quickly. Just as rapidly, she felt her muscles begin to relax. She took another drink, then looked at Con, waiting.

"I'm verra thankful the Druids were there to aid us today," Con said to the room. "But just as before, I think this is where your association with us ends. None of us want the Dark to turn their attention to MacLeod Castle."

Isla sat in the chair to Devon's right, with one leg crossed over the other. Her long, black hair fell over her left shoulder while she wore the look of a woman intent on battle.

"Let them try," Isla stated.

Hayden nodded in agreement as he stood beside his wife. "Aye. Let them try."

"You doona know what you're getting into," said a man with gray eyes and short, dark hair.

Kinsey leaned over and whispered, "That's Banan."

"We do," Fallon stated. "We've discussed it as a family. The Kings were there for us when we needed you. Now, it's time for us to return the favor."

Con finished off his whisky and set the empty glass

on the mantel. "We didna have children to worry about. You do."

"The decision's made," said a man with very long, dark brown hair and blue-gray eyes.

Once more, Kinsey leaned over. "That's Phelan. I just met him. Apparently, he's half-Fae."

"Broc has already found Anson," Fallon announced.

Devon sat straighter as she looked to the giant of a man Fallon pointed to. Beside Broc stood a flame-haired Druid who looked ethereal.

Unable to help herself, Devon asked, "Found him how?"

Broc's dark gaze slid to her. "My power is being able to find anyone, anywhere. Anson is being held deep within the Dark Palace as Con suspected."

As much as Devon wanted to get to Anson, the real problem was the Druid causing so many complications. "And the Druid? Can you find her?"

"I need a name or face," Broc said.

Isla said, "We're working on a drawing."

"That's Kellan that just moved to stand beside Con," Kinsey whispered to her. "On the other side of him is Thorn and then Asher."

The names began to run together. Devon drank more of the whisky. There were so many people in the library that she was sure she only saw half of them.

"Until then, we go to Ireland and find Anson," Phelan declared.

A woman of exceptional beauty moved from the crowd to walk toward Con. The two stared at each other for a long moment before she turned to face the room.

Her long, black hair was pulled away from her face in an intricate braid. She wore black leather pants, a beige sheer shirt that revealed her black bra, and black stilettos with a small silver skull at the base of each heel.

Silver eyes met Devon's before the woman said, "Phelan, you can't go to Ireland."

Devon's stomach dropped to her feet at the Irish accent. "You're Fae."

"Rhi," the woman said with a smile and a small curtsy. "I'm a Light Fae and here to help. I've fought the Dark many times, and I'm always eager to do it again."

Devon remembered Anson speaking of Rhi. A cursory glance at all the Dragon Kings had Devon wondering which one was the idiot who'd let the Fae go.

"I'm sorry your first encounter with the Fae was with the Dark," Rhi said, her top lip curling in disgust. Then she gave Devon a wink. "Not everyone can be as fabulous as me."

A smile formed without Devon even thinking about it. Rhi fairly sparkled. She drew a person's gaze without even trying. It was her inner light, the one that signaled she was Fae—but also someone very special.

Rhi's smile slipped as a serious expression came over her face. She looked Devon in the eyes and said, "We'll get Anson out."

"And I'll be right there with you, sweet cheeks," Phelan said.

There was a ripple of laughter throughout the room at Phelan's words. Even Rhi's smile was back in place.

The Fae turned to him and winked. "Nice try, stud. But you know only I can say things like that."

"I need to finish my description of the Druid," Isla said suddenly and stood before walking out of the library.

All of the Druids and most of the Warriors followed her. Devon watched them curiously. Her head swiveled to Fallon as she raised a brow.

"Isla and the others are determined to find this unnamed Druid," he explained. "It's driving her the hardest since the Ancients chose her."

Devon looked at the remaining people in the library, and her gaze lingered on a King who stood toward the back, a frown on his face. He ran a hand through his auburn locks before pushing away from the bookshelf.

"I'm going to help Isla," he replied.

After he'd left, Con told her, "That's Nikolai. Every painting or tapestry you see in this manor was done by him."

Asher retrieved the decanter of whisky and began re-filling everyone's drinks. "Nikolai's gift is projected thermography. He sees something once and is able to paint it, draw it, or weave it."

"Wow," Devon said, impressed.

Now she looked at the paintings with new eyes. To be surrounded by so much magic seemed surreal, and yet there was no other place she wanted to be.

"How are we going to get into the palace?" Phelan asked.

Kellan shrugged. "What about the tunnels you used when you all came for Denae and me?"

Devon's eyes widened. So this wasn't the first time a King had been taken? Kellan's rescue gave her more hope.

"No," Rhi said. "I have another way in."

Was it Devon's imagination, or had Con's jaw tightened?

"What way?" Thorn asked.

Rhi walked to the Chesterfield and sat on Devon's other side. "Let me go in alone. I'll find Anson and bring him back."

"No," Con and Phelan replied in unison.

Rhi rolled her eyes. "The more people I take, the more likely we'll be seen."

"If Rhys were here, he'd side with me," Phelan said.

Devon was cognizant of how Henry slowly moved to

be closer to Rhi. She wasn't sure if the Fae was aware of it, but since nothing seemed to get past Rhi, Devon was sure she noticed.

"I want to help," Devon said. When they all looked at her in silence, she added, "Please."

Con was shaking his head. "She doesna have any magic."

"But she's immune to them," Rhi said.

That had Devon frowning. "Immune to who?"

"The Dark," Rhi replied with a knowing grin.

Everyone seemed to get it but Devon. She looked helplessly at Kinsey, who smiled and said, "Once a woman has been with a Dragon King, they're not drawn to the Dark."

"So that's what he meant," Devon said as she thought back to when the Dark had been holding her.

Rhi sat forward, turning toward her. "Who?"

"The Dark who hurt Anson. He had two others hold me. When I didn't want him touching me, he said that I was impervious to them, but that he could make me feel pleasure anyway."

Kellan let loose a string of curses. "They did that to Denae. No other should have to endure such an experience."

"Did the Dark do anything to you?" Rhi asked.

Devon shook her head. "Before he could, Anson shifted and attacked."

"Tell me of this Dark," Rhi urged. "Every detail."

She didn't have to try very hard to conjure up an image of the Fae. His face was burned into her memory for what he'd done to Anson—and nearly to her. His face, his clothes, his hair, his voice, and even the way he talked came back to her in a flash.

Rhi's face crinkled with revulsion. "Amdir."

At first, Devon didn't know why her gaze was drawn

to Con. He didn't utter a sound or move a muscle. The reason became clear when she looked at his face.

His eyes had gone cold and violent. Before her stood a Dragon King who was about to rain death down upon the Dark. Not with loud words or an offensive show of strength, but with cool detachment and lethal might.

Kinsey wore a frown as she said, "There's something that's been bothering me. Devon told us how Upton admitted that they'd been watching her."

"He never said why," Devon added.

Kinsey's violet gaze held hers. "There's a reason. With me, it was because I was seeing Ryder."

"But I wasn't dating a Dragon King."

"Then there's another motive," Thorn said.

Devon gave a half-laugh. "There's nothing. I'm not seeing anyone. I'm a workaholic."

It unnerved her to have everyone in the room scrutinizing her, especially Rhi. Devon wished she knew what she'd done to make Kyvor take an interest in her, but without knowing, she couldn't explain anything.

"I agree with Kinsey," Rhi said. "There's a reason Kyvor was surveilling Devon."

Kellan said, "And we'll figure that out later. Right now, our focus is Anson."

"We leave in an hour," Con stated.

Devon jumped to her feet. Words locked in her throat as Con's obsidian eyes landed on her.

For long moments, he stared at her. Then he asked, "Why?"

Devon didn't hesitate to answer. "I love him."

CHAPTER THIRTY-NINE

Dark Palace, Ireland

Mikkel leashed his anger as he stared at Taraeth from his seat on the red velvet sofa. The King of the Dark didn't belong on his ostentatious throne. No one who had been bested by a mortal and had their arm cut off did.

It boggled Mikkel's mind how another Dark hadn't yet seen the opportunity to overthrow Taraeth. His gaze shifted to the left, to the Fae who was never far from the king's side—Balladyn.

Then again, maybe someone was even now plotting to take over.

As soon as the thought entered his mind, Mikkel dismissed it. If Balladyn wanted the crown, he'd have taken it by now. The longer Taraeth was in power, the harder it was to wrestle the title from him. And Taraeth was the longest reigning monarch of the Dark.

"You have nothing to say?" Taraeth asked.

Mikkel had stopped listening the moment the king told him how one of his Dark had decided to change the plan and bring a Dragon King to the palace.

"We had a deal," Mikkel said.

Taraeth's gaze hardened. "Amdir saw an opportunity."

It was a break for the Dark and no one else. They wanted the weapon hidden by the Dragon Kings and didn't want to wait for him to deliver it. Had they learned that Ulrik had all of his magic returned? Is that why the Dark changed their arrangement?

Mikkel wasn't a Dragon King yet. And unlike Ulrik, his magic was still bound—though that was about to change later that night.

"Can't you see this serves you, as well?" Taraeth asked.

Damn how Mikkel hated the Irish accent. His abhorrence ran almost as deep as it did for the Scots' brogue. It's why he made sure to sound British when he spoke.

Mikkel wanted to show the Fae just what he thought of all of this by enveloping all of them in dragon fire. But he wouldn't even if he could. Because right now, he needed them—as much as he hated to admit it.

As soon as that changed, Mikkel would relish killing every last one of the fuckers.

"Tell me," he urged Taraeth.

The king motioned to Balladyn. Mikkel enjoyed watching how Taraeth's lieutenant grudgingly accepted his task. There was growing discord between the two. It was too bad Balladyn wasn't man enough to take the crown for himself.

Then again, perhaps it was a good thing, because Mikkel was certain the Dark would never align with him.

Balladyn bowed his head in deference to Taraeth before looking at Mikkel. "With the capture of Anson, Con will be forced to see that the Dark—and thereby, you—aren't to be taken lightly."

"The Dark have taken Kings recently," Mikkel said. "That didn't turn out in your favor."

Balladyn's red eyes blazed with fury.

"This is different," Taraeth said. "This time, we will win."

First Ulrik's betrayal, and now this. The more Mikkel thought about it, the faster his control began to unravel. For centuries, he'd worked to set up this plan.

He'd watched Ulrik, never allowing his nephew knowledge of his existence until the time called for it. His reach extended all over the world in various businesses, political organizations, and crime syndicates.

Every move had been calculated and thought out. He'd anticipated Ulrik's betrayal—just not in the way it had happened.

The Dark . . . well, that hadn't been unexpected either. But it was what the Dark did.

What irritated Mikkel was that he hadn't seen this coming. Or Ulrik's move. Both needed to understand that he was in charge. It was time he proved that.

"I want Muriel," he stated.

Taraeth's brow furrowed. "Want?"

"I have the sister. I want her, as well."

"Why?"

Mikkel held Taraeth's gaze. "Consider them recompense for the change of plans."

"They're yours," Taraeth said after a moment's hesitation.

"Good. Take me to Muriel."

Taraeth looked at Balladyn. "See it done."

Balladyn didn't say a word as he walked from the room. Mikkel followed him along the corridors, down two flights of stairs, and through a maze of hallways.

Finally, Balladyn stopped before a door and rapped on it twice. The door opened, and Muriel's face appeared. The smile she wore faded when her gaze landed on him, but that didn't bother Mikkel.

"Hello," Mikkel said and pushed past her into the room.

Muriel looked between him and Balladyn. "Hello. How's my sister."

"She's doing wonderfully." Mikkel stopped in the middle of the room and clasped his hands behind his back. "You and Ulrik have kept in contact all these months. I want to know everything he's told you."

She closed the door behind Balladyn, who remained with them. "He's not one to share in the way of words."

Mikkel wanted specifics, and he couldn't get them with Balladyn hanging around. He looked to the Dark. "You can go now."

"I'll remain," Balladyn stated.

He ground his teeth together. The Fae was putting his nose in matters that didn't concern him. Certainly, the Dark was moving himself up on the first-to-be-killed list.

Mikkel turned his gaze back to Muriel. "You have one chance to tell me what I want to know."

"I don't know anything," she protested.

It was a lie. He knew it. "Take off your dress."

She hesitated at the order but proceeded to slip the slim straps from her shoulders and let the silver gown fall down her body to puddle at her feet.

"Come to me," he said, pointing to the spot before him.

She walked with her head held high, never looking at Balladyn. When she stood in front of Mikkel, she held his gaze, waiting.

"Get on your knees," Mikkel demanded.

There was a flare of anger in her red gaze before she went down on her knees. He then grabbed a fistful of hair and yanked her head back so she looked up at him.

All the rage that he'd been holding in was now focused

on a slip of a Fae who must know Ulrik's secrets. And he was going to find out what they were.

He bent until his face was even with hers. "Tell me what I want to know, and I won't make you suffer."

"I'm a whore. It's my body men want, not my mind," she said calmly.

He tightened his grip on her hair, causing her to wince. "I will get the information from you."

Her eyes flashed with anger. "Never."

If it hadn't been for the insistence of Muriel's repeated call, Ulrik would've put off his visit to the Dark Palace. He didn't want to chance running into Mikkel just yet.

Not when he was still digesting the information from his encounter with Eilish. The Druid intrigued him. Instead of their battle commencing after their exchange of words, she'd simply turned and walked away.

They'd both retreated to their corners after sizing each other up. Another meeting would happen soon. And that one would begin the battle.

Ulrik turned the corner and saw Muriel's door ahead. He lengthened his strides. If she'd asked him to come, it was because she had learned something. Hopefully, it was information he could use against his uncle.

His steps slowed when he saw the door slightly ajar. Thousands of years as a slave to Taraeth made Muriel obsessive about her private space. Her room was the one place where she could be alone. It was the only gift Taraeth had given her. There was no way she'd leave the door open.

When he lifted his hand toward the door, Ulrik spotted the edge of the silver bracelet on his wrist that she'd gifted him. He'd promised to help her kill Taraeth so she and her sister could be free. Not once had she complained that her revenge would have to wait until he'd had his.

Ulrik splayed his hand on the wood and pushed open the door. The blood was the first thing he saw. It was everywhere—the floor, the walls, the furniture, and even the ceiling.

It didn't take him long to find her. Muriel lay naked in the middle of the room, half on her side with her arms stretched out. Her eyes were open and staring at the ceiling.

Ulrik didn't have to walk into the chamber to see the blade marks on her body. Someone had taken great pleasure in making her suffer before she finally died.

He was shocked at the rage—and grief—that swallowed him. There was no need to keep it in check. He wanted, *needed* to feel it. Muriel had trusted him. She wasn't the first to do so, but she had been the first that he'd trusted in return. And he'd failed her.

If he'd gotten here sooner, she might still be alive. If only he hadn't put off answering her. He briefly thought about retrieving her soul and returning life back to her, but that would resume her to an existence of continued slavery—and allow whoever had done this to do it again.

He felt someone watching him and looked over his shoulder to find Balladyn. The Fae made his way over and stopped beside him.

"It was Mikkel, was it no'?" Ulrik asked.

Balladyn nodded. "He was rather put off that his plans had been changed."

"How?" Ulrik asked between clenched teeth.

"Amdir has a King chained below."

His head jerked to Balladyn. "Who?"

"Anson."

"I want to talk to him."

Balladyn started to turn away. "Follow me."

"Wait," Ulrik said. He walked farther inside the room

to Muriel's form and squatted down beside her. He put a hand on her cheek and closed his eyes.

He found her soul easily enough. When she saw him, she smiled and took hold of his hands. "I'm sorry," he told her.

"*Don't be. It was Mikkel. He tried to get your secrets from me, but I told him nothing.*"

She didn't owe him anything, especially that which had cost her her life. "Thank you."

"*It's time to stop playing games with him, Ulrik. He's coming for you. Show him you're the King of Silvers.*"

"I will."

"*Farewell,*" she said and dropped his hands before walking away.

Ulrik took comfort in the anger that cooled into righteous indignation. Muriel was right on all but one account. The game was just getting interesting—and it was his move. He stood and retraced his steps to Balladyn.

They walked in silence through the palace for a while before the Dark asked, "You were able to speak to her?"

"Aye."

"I didn't stop Mikkel."

He wasn't surprised to learn that Balladyn had witnessed the murder. "If you had, he would've returned later. This was a strike against me."

"So the war between the two of you has begun?" Balladyn asked as he took Ulrik down back passages to keep away from others.

There was a part of him that wondered if the Fae was leading him to a trap. Their alliance was a shaky one at best since neither trusted the other, but he had to take a chance.

"It began the moment Mikkel showed himself to me

and told me of his intentions. I knew in that second that I had to move my plans forward, as well as kill him," Ulrik explained.

"He's your family. After sending your dragons away, he's all you have left."

"Blood doesna always make family."

Balladyn descended one last stair before walking down a hallway to the door at the end. "I'll get Amdir away," he whispered.

Ulrik hid in the shadows as Balladyn entered the room and had words with Amdir, who stormed out a second later. Balladyn followed the Dark to the top of the steps.

Ulrik made his way into the lab and came to a halt when he saw Anson slouched against the wall with his arms chained over his head and his body healing from blows of Dark magic. Their gazes met.

"Hello, old friend," Ulrik said.

CHAPTER FORTY

Anson blinked, unsure if it was really Ulrik before him. Amdir's magic hadn't just burned away his skin and muscle, it had affected his mind.

Ulrik walked closer and came down on his haunches. "Can you hear me?"

"Aye," Anson replied and blinked his eyes to try and focus them.

"Some things have changed. I have all of my magic."

Then that meant Ulrik could shift. Anson grabbed the chains and tried to sit up straighter. He didn't know why Ulrik was telling him this, but Ulrik didn't do anything without reason.

That left Anson with a knot of worry in his gut. "Have you attacked Dreagan?"

"No' yet, but when I do, it'll be Con I'm after."

Anson shook his head. "We were all a part of what was done to you."

"It was Con's decision."

"It took all of us to bind your magic."

Ulrik's face tightened. "And only one word from Con to banish me from my home."

"So you want Amdir to torture me for my part?"

Silver eyes flashed with aversion. "I had nothing to do with you being taken."

Anson had wanted to look into Ulrik's eyes. Now that he was, he could see the truth of his friend's words. "And the Druid?"

"No' of my doing."

"Devon," Anson said, swallowing. "The Dark have Devon."

Ulrik was shaking his head. "I doona believe she's here."

"They wouldna have left her behind," Anson insisted.

"The Dark wanted you."

"She's my mate."

Ulrik issued a loud sigh. "Anson, Kyvor has been watching Devon for a long time."

What? That couldn't be right. "Why?"

"Devon is . . . special."

Anson jerked at his chains, his heart pounding as his mind fought against what Ulrik was telling him. "What do you mean?"

Ulrik looked over his shoulder and hurriedly said, "You can help me find her right after I release you."

To Anson's shock, Ulrik tried to break the chains. But no matter how much magic Ulrik used, the chains wouldn't budge. It was the sound of approaching footsteps that halted them.

"Go," Anson urged.

Ulrik stood. He raised his right arm enough that his sleeve shifted. Anson saw a flash of silver before Ulrik touched it and disappeared a second before Amdir returned with Balladyn.

"I heard voices," Amdir stated.

Balladyn looked around. "There's no one else in here."

Anson didn't know what to think of Ulrik's visit or

even how he'd gotten there. It almost appeared as if Balladyn had helped him, but surely that wasn't the case.

"Never mind," Amdir said angrily. "Leave so I can get back to my work."

Anson braced himself for the next round of Dark magic as Balladyn walked away. Instead, he heard Devon. She was calling his name, the pain in her voice his undoing.

He fought against the chains, straining to get to his feet and reach her. And through it all, he heard Amdir's laughter. That only drove Anson to fight harder.

The thought of his Devon being touched by the Dark enraged him. He was supposed to protect her, to keep her away from anything that could harm her.

She was too precious, too beautiful of spirit to let anything as foul as the Dark breathe the same air as her. He thought of her blue eyes, so bright and so warm. If the Dark touched her, she would be changed.

It wouldn't alter his love for her. Nothing ever could. Devon was the only one he ever wanted to hold in his arms. She was the only woman he would ever need to satisfy his body.

Even if she didn't accept the magic or him, it wouldn't change his feelings. His heart was bound to hers with unbreakable ties—the kind that would stop time itself.

Anson barely felt the pull of his chest and arms still healing from the torture. He kept yanking on the chains, his bellow of fury growing.

There was only one way to save Devon. He had to shift.

Each time he tried, the magic of the chains prevented it. Yet he felt the Dark magic begin to break. And with that, he let the rage consume him, shouting Devon's name until there were no more words, only a roar.

Anson looked to Amdir after he'd shifted and let loose

a burst of fire that engulfed the Dark where he stood. His head swung to the door when he heard someone approaching.

The room confined him. He wanted to spread his wings and straighten. He pushed against the ceiling that kept him bent. Dust and dried mortar rained down upon him. He halted as soon as a form appeared in the doorway.

"Anson," Rhi said as she raised her hands to him. "You have to stop doing that."

No. He was going to destroy the palace brick by brick if he had to.

"Stop!" she shouted.

But he was beyond hearing.

Devon gripped the knife Rhi had given her and stood beside Con as they walked through the Fae doorway. Though she couldn't see anything. Apparently, only a Fae could see the doorways.

There was no doubt that a single step had taken her into another world. Devon could hear Rhi talking about making the doorway herself and hiding it. Whatever that meant.

If only Fae could see the doorway, and one of them hid one, how did they ever find it again? It was a conundrum, and one that Devon couldn't afford to think about at the moment.

"Doona leave my side," Con ordered.

Devon looked around at the dark gray stone. The palace was dark in lighting as well as decoration. But it was the feeling of evil that seemed to seep from the very stones themselves that made her shiver. "Not going to be a problem."

Now that she was in the Dark Palace, she was more than a little terrified. It had taken her and Rhi an hour to convince Con to allow her to come. It was Rhi's statement that Devon was crucial to finding Anson that had turned the tides.

Though Devon had no idea how she could help, she was glad to be there. Yet it was the odd way Kinsey and Rhi had kept looking at her that unnerved Devon. Kinsey was sure there was a reason Kyvor had chosen to follow her.

And Devon was positive those at Kyvor were just pricks and had singled her out because they could.

Eventually, Con had relented and allowed Devon to accompany them, but he wasn't happy about it. She'd seen firsthand what the Dark could do to Anson, and she wanted to be there to help.

"This was a mistake, bringing Devon," Con whispered.

Rhi's lips flattened. "We need her."

"How?" Con demanded.

Rhi's silver gaze met Devon's before she shrugged. "I'm not sure yet."

Well, that certainly didn't give Devon any confidence. The longer she stood in the Dark Palace, the more she agreed with Con. What could a non-magical mortal do in such a situation?

Not a damn thing.

Devon swallowed, doing her best to keep a tight rein on the anxiety that threatened to cripple her. While they walked the dark halls of the Fae, a few of the Kings were in Dublin, attempting to draw the Dark to them.

Once the Dark took the bait, the Warriors would come out of hiding and join in the battle. Meanwhile, the Druids were gathered at a rock formation on an isle that she hadn't heard the name of. Evidently, it was a source of magic that could amplify theirs.

With the mates and other Dragon Kings guarding

Dreagan, that left only her—with no magic—Rhi, and Con. Against a palace full of Dark.

This was a *very* bad idea.

Then she thought of Anson, of his midnight eyes as he gazed at her with longing. He'd held her, comforted her, and protected her as the entire nightmare had unfolded. He'd walked into a trap—just for her.

The least she could do was swallow the sickening dread and be there for him.

"Remember what I told you," Rhi said to Con before she vanished.

It was going to take Devon more time to come to terms with the idea of people being able to teleport. That was one magical power she wished she possessed. It would make things so much easier.

"I can take you back," Con said.

Devon shook her head. "I'm here for Anson. Besides, I'm immune to the draw of a Fae."

"That doesna mean they can no' hurt you."

She looked at the King of Kings. "That's why you're with me."

One side of his mouth lifted in a smile. "Cheeky."

"Shall we find Anson?"

They hadn't gone a hundred yards before Rhi was suddenly there. "I found him. I think he's gone insane."

"Tell me," Con ordered.

Rhi held out her hand, and a sword appeared. "He's shifted."

"He needs to calm down," Con said.

Rhi looked her way. "He needs Devon."

"Take me to him," she said.

Con put out a hand to stop Rhi from grabbing her. "No' until he's composed."

"She may be the only thing that can soothe him," Rhi argued.

"In his rage, he could harm her. Trust me. He'll never forgive himself if that happens."

Rhi rolled her eyes. "Fine. I'll see what I can do."

When she was gone once more, Con looked Devon's way. "I can hear him. He's below us."

"We're going to get him out, right?"

"I'll no' rest until I do," he vowed.

Anson felt something slam into him. He stopped thrashing his head as wooden beams fell to the floor around him, only to break apart. He looked at Rhi to find she was glowing and flinging magic at him while she yelled his name.

He knew it was dangerous when she glowed, but his sole purpose was to get to Devon. She needed him. And he needed her.

He growled when Balladyn came up behind Rhi and wrapped his arms around her. Anson couldn't attack the Dark without hurting Rhi, which left him unable to help his friend.

Rhi shouted something that had Anson shifting back into human form. As soon as he did, the ceiling above him caved in, crushing him beneath the weight.

He used his magic and strength to blast away the rubble before shaking off the dirt. Then he started to advance on Balladyn.

Only Rhi quit glowing. And Balladyn placed a kiss on her cheek as she rested her head back against his shoulder. The shock of it went through Anson like lightning. There was no denying that the two were lovers.

"You shouldn't have come," Balladyn told Rhi. "The entire palace will be here shortly."

Anson fisted his hands. "Let them come."

"Stop," Rhi told both of them as she moved to stand between them.

Balladyn glared at him, his nostrils flaring. "If you want to end what Kyvor is doing, then you need to find Harriett. She'll lead you to the Druid."

"Why are you helping us?" Anson asked.

"I'm not helping you." The Dark's red eyes moved to Rhi. "I'm doing this for her."

Rhi smiled before cupping Balladyn's cheek and kissing him. Anson couldn't look at them. It was wrong to see Rhi with someone else when she belonged with her King.

Anson squeezed his eyes shut when he heard Devon's scream. Her fear consumed him. He dropped to his knees as he threw back his head and bellowed, "Devon!"

He had to get to her, to help her. Vaguely, he heard someone shout his name. Was it Rhi? He wasn't sure since his mind was on Devon.

Anson opened his eyes and saw Rhi battling Dark Fae, but Balladyn wasn't anywhere in sight. Just as Anson was about to join Rhi, Ulrik's words came back to him.

"Devon is special."

He hadn't elaborated on just what that meant, but it gave Anson an idea. Normally, Anson liked to have his quarry in sight before he possessed someone. He'd never attempted it otherwise, but drastic action needed to be taken.

There was no way of knowing what the Dark were doing to Devon, or even where she was. Shutting out everything else, he closed his eyes and filled his mind with only her.

Her scent, her soft skin, her blue eyes.

"Anson!"

It crushed him each time she called out to him, and he couldn't answer. There was no mental link as he had with the Dragon Kings. Even knowing that, he couldn't help but reply, *"I'm here, Devon."*

"*Where?*"

His heart missed a beat. Had she heard him? Had she answered? "*Devon?*"

"*There are Dark everywhere!*"

"*I'm here,*" he told her. "*Open your mind. Let me in.*"

Neither of them mentioned that his power was possessing a body and not the mind. Using more and more magic, he put everything he had into Devon.

It wasn't long before he could hear the sounds of battle. It was distant, as if coming through a tunnel. The next thing he knew, there was a blinding light, and he saw dozens of Dark all around him.

When he turned his head, he found himself staring at Con.

CHAPTER FORTY-ONE

Devon felt Anson within her head. There was no other way to explain it than that his mind, his *soul* was within her.

Her movements weren't hers anymore. Suddenly, she was fighting as skillfully as she'd seen Anson move. She didn't know how he controlled her, but she was happy that he was. Even if it was a tad weird.

"Devon?" Con asked.

There was no time to tell him that it was Anson helping as another Dark came at her. She held the knife tighter before she dove and rolled, coming up behind the Fae, she plunged the blade into his spine.

She bent backward as an arm swinging a sword came at her. With Anson controlling her, she was doing some serious ass kicking. And it felt good.

It also felt . . . familiar.

Which couldn't be right. The most she'd ever exerted herself was during her marathon shopping trips. Why then did the way her hand held the knife seem as though it were exactly how things were supposed to be?

After a particularly brutal kill with her knife to the

throat of a Dark, she caught Con looking at her peculiarly. He didn't ask what was going on. Instead, he accepted it.

Because that's what one did in a world of magic—as she was quickly learning.

Having Anson govern her movements wasn't enough. She wanted to see him, hear him. Was it a fluke that she'd heard his voice in her head? Because only a Dragon King could have that link, and she knew for certain she wasn't a dragon.

"*Where are you?*" she asked him.

"*I'm with you.*"

"*Not physically. I need you.*"

"*I'm here. I'll always be here,*" he said.

Her heart hammered against her ribs. She wanted to slide her hand into his, to twirl his hair around a finger. She wanted to look into his eyes once more.

This had better not be the end for them. She hadn't realized her feelings when she had the chance to tell him. No, she'd been too wrapped up in the magic to see anything else.

She let out a grunt when Con slammed her into the ground, covering her with his body. Barely able to take in a breath, it seemed like forever before he rose up on his hands.

"To the left," he ground out.

Devon jumped up and spun, slashing the Fae deeply across the chest. She took out another before glancing Con's way to find him yanking off what was left of his shirt. His back was burnt, threads of smoke rising from the edges of the wound left by Dark magic that had obliterated his dragon tattoo.

Rhi stood, staring over the eight Fae who lay dead at her feet. She waited for more to show themselves. As the seconds passed with nothing, she turned to Anson, ready to rip him a new one for not helping. Not that she needed his assistance, but that wasn't the point.

She stilled when she saw him lying motionless upon the debris. "Anson," she called as she rushed to him.

The weight of her sword reminded her that it was still in her grasp. She used magic to make it vanish before she knelt beside the King. As far as she could see, there were no burn marks on his naked form.

So it wasn't Dark magic that had made him lose consciousness. What then? It wasn't natural that he was passed out during battle. Not when there were Dark to kill.

"Anson," she said again and lightly slapped his face. "You need to wake up! We have to get to Devon. She's in trouble."

Rhi glanced over at the ash pile that was the remains of Amdir. The Dark deserved no less for what he'd done to the Dragon Kings—and what he'd planned to do to Anson.

She stuck her tongue out at the ashes. "Karma's a bitch, and she delivered one hell of a punch to you, ass-hole."

With a sigh, she turned her attention back to Anson. The longer they remained in the palace, the more Dark would find them. Besides, she was anxious to get to Dublin and make sure none of the Fae had realized who Phelan was.

The Dark would take great pleasure in hurting the half-Fae Warrior, and the Light . . . well, let's just say that Usaeil wouldn't be pleased to know that her brother had left an heir.

"Get up!" Rhi shouted and shook Anson's shoulders.

Devon's punch faltered, causing her to pitch forward. Right into the arms of a Dark. Thankfully, Anson helped her recover quickly by kicking the Fae in the balls using her leg.

So many orbs of magic flew past her. She couldn't believe she had yet to get hit by one. Though, to be fair, Con took a lot of them for her.

Despite Anson directing her actions, she was still very much a mortal. And she had no desire to be touched by Dark magic again. There mere thought of it was enough to make her blood turn to ice.

With each kill, she grew bolder, more confident. Which was silly. It was all because of Anson. But for the first time since realizing there was magic in the world and people around her, she didn't feel helpless.

And that was an amazing thing.

She would thank Anson properly later. For now, she enjoyed this badass feeling. She would have Anson train her when they returned to Dreagan.

It never entered her mind that there would be another outcome. She belonged with Anson. If need be, she'd fight to remain with him.

She withdrew the knife from a Dark's chest and turned to look for the next attacker. Except, there was none. Her gaze moved to Con, and she smiled.

"This feels wonderful," she said.

He didn't return her grin. He had just one word for her. "How?"

"It's Anson. I heard him inside my head, and then he took over my body."

Con's frown worried her. The King of Kings stared at her for a long time as if he were trying to figure her out. Devon grew uncomfortable. She wished Anson were beside her.

"How?" Con asked again.

She shrugged. "His power is possession."

"I'm referring to you hearing his voice in your head."

"I don't know."

A muscle in his jaw jumped. "We should find Anson."

His gaze moved to look behind her before narrowing. She looked over her shoulder and saw the Dark approaching from every direction. Two against thirty or more. Not very good odds, especially for a mortal.

"*We can do this,*" Anson told her.

He couldn't hear her thoughts, which she was thankful for. Luckily, he saw everything she did so he knew exactly what she and Con were up against.

At the front of the group was a Fae with long, black and silver hair. He stared at Con with such profound hatred that it almost became a visible entity between the two.

"The famed King of Kings," the Dark said with a sneer.

Con's nostrils flared. "You always did talk too much, Balladyn."

"And you, never enough."

Devon looked between the men. The other Dark appeared as though they were waiting for Balladyn to give the order to attack, and with the way he and Con were staring at each other, it could come at any second.

"*There's a lot of them,*" Devon told Anson.

"*Doona look at the group as a whole. You're going to stand your ground and let them run over their dead, tripping. When the ones coming for you make themselves known, that's who we'll focus on. One at a time.*"

"*Together.*"

"*Together.*"

Balladyn took a step closer, never taking his gaze from Con. "You made a mistake by coming here."

"This isna my first time venturing into your . . . home."

The Dark's red eyes narrowed. "It's going to be your last."

"And you think you'll be the one to stop me?" Con asked with a snort.

A sword appeared in each of Balladyn's hands. He twirled them, grinning. "Damn right, I will."

"What are you waiting for?" Con asked.

"*Easy,*" Anson said in an attempt to calm her.

Then Balladyn issued a loud shout. Devon watched as the Dark rushed toward her. She wanted to run, but Anson's control held her steady.

"*Trust me,*" he said.

It wasn't about trust, but the throng of killers coming right for her.

Anson's voice reached her once more as he widened her stance. "*I'll never let anything happen to you.*"

She swallowed, her heart pounding. She shoved aside a Dark and plunged her knife into another. There were bodies everywhere. She lost sight of Con in the chaos as the Fae tried to get to them.

With the Dark being so close together, they didn't use the balls of magic, but it also made it more difficult for her to fight. Anson had her thrusting her blade at anything that moved.

At one point, he helped her wrestle a sword out of the grip of a dying Fae to give her two blades. One by one, she faced her enemy with success. The few cuts she sustained could barely be felt with the adrenaline and rush of fear flooding her.

While she held off a few Dark, it was Con who had the majority closing in around him. She caught a glimpse of Con as he battled Balladyn and five other Dark at once.

Devon wondered where Rhi was. They could use the Light Fae's help right about now. Surely, she should've already found Anson.

With a cry, Devon went down on one knee. Pain shot

up the back of her leg. She heard Anson's voice say her name as he had her roll out of the way and stand up.

She came up between two Dark intent on her death. She raised her right arm and used the sword to block the downward stab of the Fae. With her left hand, she shoved the knife into the Dark's gut and yanked it out with a grin.

Pivoting, she faced the other Fae, using her sword to parry and attack. In her mind, she saw all the moves Anson had shown her since he'd taken over her body. It wasn't long before she began to guess what he would have her do next. Then, she was anticipating the movements.

He made sure to keep her injured leg away from her attackers. That became more of an issue with each of the Dark who died. The ground was littered with bodies, but it also opened up the area so that the remaining Dark could use magic.

And they didn't hesitate.

Devon chanced a quick look at Con to find him and Balladyn still going at it. During all of it, Con was fighting—and destroying—other Dark. She couldn't understand why he didn't just kill Balladyn.

Her gaze returned to her assailants. They surrounded her, each looking at her as if she were a prize. Time seemed to slow. A bead of blood dripping from her blade to land on the floor was loud, even to her ears.

"*Devon*," Anson said.

There was something in his rushed voice, a note of concern and distress that sent a trickle of unease winding through her. What did he see that she didn't?

She was about to ask when a Dark came at her from the side. Almost simultaneously, another rushed her from the front. With smooth movements, Anson sent her lunging with the sword before dropping to one knee to slice the other Dark with her blade.

The two fell dead. She had no time to rejoice as more attacked.

"*Devon!*"

Anson's voice sounded farther away. Her limbs grew heavier, and her body more clumsy. She misjudged a lunge and found her sword stripped from her fingers.

CHAPTER FORTY-TWO

Anson grabbed Rhi's hand before she could slap him again. His cheek stung from her many hits, but that wasn't why he let his fury show.

"She's going to die now," he said through clenched teeth.

Rhi's forehead creased in a frown. "What are you talking about?"

"Devon. I had possession of her body as she and Con fought the Dark. Including Balladyn. I have to get to her. Now!"

It was the mention of the Dark's name that made Rhi jerk out of his hold. "What are we waiting for, then?"

Anson jumped to his feet. Rhi didn't say a word as she grabbed his wrist. In the next instant, they were standing in an area with large columns and dozens of dead Fae. He ignored them and hastily searched for Devon.

When he found her still standing, he thought his heart might burst from his chest. She was still alive. He couldn't believe it.

"Anson!"

Her voice was still in his head. No longer was he controlling her body, but the connection remained. He didn't question how it was possible. When it came to magic, it couldn't be explained. All he knew was that the woman who held his heart was also linked to him mentally.

He saw a Dark creeping up behind her. Anson didn't hesitate to rush the Fae. With his hand wrapped around the Dark's neck, Anson squeezed until he felt the bones crush beneath his fingers.

Devon spun around, her knife raised. Their eyes met, and a smile broke out across her face. "You're here."

"Always."

He wanted to tell her of his feelings, of how he couldn't live without her. But now wasn't the time. They were surrounded by death and blood.

Anson took her hand in his and looked around to make sure all the Dark were dead. More would be on the way soon. A look toward Con showed that Balladyn was the only one left standing.

He didn't understand why Con hadn't killed the Fae. There were plenty of opportunities. It wasn't until Anson saw Rhi standing off to the side staring at the Dark that it hit him. He hadn't imagined his earlier sighting of Rhi and Balladyn.

"Stop," Rhi said when Balladyn and Con broke apart. She stepped between them. "Enough."

By the look of murder in Balladyn's eyes, he had no intention of ceasing. Until Rhi put a hand to his chest and said his name.

Anson couldn't believe the instant change in the Dark. For a brief moment, they saw a glimpse of what Balladyn had been like as a Light Fae. It made Anson wonder what might have become of the couple had Balladyn not fallen into the hands of the Dark.

Balladyn released a breath and nodded. His gaze then lifted to Con. There were no words spoken, but then again, none were needed. Balladyn hated all Dragon Kings for what had been done to Rhi. The fact that the Dark could love so deeply changed the way Anson viewed him.

"We should leave before more come," Anson said to the group.

Devon's hand tightened in his. "Agreed."

"Rhi," Con said.

She turned her head to the side. "Give me a sec. I can't leave Balladyn like this."

"I'll be fine," Balladyn said in a clipped voice.

Anson frowned when he saw Rhi look to her left. There was no one there, but she looked at the spot as if someone were. He was about to ask what she saw when Rhi took a step back from Balladyn and dropped her hand.

"Let's go," Rhi said.

They quickly followed Rhi to the doorway. Right as they stepped through, Anson looked back at Balladyn. The Dark was staring at them. Then something lifted Balladyn and tossed him against the wall, knocking him out.

Anson didn't have time to see who had attacked Balladyn because once they'd stepped through the doorway, Rhi teleported them to Dreagan.

Upon arrival, the manor was alive with people. Con took a second to heal Devon's injury while Anson looked around at the Warriors with their Druid wives. Before he had time to ask what was going on, a pair of jeans was shoved into his hands. Anson jerked them on and turned to Con.

"What's going on?"

Con let out a sigh. "There's a lot I need to fill you in on."

Not wanting to be parted from Devon again so soon, Anson took her hand and pulled her after him as he followed Con up the stairs to his office.

Sebastian was already there. He turned from the windows and shook his head of long, pale brown hair. "The plan didna work. Only a few Dark took the bait. The Warriors didna need to move from their hiding places."

"That's probably a good thing. We'll need that element of surprise later," Con said as he held out his hand and a dress shirt appeared. He put it on as he came around his desk and sat. He looked at Anson and motioned to the chairs as he said, "I sent a group to Dublin to draw out the Dark so we could get to you at the palace."

Sebastian's lips twisted ruefully. "I was looking forward to killing some Fae."

"It's coming," Con said.

Sebastian looked at Con before he gave a nod to Devon and Anson and walked from the room without another word. The door closed behind him.

Anson waited as Con sat silently for several long minutes. Whatever it was that had to be said couldn't be good. Though he wanted to hear it, he also wanted time alone with Devon.

"It's difficult to know where to begin," Con finally said. "First, Asher had a run-in with Ulrik in Paris at the World Whisky Consortium. Ulrik shifted."

Anson nodded. "So he wasna lying."

"Excuse me?" Con's gaze was intense as he pinned Anson with a dark look.

Anson ran a hand over his face. "I spoke with Ulrik at the palace. He told me he didna have anything to do with Kyvor or the Druid."

"You believe him?"

"I do. He also told me that he had all his magic. Then he said that Devon was special."

Her head whipped around to him. "What does that mean?"

"I think Ulrik knew I'd be able to possess you to help

you fight. Maybe he also meant the mental link. I doona know."

Devon smiled, her blue eyes softening. "I don't care how it happened. I'm just glad it did."

"I care," Con said. "What else did Ulrik say?"

Anson lifted a shoulder in a shrug. "I asked him to find Devon. I thought the Dark had taken her. He tried to break the chains holding me, but he wasna able to."

"That's the last you saw of him?"

"Aye. Right before he touched a silver bracelet and vanished."

Con leaned back in his chair and swiveled it to the side so one arm rested on the desk. "To attack Asher and Rachel, only to help you and Devon. Strange."

"It is," Anson said.

"And he can teleport."

Anson shrugged. "Apparently. What else happened here?"

"I already told you, I sent Dmitri to Fair Isle after Faith found the dragon skeleton."

Anson nodded. "How did that turn out?"

Con blew out a breath. "When the bones were dug up in the cave, Faith found a wooden dragon and brought it back with her. We didna know it at the time, but it was filled with *mie*, *drough*, Light, and Dark magic."

"How is that possible?" Anson asked.

"That's what Rhi was trying to figure out at MacLeod Castle with the Warriors and Druids. The wooden dragon was carved in my image."

Shit. This was incomprehensible. And very bad. "If it was filled with magic, what does it do?"

"Alter whoever touches it. For a Fae, they pass out from the anger. For a King, it turns us against mortals to the point where even I wanted to kill them all."

"And humans?" Anson asked.

Con gave a perturbed shake of his head. "Faith tried to kill Dmitri. It was what could've happened with Ulrik and his woman all over again."

"That's no coincidence."

"Nay. It isna."

Anson sat forward and rested his forearms on his knees. "All of this combined with a Druid who is able to alter someone's mind and project herself."

"There's more."

More? He couldn't be serious. Anson slowly sat back and waited. Devon remained silent, taking it all in. The fact that Con wasn't asking her to leave meant that he accepted her as part of the family.

"The rumors were true," Con continued. "I did take a lover."

Anson shook his head as it dawned on him who it was. "Tell me it isna true. Tell me you and Usaeil are no' together."

"We're no' anymore."

He couldn't believe Con would take the queen as his lover. Then he looked over at Devon. She held his heart, but it had been tough telling her who he was and hoping she accepted him.

With the queen, Con didn't have to worry about any of that. So in that regard, Anson could see why Con had turned to Usaeil. Though it didn't make it any easier to swallow.

"You'll see this soon enough." Con pulled open a drawer and took something out. He then reached over the desk and handed Anson a magazine.

Anson took it to see a fuzzy photograph blown up to cover the entire page. Con had his back to the photographer, but there was no doubt it was him.

"At least they didna get your face," Anson said and handed the magazine to Devon.

Devon gasped. "This woman, this famous actress is really a Fae?"

"The Queen of the Light," Anson corrected her. "Usaeil."

"Oh, my God," Devon murmured.

Con's lips flattened. "Usaeil wanted to announce our relationship to all of you and the Light. I refused. She didna listen, telling me that once we were wed, all of you would then choose a Light for your mates. She's convinced the Fae will be able to give us children."

"Right," Anson said with a snort. He then pointed to the magazine. "That came out after you told her no?"

"Rhi found pictures posted all over the Light castle."

"So Rhi knows?"

Con gave a nod. "It was the same time she told me about her and Balladyn."

"I was going to tell you I saw him kiss her. Is that why you didna kill him?"

"Aye." Con rose and moved to stare out the window. "I couldna take him from her."

Anson looked at Devon and held out his hand. She put her palm in his as they shared a smile. There was much the two of them needed to discuss. And he wasn't at all sure how things would go.

He got to his feet and pulled her up beside him. As he guided Devon to the door, Anson recalled the conversation he'd overheard between Balladyn and Amdir.

Anson stopped at the door and looked back at Con. "Do you know someone named Mikkel?"

Con turned to the side. "Nay. Why?"

"I heard Balladyn say something to Amdir about Mikkel being involved with Kyvor."

"We'll have to settle up with Amdir soon enough."

"I took care of that."

Con's lips softened into a quick smile. "Good." Then he turned back to the window.

Devon gave a tug on Anson's arm. He walked out of the office, closing the door softly behind him. Then he pushed his woman against the wall and took her lips in a fiery kiss.

CHAPTER FORTY-THREE

How had she ever lived without passion? As soon as Anson walked into her life, it was like Devon had been woken from a long sleep.

She groaned at the feel of his tongue meeting hers. Desire rose like a tidal wave. His large hands were splayed on either side of her head on the wall. She felt his arousal pressing against her stomach, causing her body to ache with need.

"Come," he said huskily and reluctantly stepped back.

She licked her lips, tasting him on her. They hurried down the hall to the stairs. She looked down at her hand, wiggling her fingers against his. She remained beside him as they ascended to the top floor.

There were no words spoken as they made their way to the very end of the corridor. Nor when he opened the door and motioned her within.

She knew from the moment she stepped inside that it was Anson's room. It was far different from the light and airy room she'd been shown to.

This chamber was utterly masculine from the dark wood used for the furniture to the various weapons

placed around the room. Her gaze halted when she saw
the sword hanging horizontally away from all the rest.

"Every King has a sword," he said as he closed the
door and came up beside her. "It's what we use to battle
each other in human form."

She glanced at him, confused. "Why would you do
that? Why not fight in your true form?"

"It's always been the way."

He took her hand and led her to the hearth where a
fire blazed. She sat on the small sofa and watched as he
went down on his haunches to stoke the fire. The flames
danced high, causing sparks to shoot up. The red-orange
glow lit his face and front half, while the rest of him was
in shadows.

His tat drew her gaze. As she stared at the two dragons seemingly forever circling each other, she jerked and
looked harder. Had they just moved?

As she scrutinized them, she saw them shift slightly.
Her lips parted in amazement. She had to touch them—
him. She scooted to the edge of the cushions and then
pushed to her knees behind him.

There was no other choice for her but to put her hands
on the tattoo. His flesh heated beneath her palms, and
he stilled. Then she leaned forward and placed a kiss on
the tat.

It was her way of letting him know that she accepted
everything that he was as well as his world of magic. Her
recognition only strengthened the bond between them.
And she could *feel* it!

Anson turned to face her, his black eyes filled with
happiness. The fire crackled between them. She slid her
hands through his thick hair, letting the cool strands slip
through her fingers.

"I don't know how this happened," she said.

He took her hand, watching, as he lifted it so they were

palm to palm. Then his gaze returned to her face. "What?"

"This. Us," she added.

His hand moved slightly so their fingers could interlock. With his gaze never leaving hers, he said, "I like this. Verra much."

"I . . . ," she hesitated, faltering. She'd never wanted something as badly as she did Anson, and she didn't want to ruin it by saying the wrong thing. "I don't want this to end."

"It doesna have to."

"What I'm trying to say—badly—is that I-I love you."

His lips curved into a sensual smile.

She waited for him to say something, anything. When he didn't, she swallowed and glanced away, her heart pounding in fear that he didn't feel the same. "Say something. Please. I'm wearing my heart on my sleeve here."

"Shh," he murmured as he pulled her against him before laying her back on the rug. "Words are no' always needed."

The desire shining in his dark eyes caused her breath to catch. Her body tingled with expectation. She knew what it was like to be loved by him, to have her body branded by his touch. She needed it like she needed air to breathe.

Effortlessly, he disrobed her until she was naked. Her chest rose and fell rapidly in anticipation. Her body pulsed with need, with a yearning that only he could deliver.

With deliberate slowness, he trailed his fingers between her breasts and down her stomach before moving back up again. His large hands massaged her breasts, never touching her nipples that stood erect, waiting for attention.

Her breasts swelled as he flattened a palm over aching

tips, massaging. For what felt like hours, he teased her before finally pinching her nipples.

She let out a cry of pleasure. It was short-lived as his hands glided down her body to her stomach and hips and then to her thighs. Her body began to tingle all over. It was then that she realized she was nothing more than a vessel of sexuality meant only for him.

A slave of pleasure.

It was a role she gladly accepted.

The more his fingers slid over her body, the more she tried to shift her hips so he'd touch her mound. Time and again, he went around it, coming close, but never touching her.

She wanted to scream in frustration as every fiber of her being was centered on her womanhood. Then, he gently spread her legs. The air that met her swollen, wet folds caused her to gasp aloud. Then moan.

Still, he avoided the core of her desire as his fingers traced around her pelvis and across her legs until she thrust her hips.

Her breath locked in her chest when she spied him settling between her thighs. His movements were so slow, so deliberate as he lowered his face to her center, that it was almost too much to bear.

Desperation caused her to clutch at the rug as she impatiently waited for his touch. The anticipation bordered on pain. His gaze met hers. It was the promise of ecstasy in his eyes that caused her mouth to go dry.

Her clit twitched as his head lowered.

"Anson," she whispered right before the first moment of contact.

With toes curled in pleasure, she cried out as his wet tongue lapped at her stiffened peak. The way he licked and suckled had her shivering with excitement.

The lips of her sex were parted and gently fondled.

Within Anson's arms, she felt worshipped. She reveled in the sexuality, in the decadence.

Desire tightened within her, bringing her close to peaking. As if sensing that, he rose up and flipped her onto her stomach. She moaned as he traced a finger down her spine to her butt before grasping her hips.

She bit her lip in eagerness when he raised her hips and held her steady. His stiff length brushed the inside of her leg before finding her entrance. Inch by inch, he slowly pushed inside her.

Devon curled her fingers in the rug and sighed as her body stretched to accommodate him. His arousal slid rhythmically in and out of her.

She was spellbound, completely enraptured by the feelings within her. There was no doubt that she loved Anson. And knowing that she could totally lose herself to him gave her strength. It allowed her to lie there and accept the pleasure he gave her, because theirs was a connection that went beyond the physical.

The hard slap of his pelvis against her backside made her cry out for more. He thrust into her with brutal precision, giving her no other choice but to give in to the bliss that awaited them both.

His rough, masculine frame pressed against her heightened her desire, propelling her toward the building orgasm that she couldn't contain.

"Say you're mine," he demanded.

"I'm yours. All yours. Only yours."

His fingers dug into her hips as he pounded her harder. "Only mine."

The climax swept through her suddenly. She screamed, her back arching even as he continued to thrust deeply. It extended her orgasm, her body convulsing and lost in a world of pleasure like no other.

The walls of her sex were still quivering when he

drove deep inside her and stilled. She felt his seed fill her before he collapsed atop her and rolled them to the side.

She stared into the flames of the fire, unable to believe her life had taken such an unexpected turn. Despite all the terror and shock, she wouldn't change a moment of it.

"I love you."

Tears gathered in her eyes at Anson's whispered confession. Now, her life was truly complete.

He rolled her onto her back and looked down at her. "I doona know how or why we were able to link our minds, but it only confirms what I've always known. You're special, Devon Abrams. Because you were meant for me."

"I do want to know how we were able to communicate telepathically, but it doesn't matter right now because I have you."

One side of his lips lifted in a smile. "I want you to be mine. Become my mate and live with me here. Because I am yours. All yours. Only yours."

She thought her heart would burst, she was so happy. Devon threw her arms around his neck and held him tightly. "Yes."

"I doona want to wait," he said, pulling back. A small frown puckered his brow in his seriousness. "You need to be sure. We doona divorce. Once a Dragon King is mated—"

"They mate for life," she finished. "I know in my heart that we're meant to be together. Even if I had doubts, what we accomplished at the Dark Palace says it all. Unless other mates can link to their Kings like I did with you."

He shook his head, smiling. "None have ever been able to do that. It's more than just our linking. You were fighting on your own."

"I know. It was like my body and mind absorbed everything you were doing. I can't explain it."

"Magic can no' always be explained."

"Like love."

"Love is magic," he said and kissed her.

Yes, love was magic. How had she ever thought that magic didn't exist? None of that mattered now. She knew the truth—the whole, beautiful truth.

And she would protect it.

"Is it over with Kyvor?"

"From what I learned, aye," he replied. "They'll find Harriett soon enough."

"And the Druid."

He blew out a breath and lay on his back. "And the Druid. It seems we gain a new enemy at every turn."

"I suspect they've been in the shadows for some time. They're just now showing themselves, thanks to Ulrik."

He turned his head to her. "Did you ever hear the name Mikkel?"

"Mikkel," she repeated. "I don't believe so. Why?"

"Ulrik wasna responsible for Kyvor."

That made her rise up on an elbow and look down at him. "I know that's what you told Con, but are you sure?"

"Aye."

"Then we need to find this Mikkel."

He wrapped his arms around her and pulled her on top of him. "That will come soon enough. Tonight, you're all mine."

There were no more words as his lips took hers.

CHAPTER FORTY-FOUR

Just Not that Into Him

Rhi needed to get her mind off Balladyn. Seeing him fighting Con had infuriated her. Mainly because she thought he was coming to see her side when it came to the Dragon Kings. Obviously, she was wrong.

She heard Balladyn call to her again.

And she ignored him. Again.

Before they had a confrontation, she needed to calm down as well as put some space between them. She walked through Dreagan Manor, bypassing groups of Warriors, Druids, and Dragons.

Phelan gave her a questioning look, but she wasn't up to admitting to him who her current lover was. It would lead to other questions—ones she wasn't in any way prepared to answer.

She saw something out of the corner of her eye right before she nearly barreled into a chest. When she looked up, Rhys was smiling down at her.

"Ugh. What?" she asked in irritation with a roll of her eyes. The look on his face told her she wasn't going anywhere until he got whatever it was he wanted.

And Rhys was as stubborn as they came.

He turned and wrapped an arm around her, guiding her toward one of the rooms where a couple of mates were gathered around a laptop. "I thought this might interest you."

She shot him a look. "Why?"

"It's a bet we have going."

"We?" she asked, raising a brow.

Rhys shrugged. "The Kings and Warriors. Broc isna allowed to be involved since he might use his powers. Neither are the Druids."

"And the mates?"

His smile widened. "They have their own wager going."

One of her worst qualities—or best, depending on how you looked at it—was her curiosity. And Rhys knew it. Damn him.

Yet it was the perfect way for her to keep her mind off Balladyn.

"What is it?" she asked.

"A blog."

She wrinkled her nose. "That's all you've got for me. Really? A blog?"

Rhys laughed and walked her into the room. "Just wait."

As they entered, Kinsey looked up from the laptop and motioned Rhi closer. Jane scooted over to make room while she and her sister, Sammi, continued their debate.

Rhi eyed them. What could this blog be to have caused such an uproar? She sat and looked around at Sophie, Faith, and Rachel, who looked at her expectantly.

Kinsey pointed to the screen. "This is a blog Devon visits daily. Esther and I went back and read from the beginning. Everyone around the world is trying to figure out who this woman is."

"What does she write about?" Rhi asked. "Sex?"

Esther walked into the room carrying a newly opened wine bottle to the cheers of everyone. "Something we can all relate to. Dating."

Rhi accepted the glass of wine from Esther and looked to the doorway where Rhys was deep in conversation with Henry. By Henry's angry expression, Rhys was doing his best to get the mortal to move on from his infatuation with her.

It saddened Rhi that she'd brought such misery to Henry, all because she'd felt lonely. One kiss had changed everything for him, while doing nothing for her. She wished she could love him. Henry was a good man. The kind of man who would never leave her, the kind of man who would always be there.

But it wasn't meant to be.

Henry stormed away angrily, and Rhys returned to the group of men who were trying to figure out why the Dark hadn't taken the bait in Dublin.

It did seem strange. Perhaps she should look into it. Balladyn would know.

She sighed. There she was thinking of him again.

"Rhi," Kinsey said. "Read this."

Her attention turned back to the women as the laptop was given to her. She looked at the name of the blog: *The (Mis)Adventures of a Dating Failure*. Then her gaze scrolled down to the newest post.

Just Not That Into Him

Ladies, we've all been there. When a man is interested in us, but we don't return the sentiment. I get that it takes some nerve to walk up and ask someone out.

But why can't we say no and they accept it? Why must some of them ask us for our number so they can call/text us later? As if we'll change our minds?

For instance, I'm at the market a few days ago, checking out the apples. I can't ever decide between green or red. I mean, there are so many options, and I love them all. I really don't think the clerk would appreciate me buying one of every kind.

Anyway, I'm going back and forth in my decision when a man walks up. I see him, but after a particularly bad date the night before, I don't want any encounters with the opposite gender at the moment.

I'll give him credit. He was persistent. When I didn't immediately notice him, he made sure to keep walking around the apples, hoping I would. He even went so far as to make some comments about the produce.

After ten minutes of this, I just wanted it to stop. Unfortunately, I made the mistake of answering him. I mean, I'm a nice person. I don't like to intentionally be rude. (side note here: sometimes you have to be mean to get your point across—and that's another blog post entirely. Is it sad that I can write about all of this? I think it is. ☹)

I gave him a brief, I'm-just-being-nice-because-that's-how-I-was-raised smile. He took that as an invitation to follow me around the store. I even went and stood at the tampons hoping he'd go away.

It didn't even faze him.

Matter of fact, he pointed out the kind his sister liked to use.

I. Kid. You. Not.

By this time, I've realized my mistake. But it's too late. He must've guessed I was about to run for the hills because then he asked me out to dinner.

It was a bold move. Most men I've just met will ask me to coffee or for my number, but not straight to dinner. So, I give him props for that.

Now it's my move. I face him and look him in the eye.

I figure he deserves that much. And then I politely decline the offer with a, "No, thank you."

I've been known to make up things like having a boyfriend, being a lesbian, or any number of other excuses to decline a date. The fact that I've always felt the need to lie instead of being truthful has bothered me for a long time.

I'm not sure why I decided to try my new honest approach with this fella, but I did. I'd hoped he'd take it like a champ. So I admit, my hopes were high.

They fell quite rapidly when he kept smiling and moved closer as if he hadn't heard me. He asked for my number. Again, I declined. To my shock, he tried to give me his in case I "changed my mind."

What I wanted to tell him was that, "Dude. That's so not going to happen."

My mother would be ecstatic to know she raised me right because I kept those harsh words to myself. Another polite refusal still didn't work.

This guy wasn't going to let me leave until I agreed to something. And I wasn't going to give in. I can be quite obstinate, as my friends will tell you. I'd made up my mind, and I wasn't going to change it simply because he was tenacious or adamant.

So I dug in and gave him a firm—and final—"no, thanks."

At this rate, my friends, I'm about to give up dating for good. Between the Ugh dates, the OMFG dates, and the can't-take-no-for-an-answer guys, I'm beginning to think there is something wrong with me.

Perhaps I have a huge sign I can't see hanging above me that draws the wrong guys my way. If you see the sign, please let me know. I'd like to take it down.

No. I'd like to rip it down. Set it on fire. Blast it to smithereens.

With that, I'm signing off for the day. I'm going home to a carton of coffee-flavored ice cream and a bottle of wine to binge watch Game of Thrones.

It's really too bad Jon Snow isn't available.

Hmm. I wonder how he'd be as a date . . .

Rhi was smiling when she finished reading. She looked up at the others, who were watching her expectantly. "I want to find out who this is. Mainly because while she's witty and puts it all out there like it is, I see something else."

"What?" Kinsey asked.

Sammi raised her glass of wine and said, "Despair."

"No," Rhi said scrolling down as there were over eight hundred replies to the post, most begging the blogger to keep dating so readers could continue to get her advice and candor. "I see hope."

"Hope?" Jane said with a raise of a brow.

Rhi nodded. "She's a cynic for sure, but then again, who wouldn't be in her situation?"

And she should know. She was in a similar situation, or rather had been for what felt like an eternity.

"I think she's American," Rachel said.

Sophie shook her head of golden hair. "British, for sure."

As the women joked and laughed, Rhi continued reading the blog. The more posts she read, the more curious she was about the woman. No names—ever—were mentioned. Not even initials.

Whoever this blogger was, she had a massive following if the comments on each of her posts were any indication. All because she'd decided to put each of her horrible dating experiences out in the world.

As soon as the whole Druid thing was taken care of, Rhi was going to see what she could dig up about this woman.

CHAPTER FORTY-FIVE

There were few things better than your mission coming to a satisfying end. And seeing Stanley Upton pacing the cavern deep below Dreagan Manor went a long way to helping Anson get some revenge for what the bastard had done to Devon.

"You can't hold me here," Upton said, his blue eyes wide as he looked at each of them.

Anson stood with his arms crossed over his chest. Beside him was Devon, and on the other side of her was Con. The rest of the Dragon Kings wanted their shot at him, most especially Ryder, and they would all get it.

"I can do whatever I want," Con said.

Stanley laughed, the sound filled with fear. "I have rights."

"You lost those rights when you decided to interfere with magical beings," Devon stated.

Upton stopped and looked at her. "We had plans for you."

"What plans?" Anson asked.

Stanley's gaze shifted to him. He smiled in delight and shook his head. "You'll never find out."

Anson dropped his arms and moved into the small cavern. He advanced on Upton, backing him against a wall. He leaned down until his face was inches from the mortal's. "Tell me everything. Now."

"I'd do it," Devon told Stanley.

Upton glanced at her and Con before his gaze returned to Anson. "Will you let me go?"

"Maybe," Con replied.

Stanley nodded nervously. "He came to us."

"Who?" Anson demanded.

"He gave us many names, all aliases. I don't know his real name."

Anson straightened and nodded. "How did he know to come to you?"

"I was doing some digging into employees. The next thing I knew, he was in my office and told me I should be interested in Kinsey Burns and who she was dating."

Devon gave a snort. "And you believed him?"

"I wanted to see for myself," Upton hurried to say. "Everything he told me about Ryder was true. Once I believed the small things, he then told me about the Dragon Kings."

Anson took a deep breath. "So you had Kinsey watched."

"Yes."

"Why Devon?"

Stanley looked over Anson's shoulder to Devon. "You don't know?"

"If I knew, would I be asking?"

At this, Upton began to laugh.

Anson pressed his forearm against the mortal's neck and leaned into it. "I'd advise a lot less maniacal laughter and more talking."

As soon as Stanley nodded, Anson released him.

Upton rubbed his neck and swallowed. Then he said, "Devon's ancestors come from the Isle of Skye."

"We know that," Devon said.

"But do you know that your ancestors were some of the most feared Druid warriors? Your ancestors traveled with a brother and sister, meeting out justice to other Druids."

Anson was glad they had some answers with regards to Devon, but it opened up a wealth of other uncertainties. "Who were this brother and sister?"

"I've told you all I know," Stanley said.

Con asked, "Then why did you want Devon?"

"We thought to bring her into the fold and have her on our side. He told us her magic might manifest itself."

Devon frowned. "Might?"

Upton shrugged. "It was a chance I was willing to take to have another Druid on our side."

"Speaking of Druids," Anson said. "I need the name of the one helping you."

Stanley began to shake his head. "I can't give you what I don't know."

"That's a load of shit," Devon said and gave a shake of her head. "Everyone that came and went at Kyvor was logged."

"No' when there's magic involved," Con said.

Upton gave a quick nod. "She always arrived whenever he summoned her. She'd just appear."

"So she can teleport," Anson said. He and Con exchanged a look.

Devon cocked her head at Upton. "Where is the Druid?"

"I don't know," he replied.

Anson narrowed his gaze. "Where is Harriet?"

"You have to believe me. I've no idea," Stanley said.

Con put his hands in his pants pockets. "I'm sure you do."

"I've told you what you wanted. Can I go?" Stanley asked.

Anson turned and walked through the invisible barrier that kept the human within the cavern. "We're no' nearly done with you yet."

"Wait!" Upton shouted.

Anson took Devon's hand, and together with Con, they walked away.

It wasn't until they were in the manor that Con stopped and looked at them. "We need information on Devon's family."

"Yes, please," Devon said. "I want to know more than you do."

Anson smiled as the constriction around his chest loosened. Ryder and Kinsey were in the process of dismantling Kyvor and erasing anything on Dreagan and the Dragon Kings. The threat Kyvor had held was gone, but now the focus had turned to the Druid.

And how Devon fit into all of it. But at least she was safe now. She was with him.

"*It's over*," she said in his head.

"*One part is.*"

Con flattened his lips as he cut them a look. "Getting used to you two communicating telepathically is going to take some doing."

Anson grinned as he pulled Devon against him. "I think I left something in my room."

"Yeah," she hurried to say as she put her hand on his butt and squeezed. "That . . . thing. It's there."

"Just go already," Con said with a shake of his head.

Anson winked at Con as he lifted Devon in his arms and ran up the stairs.

CHAPTER FORTY-SIX

Four days later . . .

Finally! Con had discovered who the spy at Dreagan was. Before he could enjoy the satisfaction, he heard approaching footsteps. He wanted Kellan and Asher to confirm it. Then they could take action. The sooner, the better.

But it couldn't be today. Today was a celebration.

"Con," Asher said as he walked into the office, followed by Kellan. "We have a name for you."

He grabbed one of the gold dragon head cufflinks and put it on before reaching for the other. "I'm all ears."

"You're no' going to believe who the spy is." Kellan then tossed down a file.

Con flipped it open and stared at the picture, the same woman he'd discovered just seconds before. "She's worked for us for over twenty years."

"That family has worked with us for over five generations," Asher stated angrily. "How could she do this?"

Tugging his shirtsleeves down and adjusting the cufflinks, Con looked at his men. "We'll find out tomorrow."

"Ryder is watching her every move on the estate," Kellan said.

Con nodded in approval. Then he looked at Asher. "You should be with the other Kings."

"I'm on my way," Asher replied with a wide smile before hurrying out.

Con watched Kellan follow Asher with a heavy heart. Con's time was running short. Any day, Ulrik would issue the challenge. What would happen after was anyone's guess.

He'd always known Ulrik had the ability to best him. Now that his old friend had anger and vengeance goading him, the odds were in Ulrik's favor.

But Con wouldn't go down without a fight. He hadn't given up everything to lead his men only to be defeated now. He hadn't fought in wars, sent the dragons away, and forged a new life for the Kings for nothing.

He was prepared to kill the man he'd once considered a brother. Perhaps it would've been easier for him to end Ulrik's life instead of banishing him all those ages ago, but he hadn't been able to.

It had been the desolation and torment in Ulrik's eyes that had stayed his hand. He'd known it was a mistake. He'd seen the way Ulrik's heart had begun to grow chilly to anyone and anything.

And he'd foreseen his friend's quest for revenge.

Con gave himself a mental shake. Those worries were for later. Now, he had to get ready for the mating ceremonies. Five Kings were taking humans as their mates, and the manor was buzzing with excitement.

He stood and put on a black suit jacket and adjusted his kilt. After a quick tug of the gold pocket square in his breast pocket, he opened the middle drawer of his desk and took out the five velvet boxes.

The family was expanding again. It pleased him that

the Kings had found love and happiness. After so much heartache and sorrow, they deserved this moment.

Though he would admit it to no one, he liked having the women around. They had become like sisters to him. It reminded him of the family he'd once had. Despite what might come in the future, the mates were family. And he always protected family.

Palming one box, he tucked the others in his sporran before walking out of the office. He turned right and headed down to the opposite side of the hall where he rapped his knuckles upon the door.

Sophie opened it, smiling when she saw him. "Come in."

"Thank you." He looked over the dark purple, strapless gown that hugged her upper body before falling into a full skirt. The top had black beading in a large, elegant, floral pattern that didn't detract from the overall design of the dress. Sophie's golden hair was left to hang sophisticatedly midway down her back.

He saw the picture of her with her best friend, Claire, sitting on a table. "I'm sorry Claire couldna be involved."

"I'd rather keep her in the dark about everything. It's safer that way. We'll have a party that includes her later." Sophie walked to the dressing mirror and checked her hair. "Is it time?"

"Nearly."

She rubbed her hands together as she straightened. "I'm ready."

"No' completely." He held out the small box to her.

Sophie accepted the gift and opened the lid. Her lips parted in an *O* as she gazed at the cushion cut dangle earrings. Weighing in at over five carats each, the Siberian amethysts were a rare find.

"The color is so dark," she whispered. "They match Darius perfectly. Thank you, Con."

He bowed his head in reply and watched as she put them on. "I'm pleased Darius has found such a woman to love."

She looked at him in the mirror, her lips turning up in a smile. "He's a special dragon. I'm going to love him with everything I am."

"I know," he replied.

Con left her and walked down the hall to another room. This time when he knocked, he heard a voice call for him to enter. He opened the door and poked his head in to find Lily helping to finish buttoning the dozens of buttons at the back of the gown.

"Con," Faith said with a welcoming grin as she stood in front of the mirror. "What do you think?"

He looked over the white, long-sleeved mermaid gown with an appreciative eye. The top of the gown was nude and lace, but instead of being revealing, it was classy and beautiful. The lace continued down the skirt as it flared and ended in a train.

"You look stunning," he said.

Faith beamed and turned her head from side to side, looking at her shoulder-length blonde hair that was in tousled waves with the sides gathered at the back of her head and held together with a glittering clip. "I feel like a princess."

"You are one," Lily said with a grin. She then stood back and looked at Faith. "You're ready. I'll wait outside."

When Lily was gone, Faith turned to face him. "Is this the time where you tell me how important it is that I love Dmitri? Because I do."

"Nay, lass. This is where I welcome you into our family." He handed her the box.

"Lily showed me the ring you gave her, but I wasn't expecting anything."

That made him grin. "It's tradition. If it isna to your liking, I can have something else made."

"I'm going to love it," she declared. Then she opened the box.

He watched her eyes widen before she pulled out the bracelet. Then she slipped her hand through the narrow band of gold that interlocked with a single pearl.

It hadn't taken him long to realize that Faith loved the simple things. Her gift was the first he'd designed as soon as he knew she and Dmitri would be mated.

To his shock, she threw her arms around him, hugging him tightly. "Thank you for letting me be a part of this wonderful family," she whispered.

He returned her embrace. "You claimed Dmitri's heart. There was never any choice in the matter."

She laughed, sniffing as she pulled back. "Stop. You're going to make me cry, and I don't want to mess up my makeup."

"We wouldna want that. I'll see you below, then."

She gave a wave before he walked out. His next stop was Kinsey. He found her sitting in her room with her laptop open, watching cameras from around the estate.

When she looked up and saw him, she laughed. "I can't help myself. I have to help Ryder make sure there's no one trespassing."

"The magic barrier will tell us that."

She shot him a droll look. "I know. I just like to allow myself to think I'm needed."

"But you are. Now, stand up and let me get a look at you."

She smiled and got to her feet before twirling around. The gray tulle dress was perfection for Kinsey. A little fanciful with the ball gown style and some sensuality added with the off-the-shoulder tulle bodice, with it coming together in sophistication that was all Kinsey.

"Flawless," he said.

She beamed and tossed her long, dark hair over her shoulder. The top half was a series of braids—some thick, some thin—that came together, bound by a small, white flowers that then trailed down with the rest of her hair.

"After everything that's happened, I didn't think this day would ever get here." The smile was gone and her expression serious. "I know what's coming. Ryder and I have spoken about it at length. What happened at Kyvor with Devon made me realize how quickly life can be taken."

Con reached into his pocket and took out her box. "You went to London as a mortal, knowing things could go sideways. You did it for Ryder."

"I did it for all of you," she corrected.

"You were verra brave."

She wrinkled her nose. "Or foolish, depending on how you look at it."

"I'm no' changing my opinion. I'm glad to have you with us," he said and gave her the box.

She glanced at him before opening the lid. Without hesitation, she drew out the gray star sapphire and slipped it on her finger. The large oval gem was set in a thick platinum filigree band.

"Wow," she murmured. "It's beautiful. Thank you."

"My pleasure."

He watched her play with the ring for a moment before he quietly slipped out to let her finish getting ready. His steps took him to yet another door.

After being bidden to enter, he found Rachel standing in front of the window, watching the snow fall in a strapless, dark green velvet gown. Her wealth of black hair was pulled back in an array of loose curls with tendrils falling around her face and neck.

"I can't believe I never visited Scotland in all of my travels," she said without turning around. "I listened as Asher spoke of Dreagan, and the love and longing I heard in his words made me want to know what I was missing. Now that I'm here, I don't ever want to leave."

"It's a good thing you belong here, then," Con said as he moved closer.

She turned to face him. "I do belong here. Really, I belong anywhere Asher is, but this place is . . . I have no words for how it makes me feel."

"Magic," he supplied.

Rachel laughed softly. "Yes. It's magical. I can feel it. Everywhere."

Of all the women, Rachel was the one who had seen Ulrik in his true form when he attacked her and Asher. It was only because of Asher that she hadn't died.

"This war will get worse before it gets better," Con said.

She licked her lips. "I expect as much."

"You've seen a lot with your work. Your presence will help keep the other mates calm."

"I promise to do my best."

He held out the large box. "I know you will."

Surprise flashed in her dark eyes as she accepted the gift. Then she opened it. Without a word she took the four strands of faceted chrome diopside to the mirror and clasped them around her neck.

With her fingers running over the deep green beads, she turned back to him. "These are the perfect gift. Each time I wear them, I'll feel as if I'm wearing a part of Asher. Thank you so much, Con."

"Welcome to the family." He smiled and turned to the door as he said, "I've got one more person to see."

"Hurry. I can't wait to see Asher."

Con was smiling when he closed the door. He gave a

quick knock when he stood in front of his last stop. Almost immediately, the door opened.

Devon moved back for him to enter. "Is it time? Please tell me it's time because I don't think I can wait any longer."

"Just a moment more," Con said, hiding his grin.

She closed the door, her long, mocha skirts rustling as she walked to the dressing table, then to the bed, and back to the table.

Her two-piece gown accentuated her lithe figure and showed a hint of skin at her waist. The top of the gown was beaded and in a halter style with a low back.

"Devon," he said, stopping her with a hand on her arm before she could move away again. "Are you nervous?"

She gaped at him. "Not at all. I can hear Anson in my head, and he keeps saying he's about to come up here and get me if I don't hurry."

It still amazed Con that those two were linked in such a way. It had never happened before, and he wasn't sure it would again.

Ryder had done extensive research into Devon's family. It had taken a lot of work, but he'd discovered a link to the Druids on Skye that surprised everyone—and explained so much.

But that connection was so distant, it didn't seem as if it should matter. Yet it was the only explanation for what Devon had been able to do.

Magic, as Con had just told Rachel, couldn't be explained. It simply was. It worked in various, wondrous ways.

"Then we should hurry," Con said. "First, this is for you."

She stared at the velvet box for a moment before taking it. Shooting him an excited grin, she opened it. Her smile widened when she took out the smoky quartz bracelet.

He held out his hand. "Shall I?"

"Please," she asked, handing him the bracelet.

"I designed it with both round and princess cut stones because I couldna decide on which suited you better. I also think it matches you. You're of two worlds."

Once it was clasped in place, Devon held up her arm and gazed lovingly at the piece. "You put a lot of effort into this." She lowered her arm and looked at him. "I'm honored by your gift."

"I'm glad you like it. Now, come," he said as he heard Anson in his head. "Anson is losing patience."

Devon laughed as she took his arm and they walked from the room. When they reached the main floor, the other four women were already gathered. He looked at each before leading them through the solarium to the hidden door into the mountain.

"I'm here."

Anson's gaze jerked to the opening in the cavern at the sound of Devon's voice in his mind. He didn't see anyone but his woman, the love of his life.

The sight of her in the dress that matched his dragon stirred his blood. He held out his hands to her. As soon as she touched him, he fought not to kiss her.

They stared into each other's eyes. He was smiling like a fool, but it was only because he was deliriously happy. Con had been right all those years ago when he'd said that Brenna wasn't his mate. The proof stood before him now.

Devon was the other half of his heart. She made him whole. And together, they would do amazing things. With their mental link, she was a part of him, and he was a part of her. The yin to his yang.

Just like his dragons.

He'd always wondered why he had such a tattoo. Now he knew.

Con's voice rang out in the cavern. "It's a joyous day when we gather for such a ceremony. Today, we welcome five more into our family. It takes a special kind of woman to claim the heart of a Dragon King and agree to be a mate."

"I love you," Anson whispered to Devon as Con stopped before Darius and Sophie for their vows.

Devon gazed at him so adoringly that it caused Anson's heart to miss a beat. "I love you."

Not once did he take his gaze from her. He wanted to remember every detail of the moment from the way her blue eyes shone in the low light to how exquisitely tempting she was by baring a portion of her stomach, her shoulders, and nearly her entire back.

His woman was hot.

And all his!

Finally, Con stood before them. "Anson, do you bind yourself to the mortal, Devon Abrams? Do you vow to love her, protect her, and cherish her always?"

"With all my heart," he readily answered.

Devon's eyes filled with tears. Anson squeezed her hands when Con turned to her.

"Devon, do you bind yourself to the Dragon King, Anson, King of Browns? Do you swear to love him, care for him, and cherish him always?"

"With all my heart," she said, repeating his words.

In the next heartbeat, she gasped in pain as the dragon eye tattoo burned itself into her skin on her upper left arm. Anson looked at the tat and wanted to shout with joy.

"The proof of your vows and your love," Con stated. "Devon is officially marked as Anson's!"

The cavern erupted in thunderous cheers for all five matings.

Anson quickly pulled Devon to the side before anyone could find them. He looked closer at her new tat that had the same black and red ink as his own.

"I'm finally yours," she said breathlessly.

He pulled her against him. "You've been mine from the moment I first took your body."

"Well, we're official now."

"That's right. I have you for eternity."

She closed her eyes and sighed. "I like the sound of that."

Anson covered her mouth with his for a long, slow kiss to seal their vows. He craved her, and now that they were bound, he ached for her even more.

"Let's leave," he said between kisses.

She laughed. "We're supposed to be celebrating."

"There are four other couples. They willna miss us. I need you," he added.

She moaned as he kissed down her neck. "Let's go."

He took her hand and hurriedly led her out of the cavern. When they glanced back, the other newly mated couples were making their escape, as well.

Anson laughed as they ran through the mountain, into the manor, and up the stairs to his—no, *their*—rooms. He grabbed her against him, turning around in the room.

"This is the first day of our lives together," he said.

She kicked off her shoes and gave him a saucy look. "Then I think we need to do some celebrating of our own. Come here, husband."

He didn't need to be told twice.

EPILOGUE

Rhi stood veiled in the corner of the cavern, watching the mating ceremony. She hadn't looked Daire's way since the Dark Palace when he'd knocked Balladyn unconscious.

She was still so angry that Death had erased her memories, and Rhi wasn't yet ready to talk to any of the Reapers—especially Daire.

He'd seen her at her most vulnerable. She'd told him things she hadn't shared with anyone else. He knew her secrets. How long would he keep all of that to himself? Because there was a reason he was following her.

And she intended to discover what that was.

She wasn't sure why she'd come to the ceremony. If Con knew she was there, he'd be furious. Then again, he was always angry at her for something or other.

With each King who bound their hearts to their mortal, she felt a sting of remorse and sadness so great she found tears welling up.

At one time, she'd dreamed of her own mating ceremony. She'd known exactly what she would've worn. Though it mattered little now. Everyone had moved on.

She stilled when *he* approached. He kept his back to the others as he faced the wall. She hated herself for remaining near him, but she couldn't seem to leave.

"I know you're here," he whispered.

He'd always been able to sense when she was veiled. She should've remembered that. If only she hadn't needed to feel a part of something.

His face turned her way. Her hands itched to cup his jaw, to run her hands through his hair.

"Rhi!"

Balladyn's call went out to her again. She'd ignored him for too long. He was becoming impatient. And she had no business at Dreagan.

She glanced in Daire's direction, curious as to what the Reaper thought of her actions. Because she didn't know what she was doing. She was supposed to be over her King.

With one last look at *him*, she teleported away.

Esther read over the description of the Druid for the hundredth time. She could hear the celebration of the newly mated couples below. Now that the official ceremony was over, she was invited to join in the festivities, but she didn't go down.

She'd been welcomed at Dreagan because of her brother, but she didn't feel as if she really belonged—not after what had brought her to the estate. Once she helped bring down the Druid, then she might think differently.

Her gaze lifted to the empty chair across from her. Henry had stormed off thirty minutes earlier to disappear somewhere around Dreagan.

The living area that connected their rooms was one of Henry's favorite places. His need to blow off steam had nothing to do with her and everything to do with the Fae he was in love with.

She tossed down the paper and blew out a breath. A second later, there was a soft knock at her door. "Come in," she bade.

The door opened, and Nikolai poked his auburn head in. When he saw her, he pushed the door wider and stepped inside. "Alone?" he asked.

She took in the formal kilt showing his muscular legs and had to admit that he looked damn good in it. Esther licked her lips and looked into his baby blue eyes. "Yes. I really want to find out what the Druid looks like, but every time I read the description Isla gave, I come up with a different person."

"Perhaps I can help."

Esther stared at his outstretched hand for a heartbeat before she accepted it and stood. He released her almost immediately as he walked out the door.

She ignored the pounding of her heart. Given what Henry was going through, she was determined not to fall into the same hole. It wasn't easy, considering hunky men surrounded her.

They went downstairs, avoiding the areas where the celebration was happening, and entered the library. Esther was surprised to find Isla and Hayden already inside.

"I didna want to disturb Devon," Nikolai told her.

Well, of course, he didn't. It was her wedding day. Esther smiled up at Nikolai as she came to a stop beside the Druid and Warrior. Nikolai moved to stand before them next to four easels that were covered.

The Dragon King looked at each of them, his shoulders bunching beneath the tux jacket. Finally, he removed it and ran a hand over his chest.

Esther's gaze followed his large hand, noticing the hard lines of his wide shoulders. Their gazes briefly met. She hastily looked away, disconcerted by the flutter in her stomach.

Nikolai cleared his throat. "I've never done anything like this before. My gift allows everything I see to imprint upon my mind so that I can paint, draw, or craft it later. I've never tried to read a description and create something until now."

Esther looked at the four easels with interest. One of those four could be the Druid. They might actually have a face, and with it, Broc could then locate her.

Nikolai removed the cover from the first canvas. Esther noted the drawing had everything on the list she'd been reading, but since she'd never seen the Druid herself, she didn't know for sure. Her head swiveled to look at Isla.

Isla moved closer to the easel, her brow furrowed. She touched the forehead of the sketch, then the chin. "You're close, Nikolai, but not quite."

Without a word, he pulled the cover off the second canvas. Once more, Isla stared at it for a long moment before shaking her head. The same thing happened with the third canvas.

Esther focused on the fourth easel. This had to be it. Isla had said Nikolai was close on all the other three. Surely the last one would be right.

"Ready?" Nikolai asked her and Isla.

Esther nodded hurriedly, ready to rip the cover off herself. Thankfully, Nikolai didn't keep her waiting long.

She gazed at the face for a long time before looking at each of the other three drawings. It looked like almost the same face with only subtle differences, but she knew from experience that subtle was important.

Esther jerked her gaze to Isla to gauge her reaction. The Druid stared at the picture wordlessly. The seconds ticked into minutes. The anticipation was killing Esther.

"It's her," Isla finally announced.

Esther wanted to jump for joy she was so excited. She turned to Nikolai, smiling. "You did it!"

"It's a start," he replied, his blue eyes shining with delight.

But she knew how big of a start it was for them. Because of Nikolai, they could find the Druid who had nearly destroyed her life.

"Finally," she said. "Let's find Con."

Nikolai grabbed her hand, halting her. She looked down at his long fingers curling around hers and felt something move between them.

"Let the others have this night to celebrate their love," he said softly.

The argument died on her lips when she gazed into his pale blue eyes. She was so used to only having her work that she forgot others actually liked to have fun. "Of course."

She tried to tug her hand free, but he held tight. That's when she realized Hayden and Isla were gone.

"Where do you think you're going, lass?" Nikolai asked.

With a shrug, she said, "To my room."

"I have something better in mind."

She couldn't find the words to refuse him as he led her out of the library and straight to the party.

Dublin

Ulrik stood on the Ha'penny Bridge, overlooking the River Liffey as the sun sank into the horizon. The red sky reflected in the water wasn't what kept him engrossed—it was memories of the events of last week.

He knew being so near the Druid was asking for trouble, but he hoped to see her in action to better understand just how powerful she was.

"Still in Ireland, I see," Balladyn said as he leaned against the railing. "Just can't stay away."

Ulrik braced his hands on the barrier. "Something like that."

"Why did you help Anson?"

He turned his head to look at the Dark. "Why did you help Rhi?"

"I had to," Balladyn explained as he faced Ulrik. "I'd do anything for her."

"Because you love her."

The Fae nodded. "More than life itself."

"That's a fraction of what a Dragon King feels for his mate. Devon is Anson's mate."

"How do you know?"

"All I had to do was look into Anson's eyes when he spoke of her. It's there for anyone to see."

Balladyn leaned a hip against the rail. "But you hate the Dragon Kings."

"I hate Con. He's the one I want to bring down."

"Yet the others sided with him."

Ulrik shrugged indifferently. "It was Con's decision. He has to pay for what he did. I'll no' take it out on other Kings in the meantime."

"I came to tell you that Taraeth has called for your head. He blames you for Muriel's murder."

"Of course, he does."

"Every Dark is now looking for you."

Ulrik narrowed his gaze on Balladyn. "Including you?"

The Fae held his gaze for a long moment before issuing a snort. "I wouldn't be talking to you if I were going to bring you in."

"It seems my alliance with the Dark is no longer valid."

Balladyn pushed away from the metal and smiled. "I wouldn't say that. Taraeth's time has come to an end."

"So has Mikkel's."

"It looks like we've got a couple of messes to clean up."

Ulrik gave a nod. "Let's get started."

"About fekking time," Balladyn murmured.

Read on for an excerpt from the next book by
Donna Grant

HEAT

Coming soon from St. Martin's Paperbacks

It was while he was making up his bed that there was a soft knock upon his door. He didn't look up as he bade them enter while he bent, tidying the comforter.

The door opened, but it took him a second to realize that no one had spoken. When he straightened, he was shocked to find Esther North standing there.

The British beauty was still in the doorway, her hand upon the knob as her gaze was locked on the various drawings that were scattered about his room, hung on lines he had strung, or sitting on easels.

Her lustrous brunette tresses hung free about her shoulders. She wore an oversized gray sweater that hid her curves and dropped past her hips over a pair of black leggings. Thick, fuzzy white socks that had a kitten face atop them, complete with a pink nose and whiskers, covered her feet.

The longer she stood staring, the more he was able to gaze at her striking features at his leisure. The MI5 agent had captivated him from the very beginning when a Druid had gotten into Esther's mind and controlled her with magic.

The Dragon Kings had managed to undo the magic of

the Druid, but there was more damage. The memories of the time Esther spent with the Druid were missing. It made her a liability, but she was allowed to remain because of one very important reason—she was the sister of Henry North.

Henry, also MI5, worked with the Dragon Kings to track the movements of the Dark Fae to try and figure out their next move. It was uncommon for the Kings to trust humans, but Henry was an exception.

And so was his sister.

Nikolai knew Esther's face. His power allowed him to conjure every detail about her. From the small, nearly hidden scar at her wrist from some childhood accident, to the confident way she held herself.

He knew her hair wasn't just brown. It held strands the softest shade of walnut, darker tones that deepened into chocolate, and the lighter shades of amber.

He knew the curve of her face and how she lifted her chin when she was angry. He knew her small nose and the lines in her brow from the expressive way she spoke. He knew her mouth and how her bottom lip was slightly fuller than the top.

He knew her round eyes and the deep shade of brown along with the band of black that encircled her irises. He knew the slope of her breasts, the indent of her waist, and the flare of her hips. He knew the way she preferred to wear muted colors to help her blend in with a crowd.

It had taken one look to put all that to memory, but he found his eyes going to her again and again, as if he couldn't get enough.

That fact was only one reason he kept drawing Esther. The other was that he had no choice. She filled his mind like no other before.

Esther was shocked. And that wasn't an easy thing to do. Her eyes moved from one sketch of her to another, each depicting different areas of Dreagan she had been to, from the manor, the distillery, or strolling through the snow in the Dragonwood.

There was even pictures of her walking the caves inside the mountain connected to the manor. The picture she stared at the longest was the one where she had stood at the entrance to the cavern where four of Ulrik's largest silver dragons were kept sleeping within a cage.

The look on her face was one of awe and curiosity. Though, she remembered feeling fear at the idea of Ulrik killing Con and releasing those dragons to wipe out humans.

But in many of these instances, she knew Nikolai hadn't been there. How then had he drawn them? His power of projected thermography allowed him to see something once and paint it, draw it, or weave it.

As her eyes moved from one side of the room to another, they clashed with a bare chested Nikolai that made her mouth go dry as she stared at his chiseled form.

The Dragon King had a way of making her forget whatever she was thinking every time she looked into his baby blue eyes.

But that's not what her gaze lingered on now. It was his tattoo. She knew every Dragon King had one, but this was her first time to see Nikolai's, and it was stunning.

Starting at his wrist was the tail of the dragon that snaked up his arm to his bicep where the body of the dragon began. The back claws of the dragon looked as if they were digging into Nikolai's arm as its wings were tucked.

The dragon turned and leaned over Nikolai's shoulder. The head of the beast was on Nikolai's chest with its mouth open as if roaring. One of the dragon's arms was outstretched as if reaching for something.

It was the intricacy of the tat along with the mix of

red and black ink that would ensure it was never duplicated in any way.

It was impossible not to ogle his finely shaped chest or the washboard stomach. Drops of water had fallen from his hair to his shoulders before they wound their way down his amazing chest. She bit her lip, her blood heating when she noticed that his jeans were unbuttoned and hanging precariously upon his narrow hips.

Unable to look away, she followed the trail of hair from his navel until it disappeared in his jeans. She swallowed, not quite sure how to feel about her blatant carnal reaction to Nikolai.

As she raised her gaze, she noticed that his hands were clenched tightly. That caused her eyes to jerk upward and clash with his.

His features were strong and perhaps a bit harsh, but she found them disarmingly so. From his jawline, to the wide lips to his hallowed cheeks.

She wanted to run her fingers through his subtle cinnamon red locks. He kept the hair around his face shorter than the rest that was full of body and thickness. Even now with it wet, the strands held a wave as they fell to the back of his neck.

It took her several minutes to remember what she was doing in his room she was so consumed by him and the lascivious thoughts that kept running through her head. Of all the men at Dreagan, it had been Nikolai who had caught her eye, even as she fought against it.

Nikolai was one of the quiet ones. She'd noticed right from the start how he stood to the side observing everything and everyone. She'd mistakenly assumed he was like her and trained for such things.

The real reason was because of his power. Everything he witnessed was filed away in his brain to be sorted through later.

The longer they stared at each other, the more aroused she became. She knew she should speak, but she couldn't think of anything to say. Which was a first for her. The one thing she had never lacked was words.

"Esther."

Her name had been passed down through generations of North's. She'd always hated it. Right up until Nikolai said it in that deep, husky brogue. Her name had never sounded sexy until he spoke it.